Ocean of Secrets

VOLUME 2

STORY AND ART BY
SOPHIE-CHAN

TOKYOPOP®

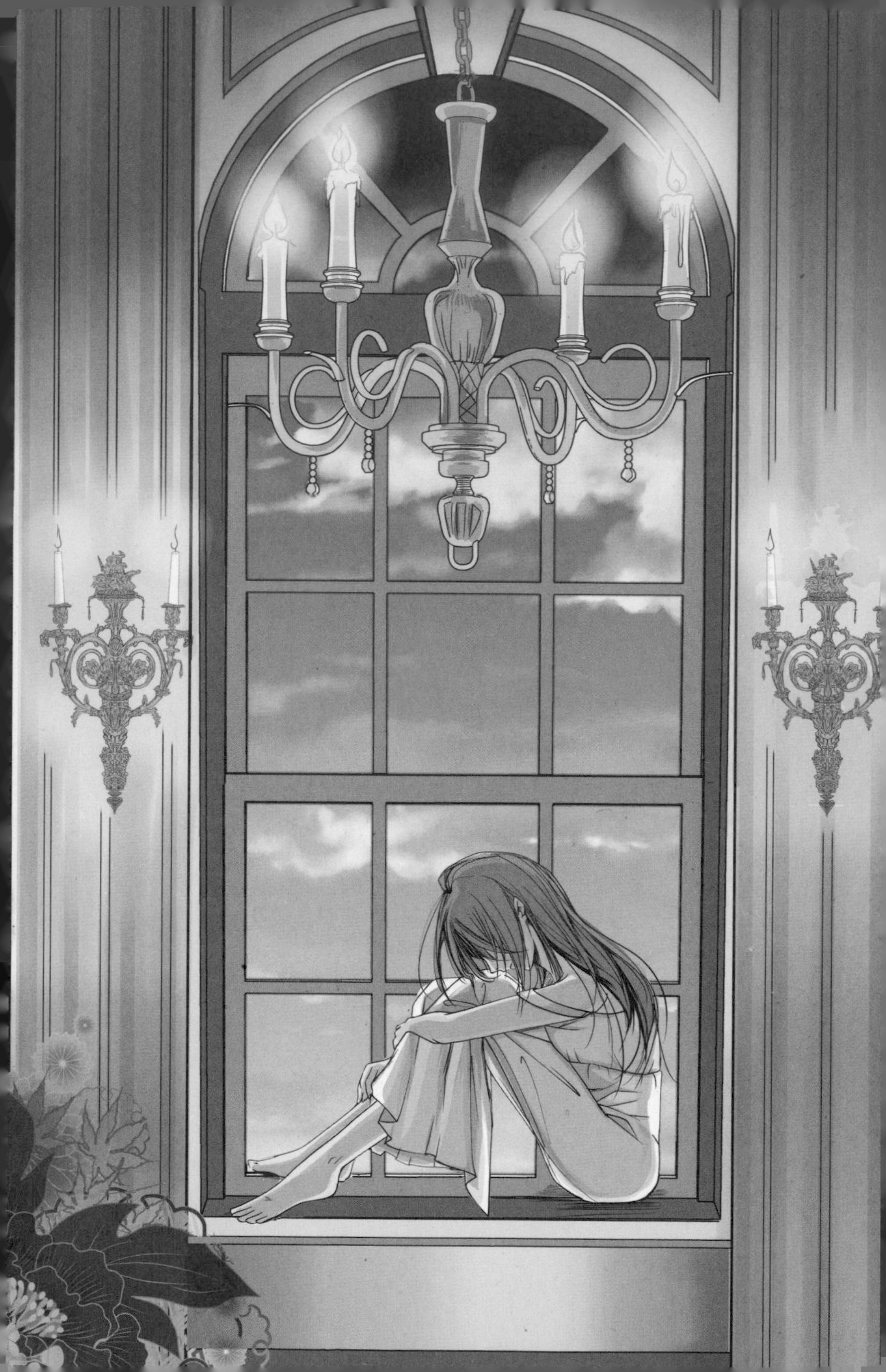

THIS VOLUME IS DEDICATED TO
SENPAI!

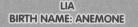

ABOUT THE CHARACTERS

LIA
BIRTH NAME: ANEMONE

A 17-YEAR-OLD ORPHAN RESCUED FROM DROWNING AND BROUGHT TO THE FLYING KINGDOM OF LYRONAZ. HER COURAGE AND FEARLESSNESS HELP HER TO UNRAVEL THE MYSTERY BEHIND HER TRUE IDENTITY: THE KIDNAPPED PRINCESS OF LYRONAZ.

ALBERT H. CHARLES

A BENEVOLENT SHIP CAPTAIN ON THE RUN AFTER BEING FALSELY ACCUSED OF KILLING THE BELOVED LYRONAZ QUEEN. AFTER THE CHARGES AGAINST HIM WERE DROPPED, HIS NEW MISSION IS TO FIND THE QUEEN'S MURDERER.

MORIA H. CHARLES

ALBERT'S STRONG-WILLED LITTLE SISTER, WHO JOINED HIM IN HIS ESCAPE FROM LYRONAZ. SHE BECAME LIA'S BEST FRIEND AND REVEALED THE TRUTH OF LIA'S IDENTITY WHEN LIA WAS ARRESTED.

THE ROYAL FAMILY OF LYRONAZ

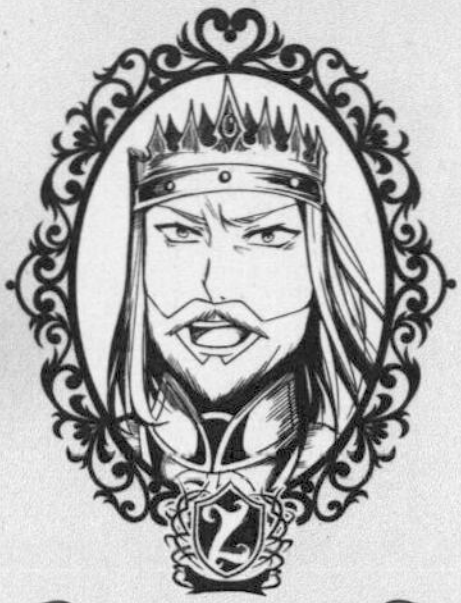

KING DEMETRIUS

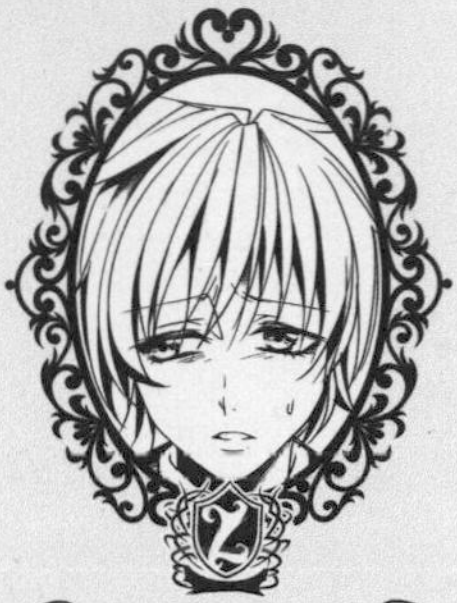

PRINCE LEWIS

THE PEACEMAKERS

THE PROTECTORS OF THE MAGICAL KINGDOMS

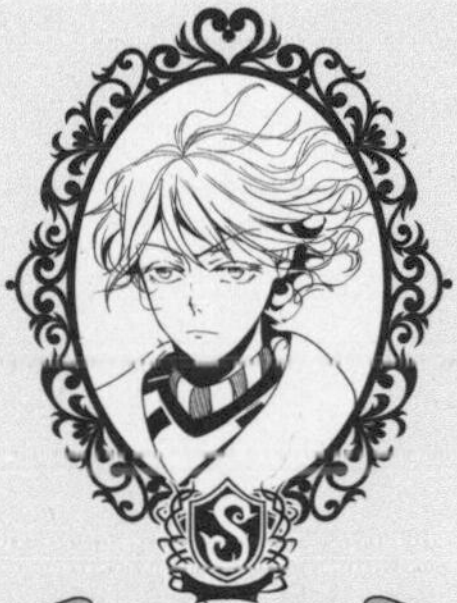

CIAN OF SYRONAZ

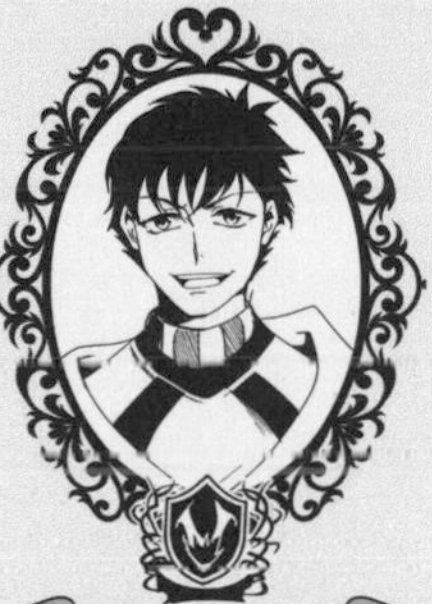

AIDEN OF VYRONAZ

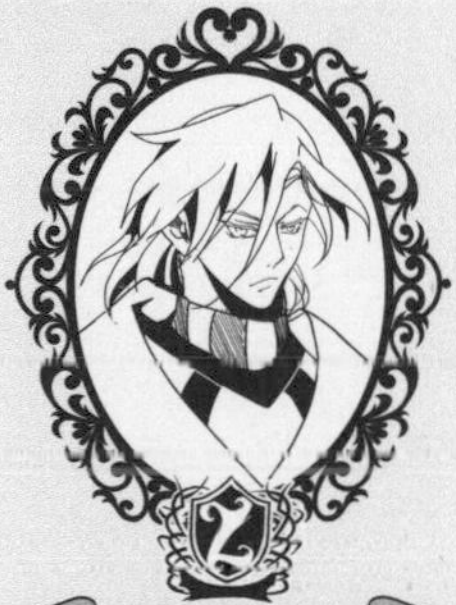

LUCAS OF LYRONAZ

THE STORY

AFTER BEING SWEPT AWAY BY THE OCEAN CURRENT, LIA IS SAVED BY ALBERT, A RUNAWAY WHO FLED HIS HOMELAND WITH HIS SISTER MORIA AFTER BEING FALSELY ACCUSED OF MURDERING THE QUEEN OF LYRONAZ. THEY WERE SOON LOCATED AND CAPTURED BY THE PEACEMAKERS OF THE THREE MAGIC KINGDOMS. WITH ALBERT TAKEN INTO CUSTODY AND MORIA BADLY INJURED FROM THE ALTERCATION, LIA SETS OUT ON AN ADVENTURE INTO THE FLYING KINGDOM OF LYRONAZ TO RESCUE ALBERT. THERE SHE LEARNS THE SECRET OF HER BIRTH, AND HER NEW-FOUND MEMORIES ARE PROOF THAT ALBERT IS INNOCENT. WITH ALBERT'S CHARGES DROPPED, HIS NEW MISSION IS TO FIND THE PERSON RESPONSIBLE FOR THIS TRAGEDY.

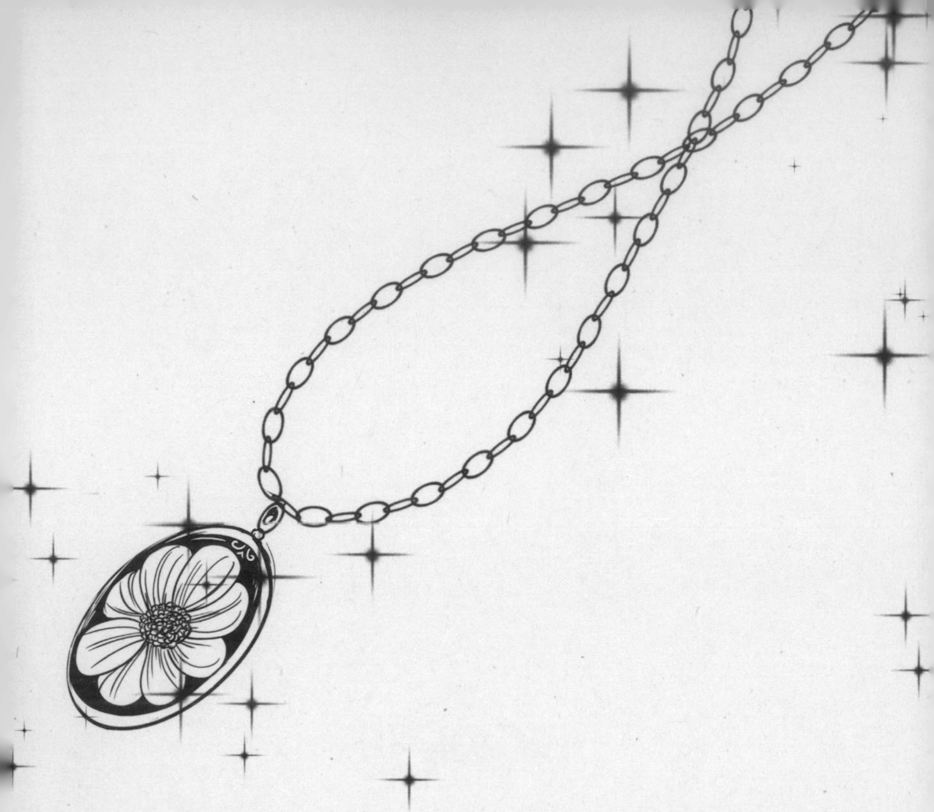

CONTENTS

Ocean of Secrets

CHAPTER 5

DISCOVERY

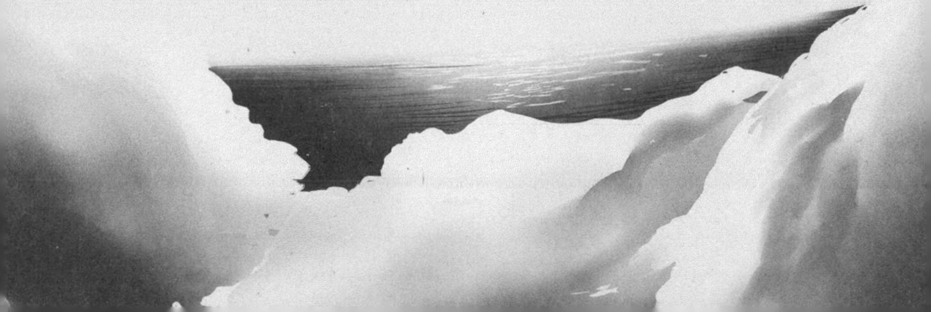

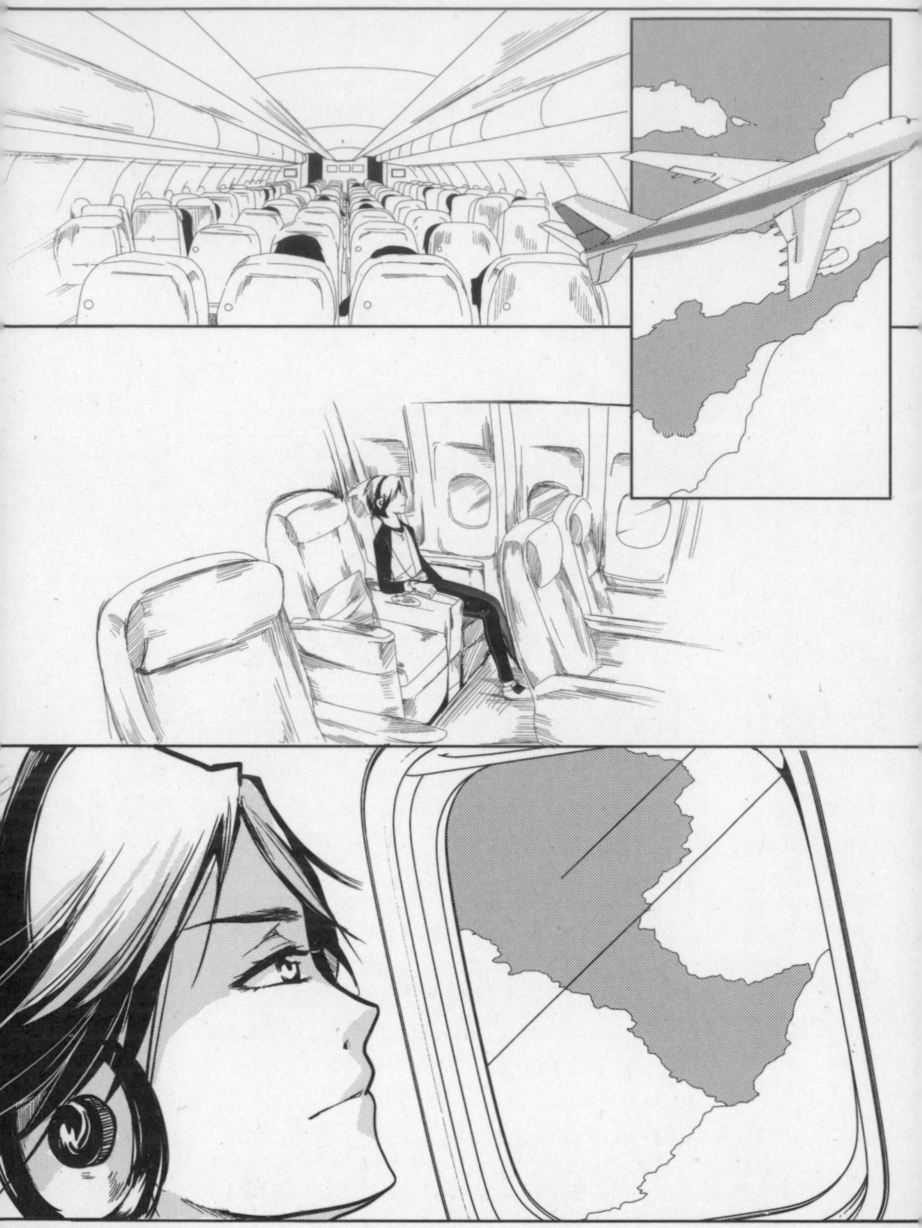

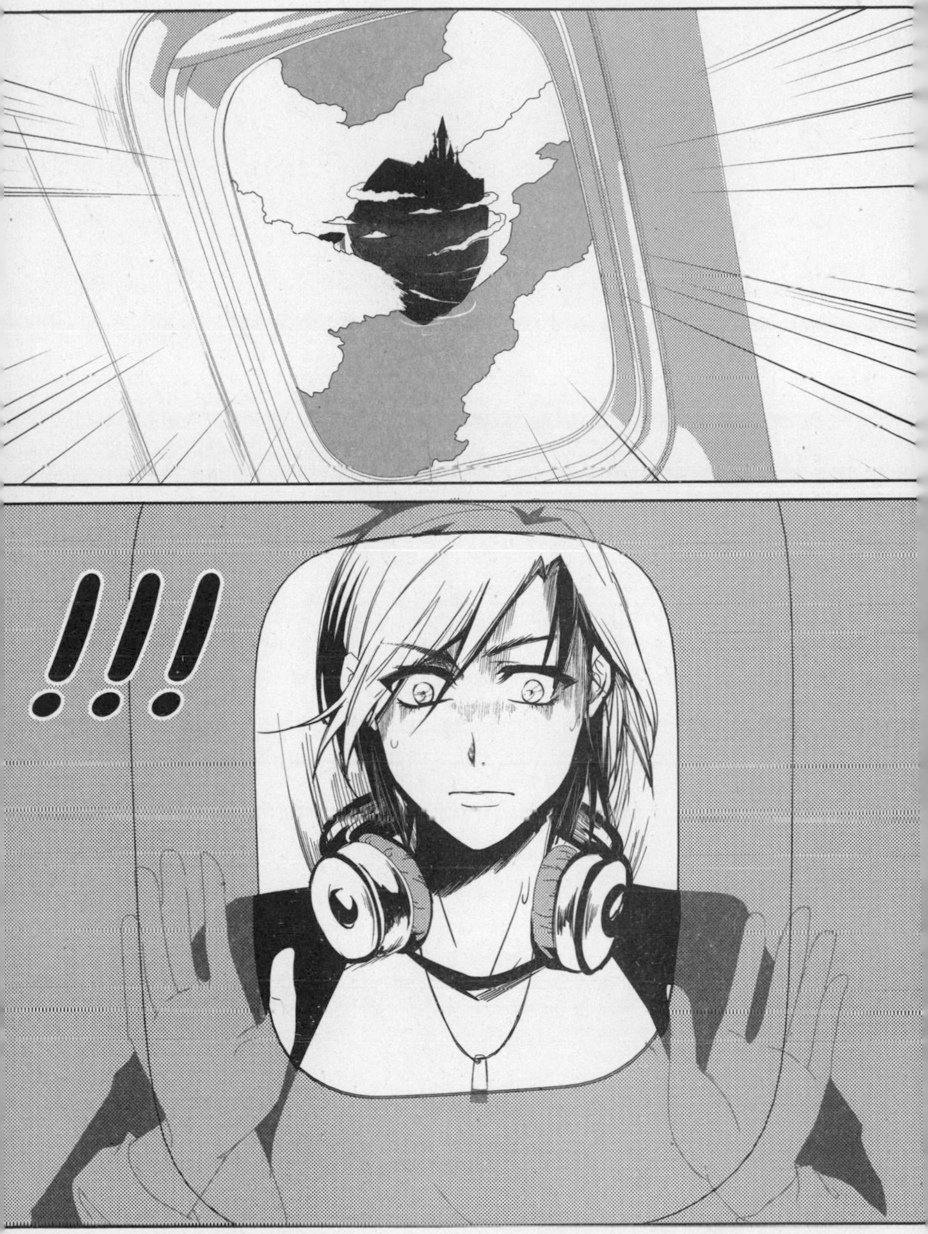
!!!

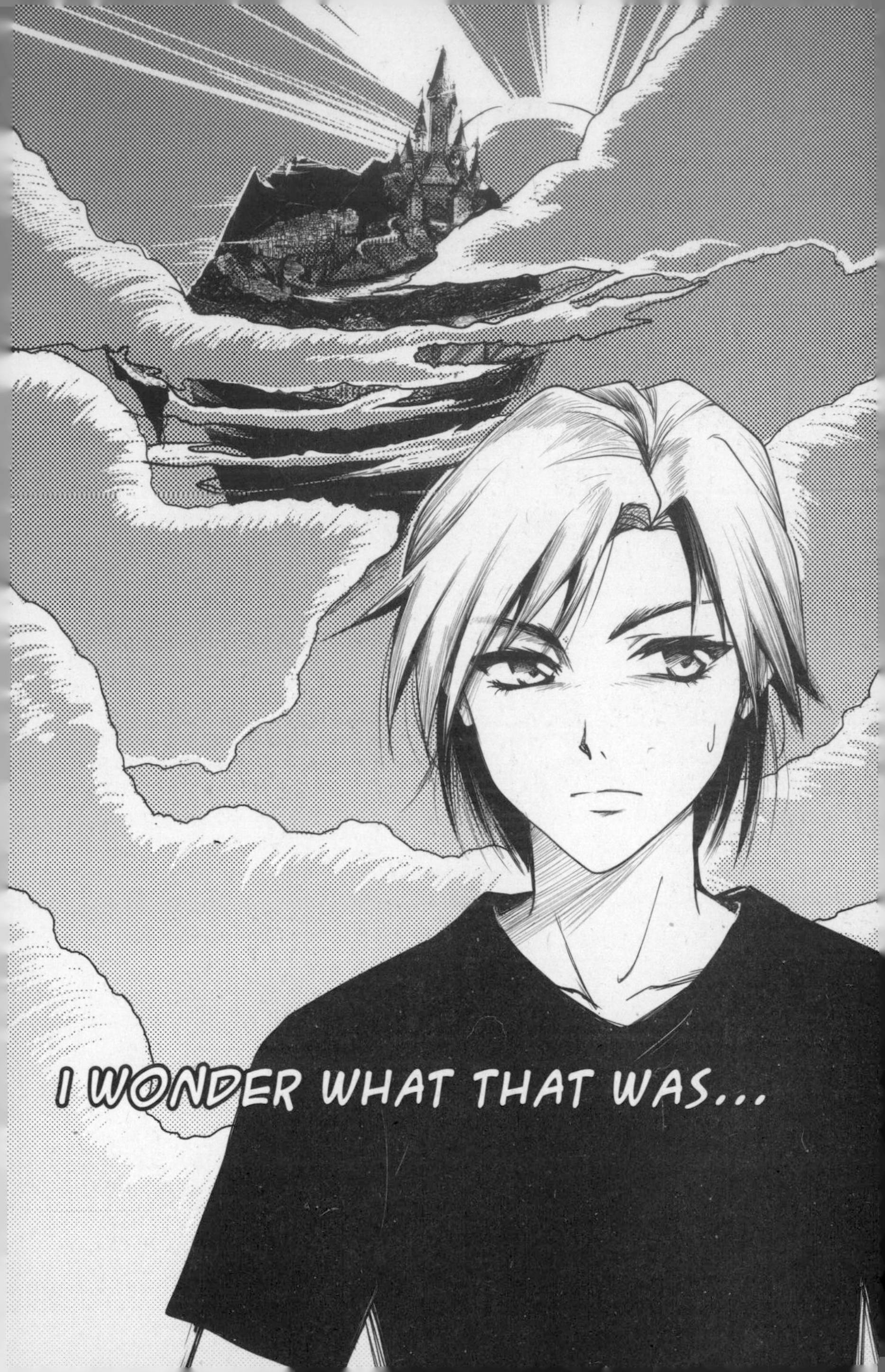
I WONDER WHAT THAT WAS...

READ THIS WAY

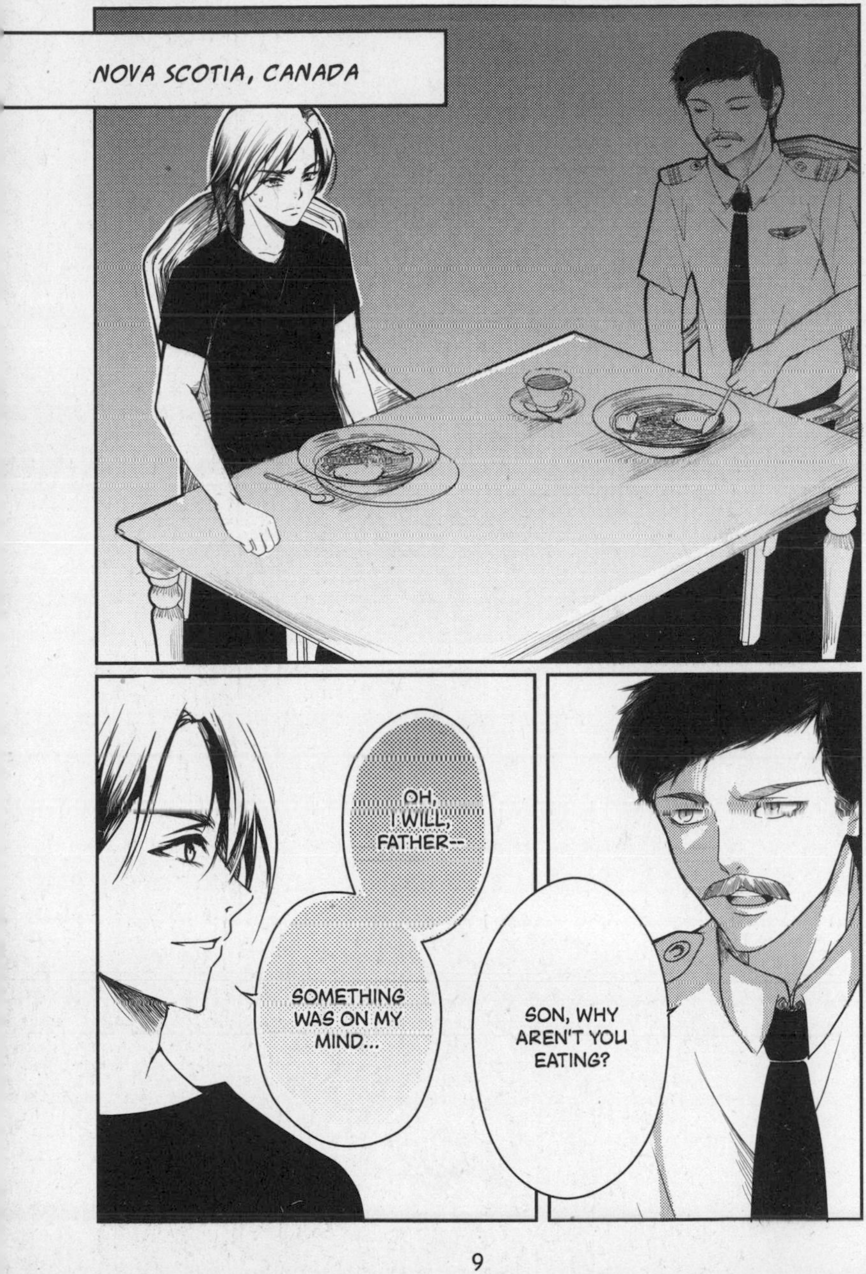
NOVA SCOTIA, CANADA
SON, WHY AREN'T YOU EATING?
OH, I WILL, FATHER--
SOMETHING WAS ON MY MIND...

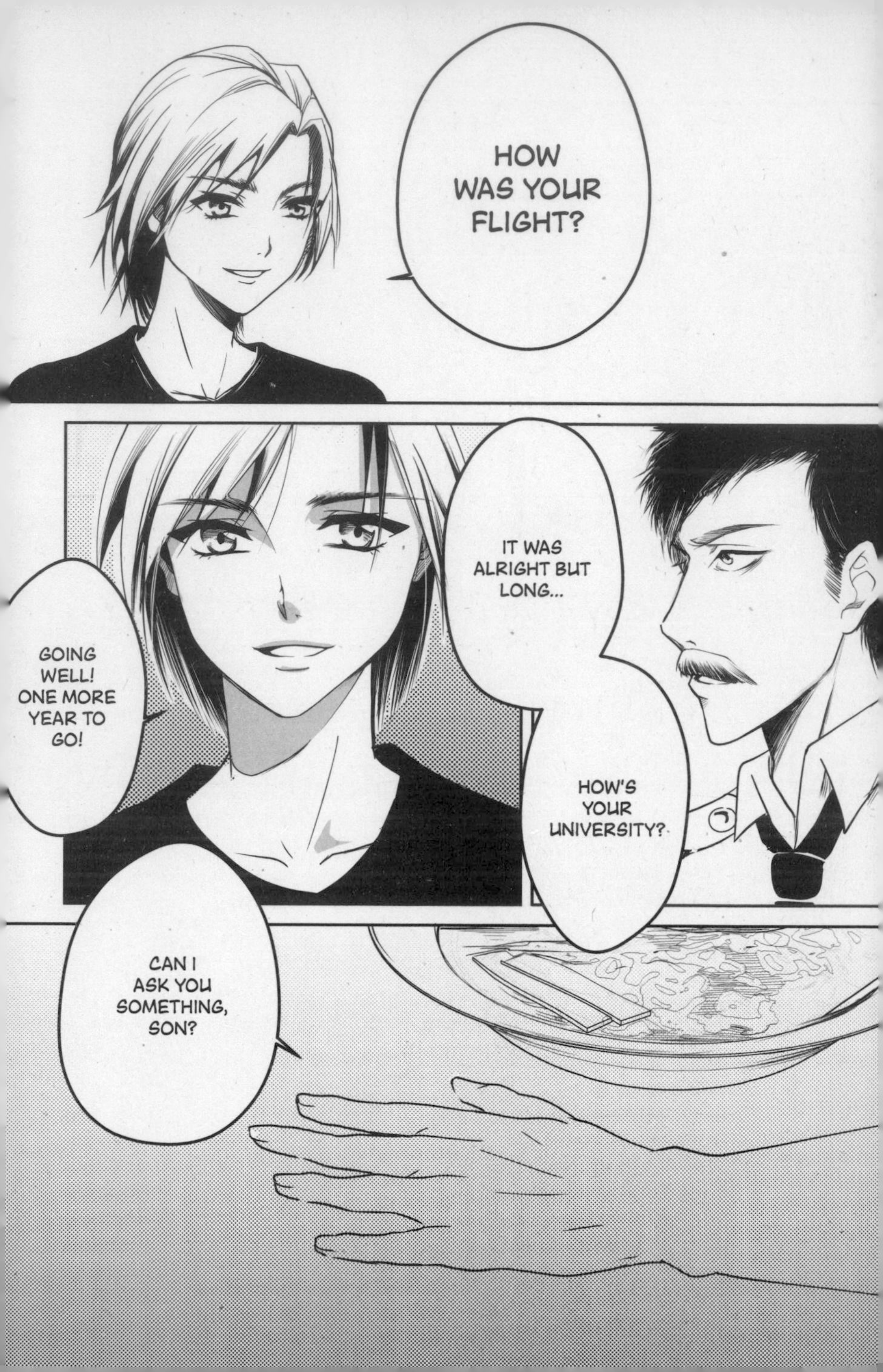
HOW WAS YOUR FLIGHT?
IT WAS ALRIGHT BUT LONG...
HOW'S YOUR UNIVERSITY?
GOING WELL! ONE MORE YEAR TO GO!
CAN I ASK YOU SOMETHING, SON?

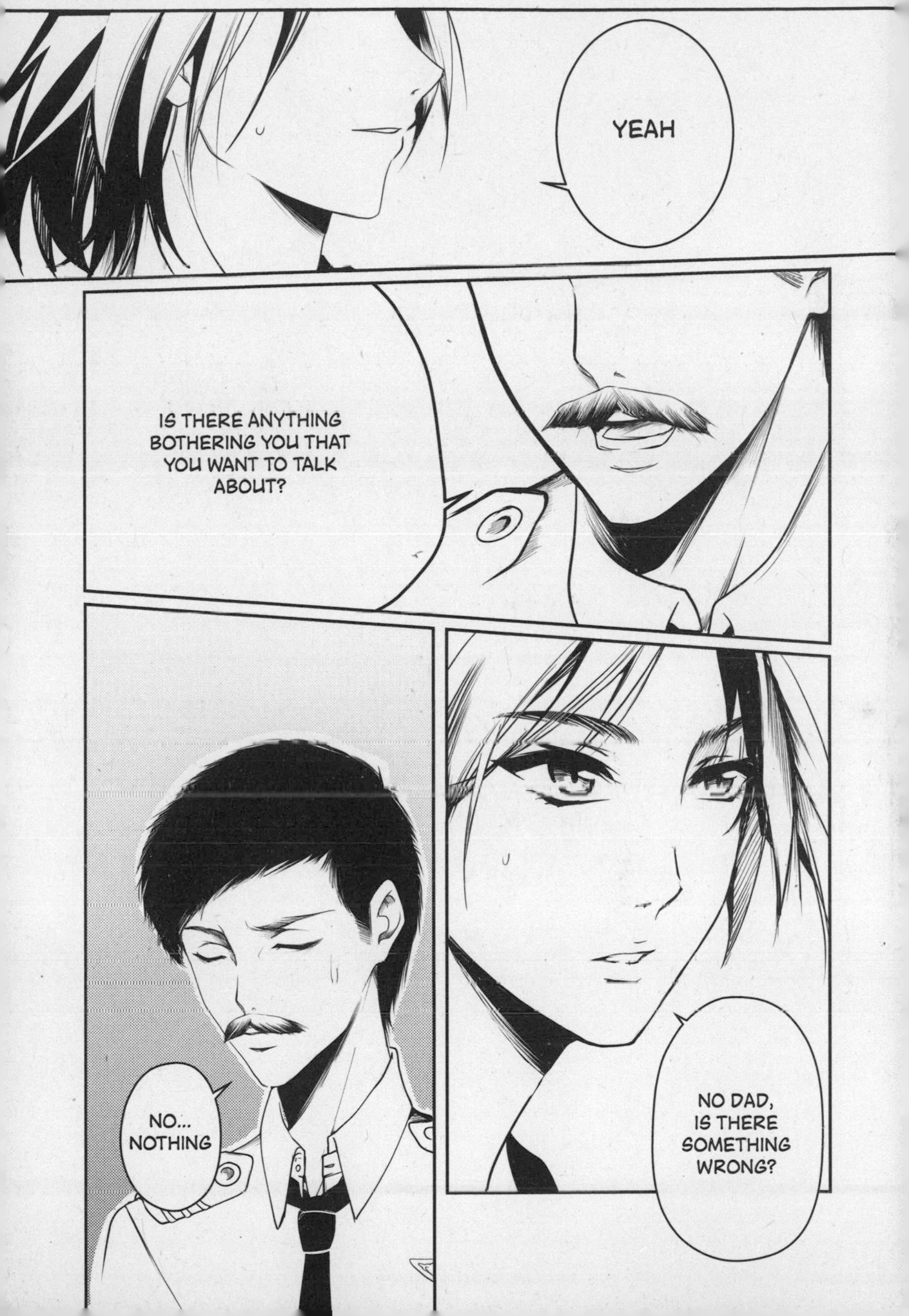
YEAH
IS THERE ANYTHING BOTHERING YOU THAT YOU WANT TO TALK ABOUT?
NO DAD, IS THERE SOMETHING WRONG?
NO... NOTHING

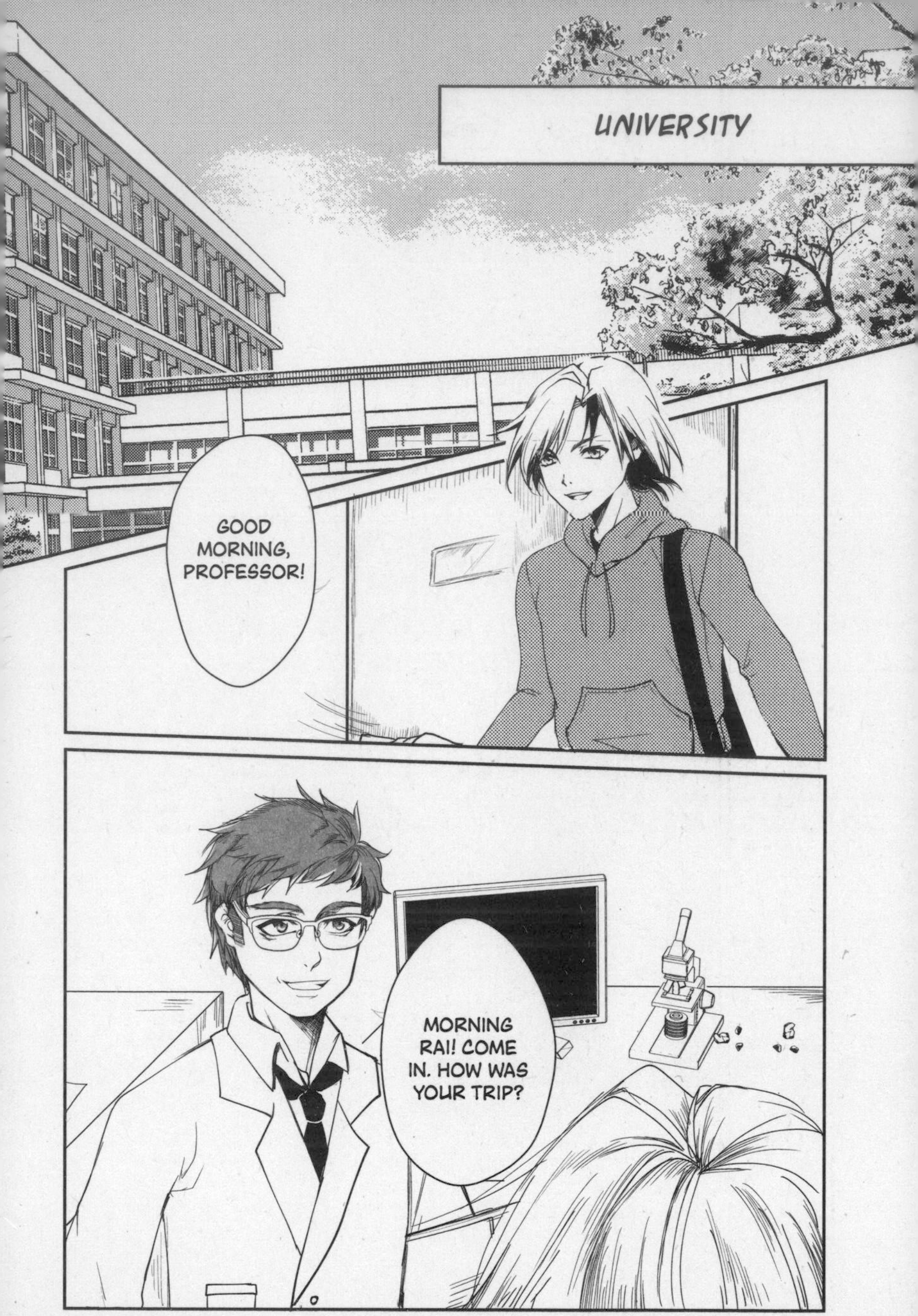
UNIVERSITY
GOOD MORNING, PROFESSOR!
MORNING RAI! COME IN. HOW WAS YOUR TRIP?

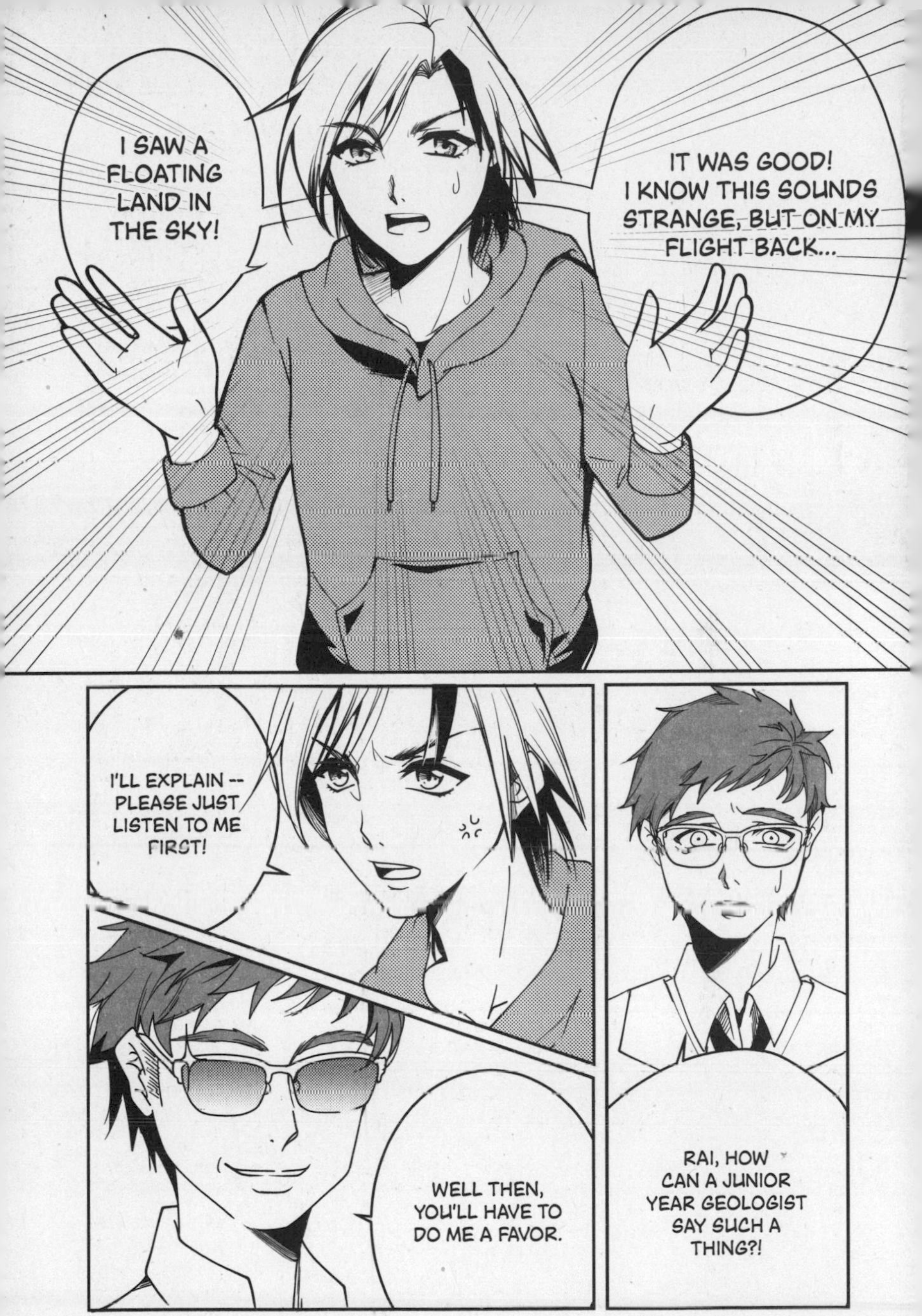
IT WAS GOOD! I KNOW THIS SOUNDS STRANGE, BUT ON MY FLIGHT BACK...
I SAW A FLOATING LAND IN THE SKY!
RAI, HOW CAN A JUNIOR YEAR GEOLOGIST SAY SUCH A THING?!
I'LL EXPLAIN -- PLEASE JUST LISTEN TO ME FIRST!
WELL THEN, YOU'LL HAVE TO DO ME A FAVOR.

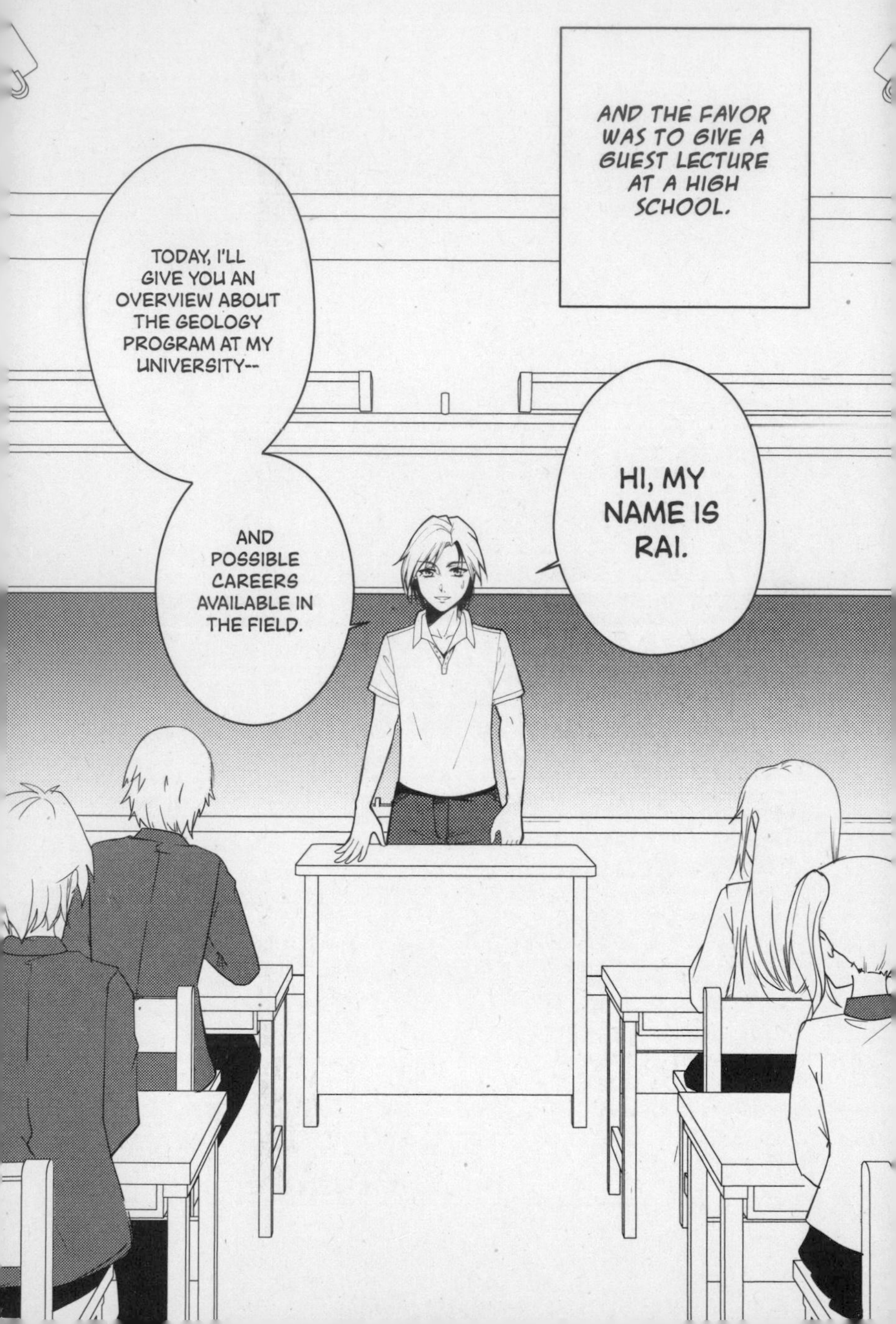
AND THE FAVOR WAS TO GIVE A GUEST LECTURE AT A HIGH SCHOOL.
HI, MY NAME IS RAI.
TODAY, I'LL GIVE YOU AN OVERVIEW ABOUT THE GEOLOGY PROGRAM AT MY UNIVERSITY--
AND POSSIBLE CAREERS AVAILABLE IN THE FIELD.

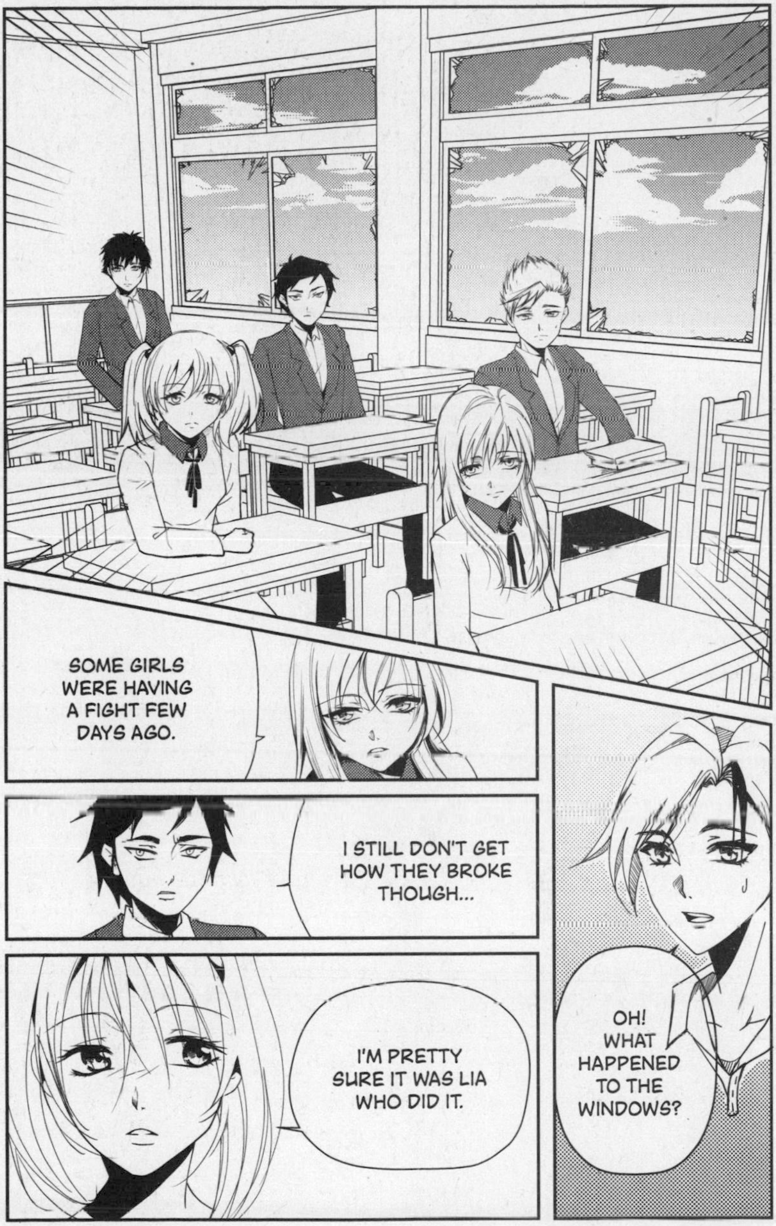
OH! WHAT HAPPENED TO THE WINDOWS?
SOME GIRLS WERE HAVING A FIGHT FEW DAYS AGO.
I STILL DON'T GET HOW THEY BROKE THOUGH...
I'M PRETTY SURE IT WAS LIA WHO DID IT.

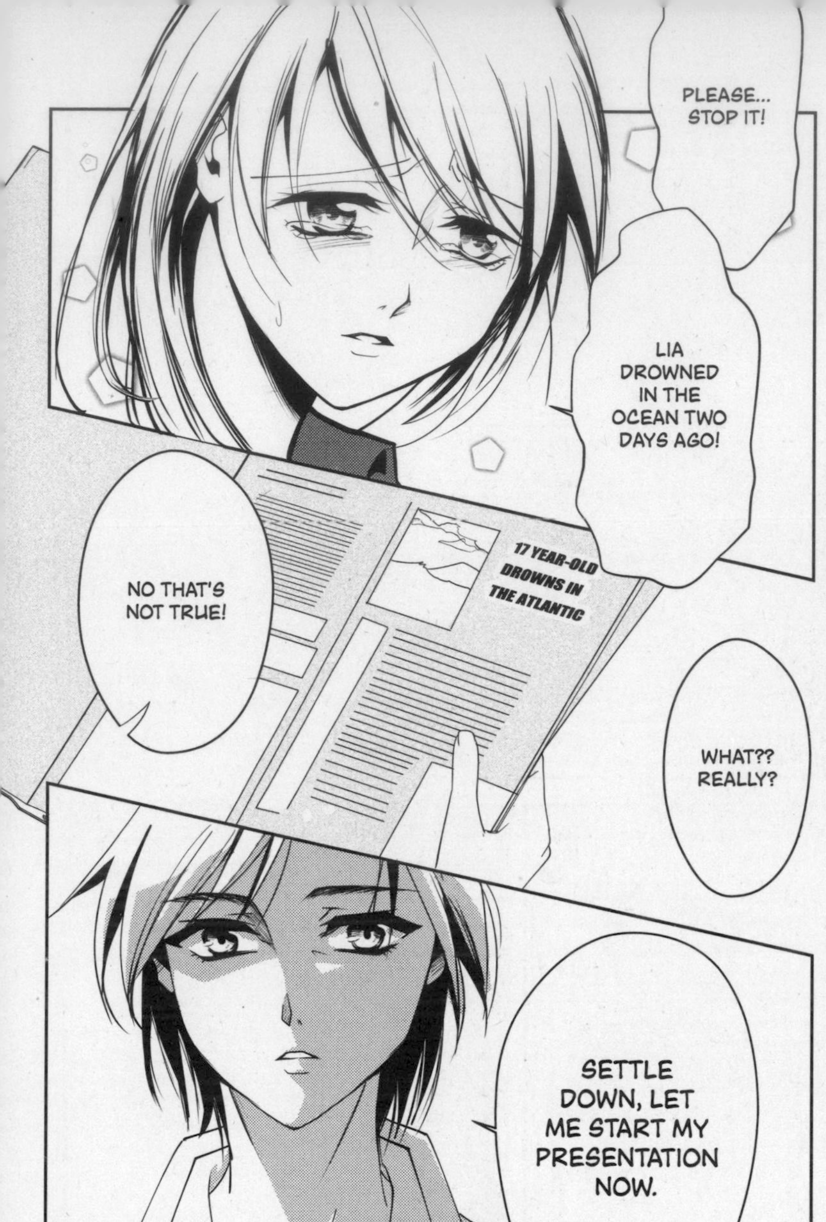
PLEASE... STOP IT!
LIA DROWNED IN THE OCEAN TWO DAYS AGO!
17 YEAR-OLD DROWNS IN THE ATLANTIC
NO THAT'S NOT TRUE!
WHAT?? REALLY?
SETTLE DOWN, LET ME START MY PRESENTATION NOW.

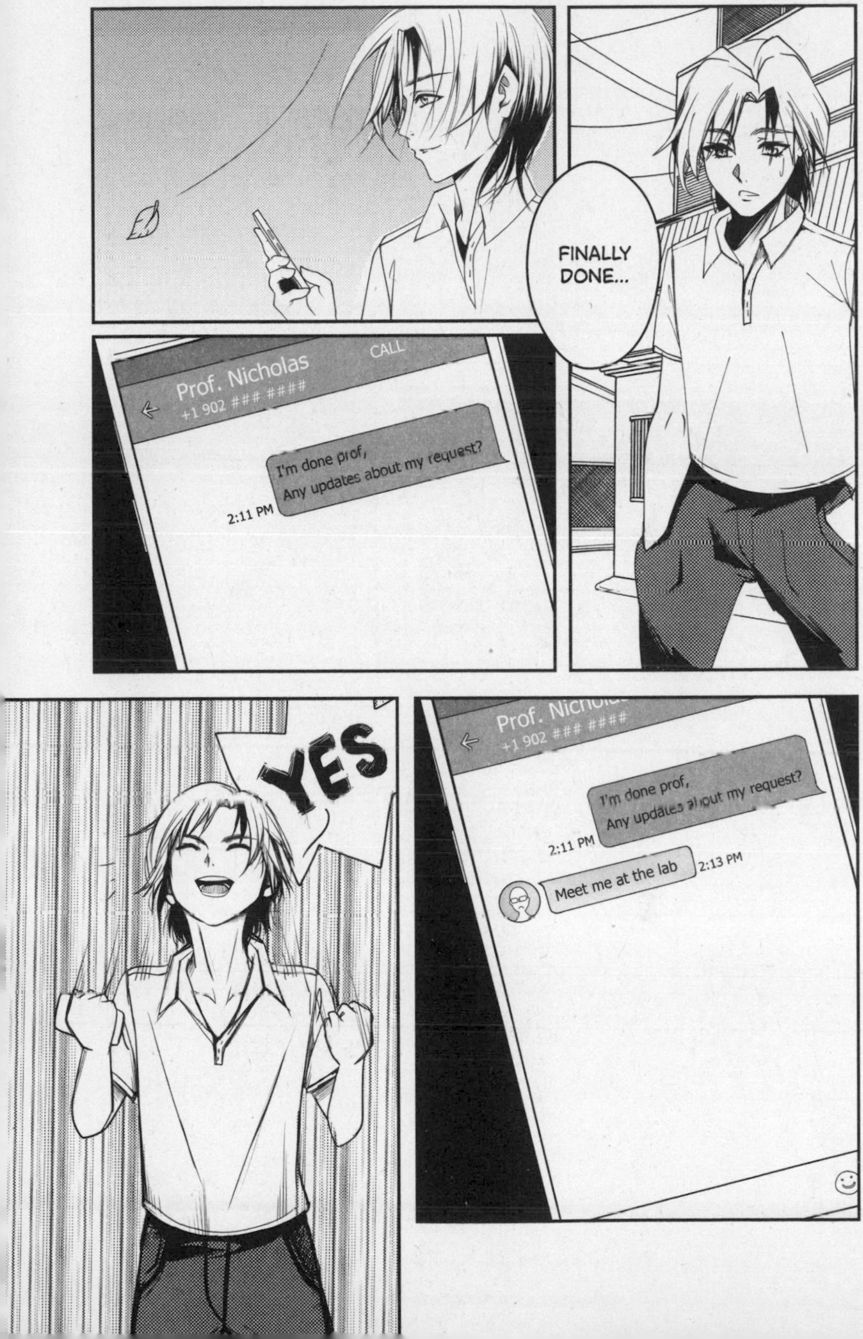
FINALLY DONE...
Prof. Nicholas
CALL
+1 902 ### ####
I'm done prof,
Any updates about my request?
2:11 PM
Prof. Nichola
+1 902 ### ####
I'm done prof,
Any updates about my request?
2:11 PM
Meet me at the lab
2:13 PM
YES

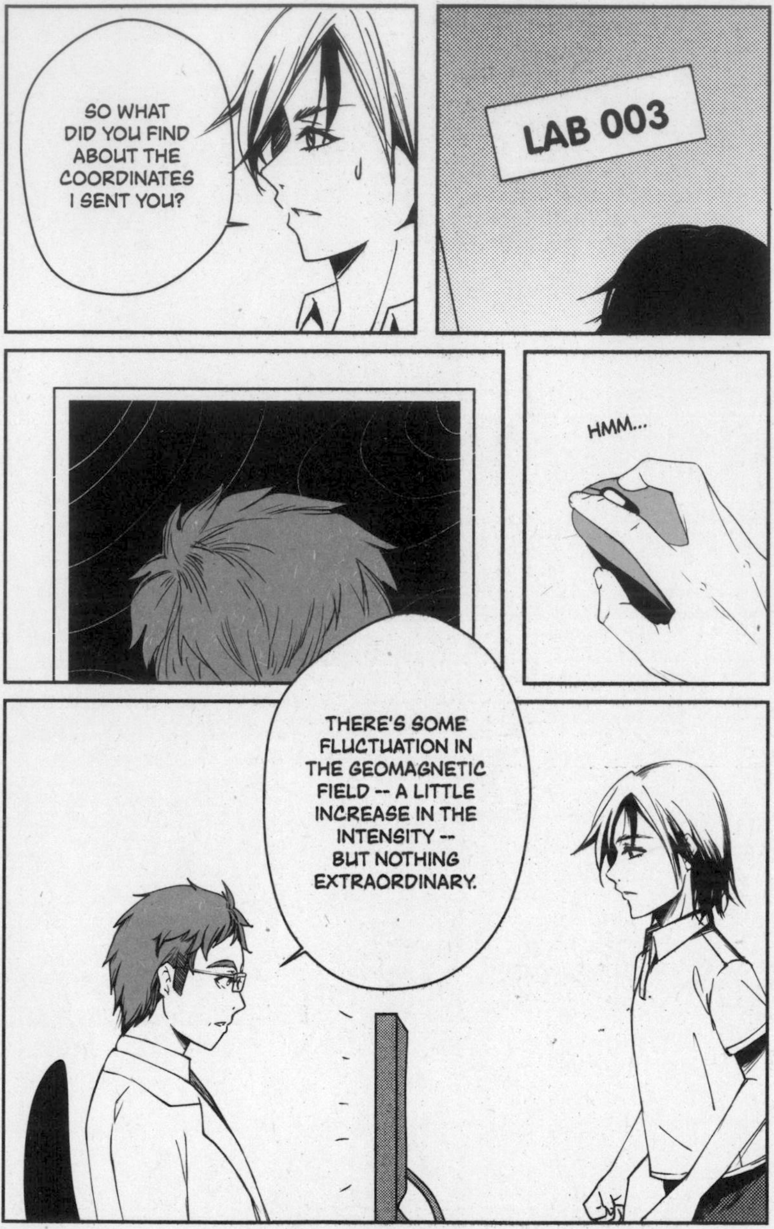
LAB 003
SO WHAT DID YOU FIND ABOUT THE COORDINATES I SENT YOU?
HMM...
THERE'S SOME FLUCTUATION IN THE GEOMAGNETIC FIELD -- A LITTLE INCREASE IN THE INTENSITY -- BUT NOTHING EXTRAORDINARY.

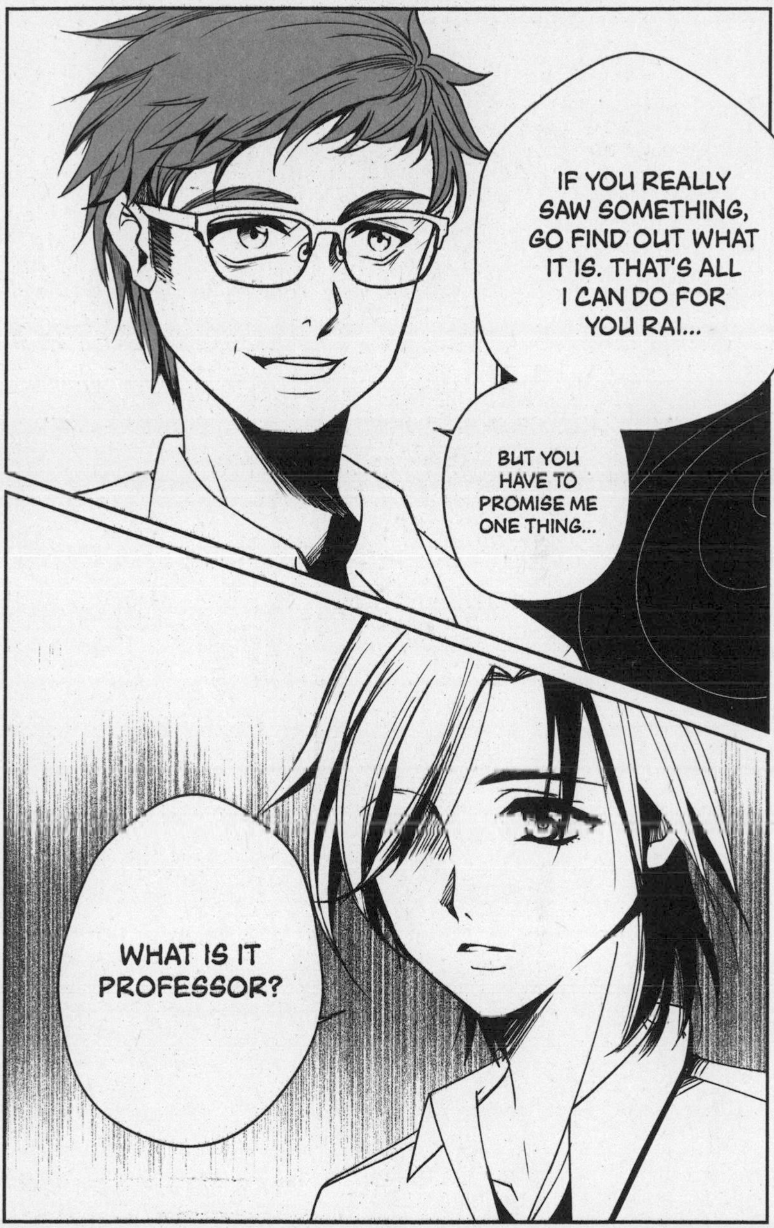
IF YOU REALLY SAW SOMETHING, GO FIND OUT WHAT IT IS. THAT'S ALL I CAN DO FOR YOU RAI...
BUT YOU HAVE TO PROMISE ME ONE THING...
WHAT IS IT PROFESSOR?

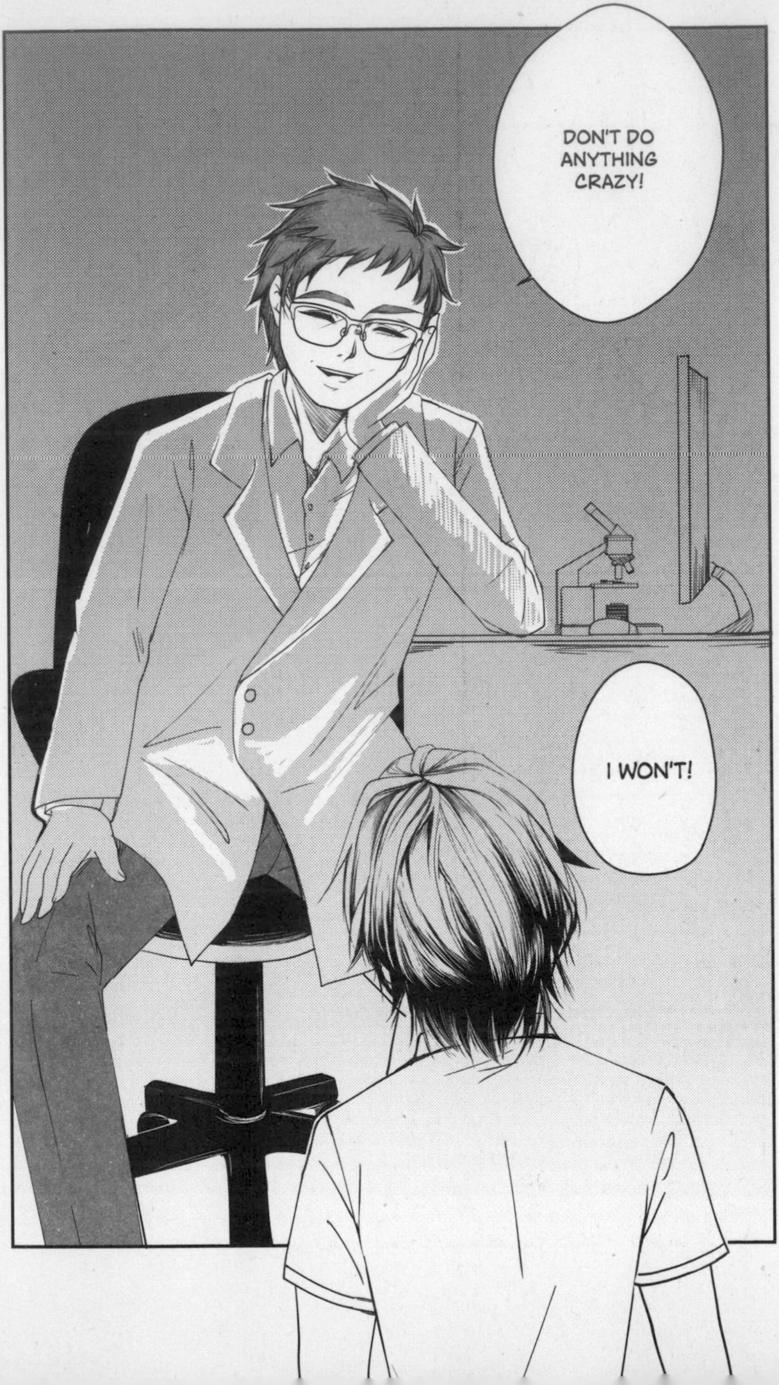
DON'T DO ANYTHING CRAZY!
I WON'T!

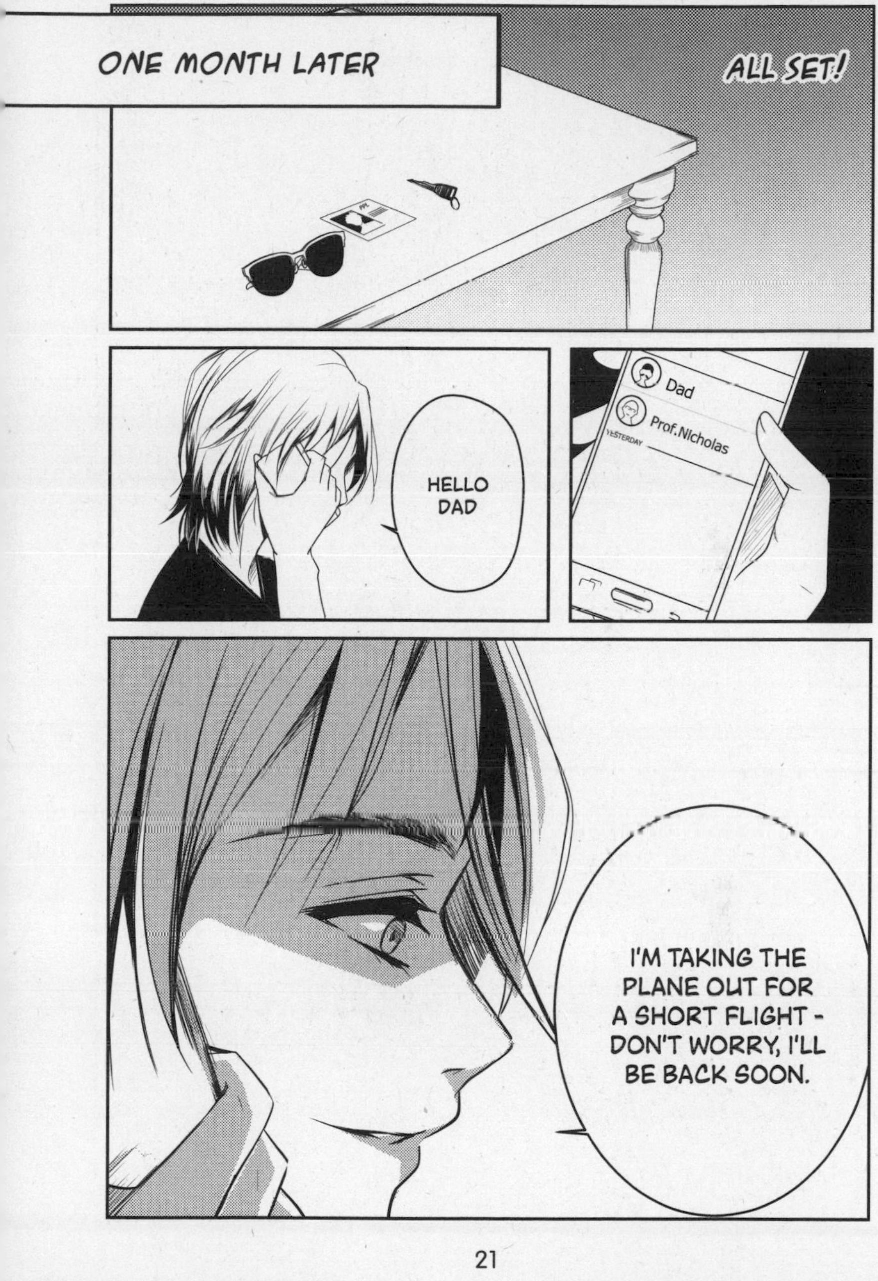
ONE MONTH LATER
ALL SET!
Dad
Prof.Nicholas
YESTERDAY
HELLO DAD
I'M TAKING THE PLANE OUT FOR A SHORT FLIGHT - DON'T WORRY, I'LL BE BACK SOON.

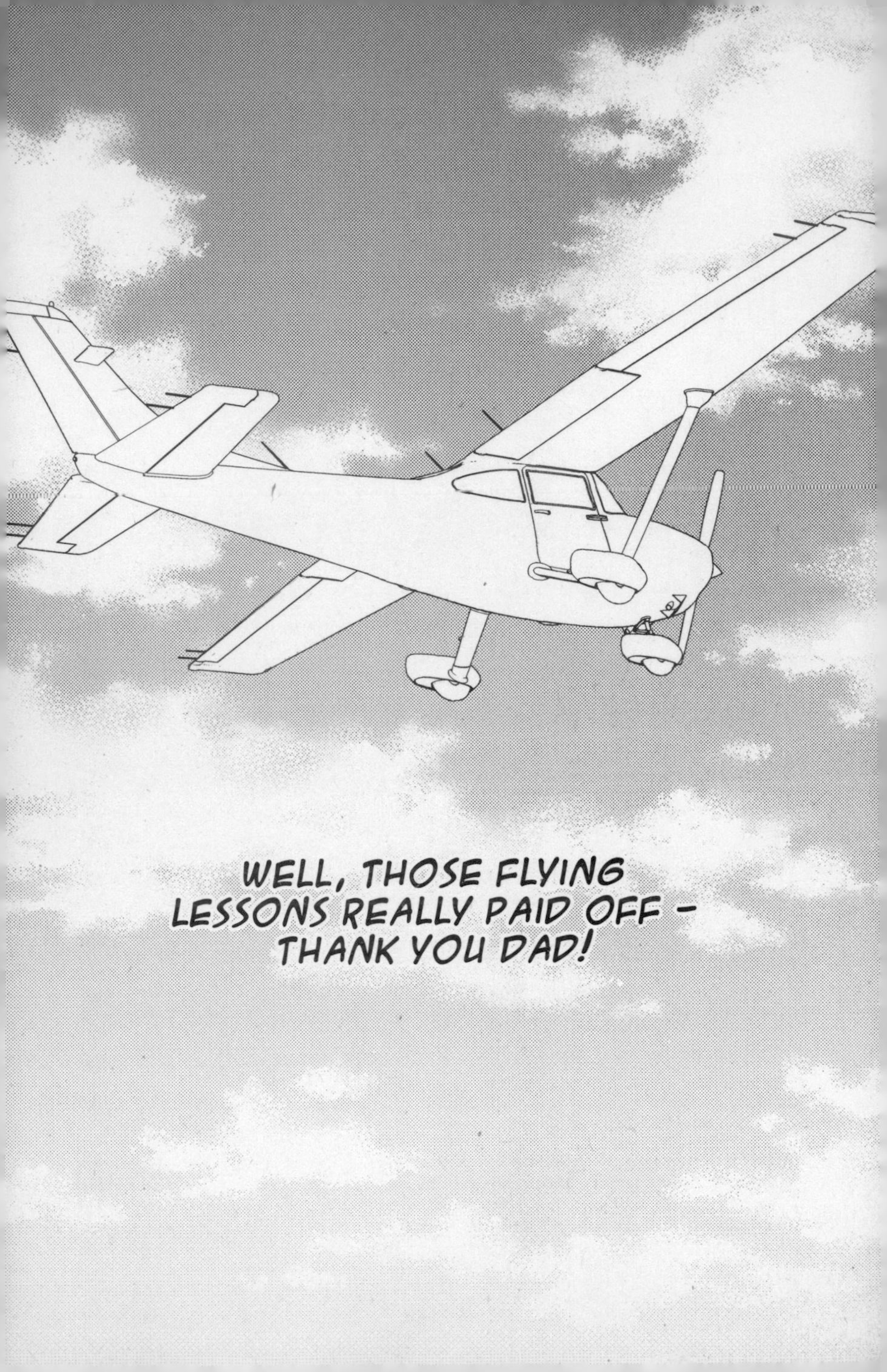
WELL, THOSE FLYING LESSONS REALLY PAID OFF - THANK YOU DAD!

Ocean of Secrets

CHAPTER 6

A DARK SECRET

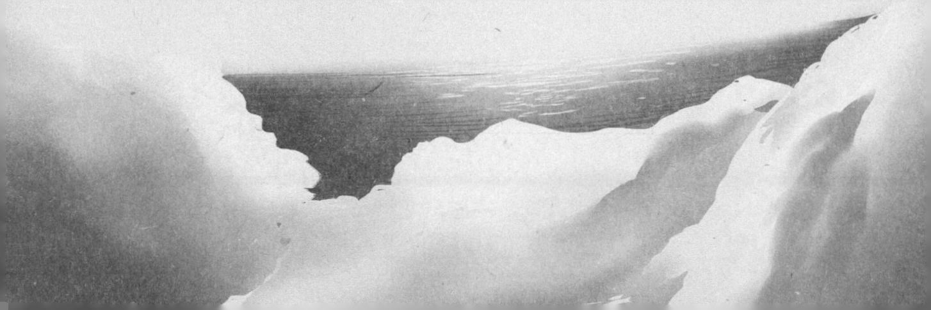

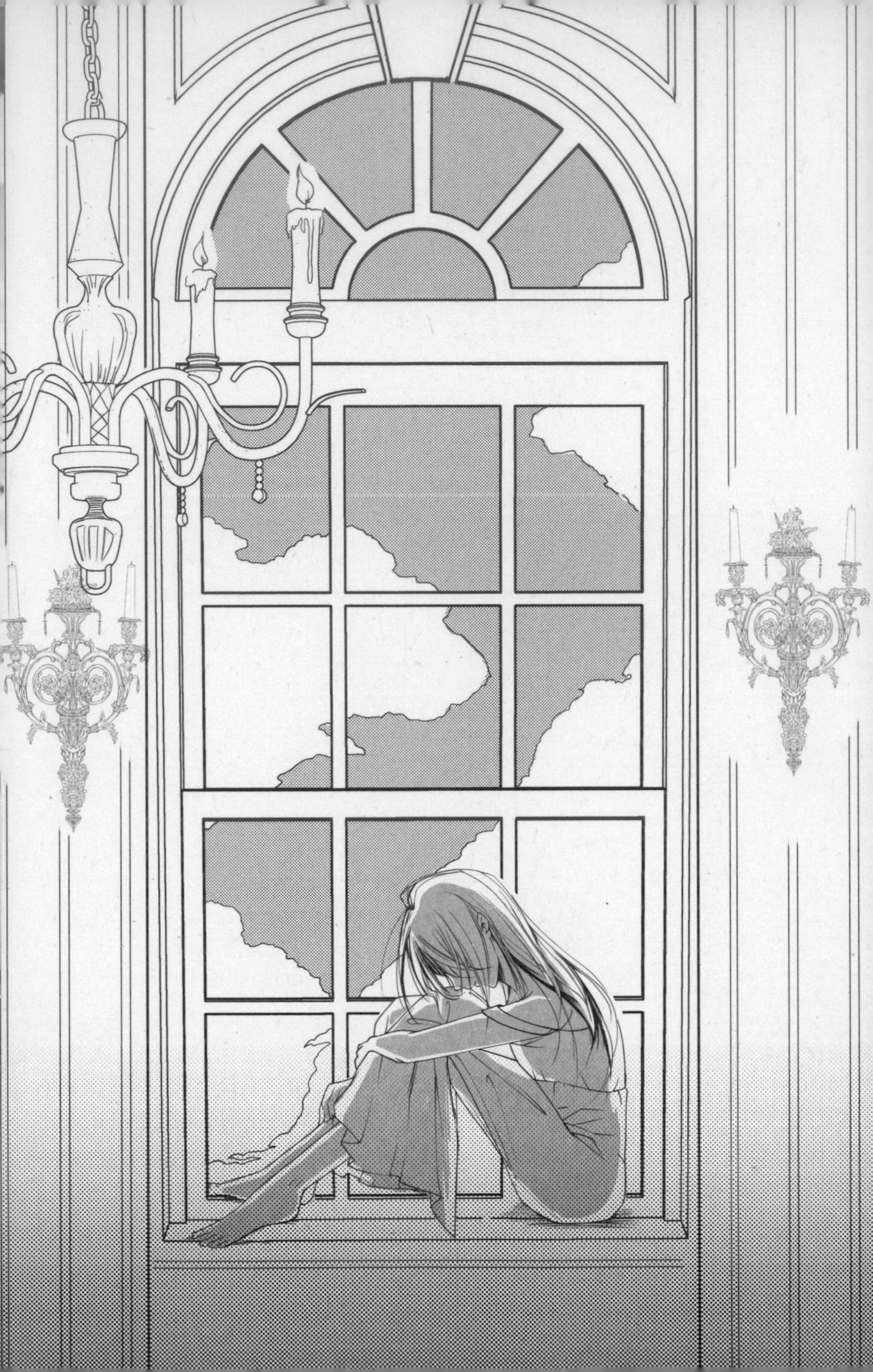

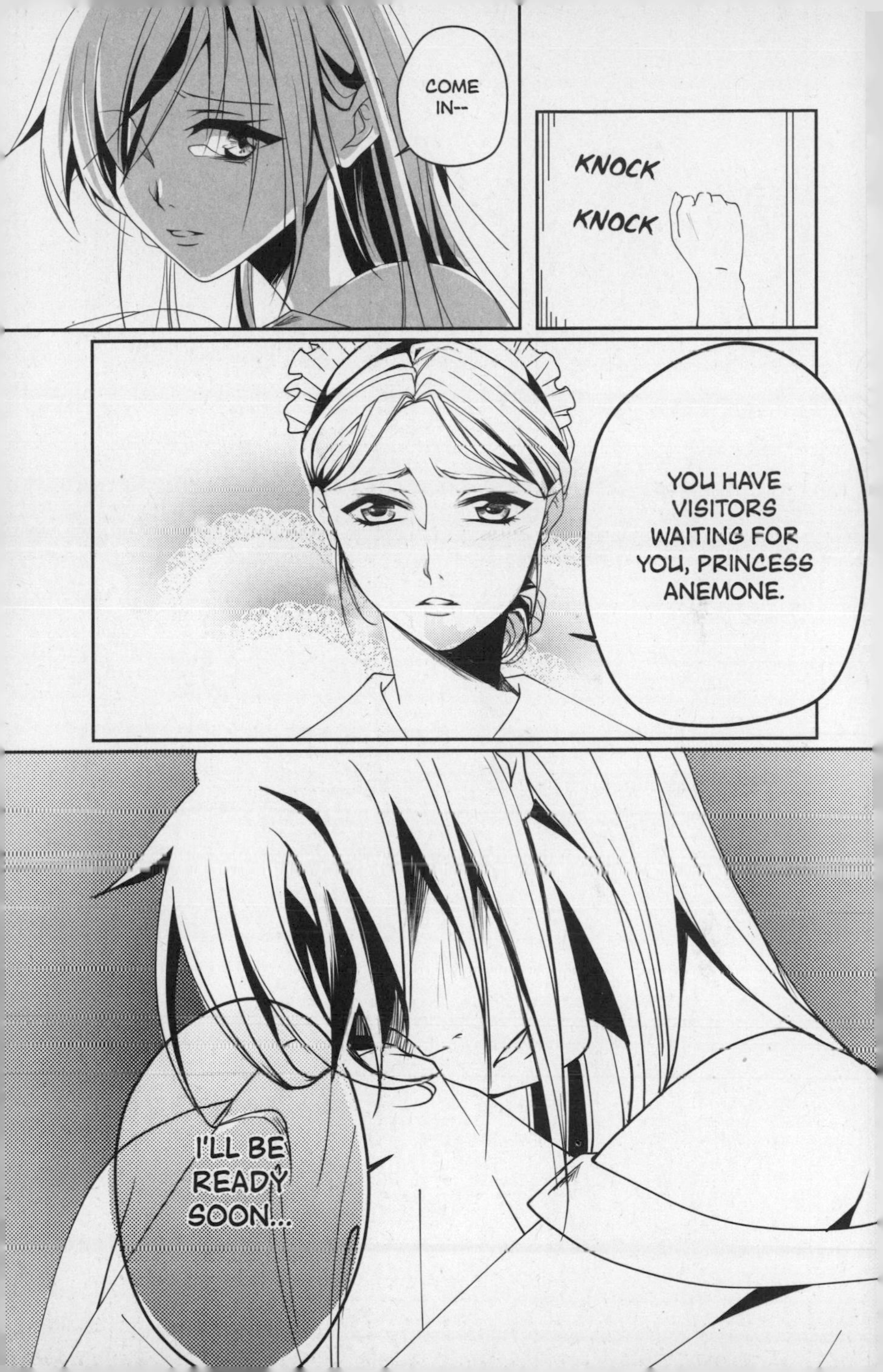
KNOCK
KNOCK
COME IN--
YOU HAVE VISITORS WAITING FOR YOU, PRINCESS ANEMONE.
I'LL BE READY SOON...

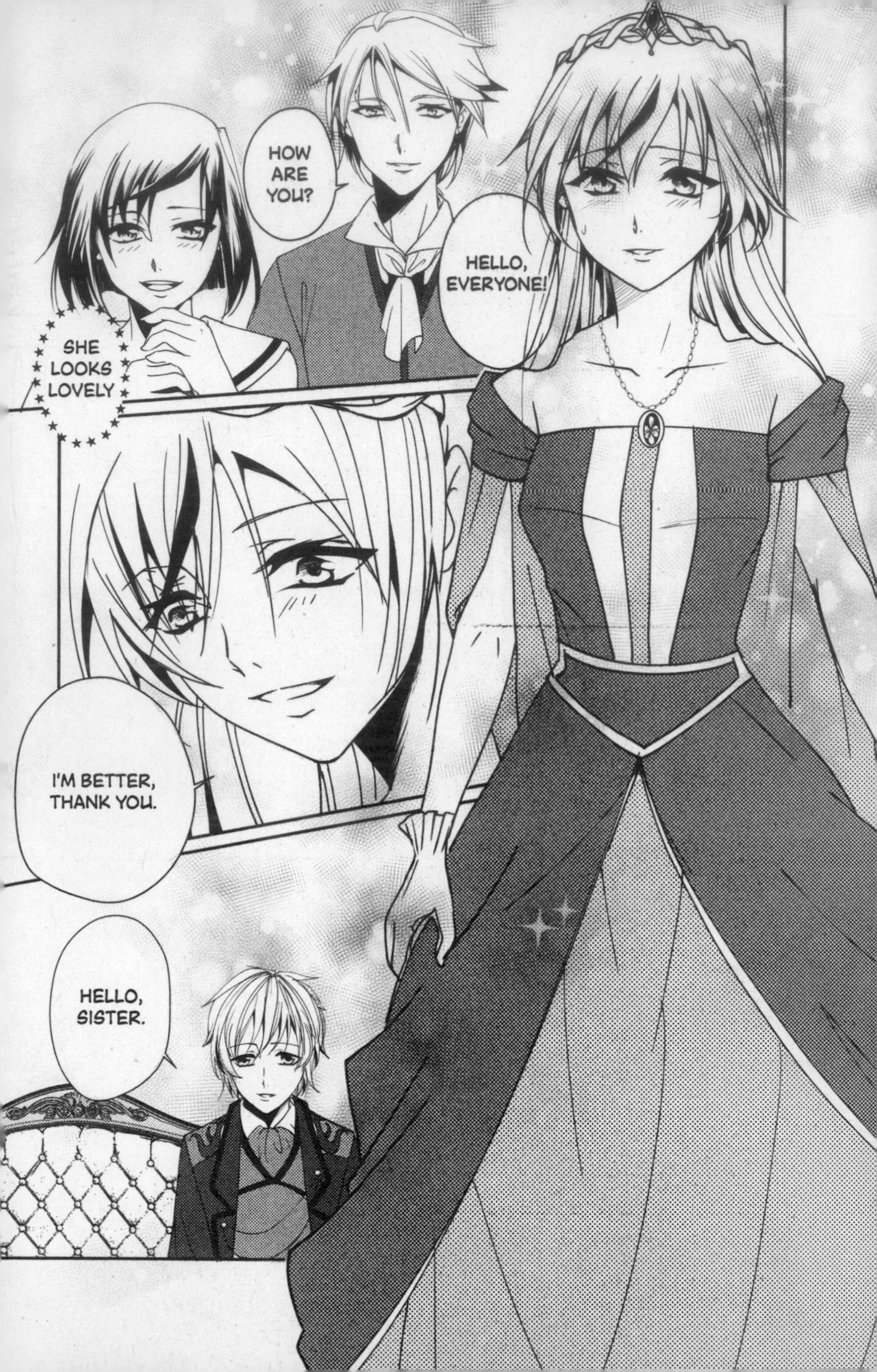
HELLO, EVERYONE!
HOW ARE YOU?
SHE LOOKS LOVELY
I'M BETTER, THANK YOU.
HELLO, SISTER.

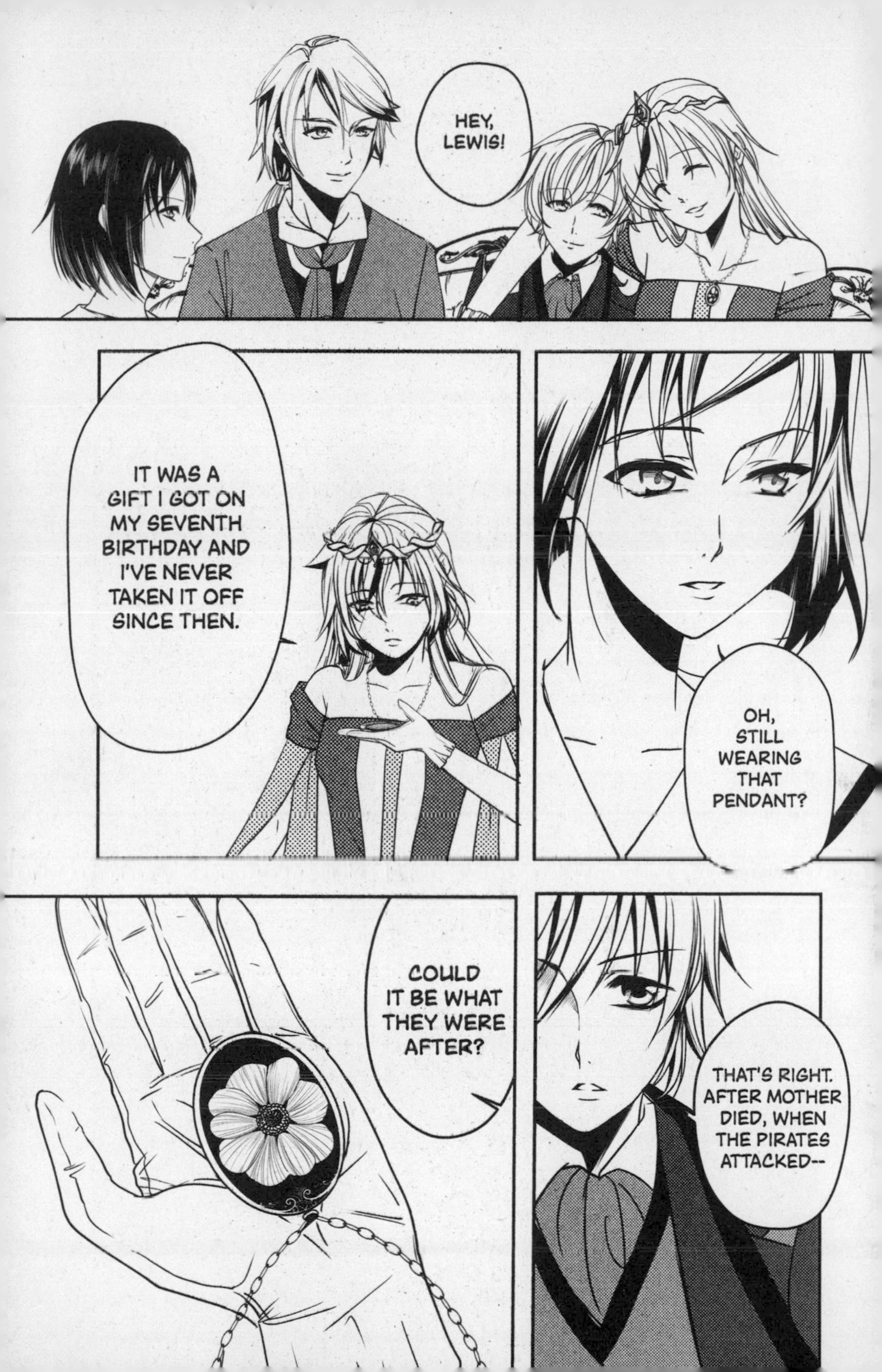
HEY, LEWIS!
OH, STILL WEARING THAT PENDANT?
IT WAS A GIFT I GOT ON MY SEVENTH BIRTHDAY AND I'VE NEVER TAKEN IT OFF SINCE THEN.
THAT'S RIGHT. AFTER MOTHER DIED, WHEN THE PIRATES ATTACKED--
COULD IT BE WHAT THEY WERE AFTER?

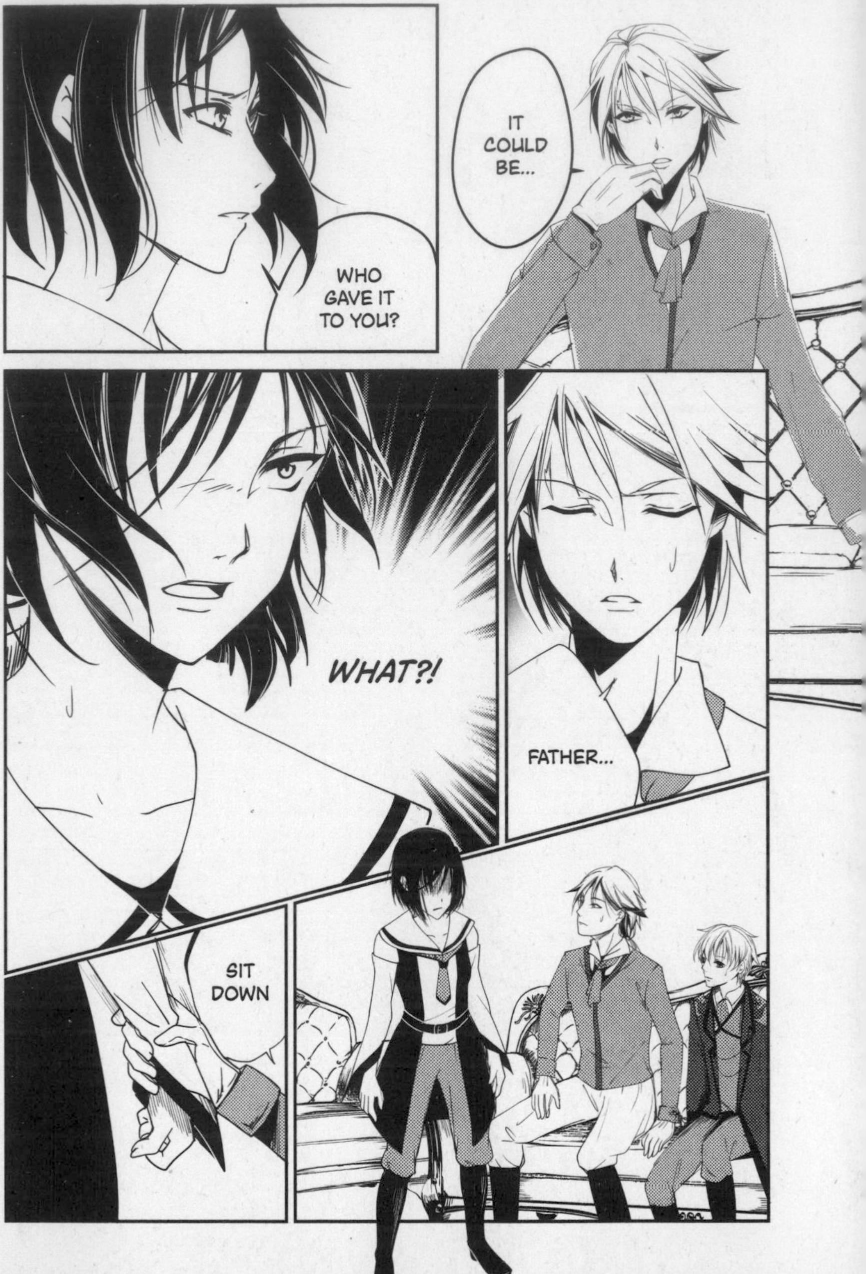
IT COULD BE...
WHO GAVE IT TO YOU?
FATHER...
WHAT?!
SIT DOWN

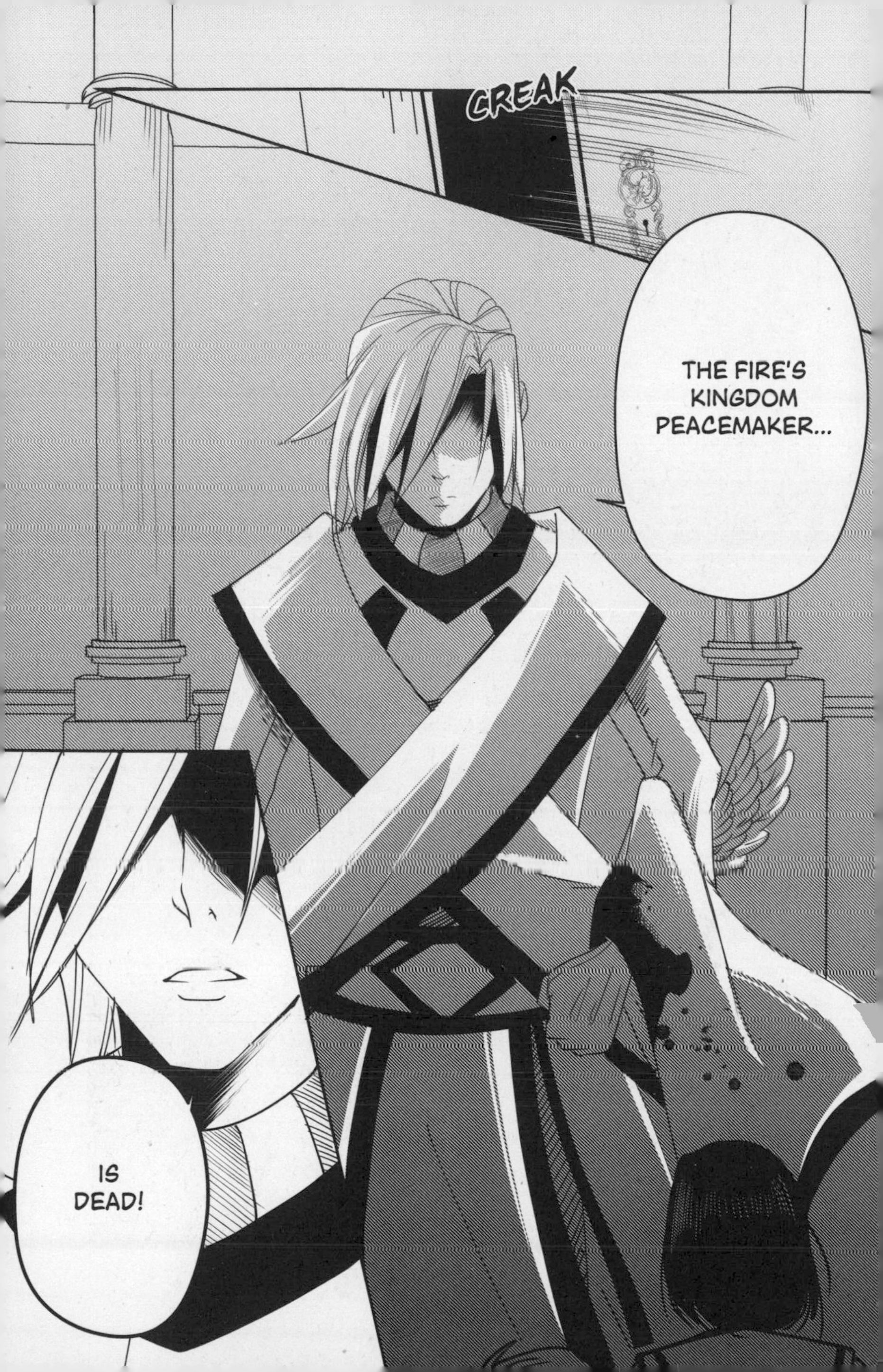
CREAK
THE FIRE'S KINGDOM PEACEMAKER...
IS DEAD!

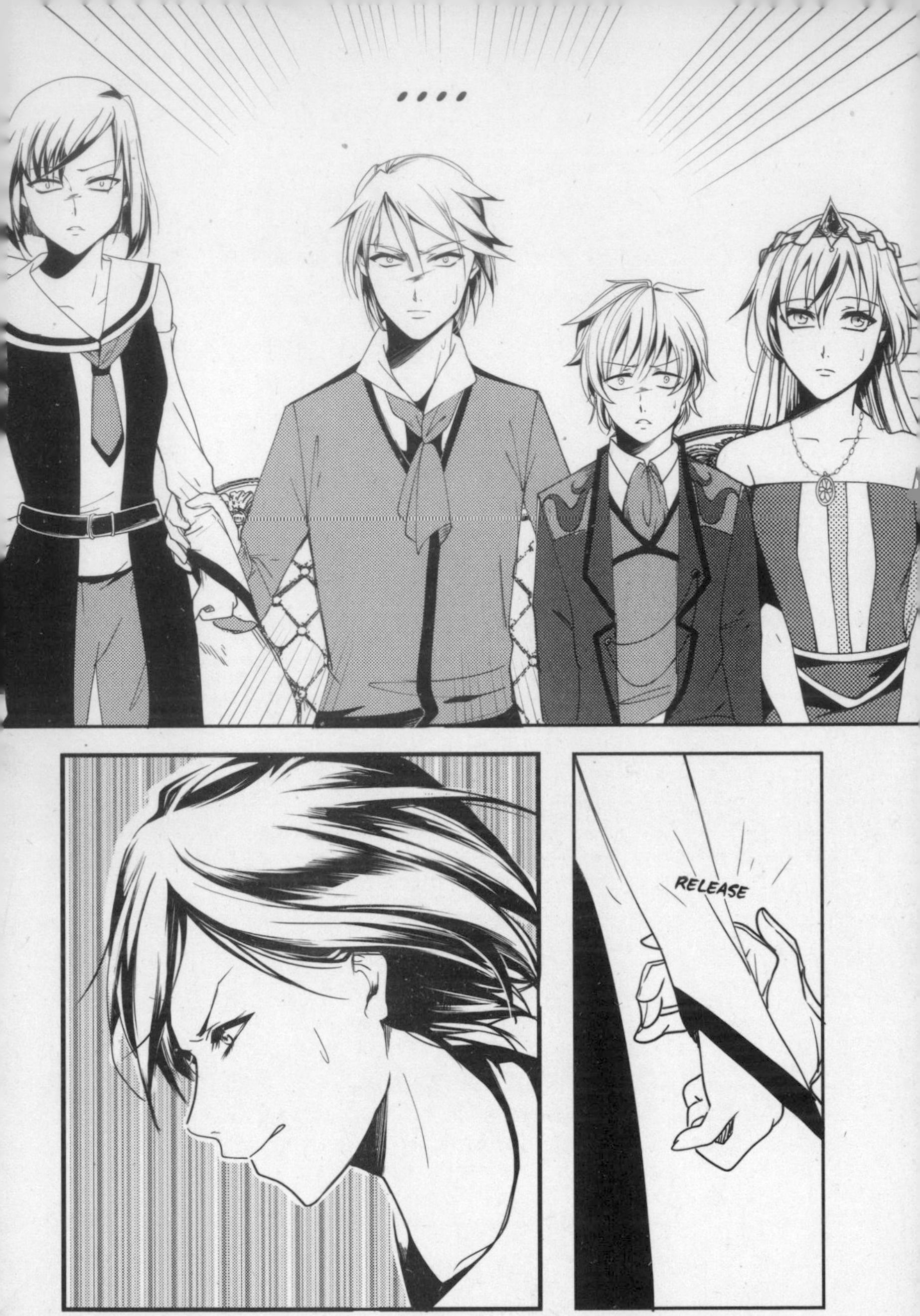
....
RELEASE

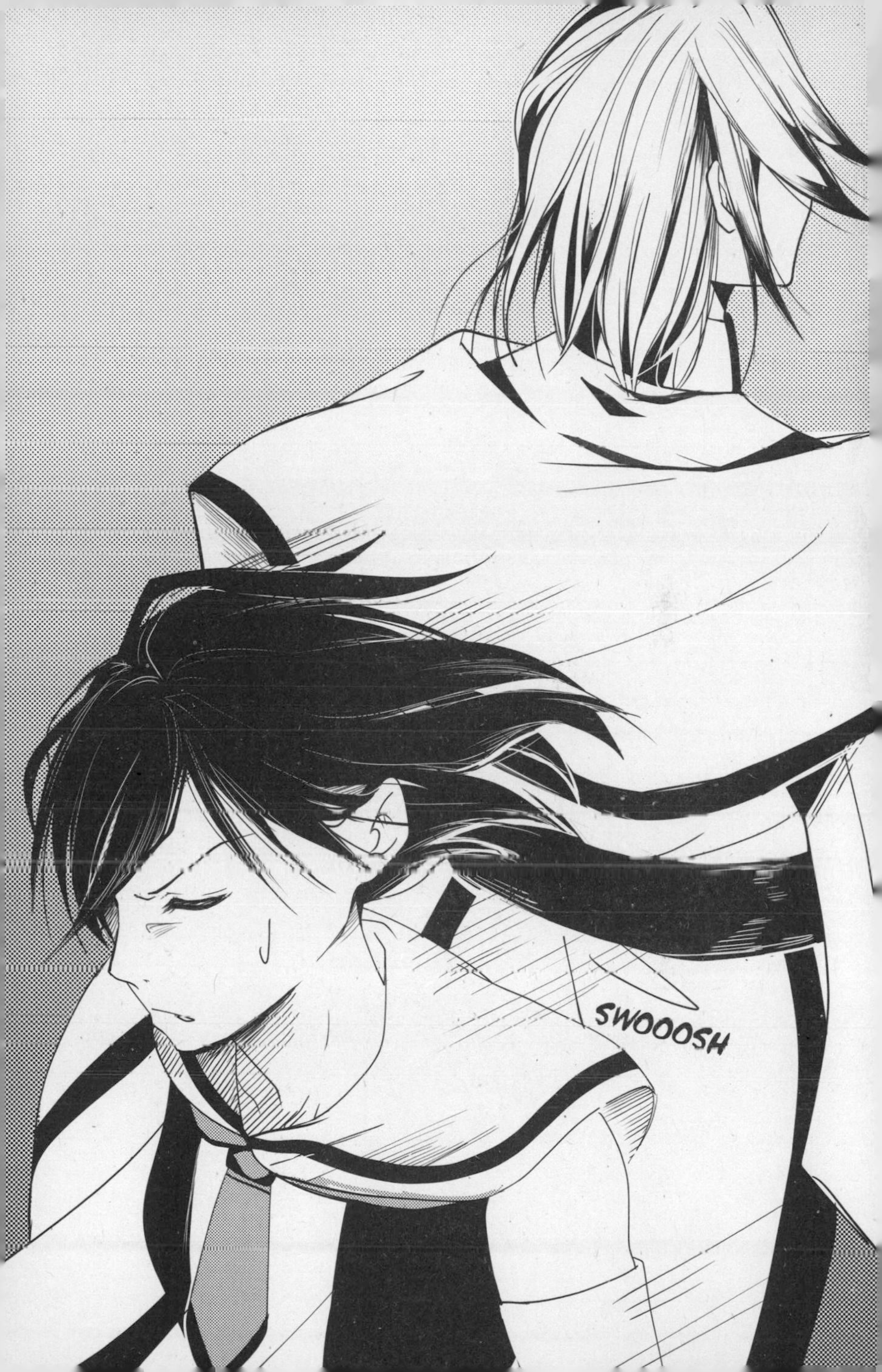
SWOOOSH

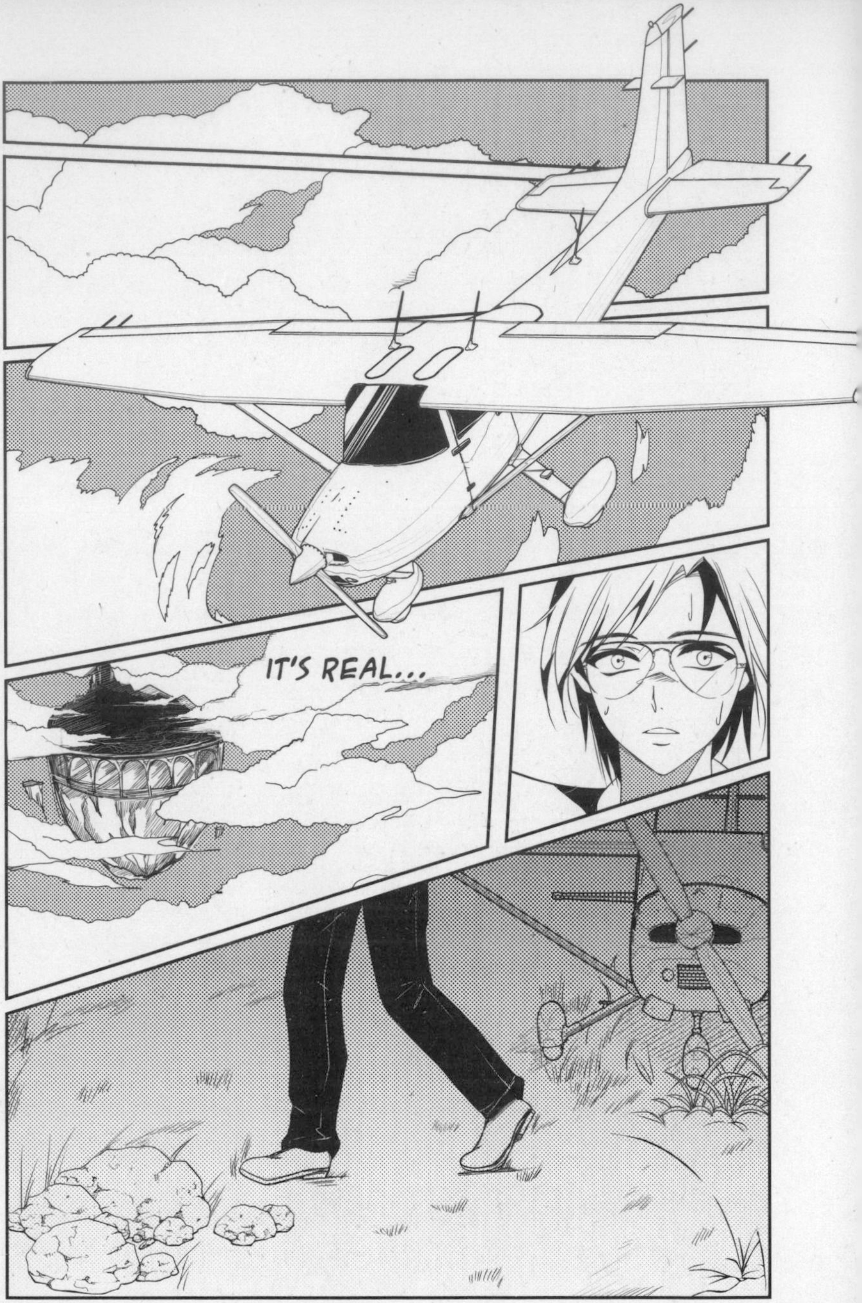
IT'S REAL...

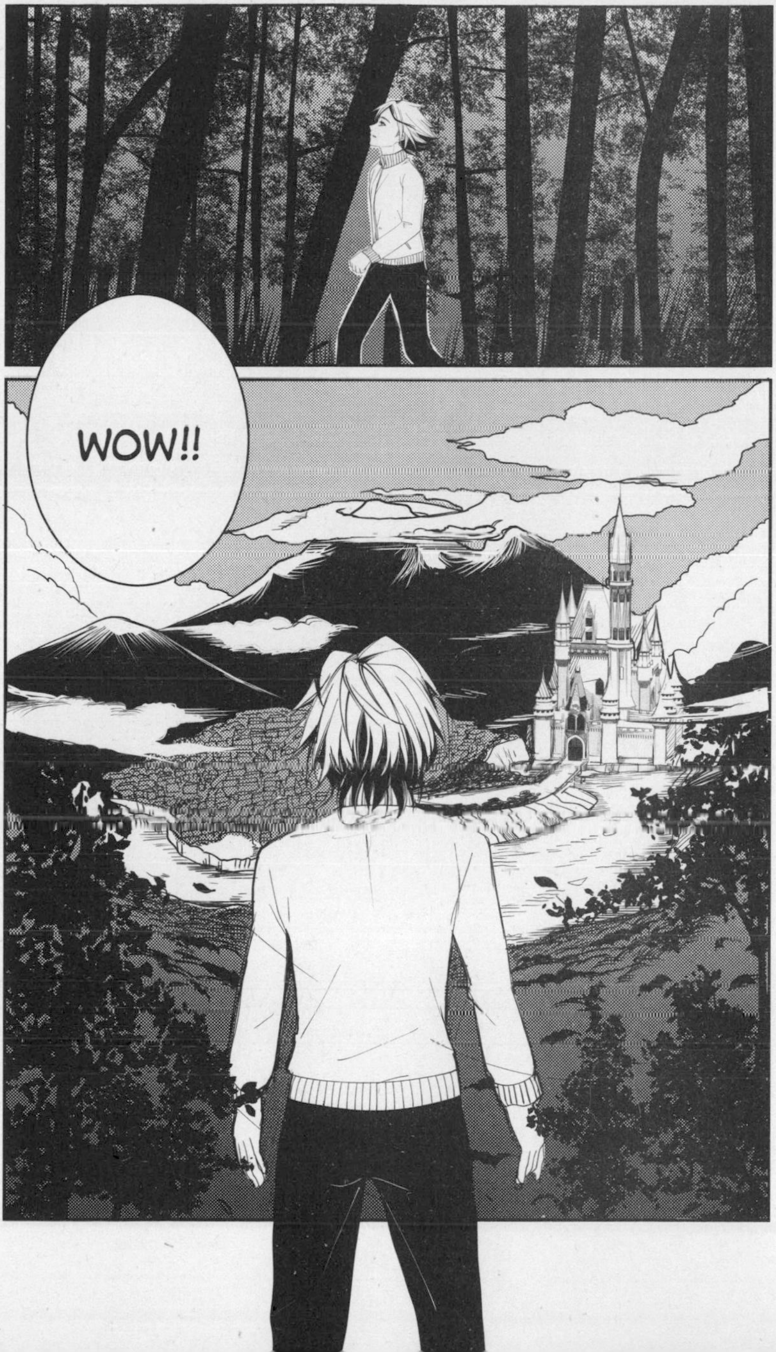
WOW!!

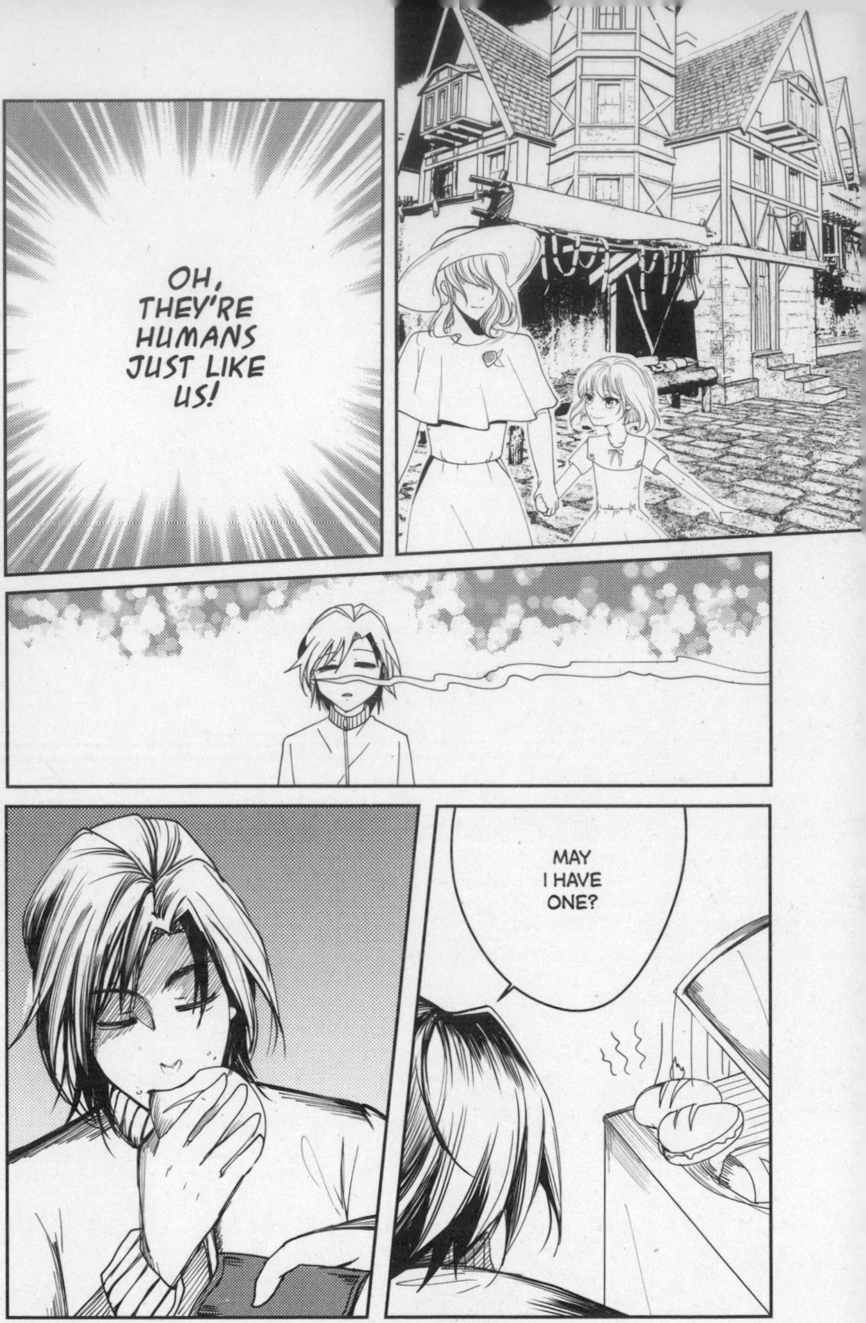
OH, THEY'RE HUMANS JUST LIKE US!
MAY I HAVE ONE?

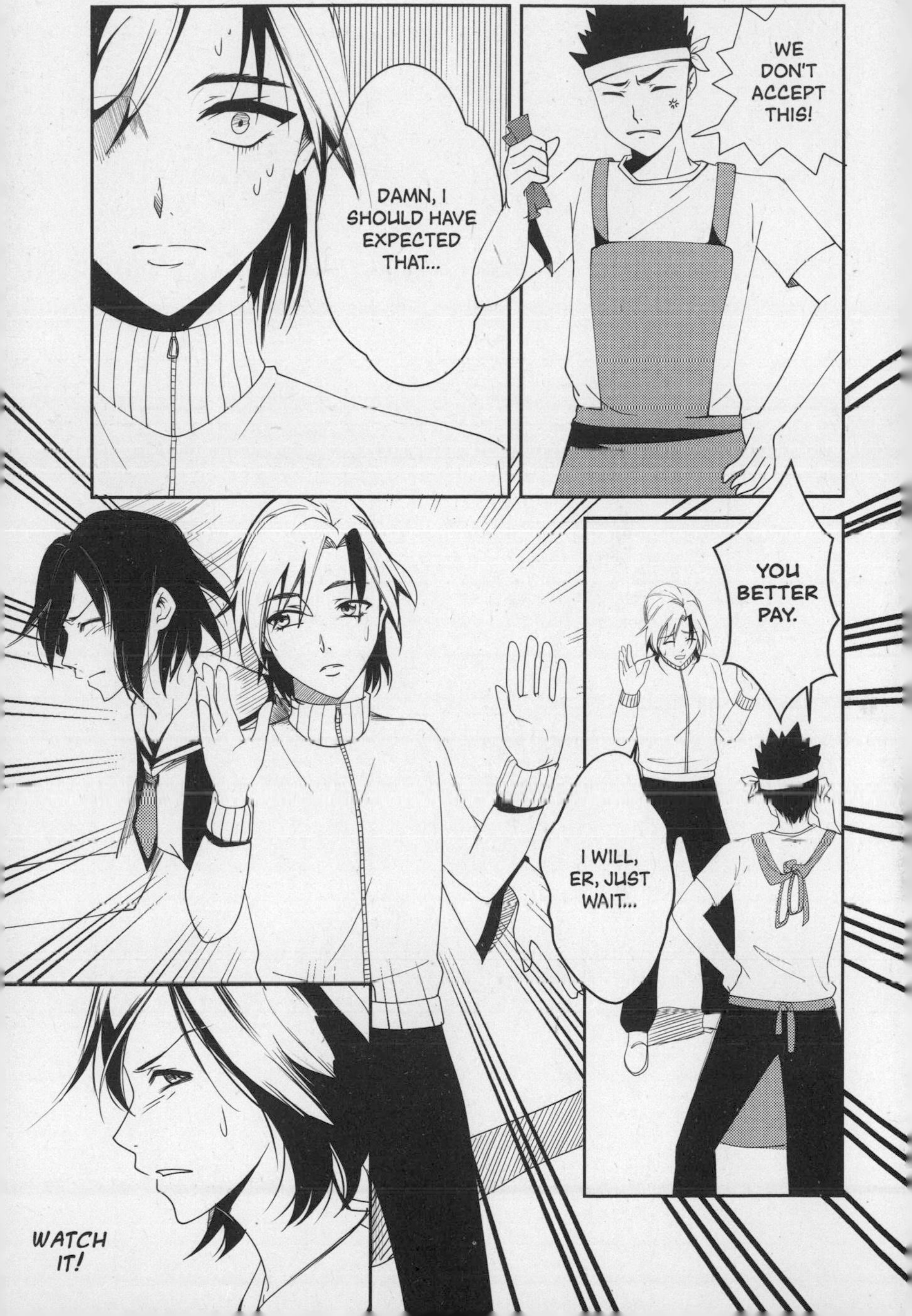
WE DON'T ACCEPT THIS!
DAMN, I SHOULD HAVE EXPECTED THAT...
YOU BETTER PAY.
I WILL, ER, JUST WAIT...
WATCH IT!

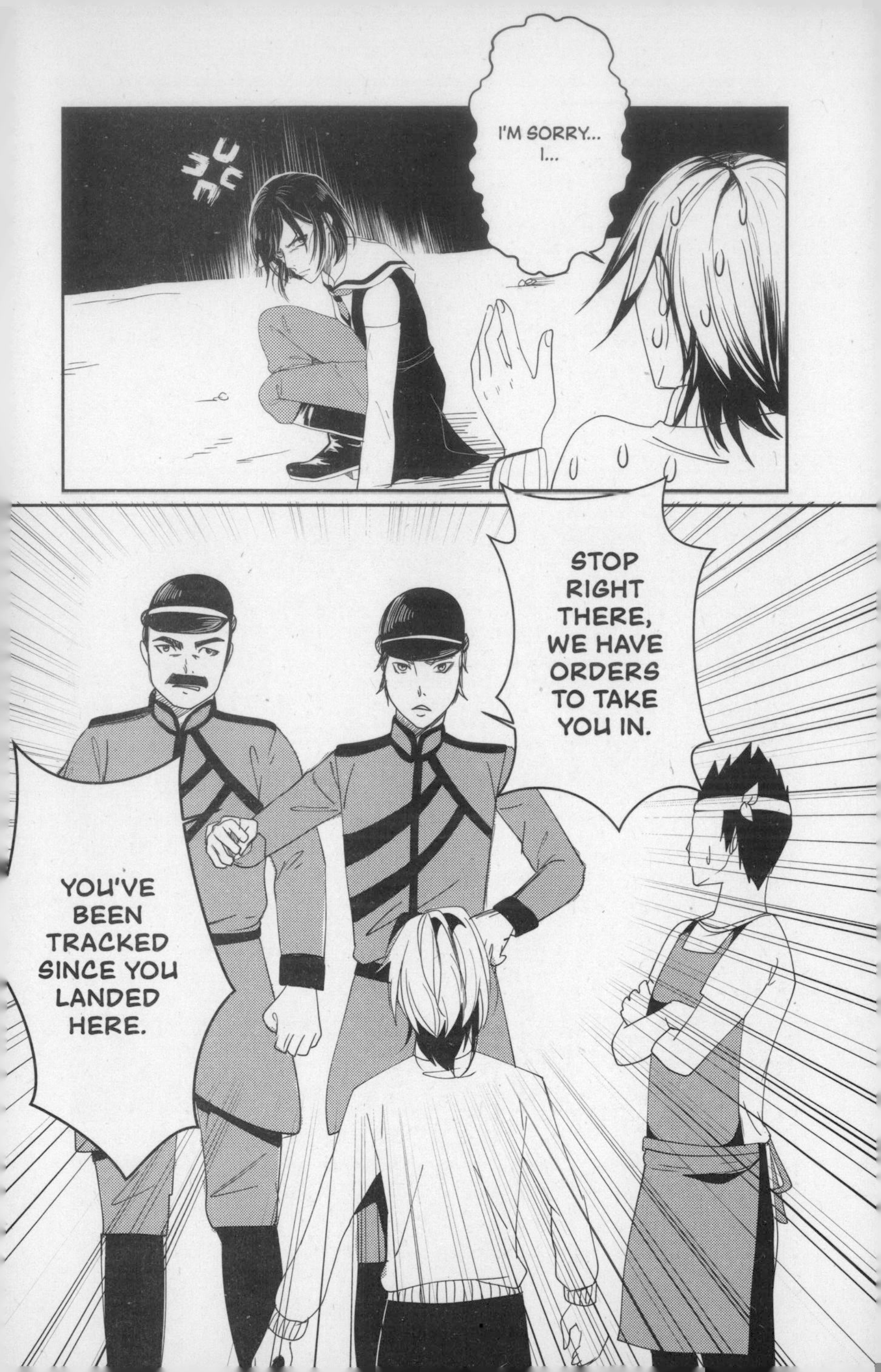
I'M SORRY... I...
STOP RIGHT THERE, WE HAVE ORDERS TO TAKE YOU IN.
YOU'VE BEEN TRACKED SINCE YOU LANDED HERE.

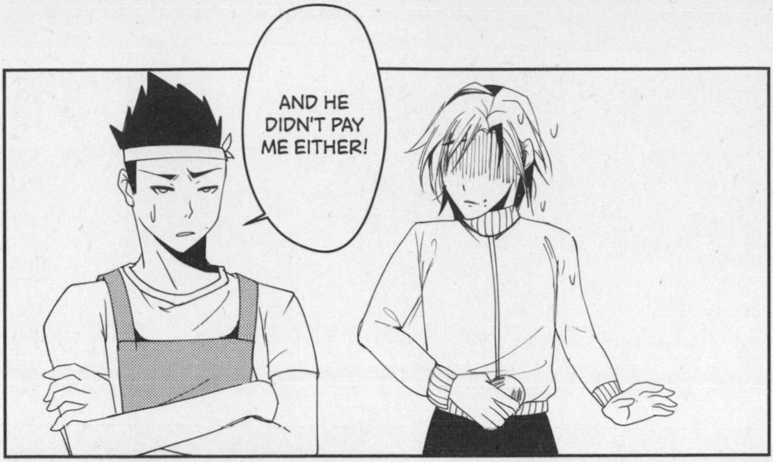
AND HE DIDN'T PAY ME EITHER!

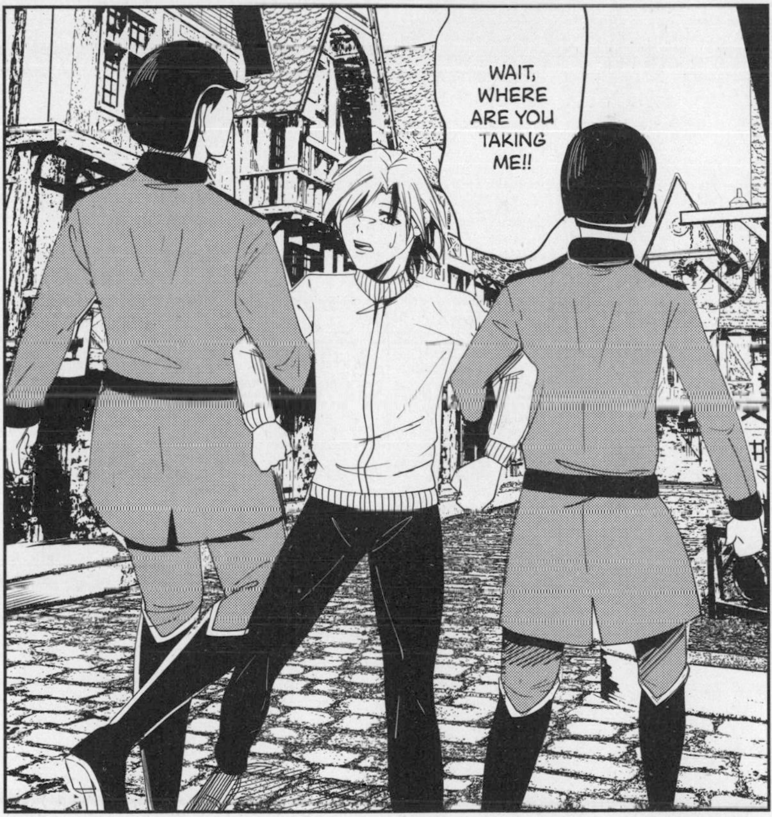
WAIT, WHERE ARE YOU TAKING ME!!

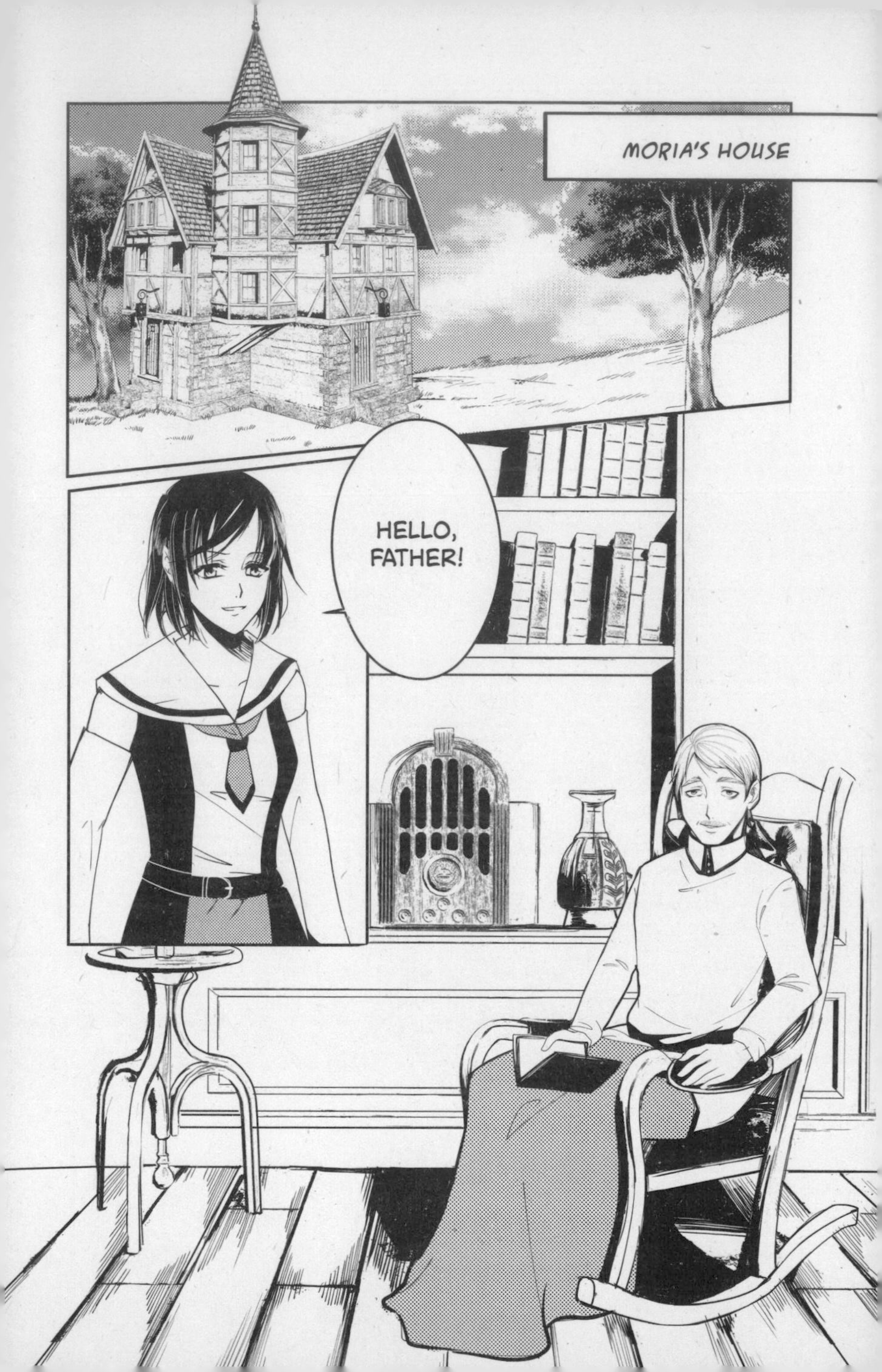
MORIA'S HOUSE
HELLO, FATHER!

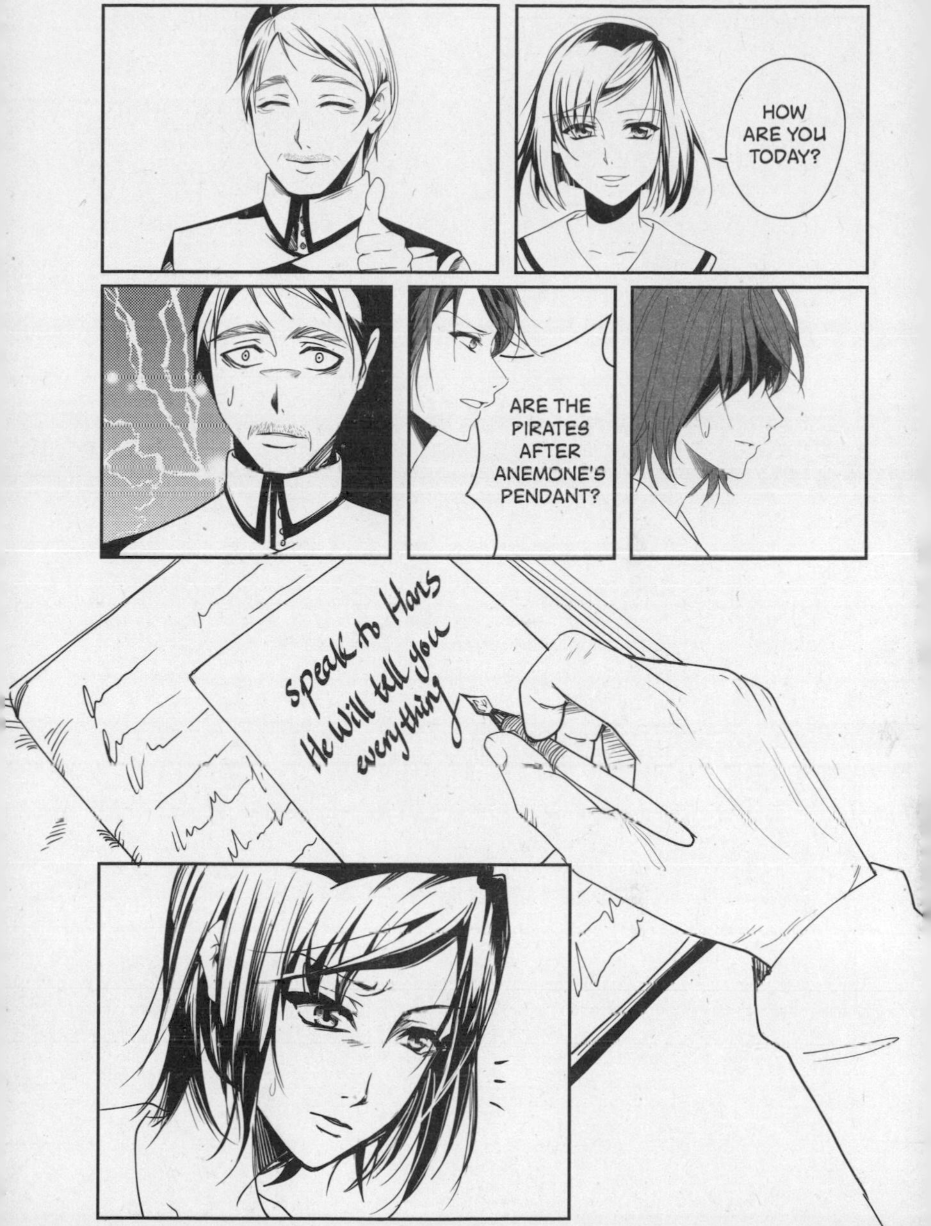
HOW ARE YOU TODAY?
ARE THE PIRATES AFTER ANEMONE'S PENDANT?
Speak to Hans
He Will tell you
everything

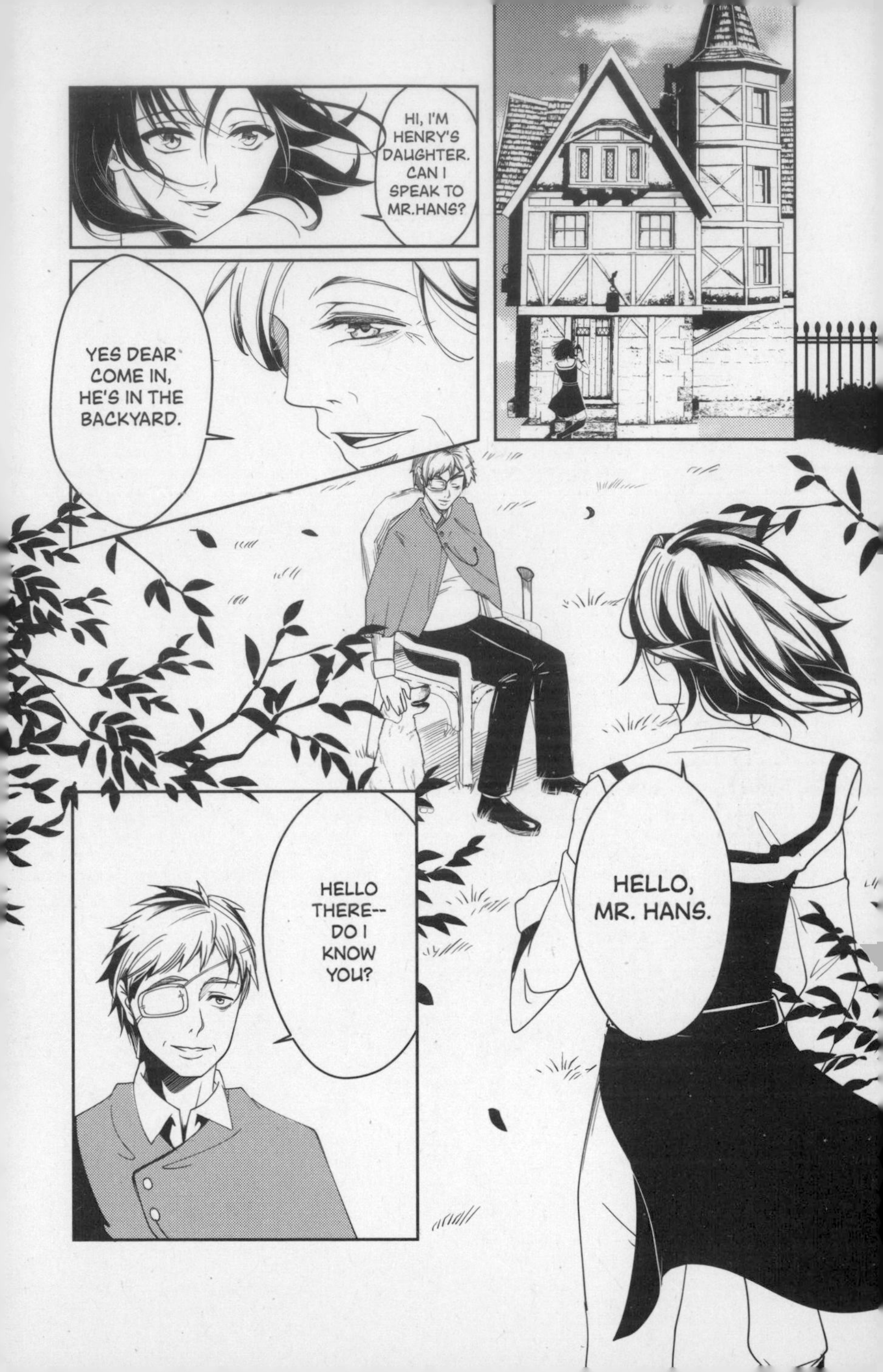
HI, I'M HENRY'S DAUGHTER. CAN I SPEAK TO MR.HANS?
YES DEAR COME IN, HE'S IN THE BACKYARD.
HELLO, MR. HANS.
HELLO THERE-- DO I KNOW YOU?

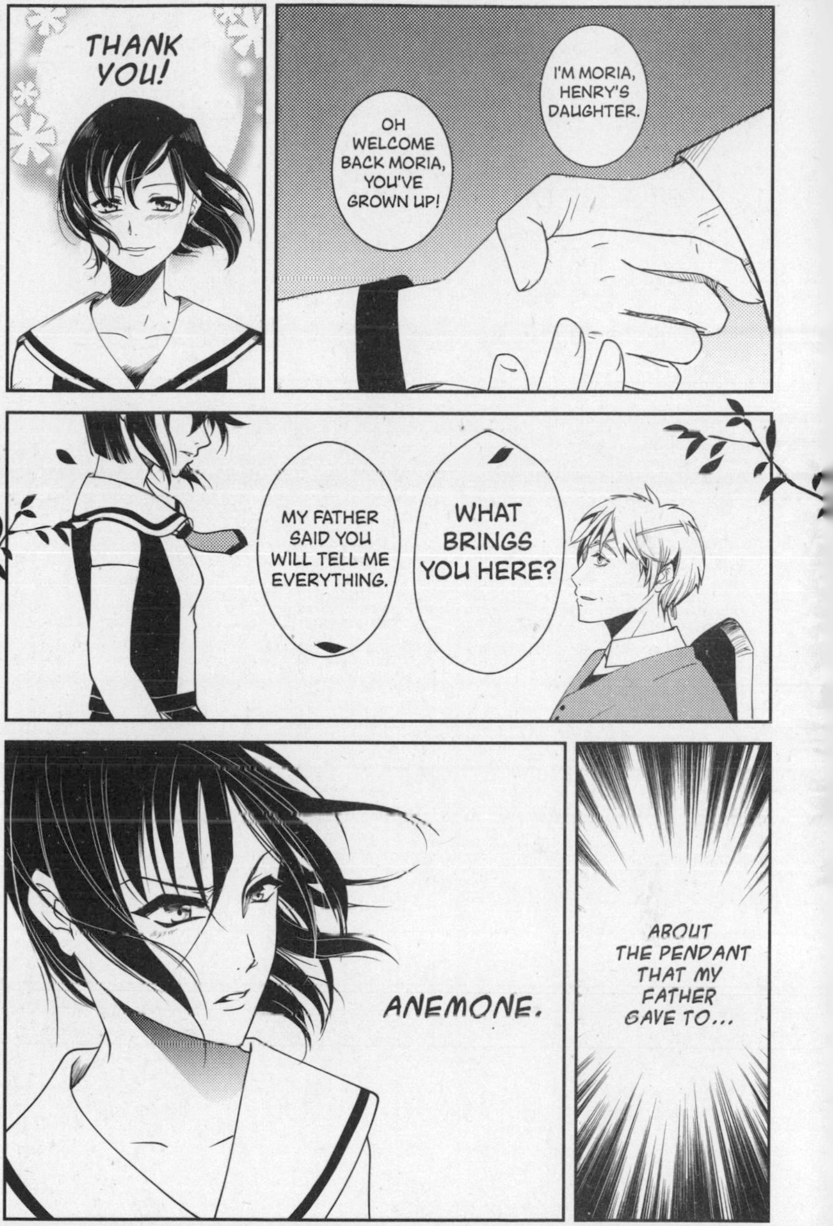
I'M MORIA, HENRY'S DAUGHTER.
OH WELCOME BACK MORIA, YOU'VE GROWN UP!
THANK YOU!
WHAT BRINGS YOU HERE?
MY FATHER SAID YOU WILL TELL ME EVERYTHING.
ABOUT THE PENDANT THAT MY FATHER GAVE TO...
ANEMONE.

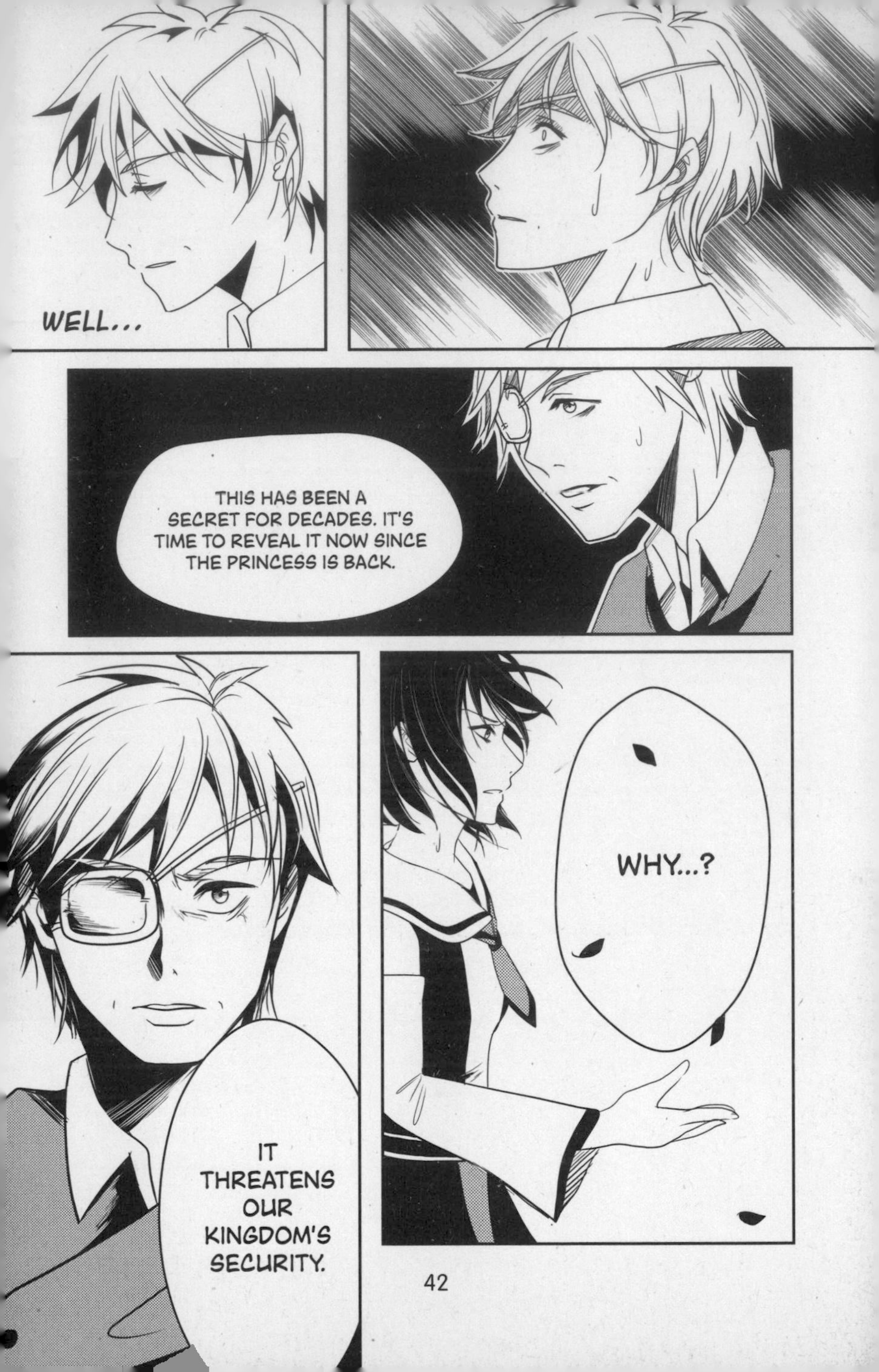
WELL...
THIS HAS BEEN A SECRET FOR DECADES. IT'S TIME TO REVEAL IT NOW SINCE THE PRINCESS IS BACK.
WHY...?
IT THREATENS OUR KINGDOM'S SECURITY.

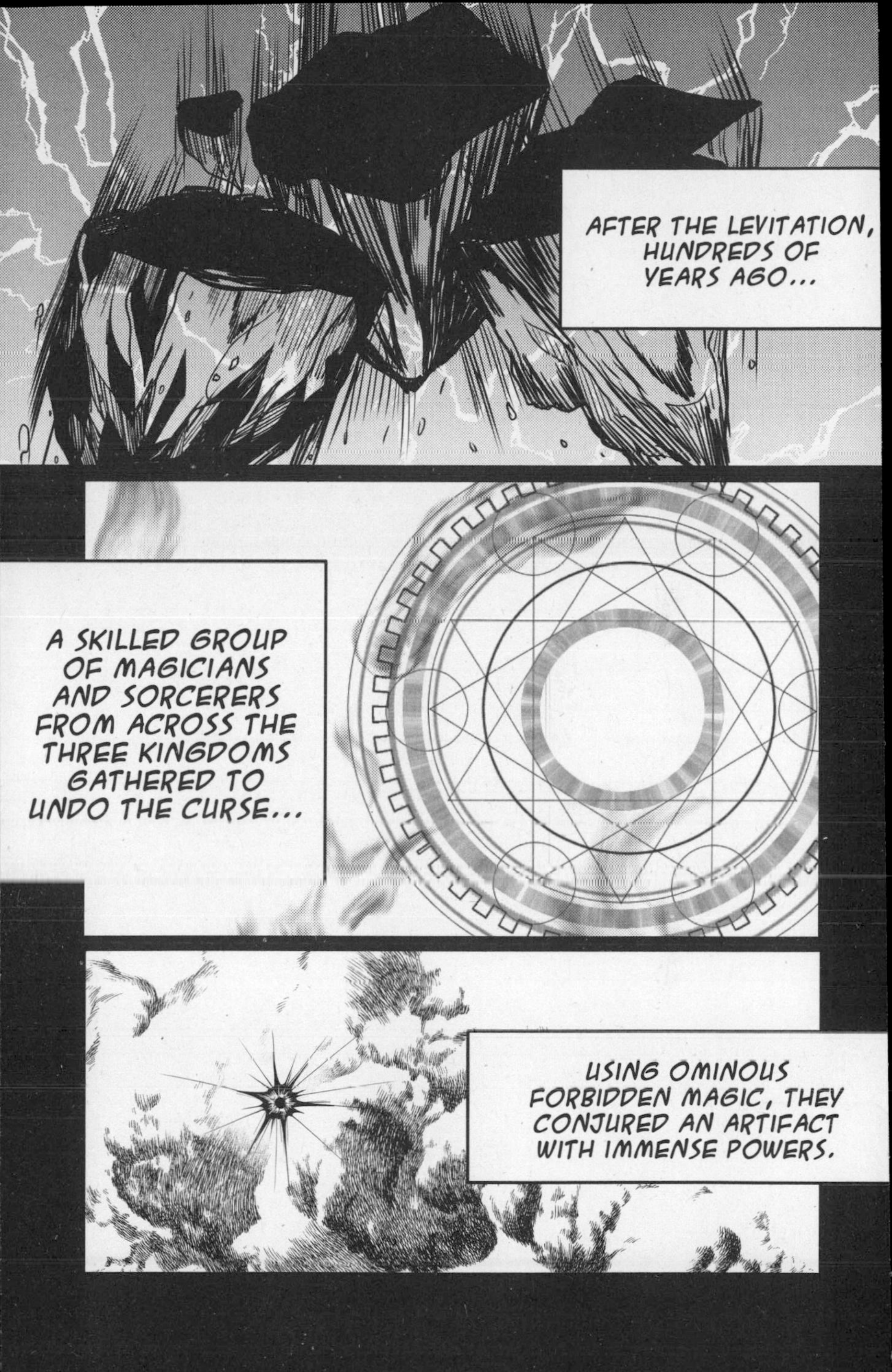
AFTER THE LEVITATION, HUNDREDS OF YEARS AGO...
A SKILLED GROUP OF MAGICIANS AND SORCERERS FROM ACROSS THE THREE KINGDOMS GATHERED TO UNDO THE CURSE...
USING OMINOUS FORBIDDEN MAGIC, THEY CONJURED AN ARTIFACT WITH IMMENSE POWERS.

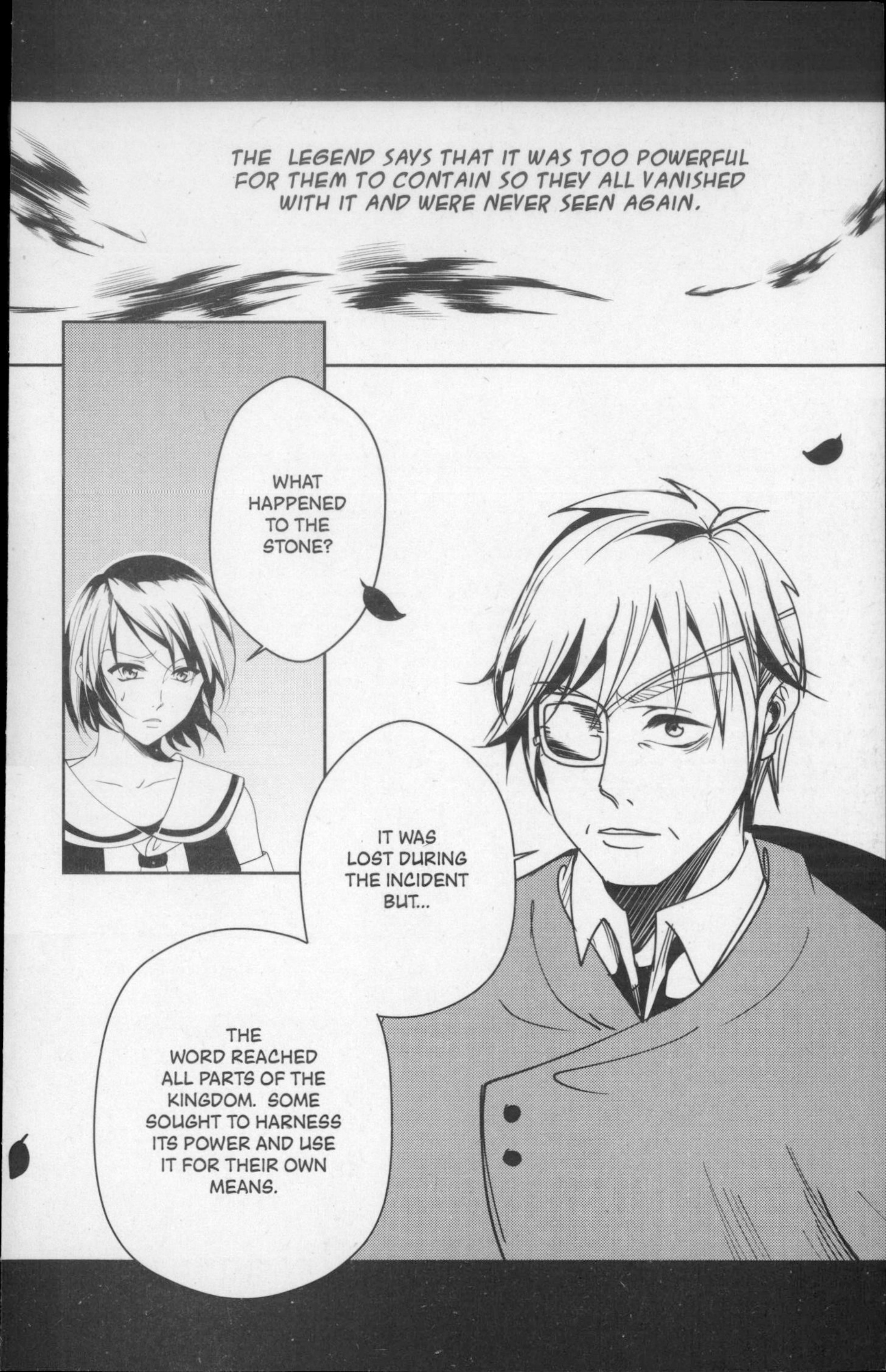
THE LEGEND SAYS THAT IT WAS TOO POWERFUL FOR THEM TO CONTAIN SO THEY ALL VANISHED WITH IT AND WERE NEVER SEEN AGAIN.
WHAT HAPPENED TO THE STONE?
IT WAS LOST DURING THE INCIDENT BUT...
THE WORD REACHED ALL PARTS OF THE KINGDOM. SOME SOUGHT TO HARNESS ITS POWER AND USE IT FOR THEIR OWN MEANS.

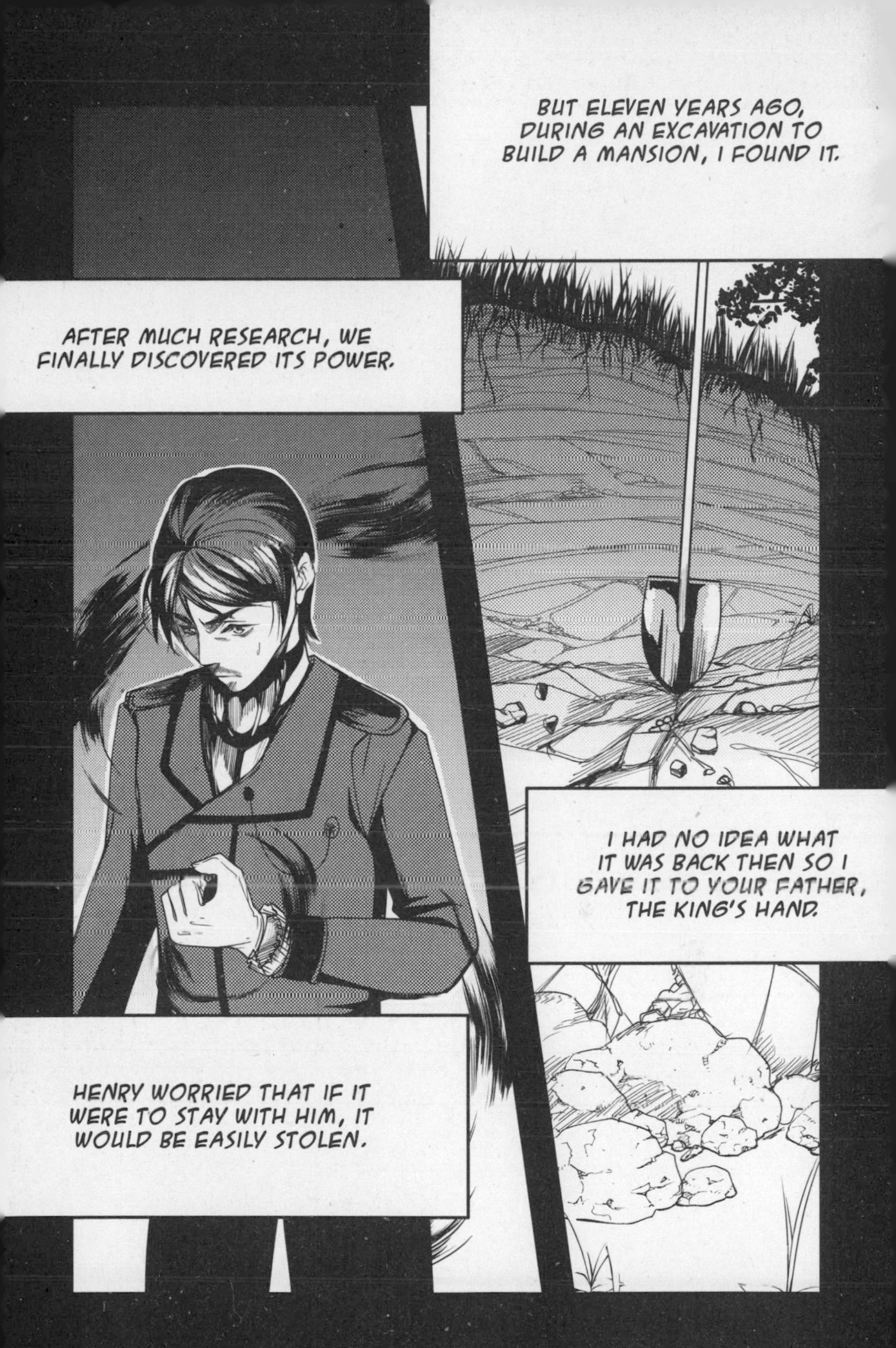
BUT ELEVEN YEARS AGO, DURING AN EXCAVATION TO BUILD A MANSION, I FOUND IT.
I HAD NO IDEA WHAT IT WAS BACK THEN SO I GAVE IT TO YOUR FATHER, THE KING'S HAND.
AFTER MUCH RESEARCH, WE FINALLY DISCOVERED ITS POWER.
HENRY WORRIED THAT IF IT WERE TO STAY WITH HIM, IT WOULD BE EASILY STOLEN.

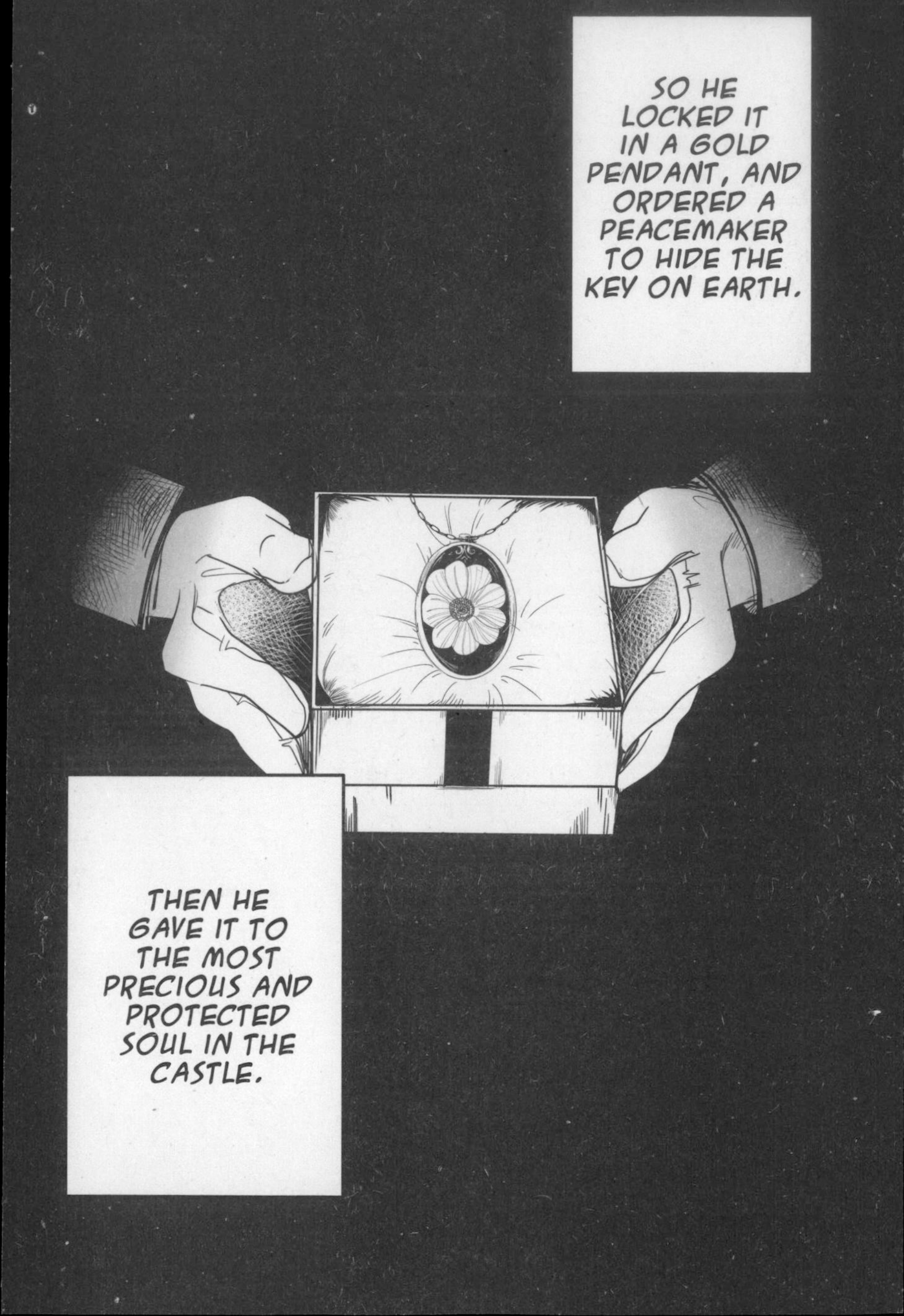
SO HE LOCKED IT IN A GOLD PENDANT, AND ORDERED A PEACEMAKER TO HIDE THE KEY ON EARTH.
THEN HE GAVE IT TO THE MOST PRECIOUS AND PROTECTED SOUL IN THE CASTLE.

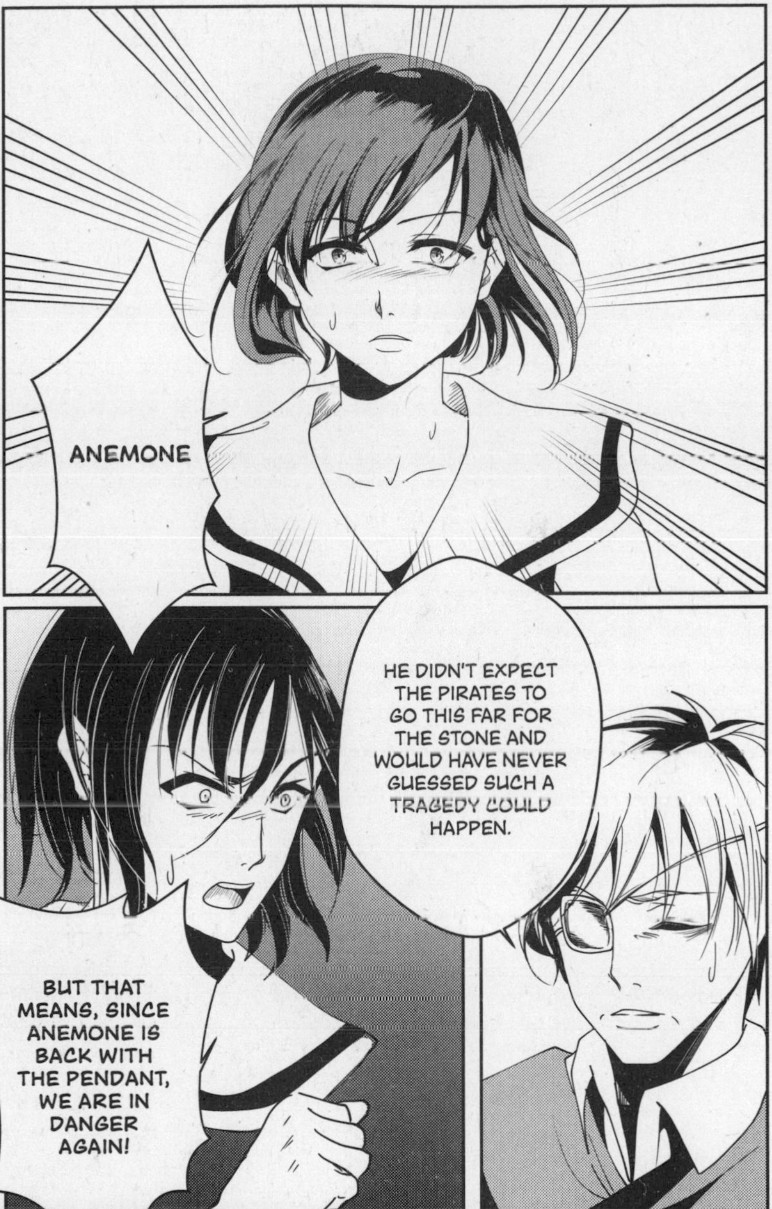
ANEMONE
HE DIDN'T EXPECT THE PIRATES TO GO THIS FAR FOR THE STONE AND WOULD HAVE NEVER GUESSED SUCH A TRAGEDY COULD HAPPEN.
BUT THAT MEANS, SINCE ANEMONE IS BACK WITH THE PENDANT, WE ARE IN DANGER AGAIN!

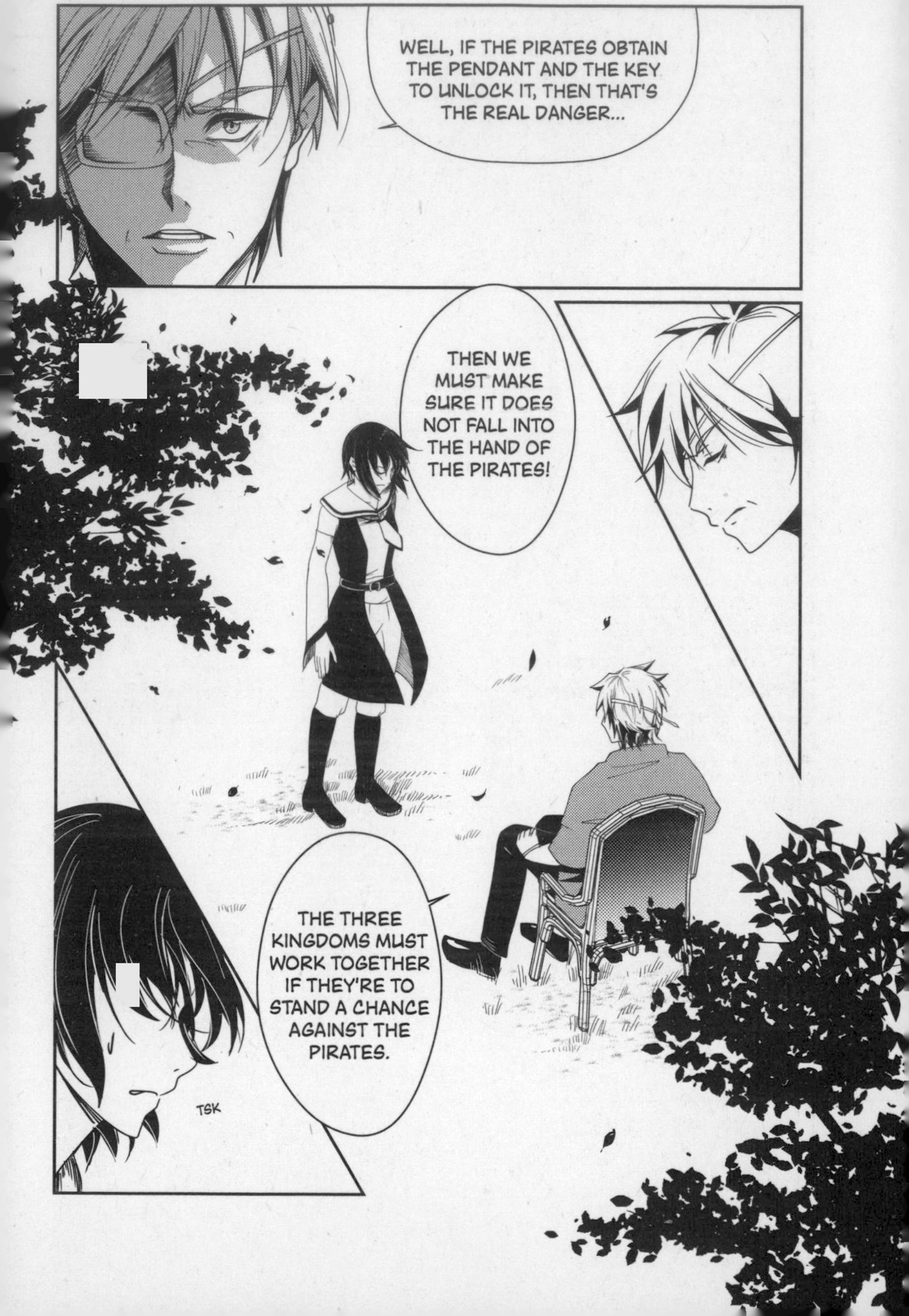
WELL, IF THE PIRATES OBTAIN THE PENDANT AND THE KEY TO UNLOCK IT, THEN THAT'S THE REAL DANGER...
THEN WE MUST MAKE SURE IT DOES NOT FALL INTO THE HAND OF THE PIRATES!
THE THREE KINGDOMS MUST WORK TOGETHER IF THEY'RE TO STAND A CHANCE AGAINST THE PIRATES.
TSK

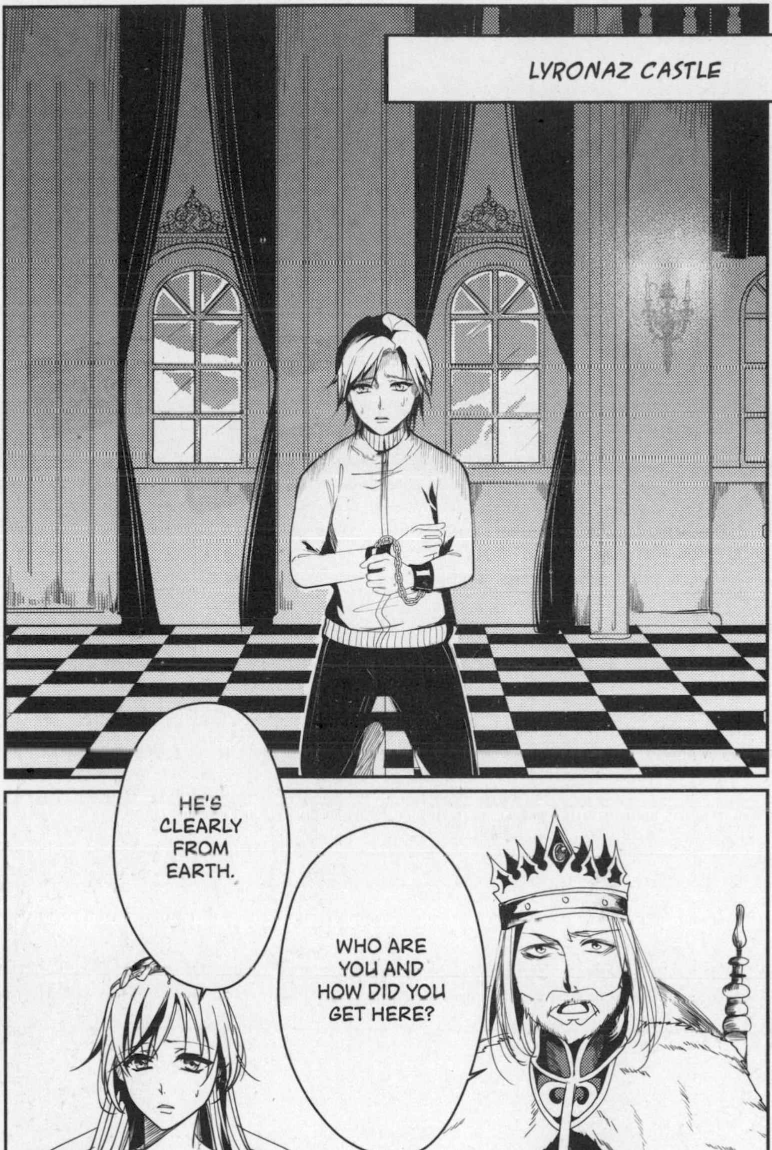
LYRONAZ CASTLE
WHO ARE YOU AND HOW DID YOU GET HERE?
HE'S CLEARLY FROM EARTH.

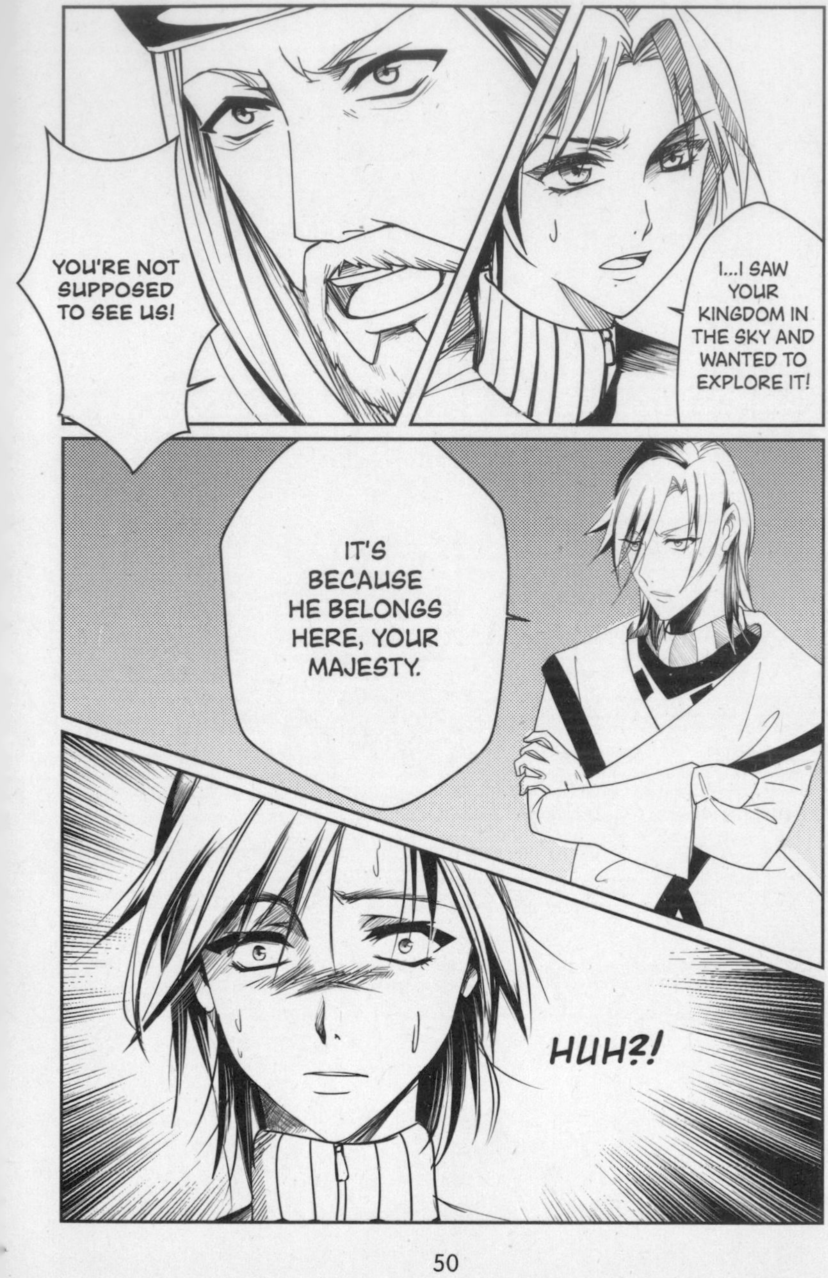

I...I SAW YOUR KINGDOM IN THE SKY AND WANTED TO EXPLORE IT!
YOU'RE NOT SUPPOSED TO SEE US!
IT'S BECAUSE HE BELONGS HERE, YOUR MAJESTY.
HUH?!

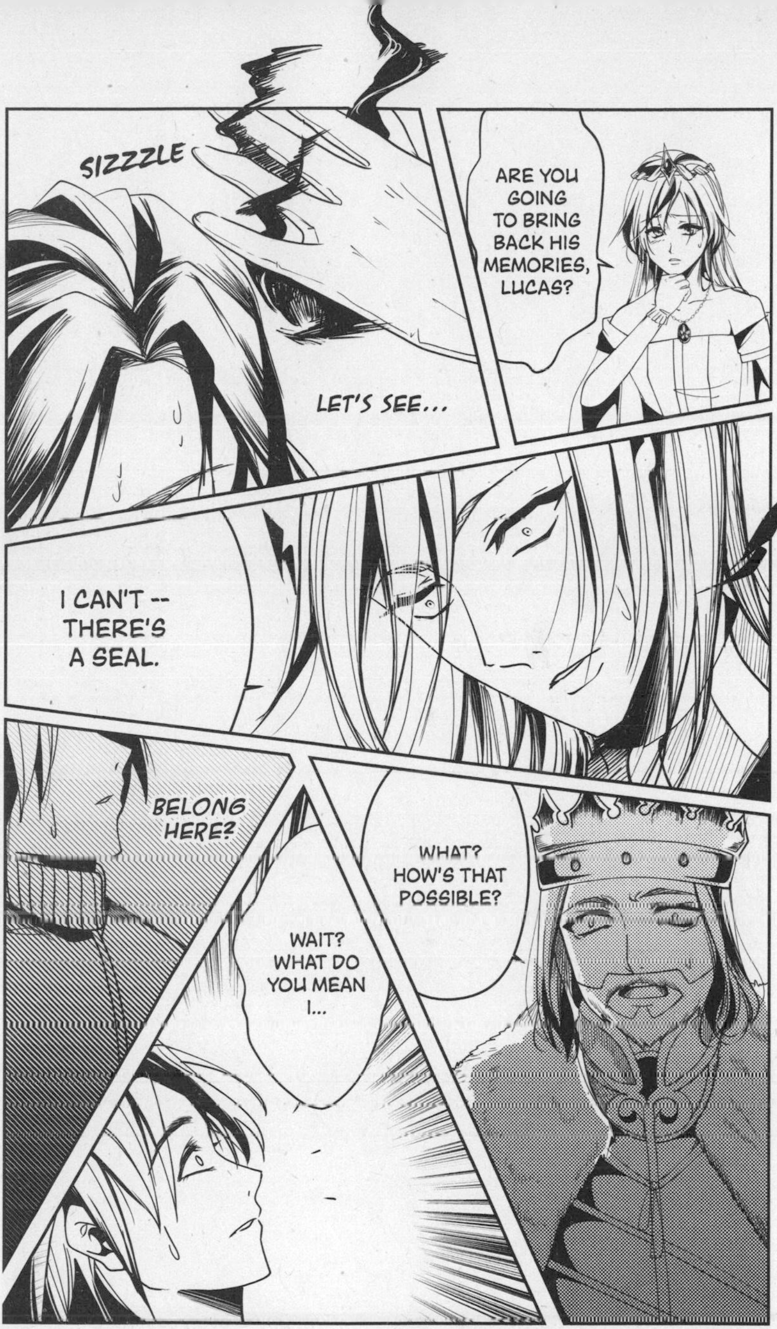
ARE YOU GOING TO BRING BACK HIS MEMORIES, LUCAS?
SIZZZLE
LET'S SEE...
I CAN'T -- THERE'S A SEAL.
WHAT? HOW'S THAT POSSIBLE?
WAIT? WHAT DO YOU MEAN I...
BELONG HERE?

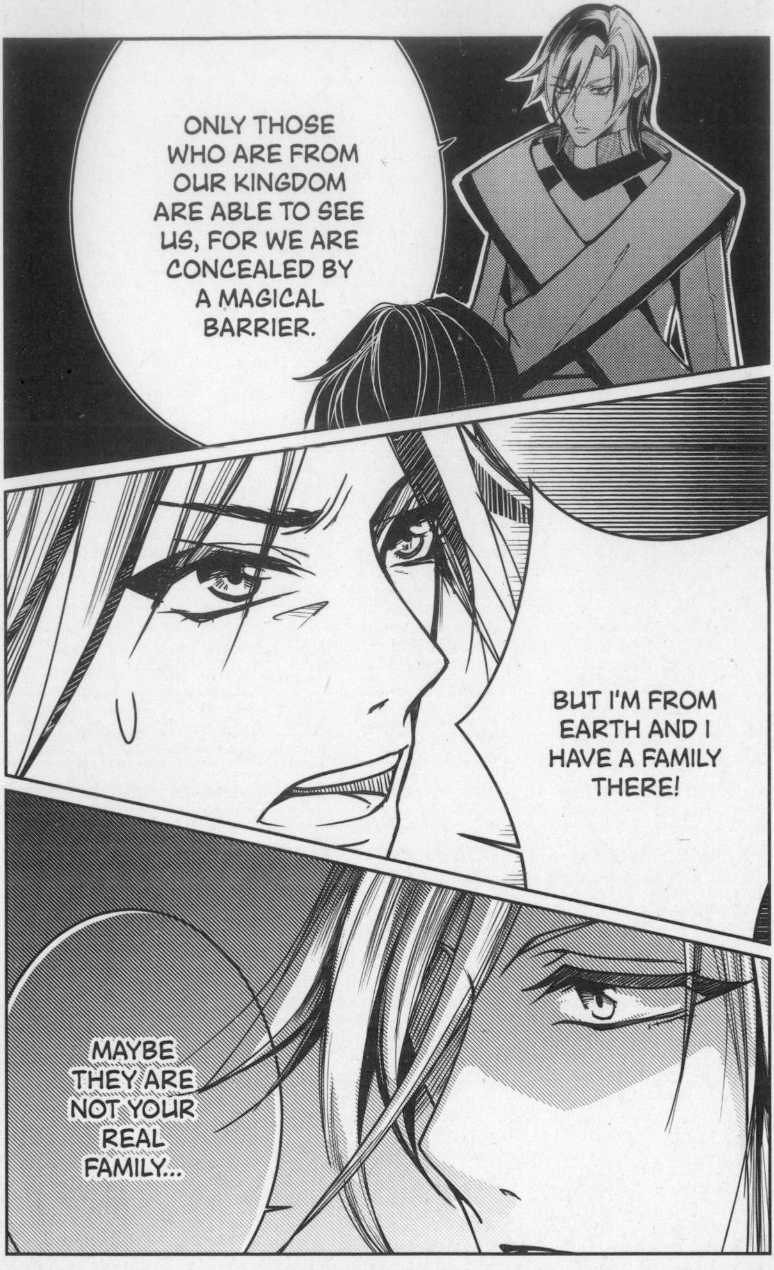
ONLY THOSE WHO ARE FROM OUR KINGDOM ARE ABLE TO SEE US, FOR WE ARE CONCEALED BY A MAGICAL BARRIER.
BUT I'M FROM EARTH AND I HAVE A FAMILY THERE!
MAYBE THEY ARE NOT YOUR REAL FAMILY...

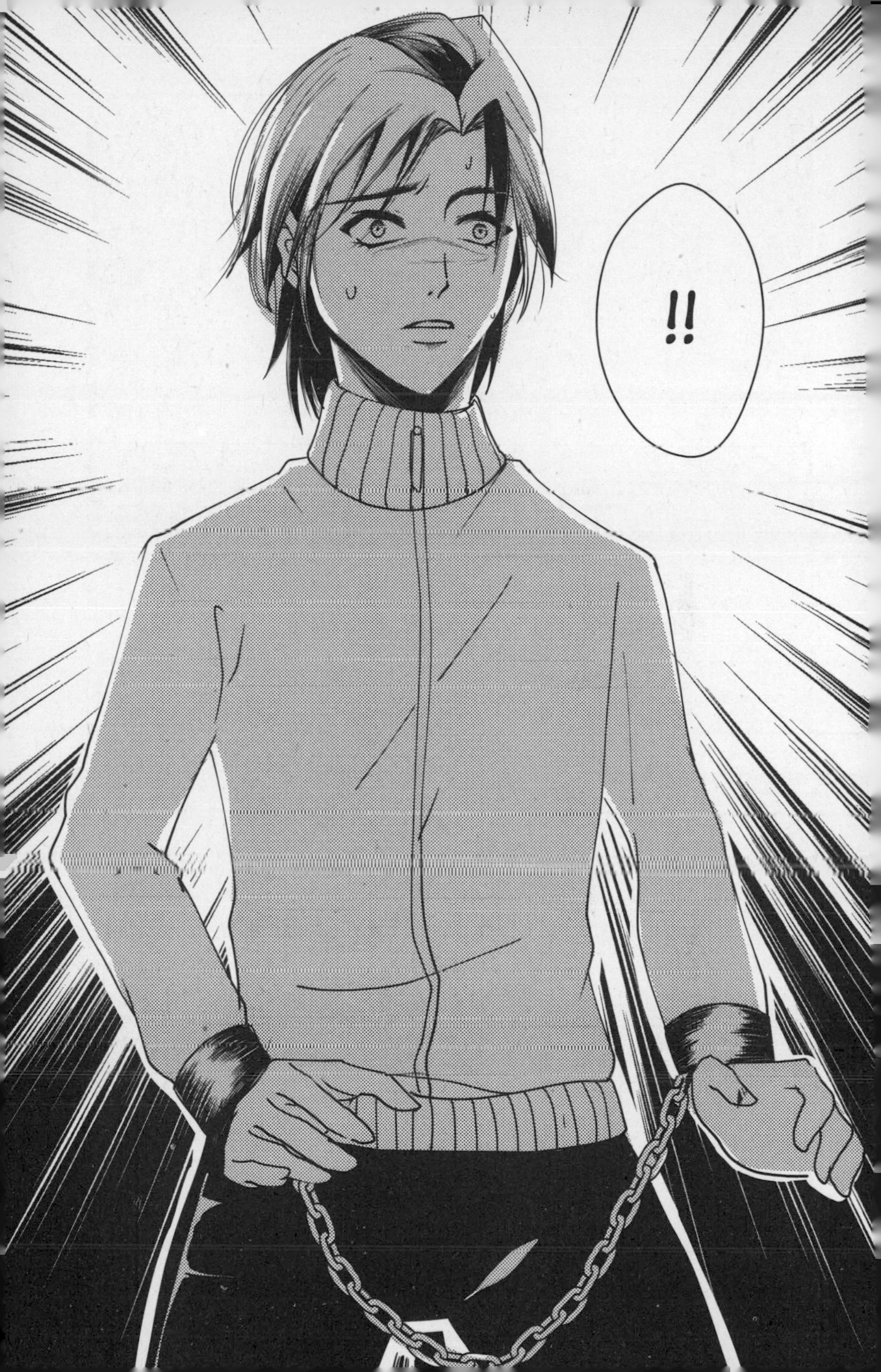
!!

Ocean of Secrets

CHAPTER 7

THE STRANGER

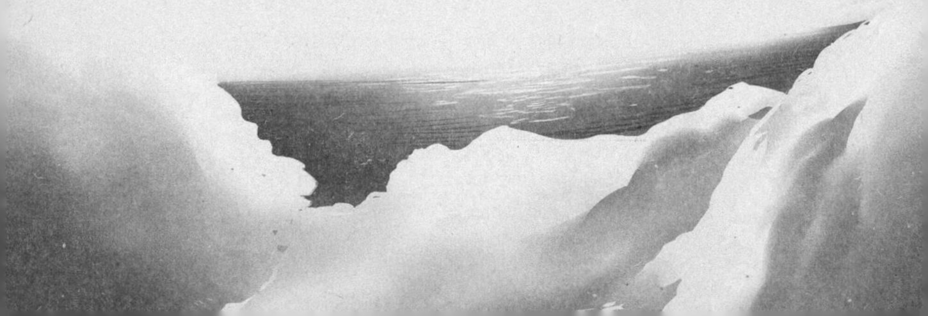

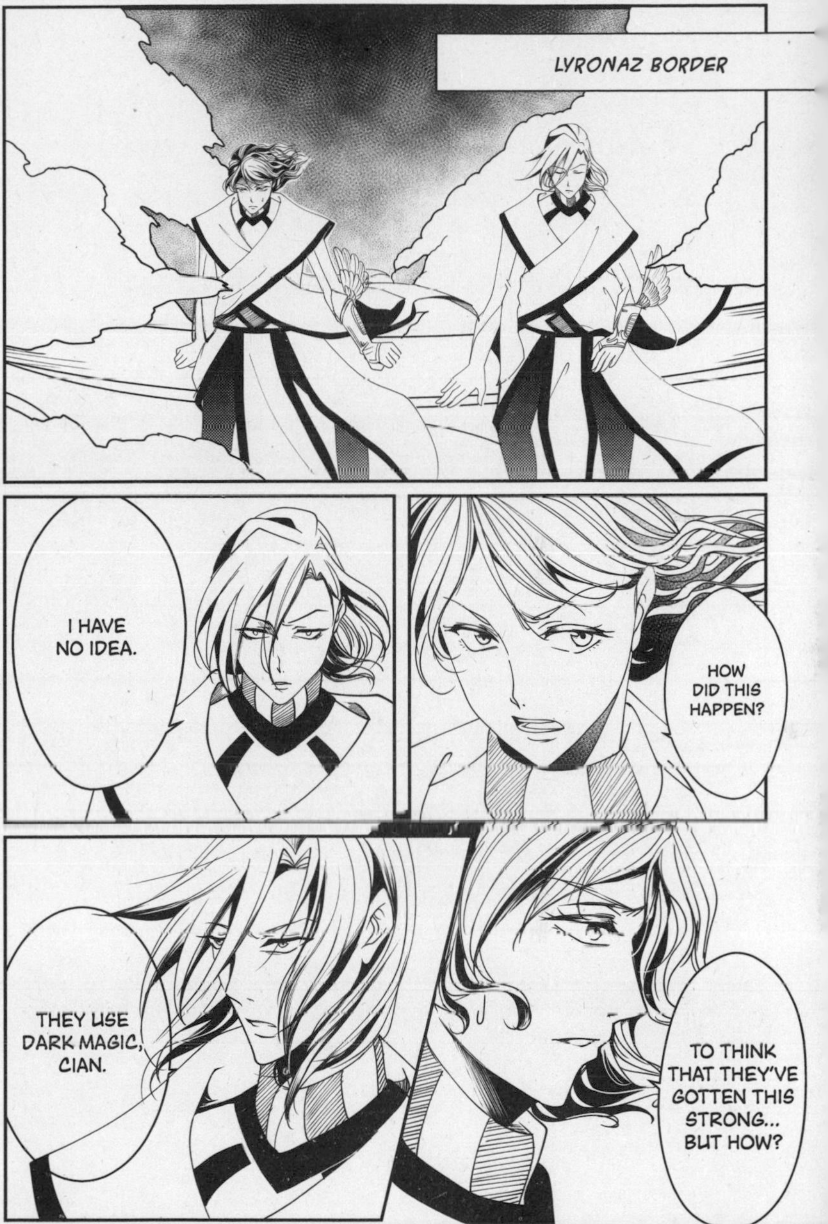
LYRONAZ BORDER
HOW DID THIS HAPPEN?
I HAVE NO IDEA.
TO THINK THAT THEY'VE GOTTEN THIS STRONG... BUT HOW?
THEY USE DARK MAGIC, CIAN.

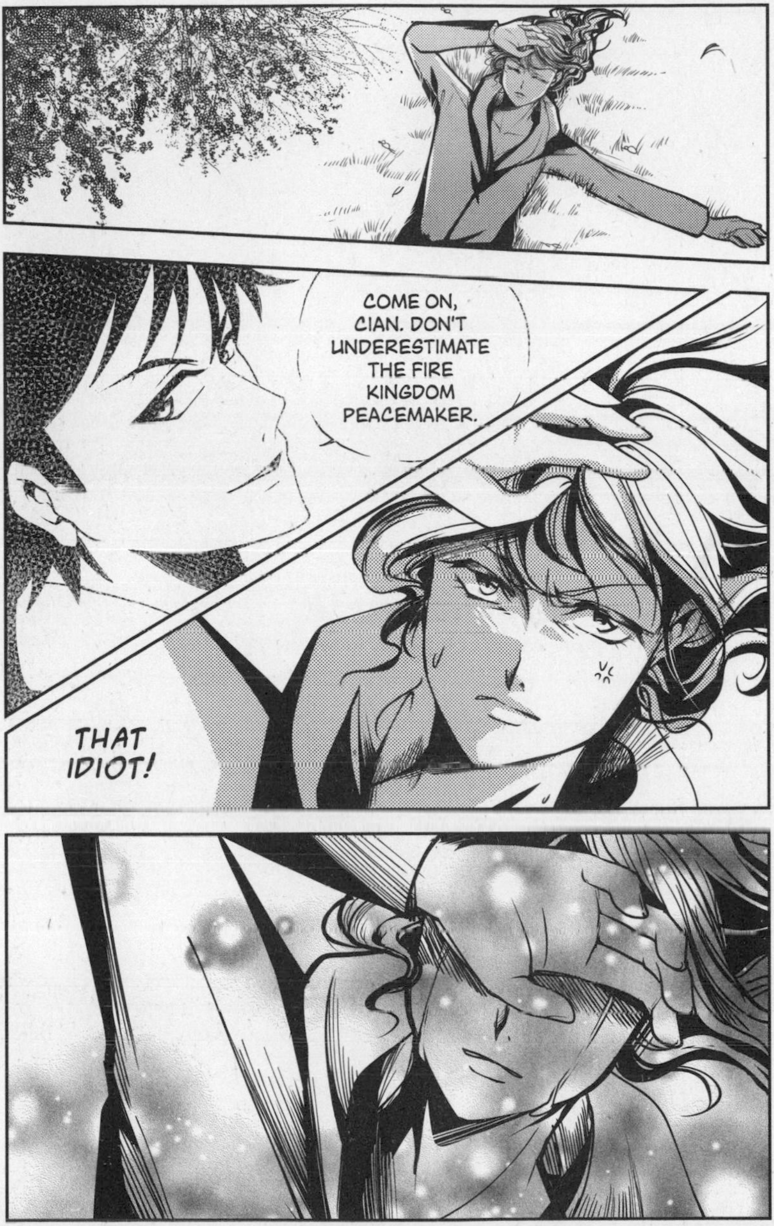
COME ON, CIAN. DON'T UNDERESTIMATE THE FIRE KINGDOM PEACEMAKER.
THAT IDIOT!

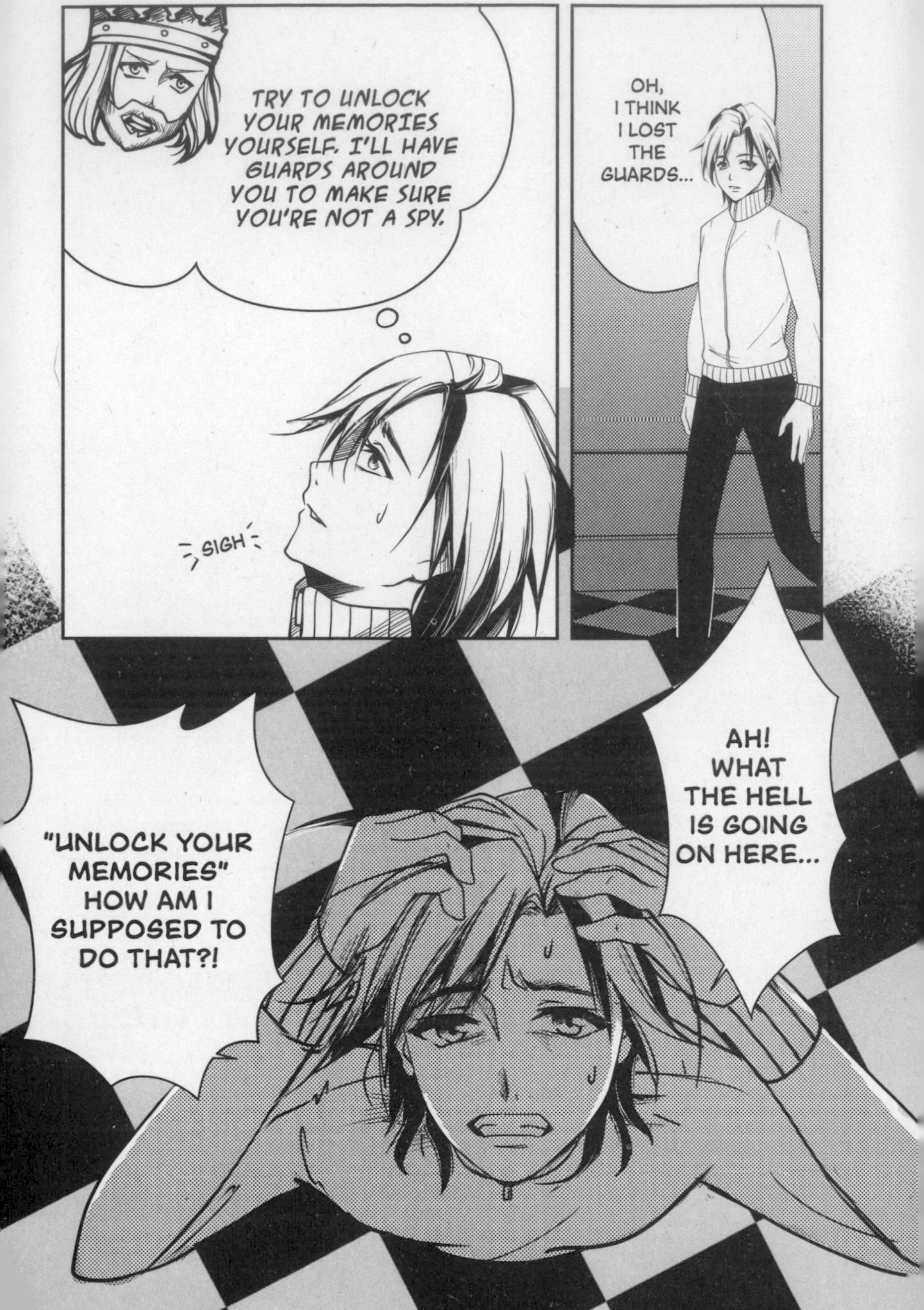
OH, I THINK I LOST THE GUARDS...
TRY TO UNLOCK YOUR MEMORIES YOURSELF. I'LL HAVE GUARDS AROUND YOU TO MAKE SURE YOU'RE NOT A SPY.
SIGH
AH! WHAT THE HELL IS GOING ON HERE...
"UNLOCK YOUR MEMORIES" HOW AM I SUPPOSED TO DO THAT?!

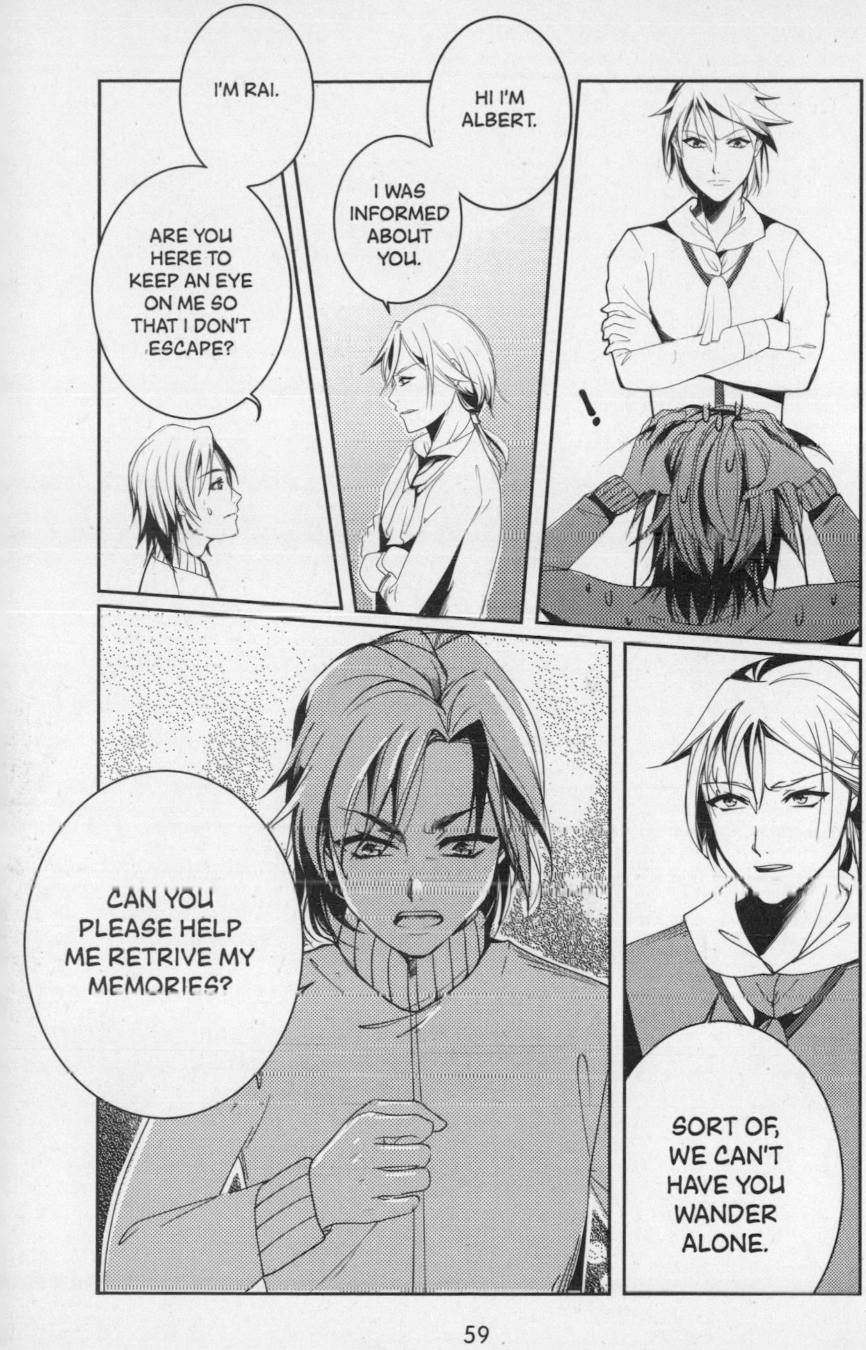
!
HI I'M ALBERT.
I WAS INFORMED ABOUT YOU.
I'M RAI.
ARE YOU HERE TO KEEP AN EYE ON ME SO THAT I DON'T ESCAPE?
SORT OF, WE CAN'T HAVE YOU WANDER ALONE.
CAN YOU PLEASE HELP ME RETRIVE MY MEMORIES?

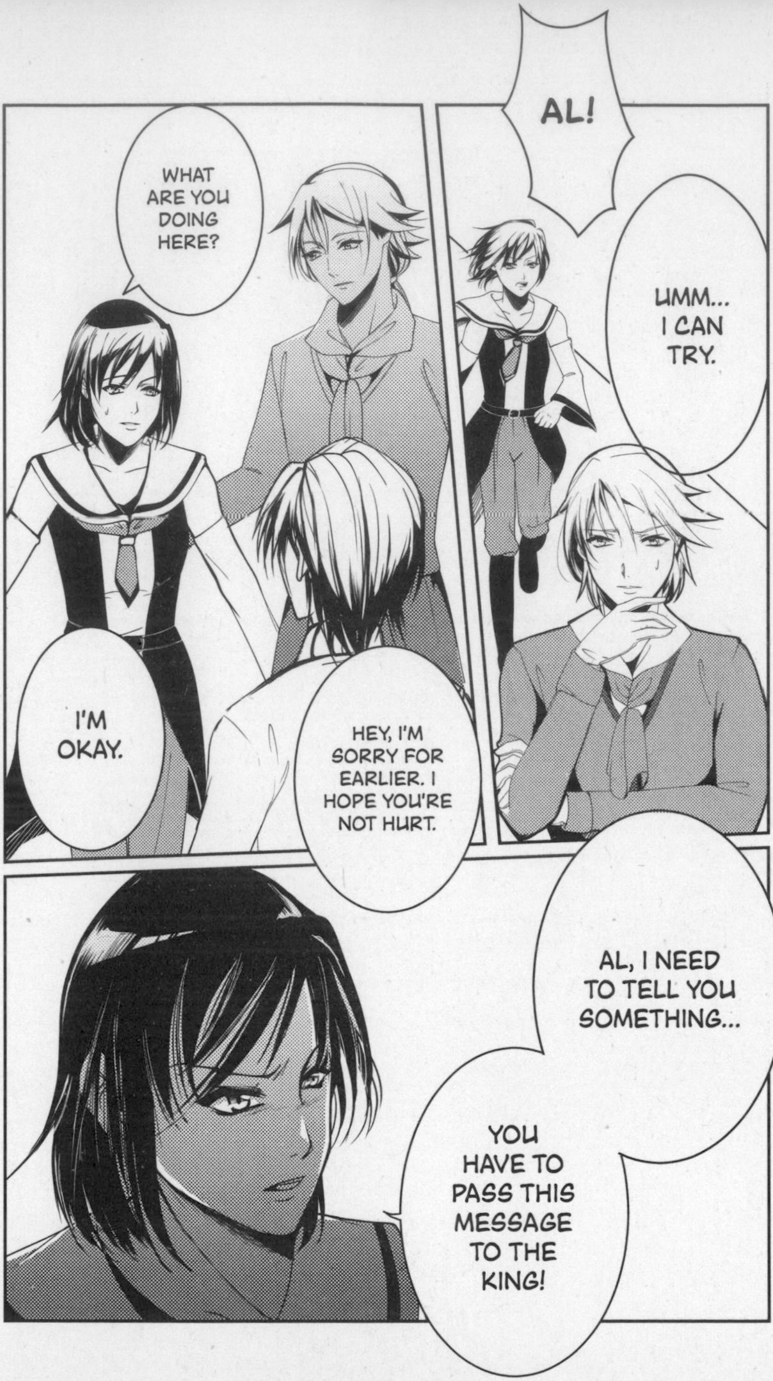
AL!
UMM... I CAN TRY.
WHAT ARE YOU DOING HERE?
HEY, I'M SORRY FOR EARLIER. I HOPE YOU'RE NOT HURT.
I'M OKAY.
AL, I NEED TO TELL YOU SOMETHING...
YOU HAVE TO PASS THIS MESSAGE TO THE KING!

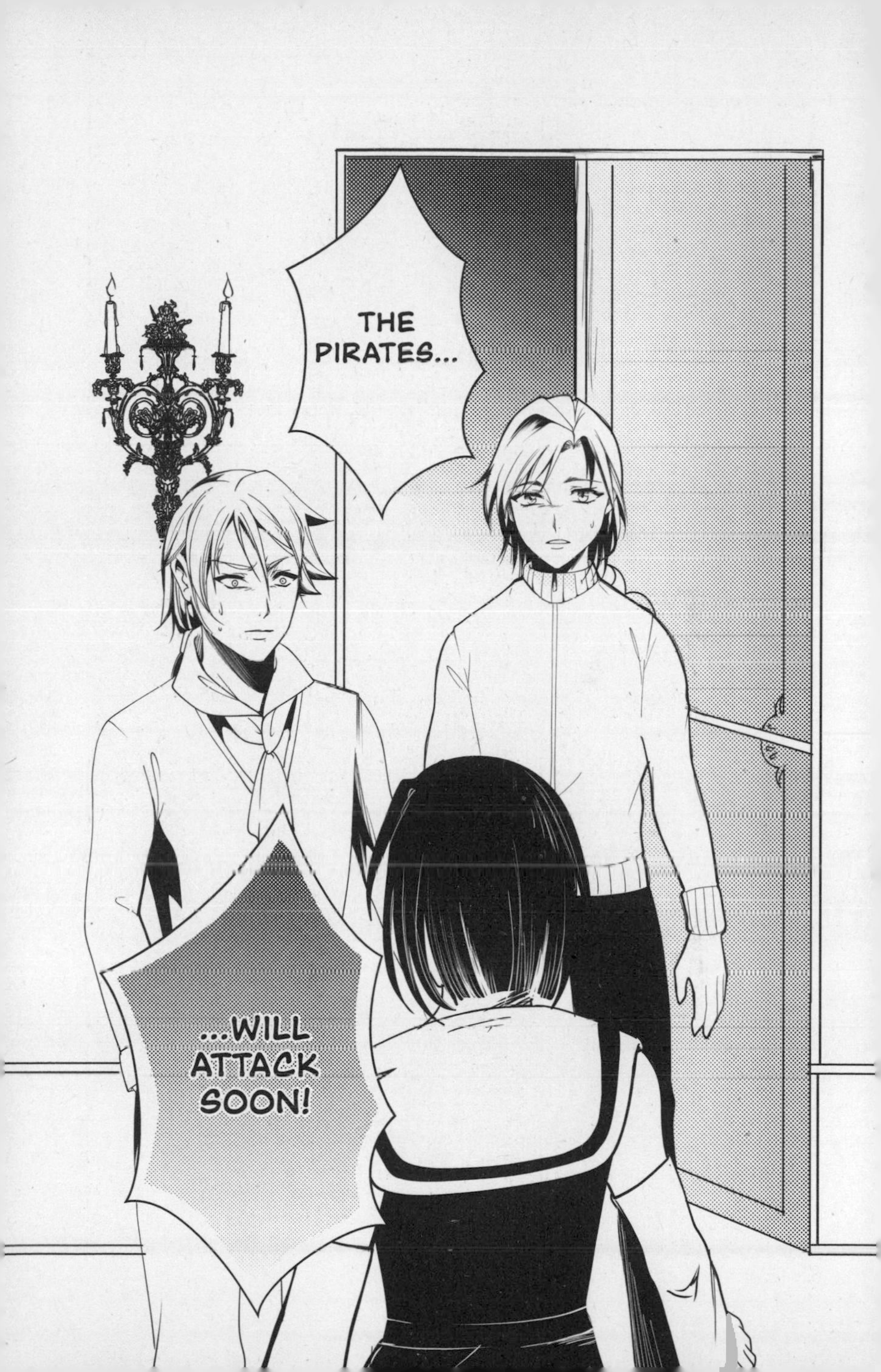
THE PIRATES...
...WILL ATTACK SOON!

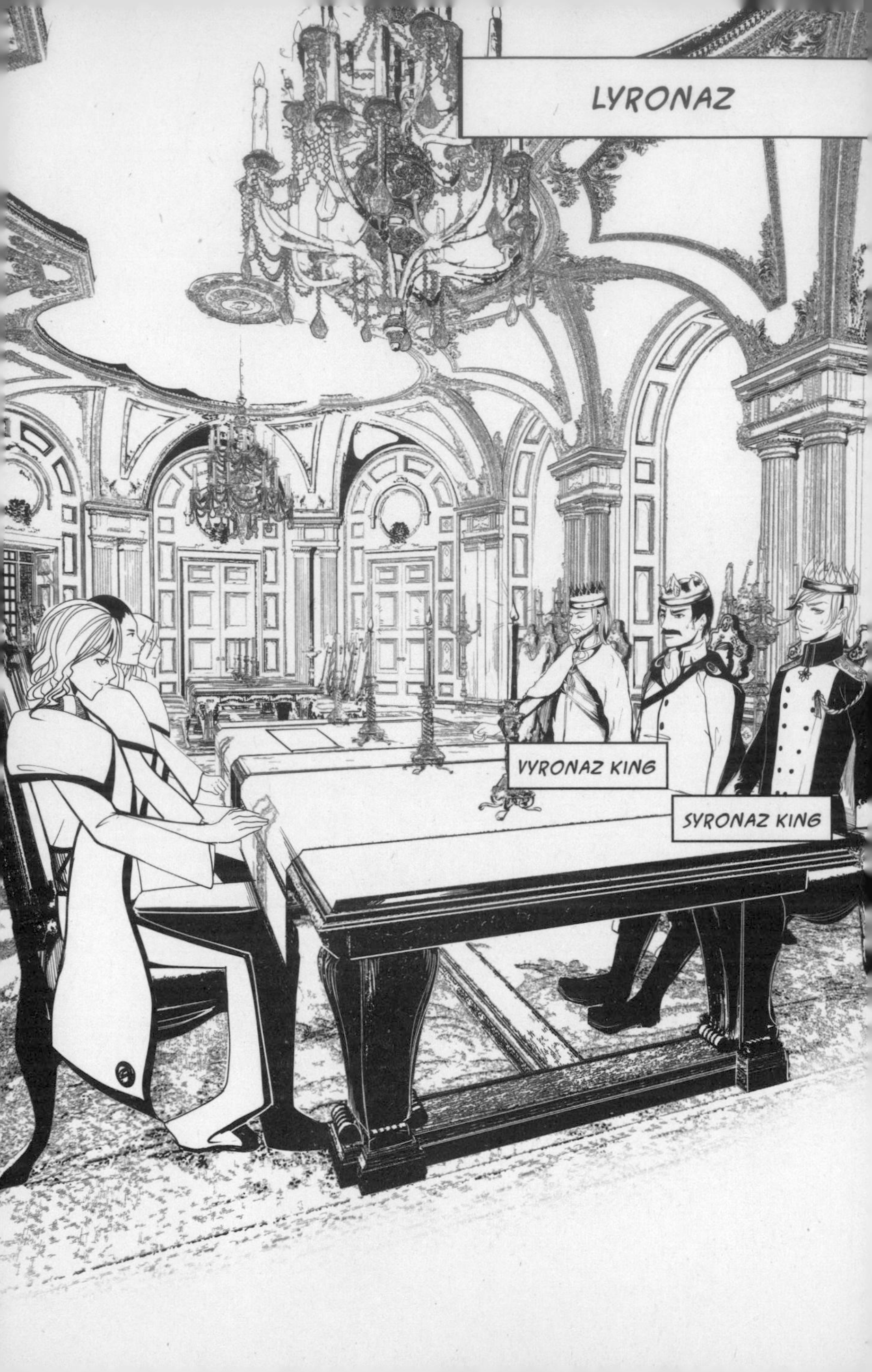
LYRONAZ
VYRONAZ KING
SYRONAZ KING

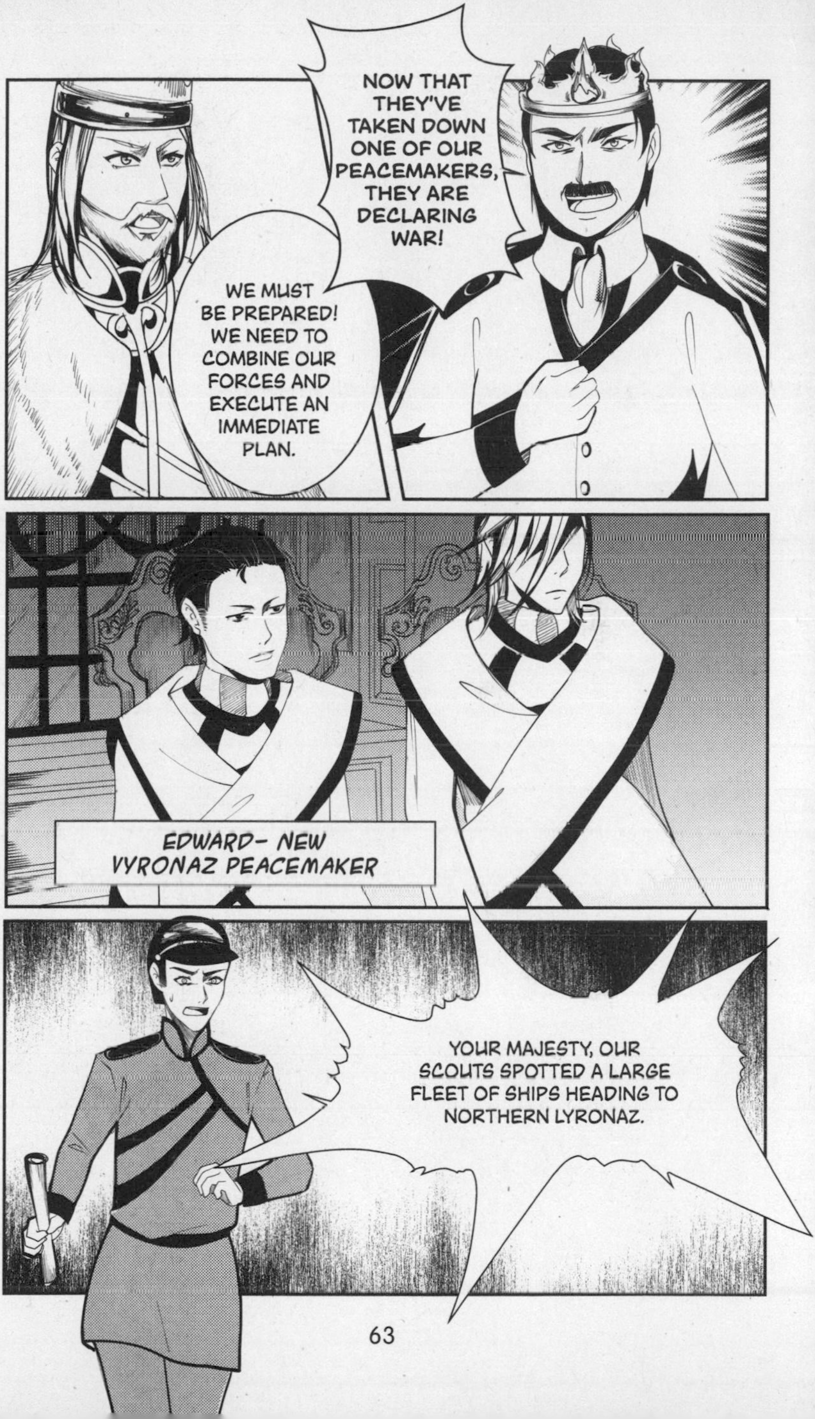
NOW THAT THEY'VE TAKEN DOWN ONE OF OUR PEACEMAKERS, THEY ARE DECLARING WAR!
WE MUST BE PREPARED! WE NEED TO COMBINE OUR FORCES AND EXECUTE AN IMMEDIATE PLAN.
EDWARD- NEW VYRONAZ PEACEMAKER
YOUR MAJESTY, OUR SCOUTS SPOTTED A LARGE FLEET OF SHIPS HEADING TO NORTHERN LYRONAZ.

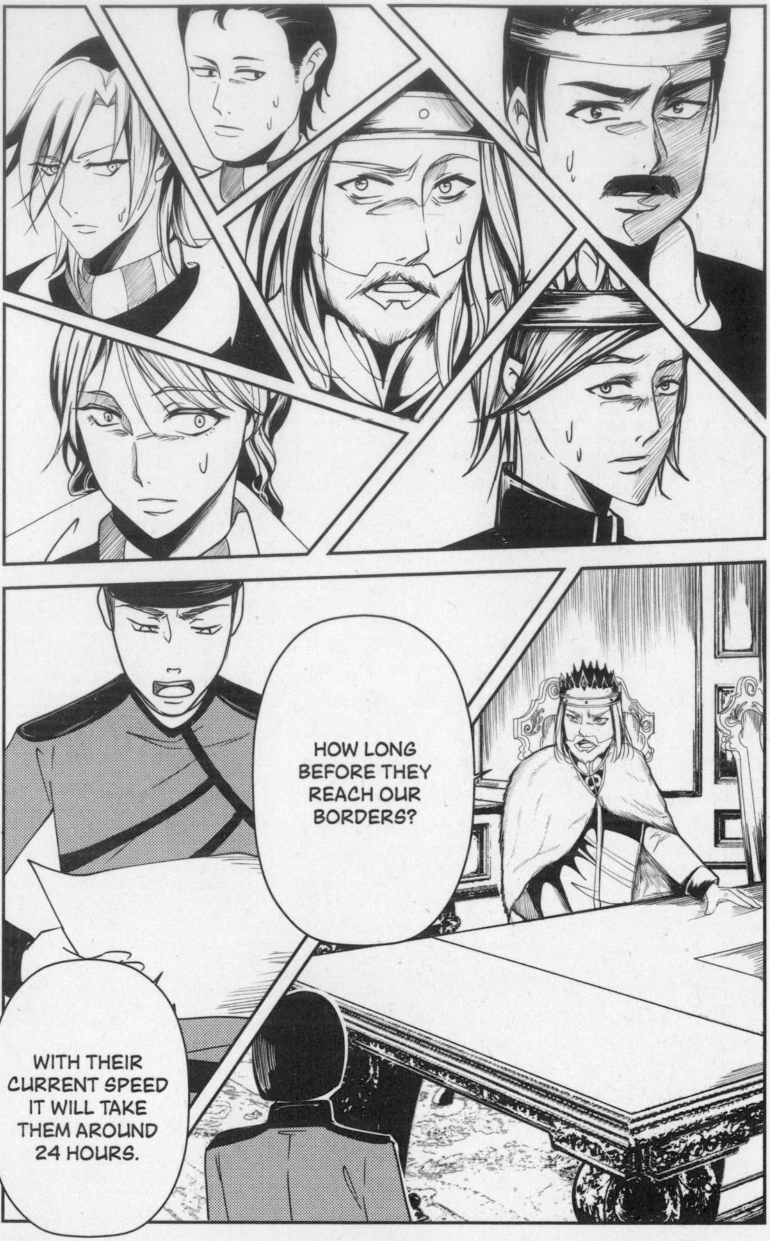
HOW LONG BEFORE THEY REACH OUR BORDERS?
WITH THEIR CURRENT SPEED IT WILL TAKE THEM AROUND 24 HOURS.

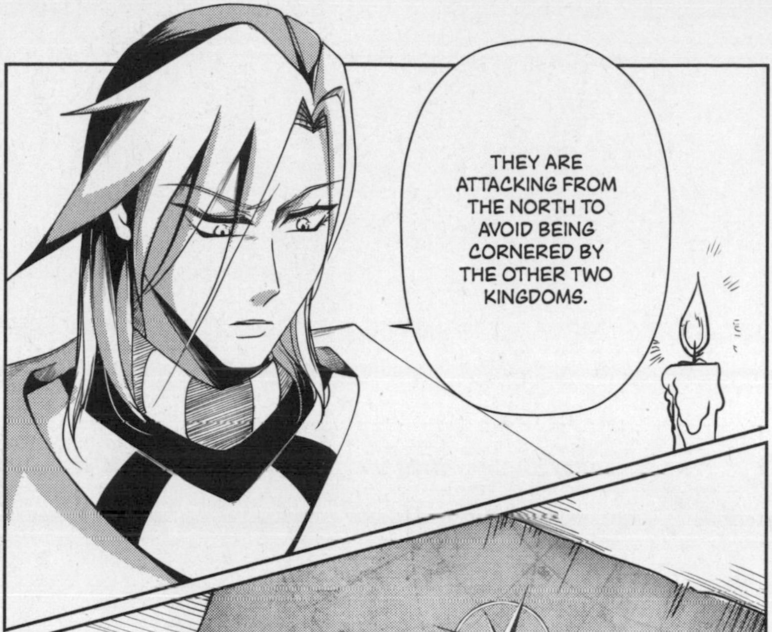
THEY ARE ATTACKING FROM THE NORTH TO AVOID BEING CORNERED BY THE OTHER TWO KINGDOMS.
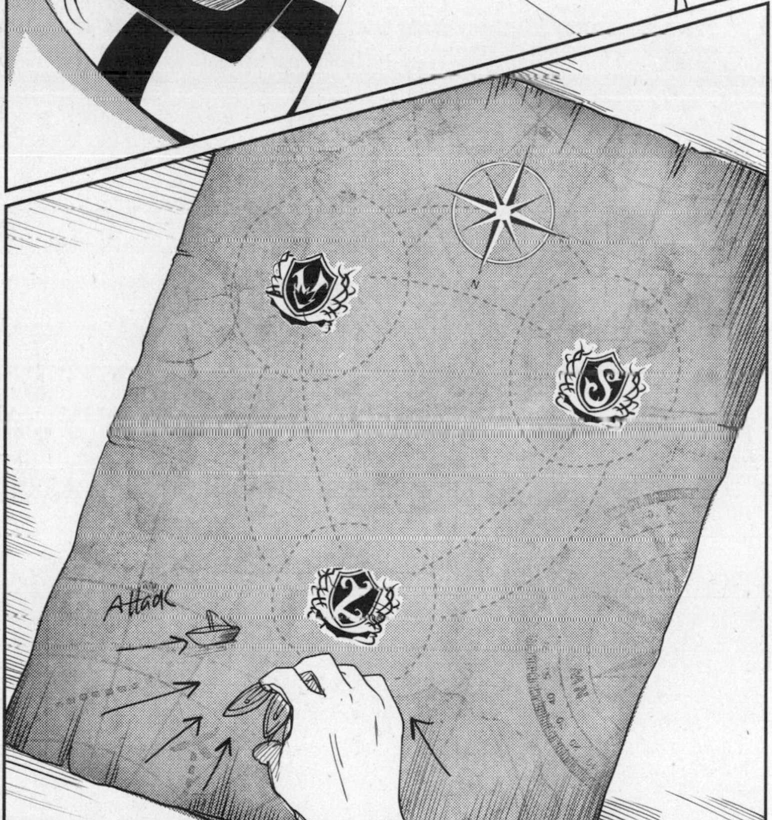
Attack

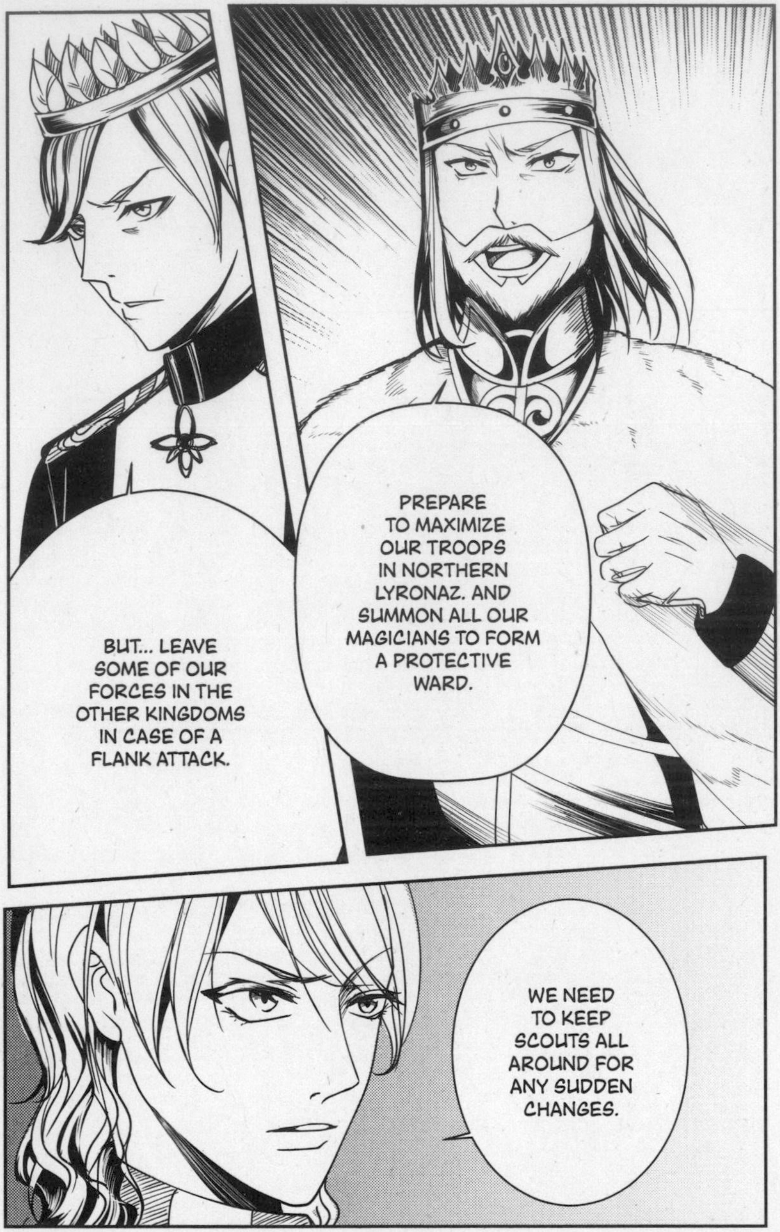
PREPARE TO MAXIMIZE OUR TROOPS IN NORTHERN LYRONAZ. AND SUMMON ALL OUR MAGICIANS TO FORM A PROTECTIVE WARD.
BUT... LEAVE SOME OF OUR FORCES IN THE OTHER KINGDOMS IN CASE OF A FLANK ATTACK.
WE NEED TO KEEP SCOUTS ALL AROUND FOR ANY SUDDEN CHANGES.

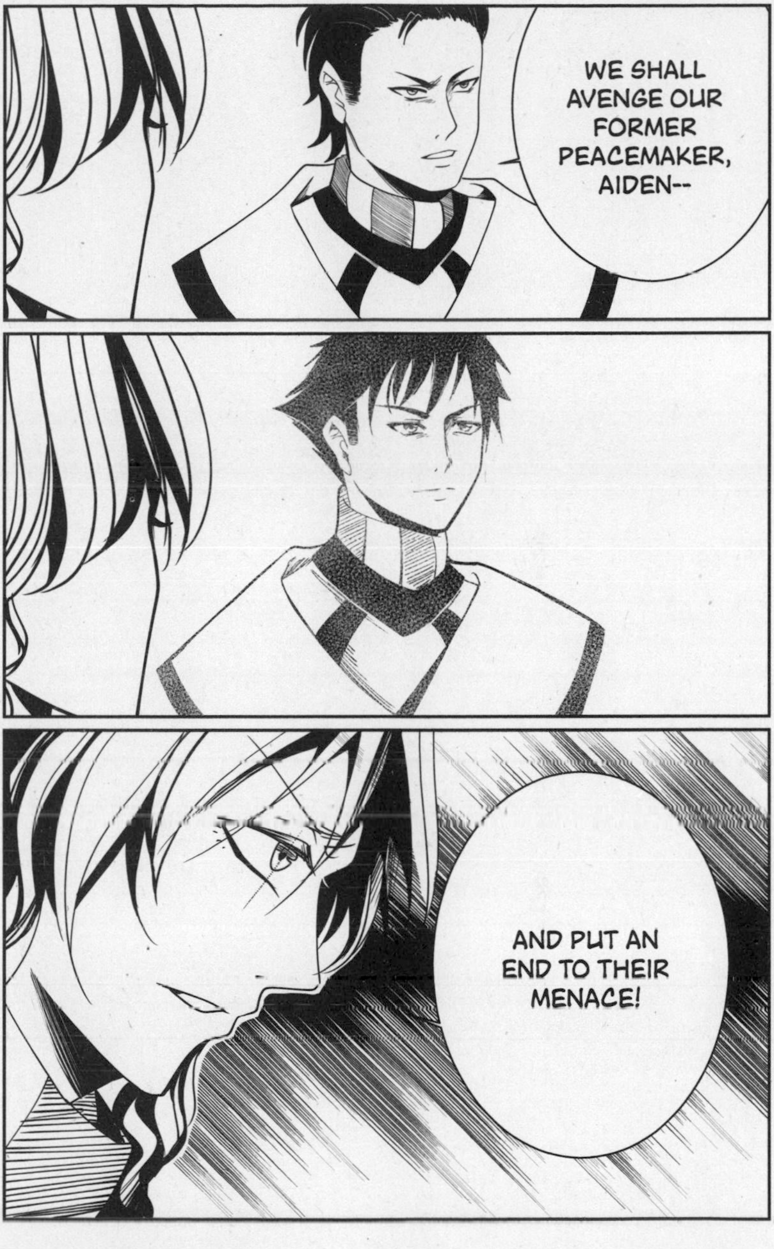
WE SHALL AVENGE OUR FORMER PEACEMAKER, AIDEN--
AND PUT AN END TO THEIR MENACE!

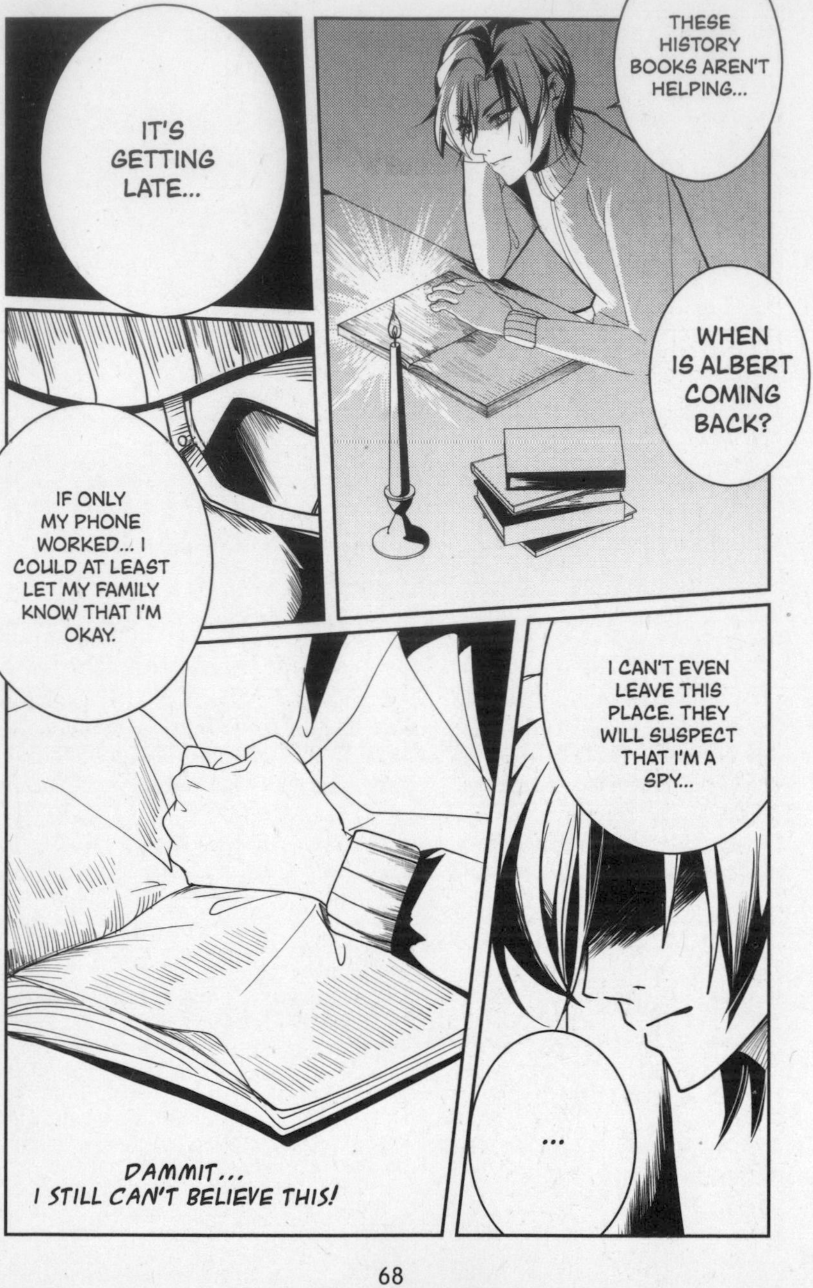
THESE HISTORY BOOKS AREN'T HELPING...
WHEN IS ALBERT COMING BACK?
IT'S GETTING LATE...
IF ONLY MY PHONE WORKED... I COULD AT LEAST LET MY FAMILY KNOW THAT I'M OKAY.
I CAN'T EVEN LEAVE THIS PLACE. THEY WILL SUSPECT THAT I'M A SPY...
...
DAMMIT... I STILL CAN'T BELIEVE THIS!

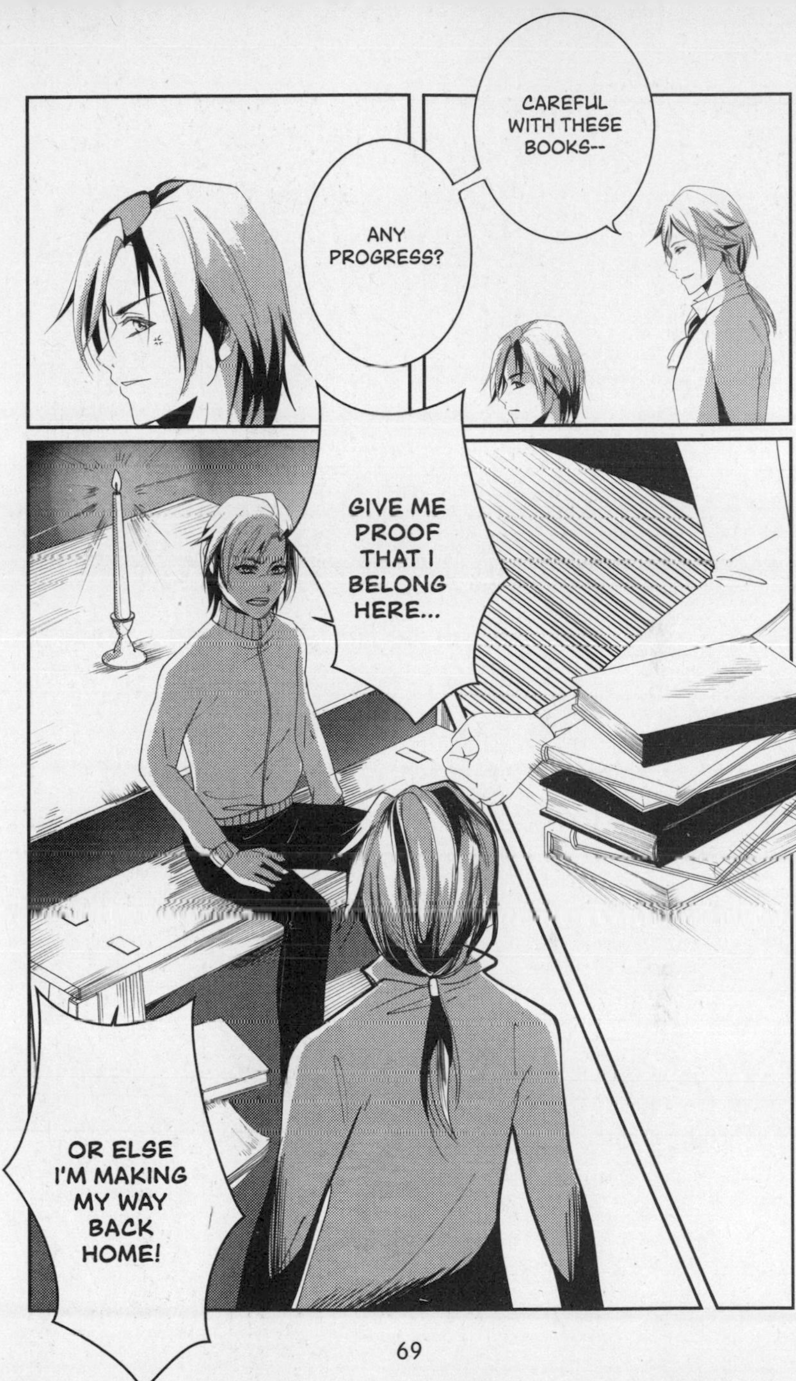
CAREFUL WITH THESE BOOKS--
ANY PROGRESS?
GIVE ME PROOF THAT I BELONG HERE...
OR ELSE I'M MAKING MY WAY BACK HOME!

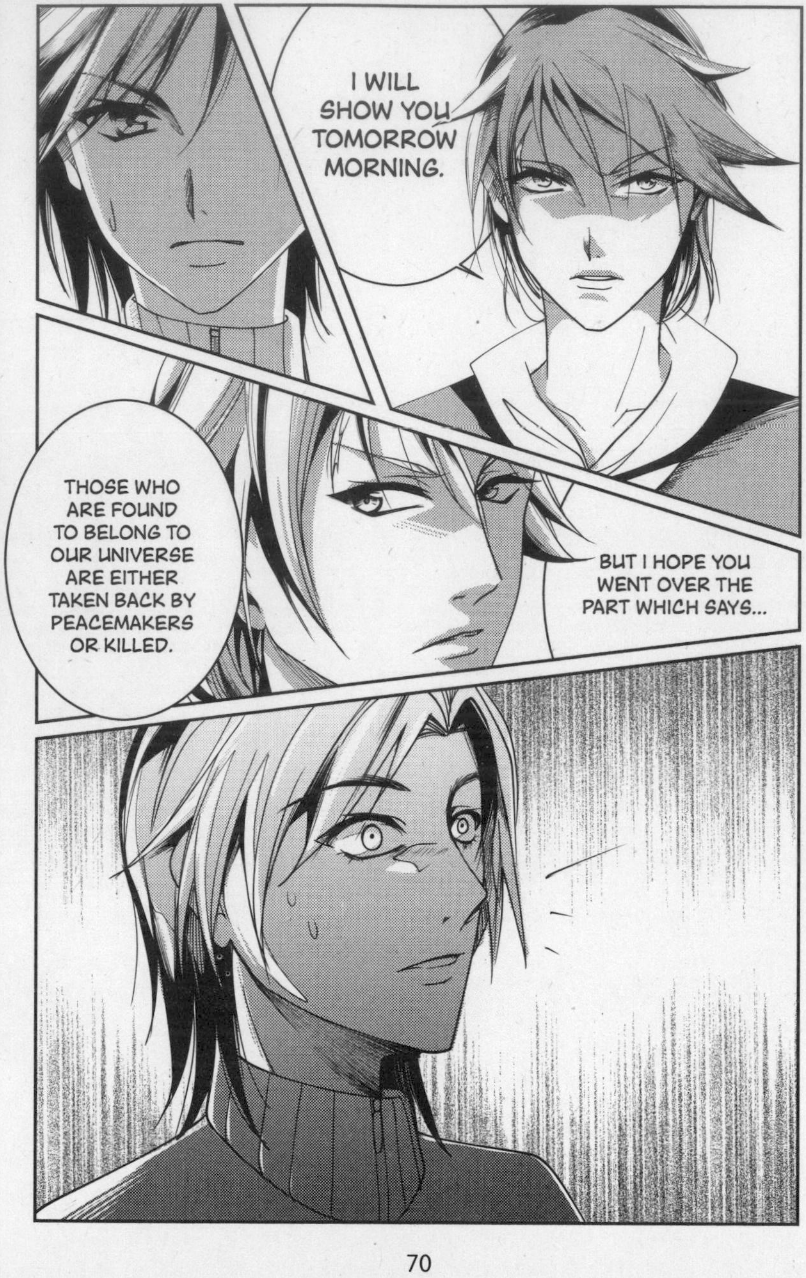
I WILL SHOW YOU TOMORROW MORNING.
BUT I HOPE YOU WENT OVER THE PART WHICH SAYS...
THOSE WHO ARE FOUND TO BELONG TO OUR UNIVERSE ARE EITHER TAKEN BACK BY PEACEMAKERS OR KILLED.

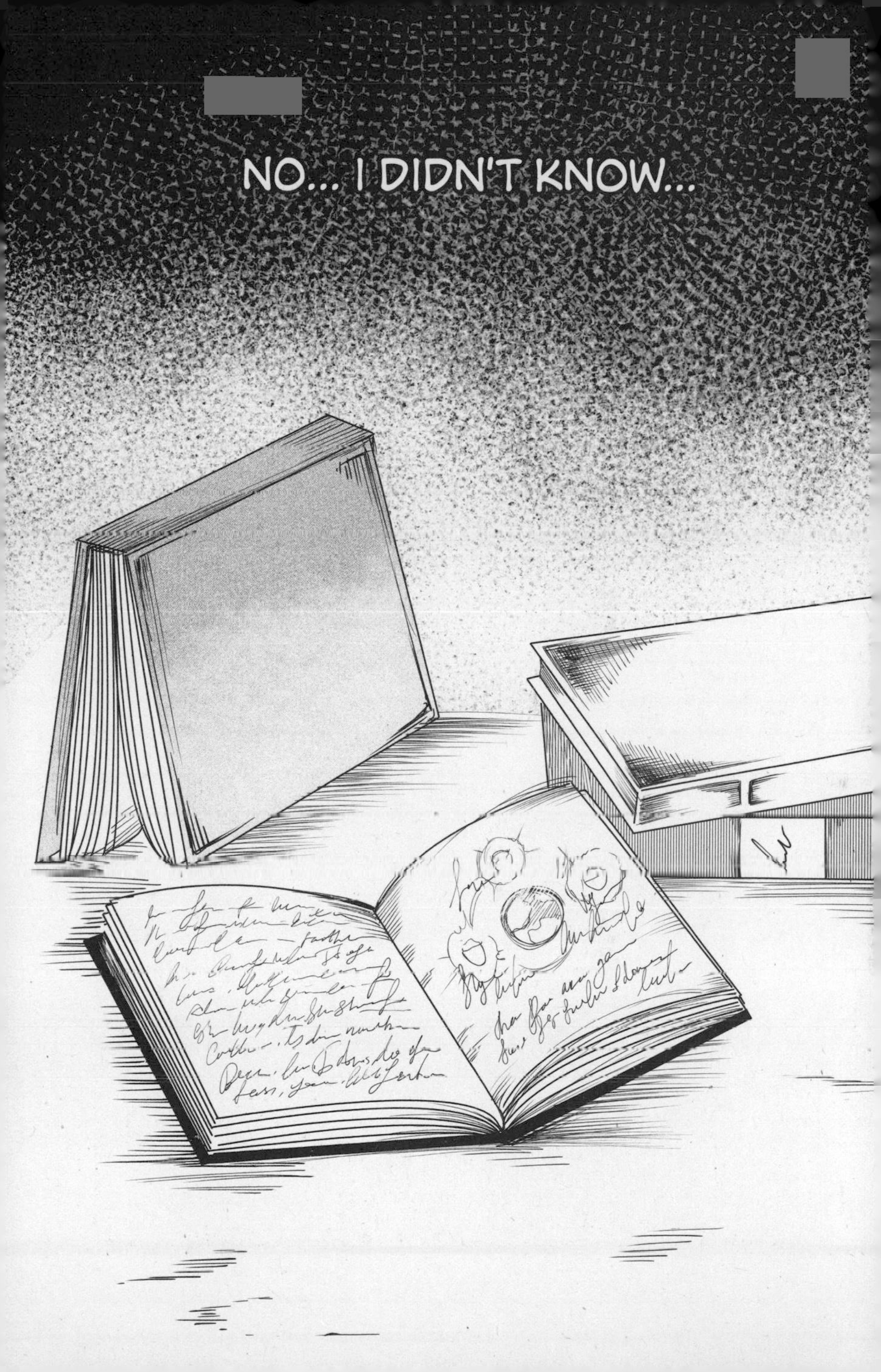
NO... I DIDN'T KNOW...

Ocean
of
Secrets

CHAPTER 8

A STORM FROM THE SOUTH

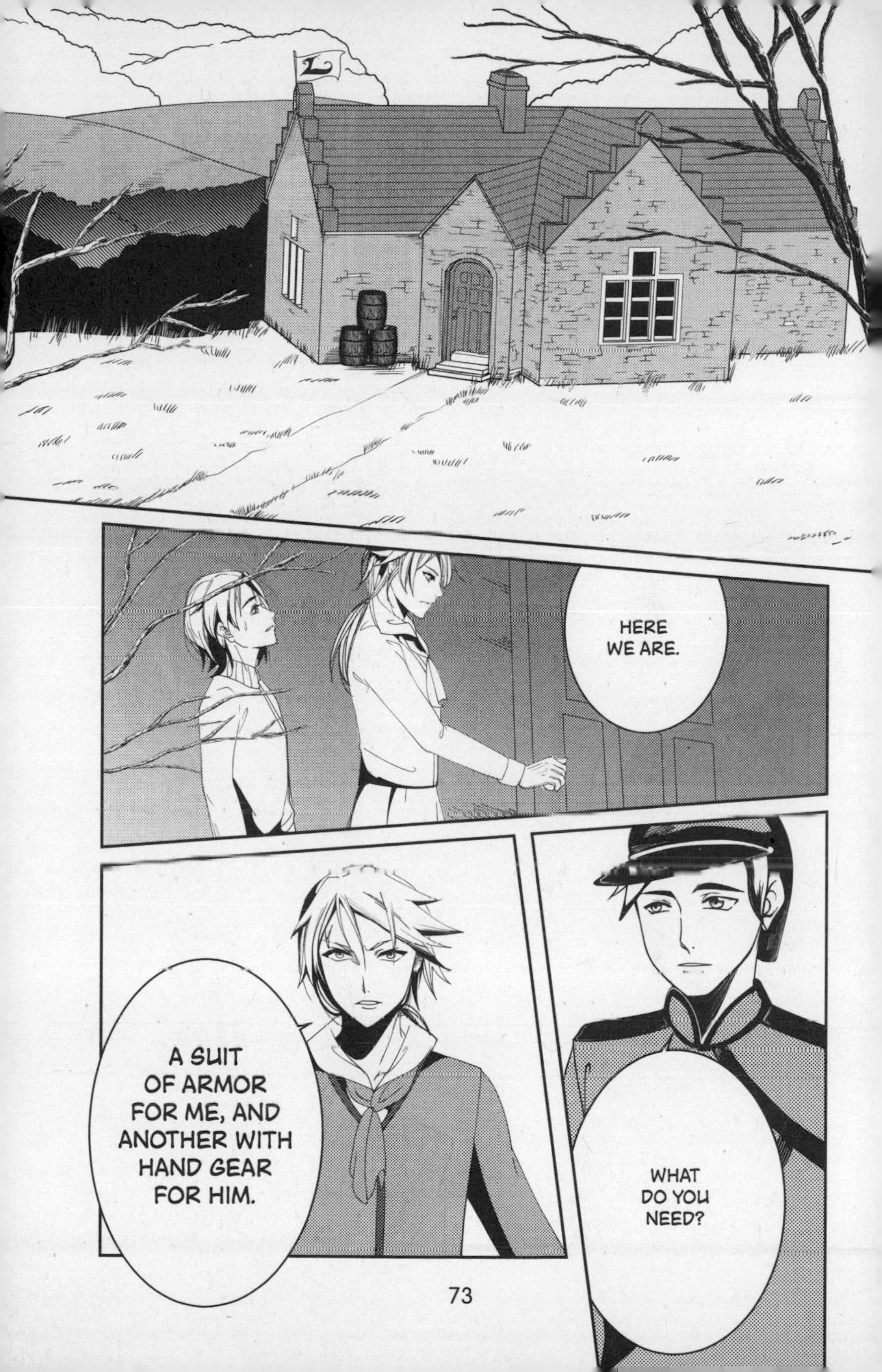
HERE WE ARE.
WHAT DO YOU NEED?
A SUIT OF ARMOR FOR ME, AND ANOTHER WITH HAND GEAR FOR HIM.

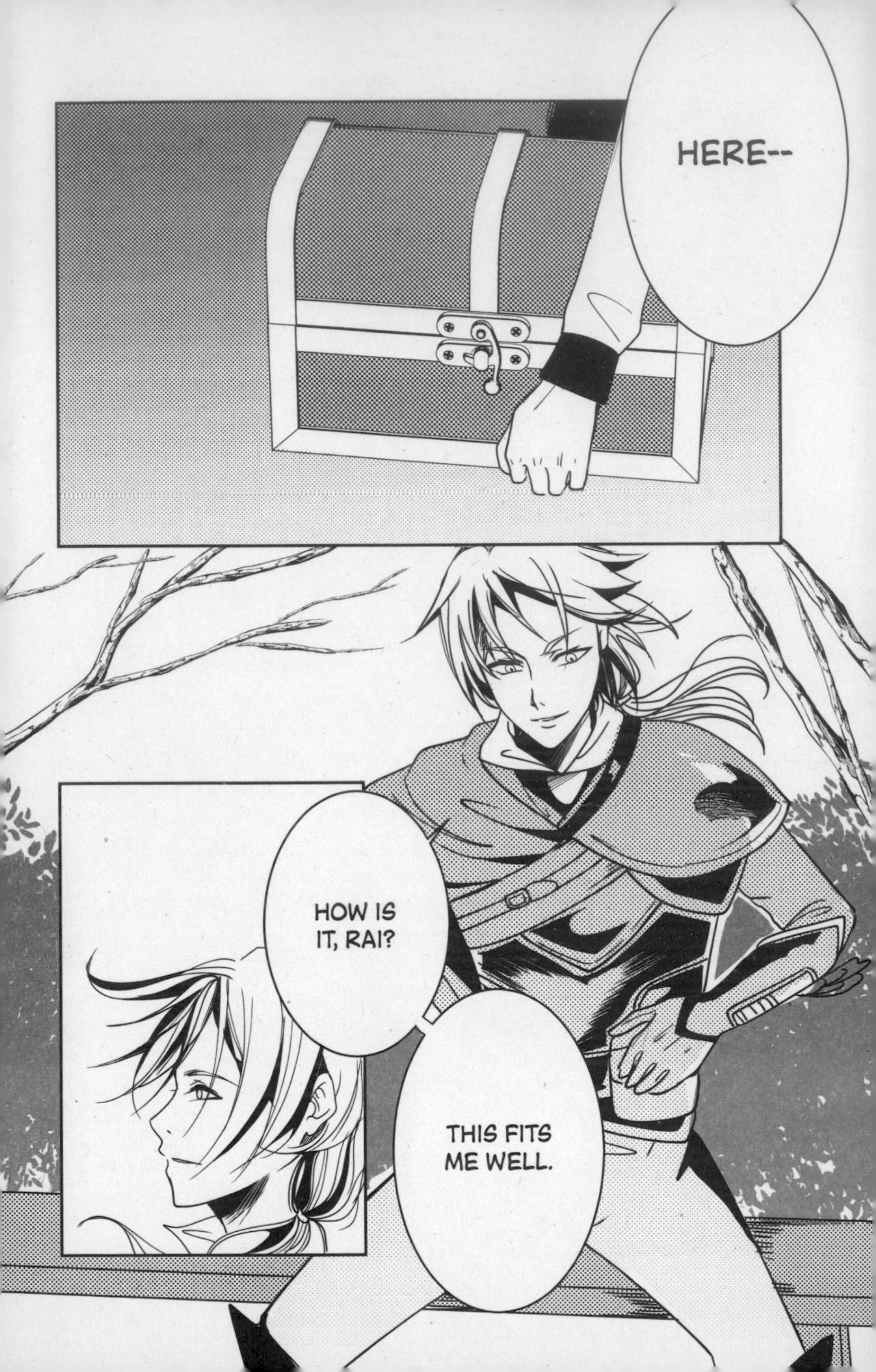
HERE--
HOW IS IT, RAI?
THIS FITS ME WELL.

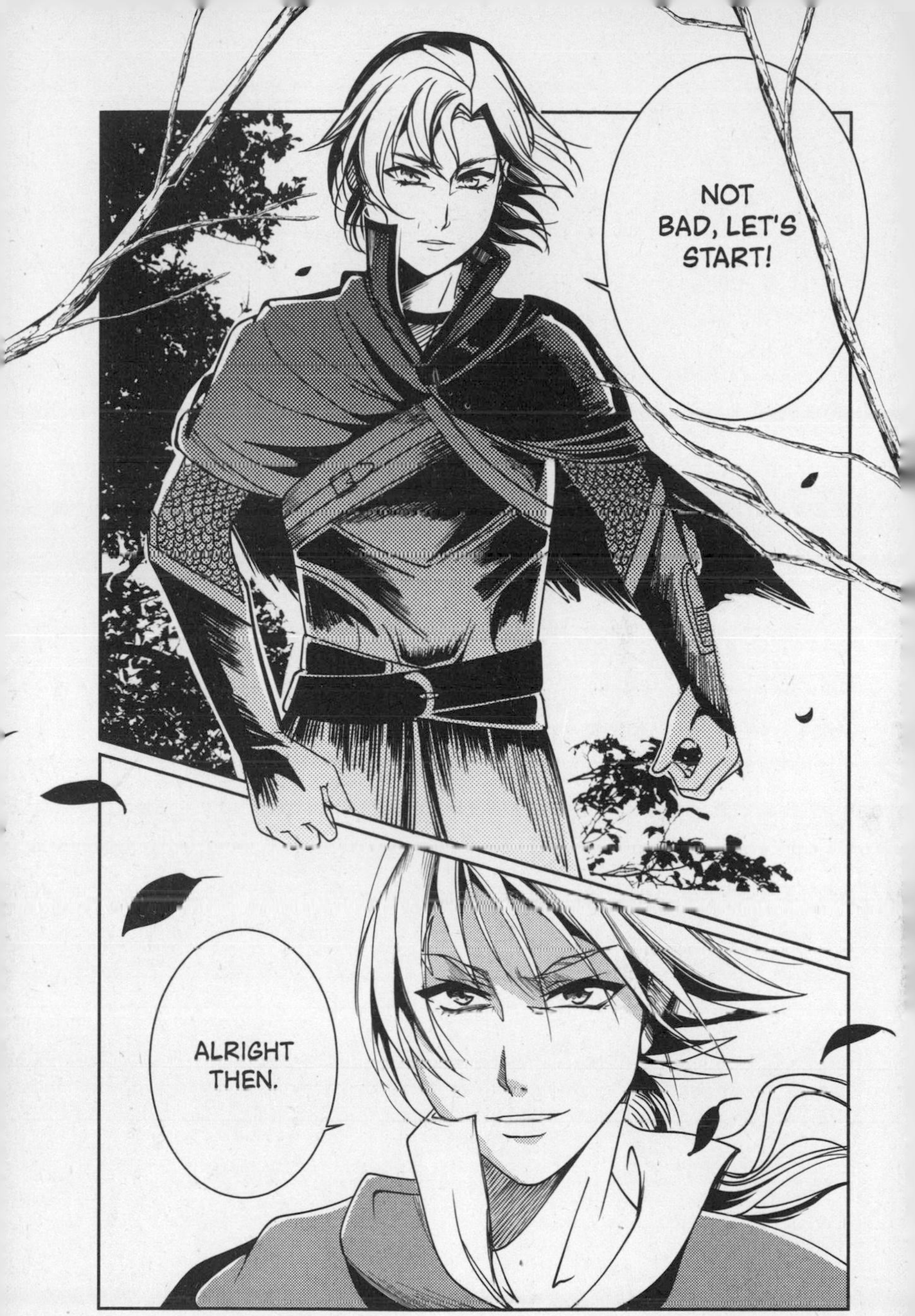
NOT BAD, LET'S START!
ALRIGHT THEN.

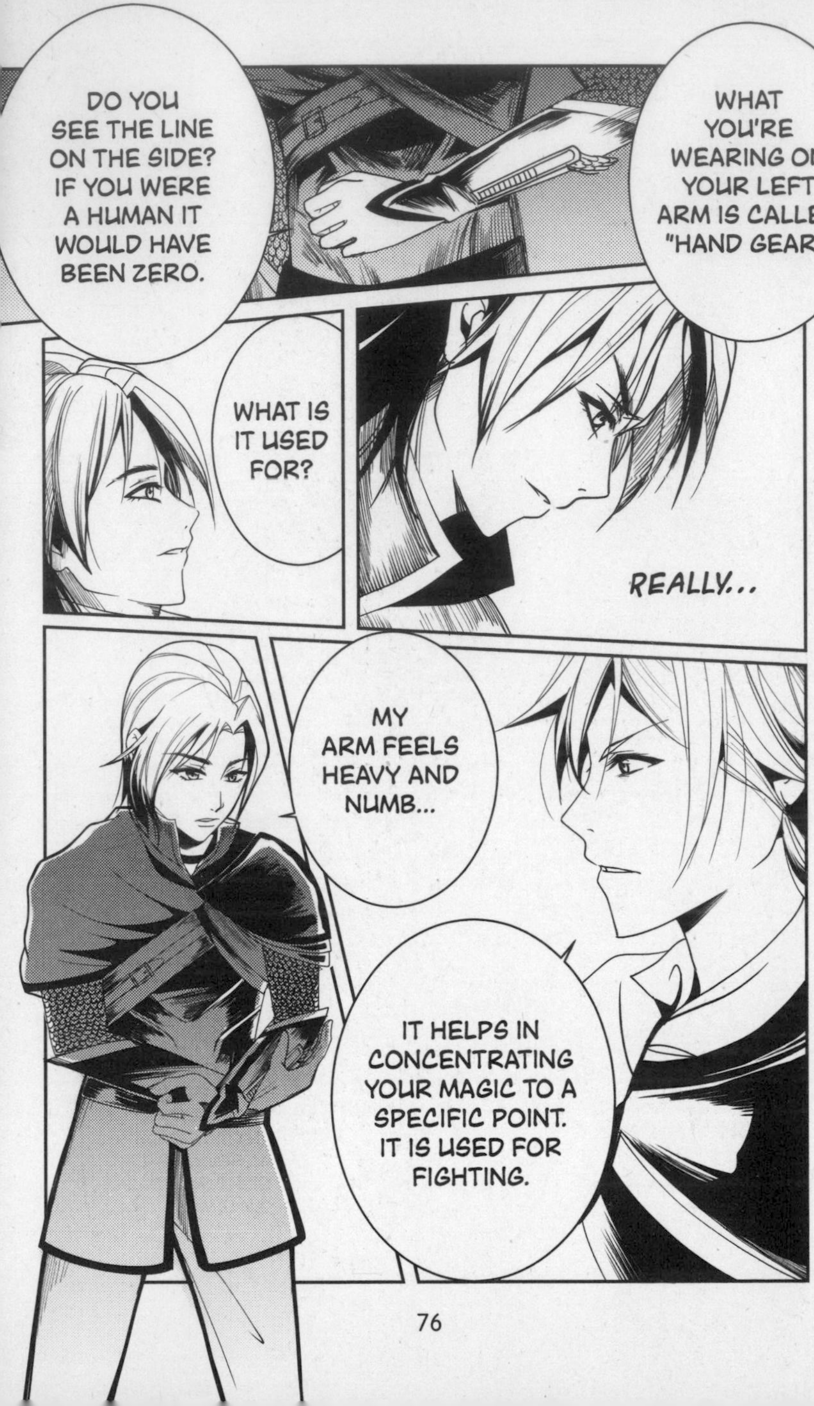
WHAT YOU'RE WEARING ON YOUR LEFT ARM IS CALLED "HAND GEAR".
DO YOU SEE THE LINE ON THE SIDE? IF YOU WERE A HUMAN IT WOULD HAVE BEEN ZERO.
REALLY...
WHAT IS IT USED FOR?
MY ARM FEELS HEAVY AND NUMB...
IT HELPS IN CONCENTRATING YOUR MAGIC TO A SPECIFIC POINT. IT IS USED FOR FIGHTING.

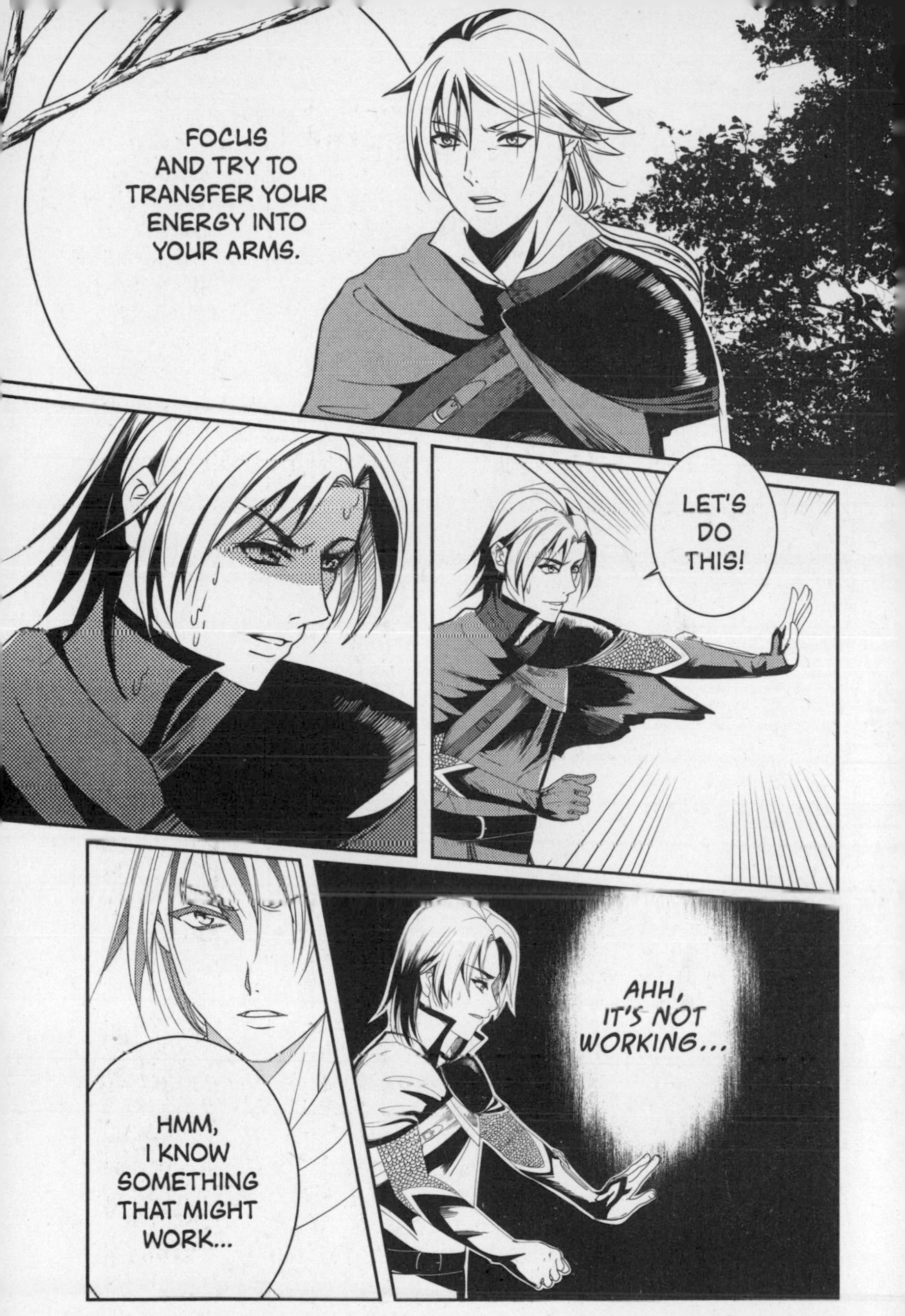
FOCUS AND TRY TO TRANSFER YOUR ENERGY INTO YOUR ARMS.
LET'S DO THIS!
AHH, IT'S NOT WORKING...
HMM, I KNOW SOMETHING THAT MIGHT WORK...

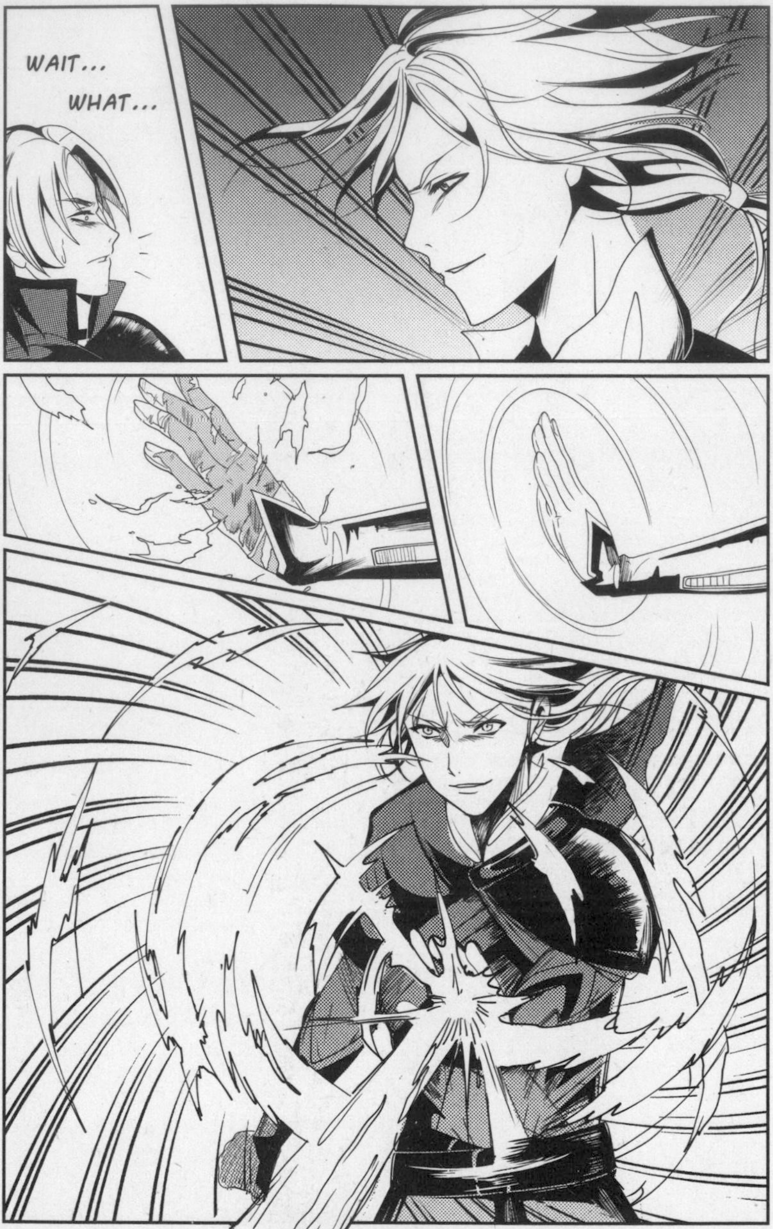
WAIT...
WHAT...

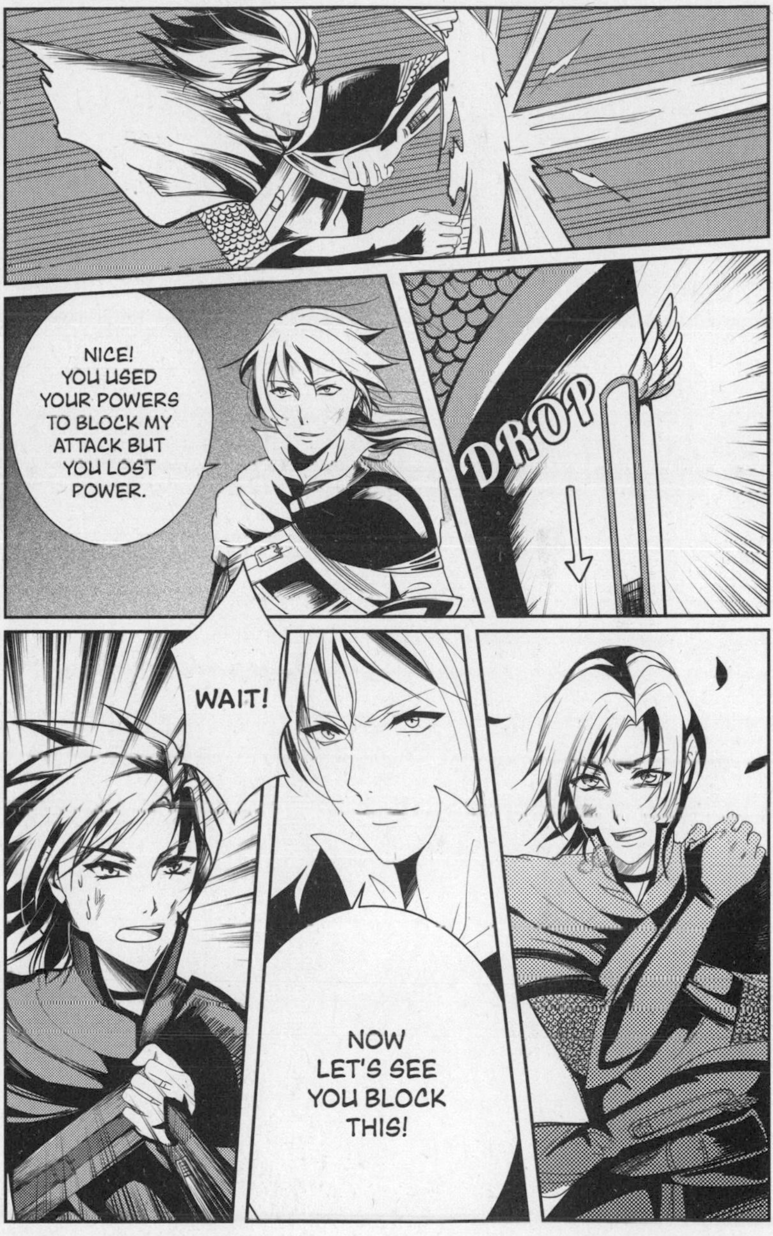
DROP
NICE! YOU USED YOUR POWERS TO BLOCK MY ATTACK BUT YOU LOST POWER.
NOW LET'S SEE YOU BLOCK THIS!
WAIT!

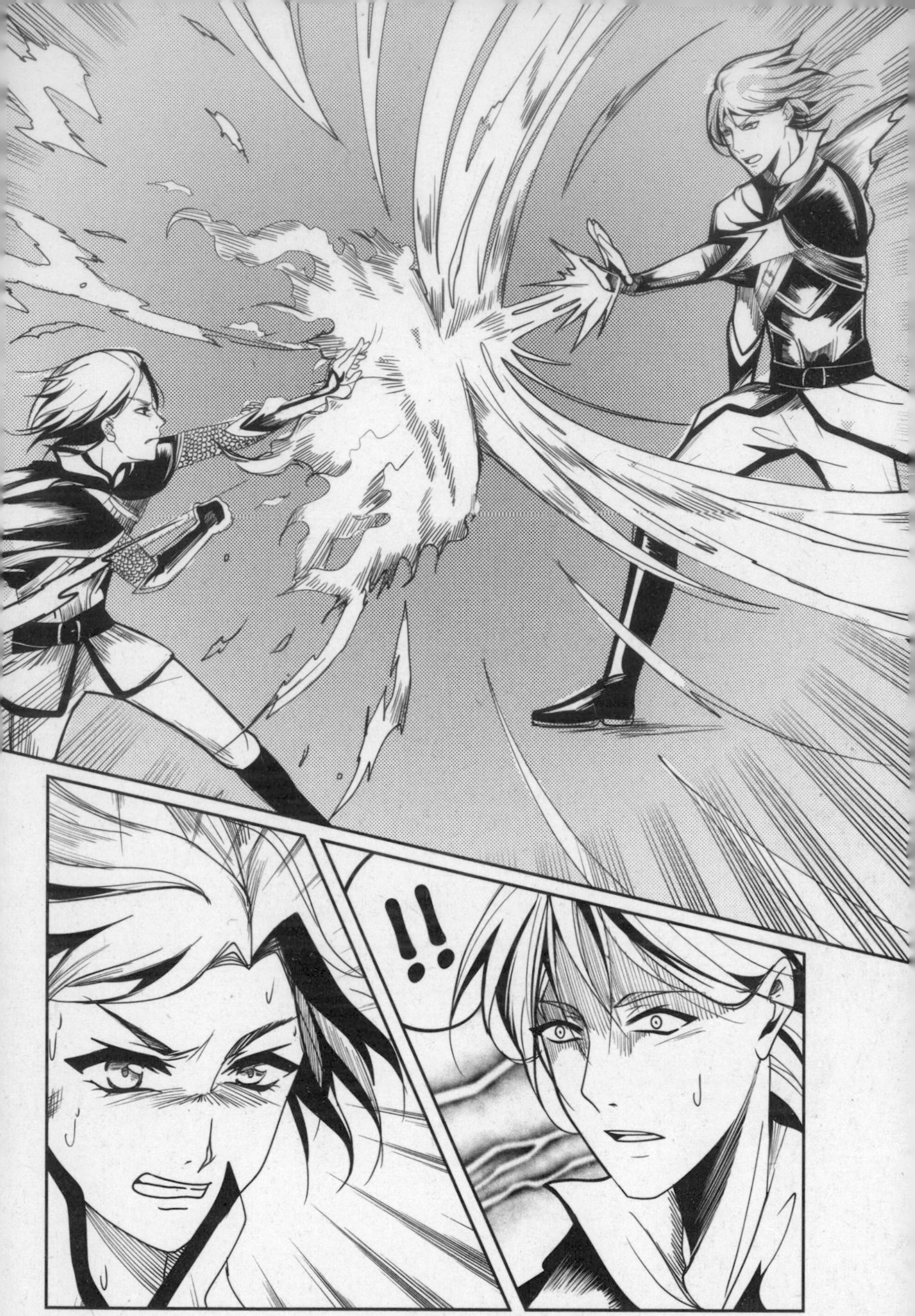
!!

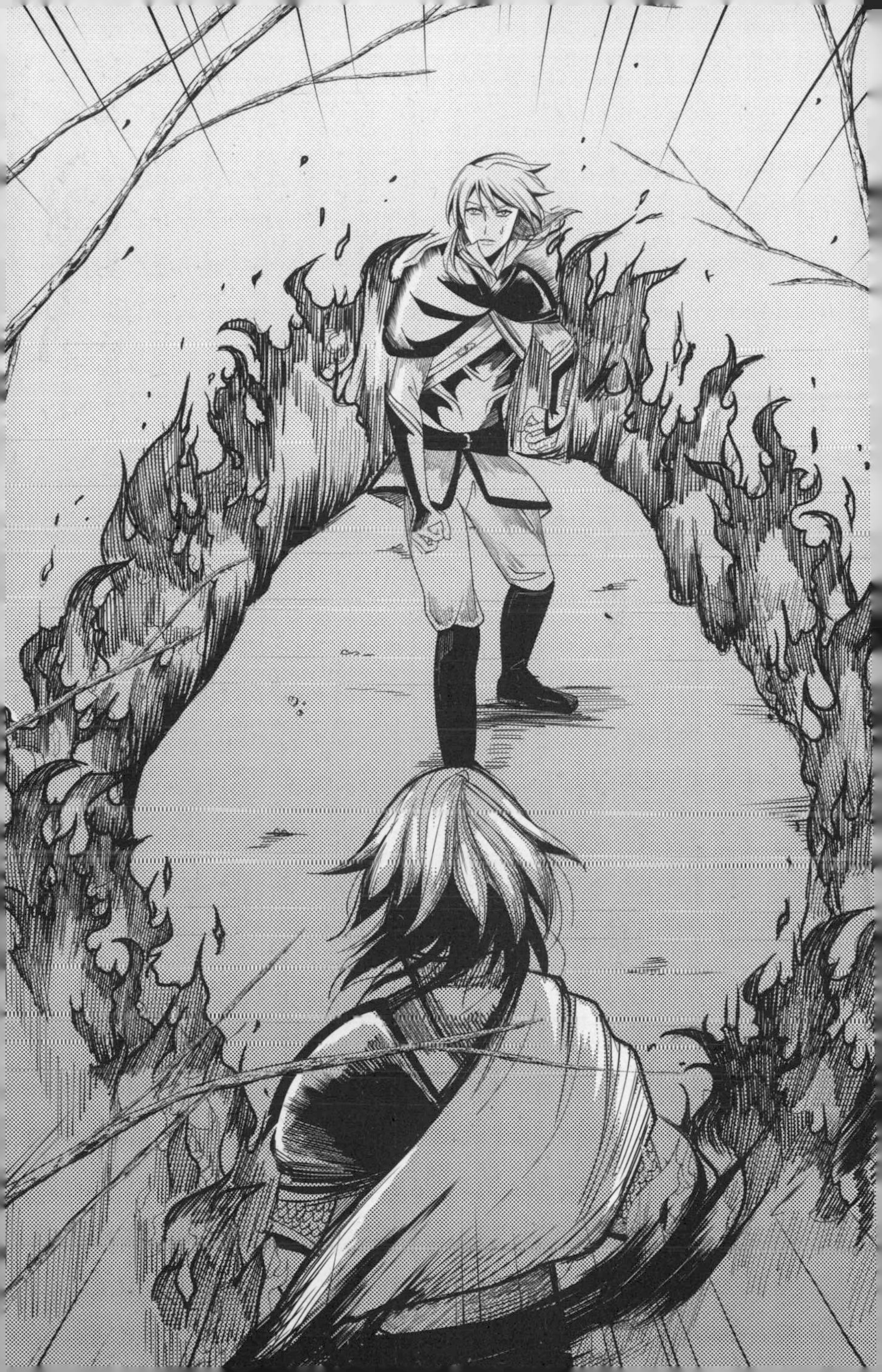

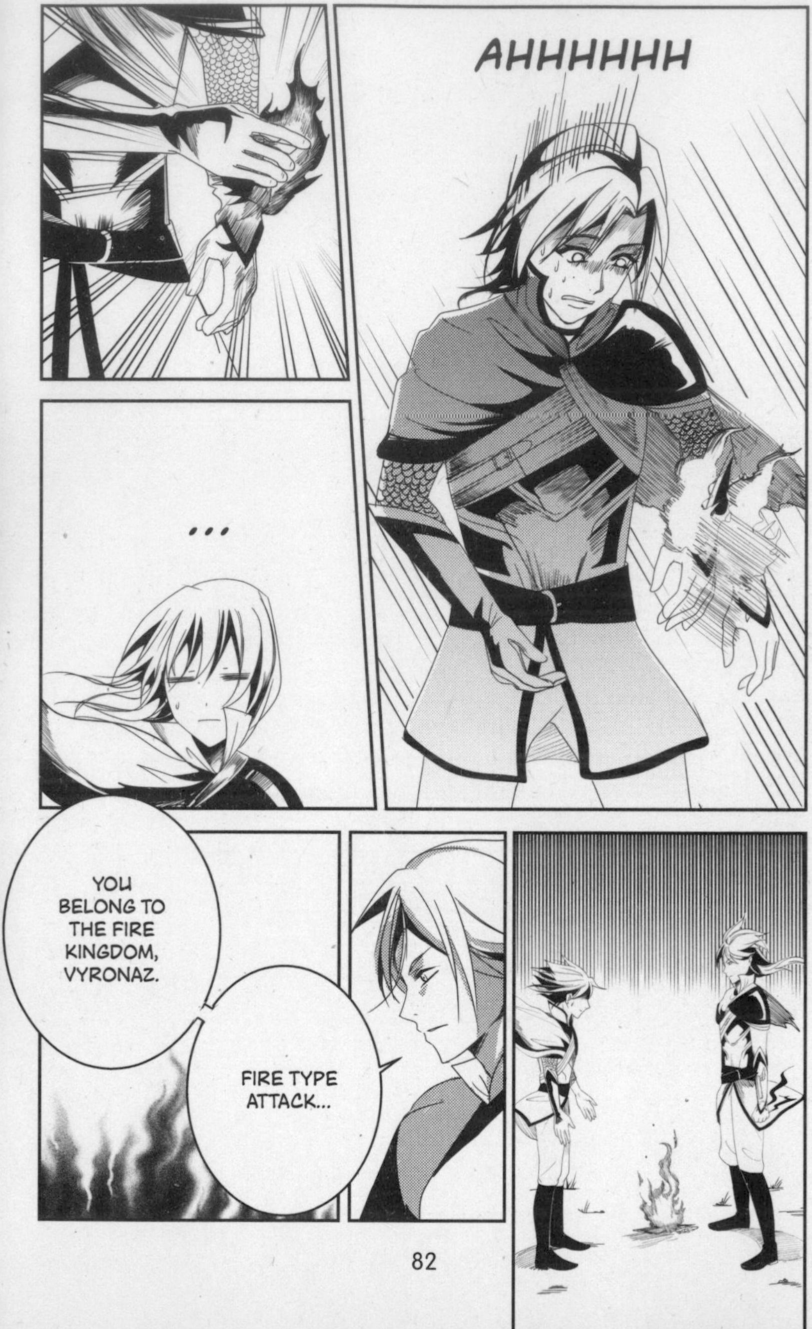
AHHHHHH
...
FIRE TYPE ATTACK...
YOU BELONG TO THE FIRE KINGDOM, VYRONAZ.

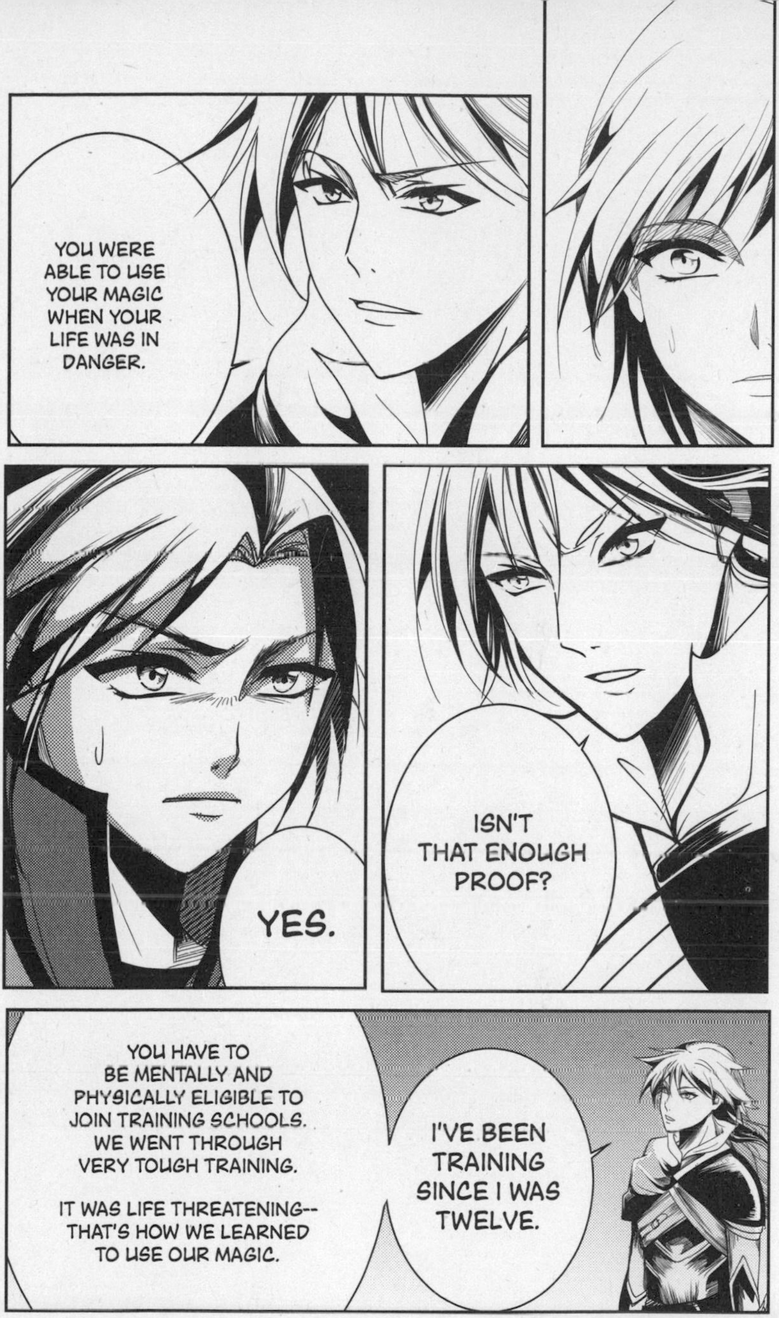
YOU WERE ABLE TO USE YOUR MAGIC WHEN YOUR LIFE WAS IN DANGER.
ISN'T THAT ENOUGH PROOF?
YES.
I'VE BEEN TRAINING SINCE I WAS TWELVE.
YOU HAVE TO BE MENTALLY AND PHYSICALLY ELIGIBLE TO JOIN TRAINING SCHOOLS. WE WENT THROUGH VERY TOUGH TRAINING.
IT WAS LIFE THREATENING--THAT'S HOW WE LEARNED TO USE OUR MAGIC.

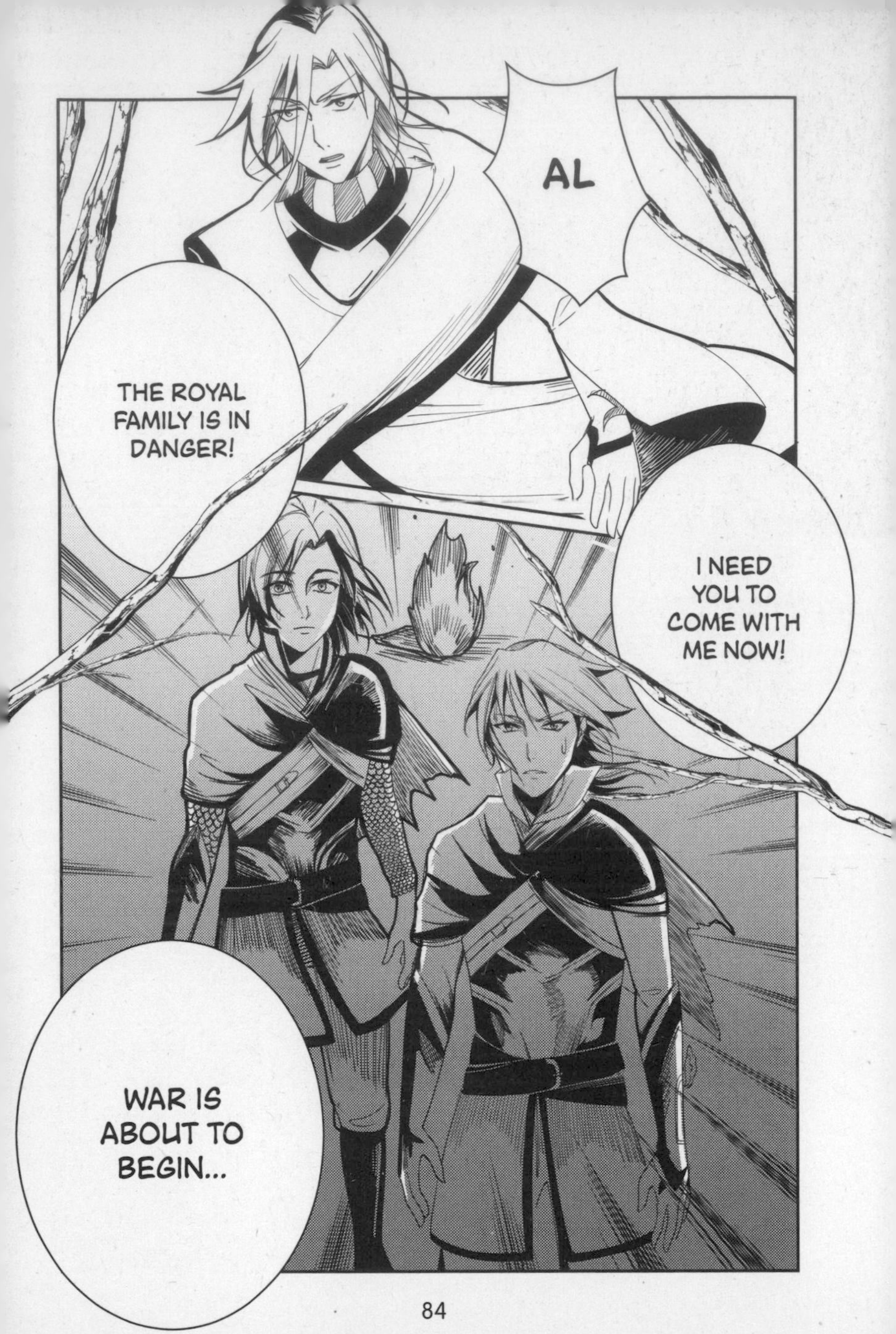
AL
THE ROYAL FAMILY IS IN DANGER!
I NEED YOU TO COME WITH ME NOW!
WAR IS ABOUT TO BEGIN...

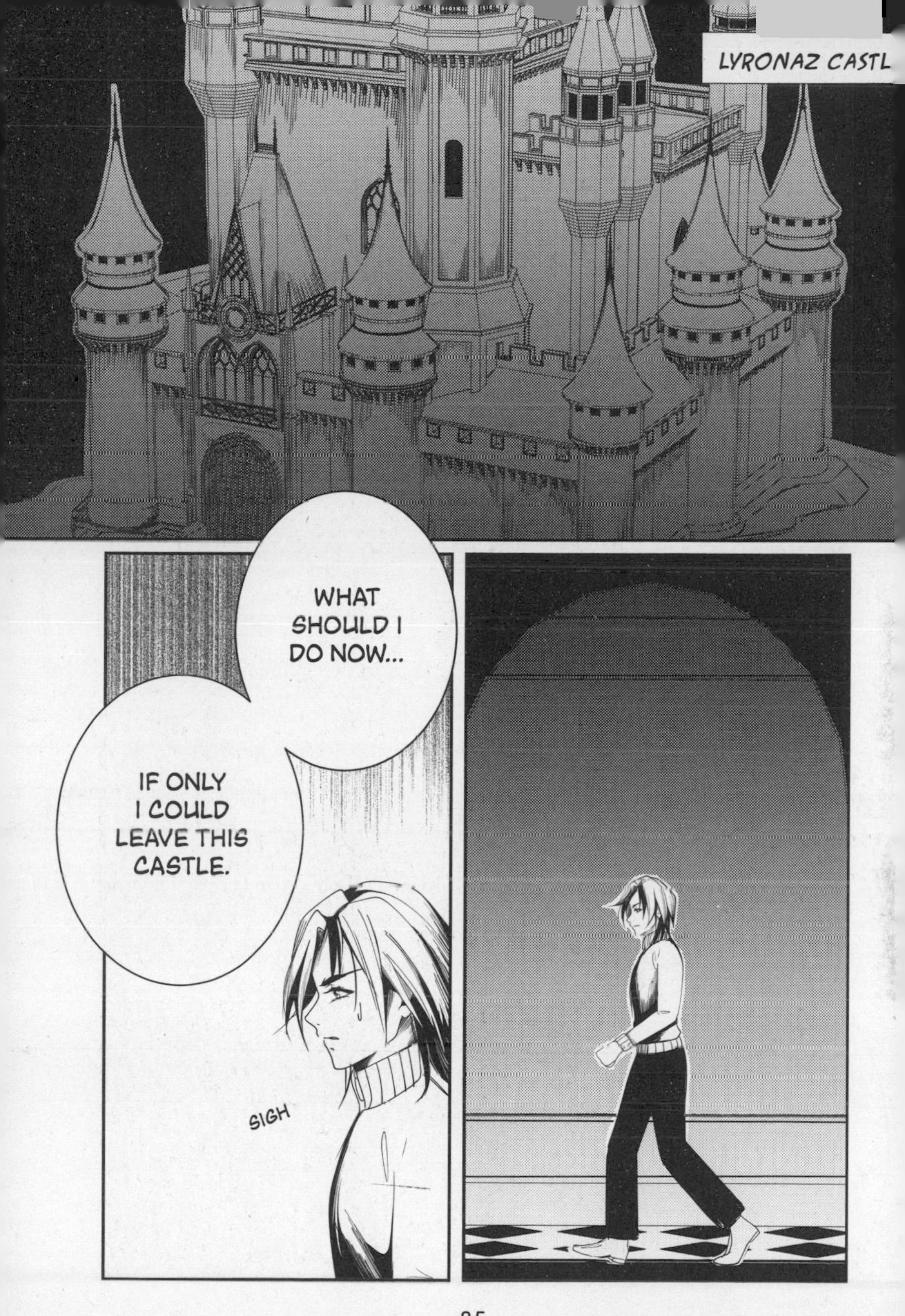
LYRONAZ CASTL
WHAT SHOULD I DO NOW...
IF ONLY I COULD LEAVE THIS CASTLE.
SIGH

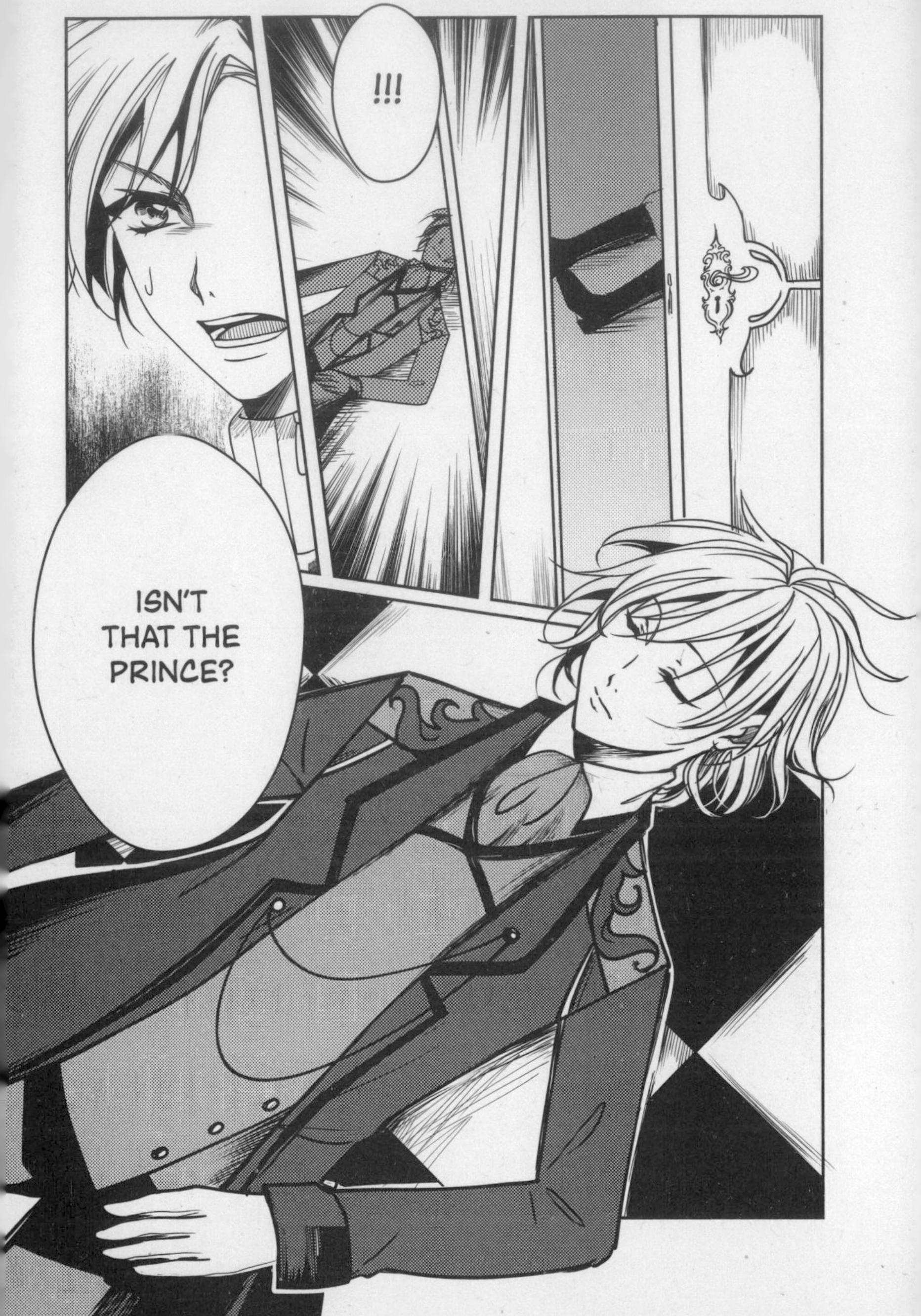
!!!
ISN'T THAT THE PRINCE?

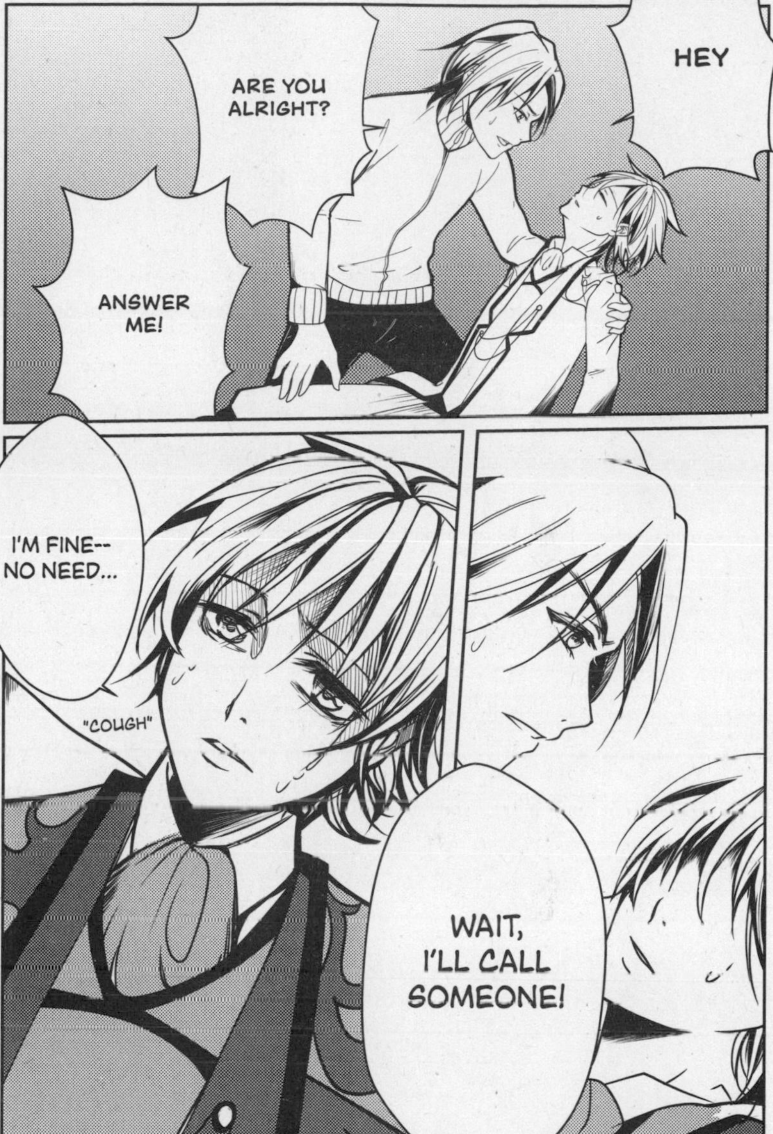
HEY
ARE YOU ALRIGHT?
ANSWER ME!
I'M FINE-- NO NEED...
"COUGH"
WAIT, I'LL CALL SOMEONE!

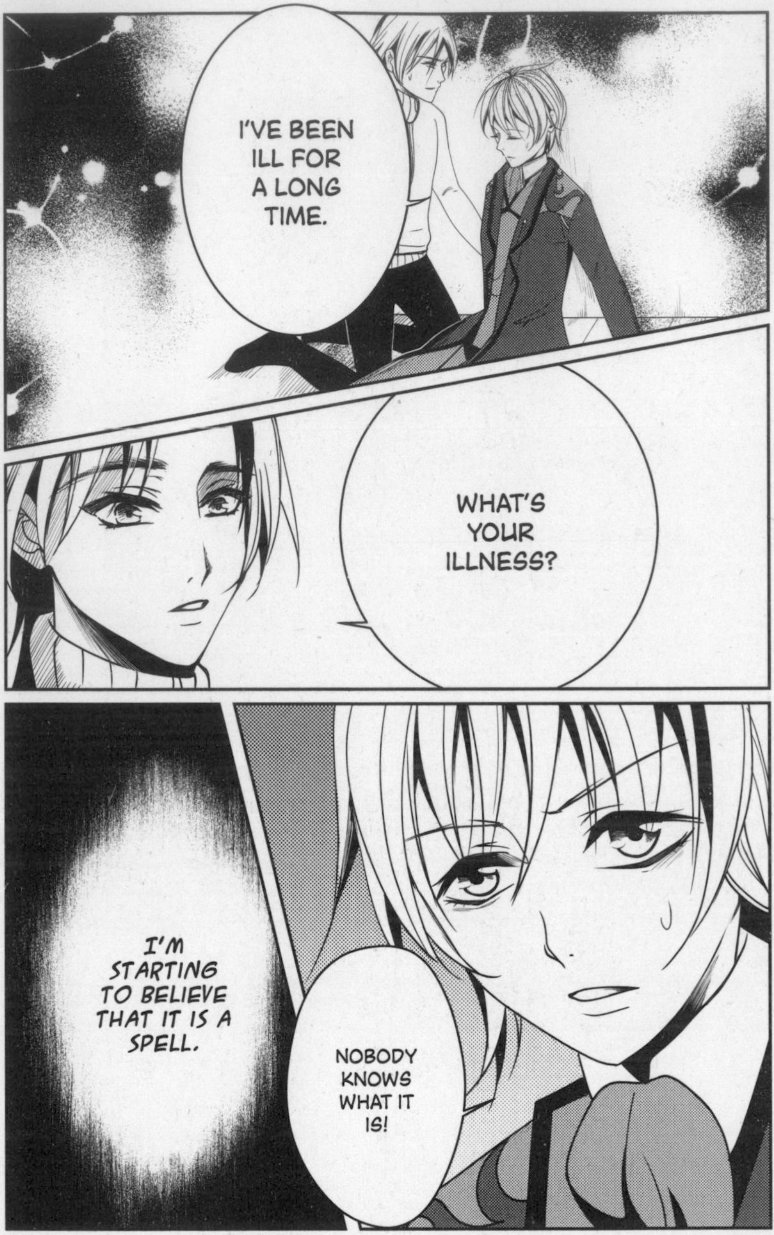
I'VE BEEN ILL FOR A LONG TIME.
WHAT'S YOUR ILLNESS?
NOBODY KNOWS WHAT IT IS!
I'M STARTING TO BELIEVE THAT IT IS A SPELL.

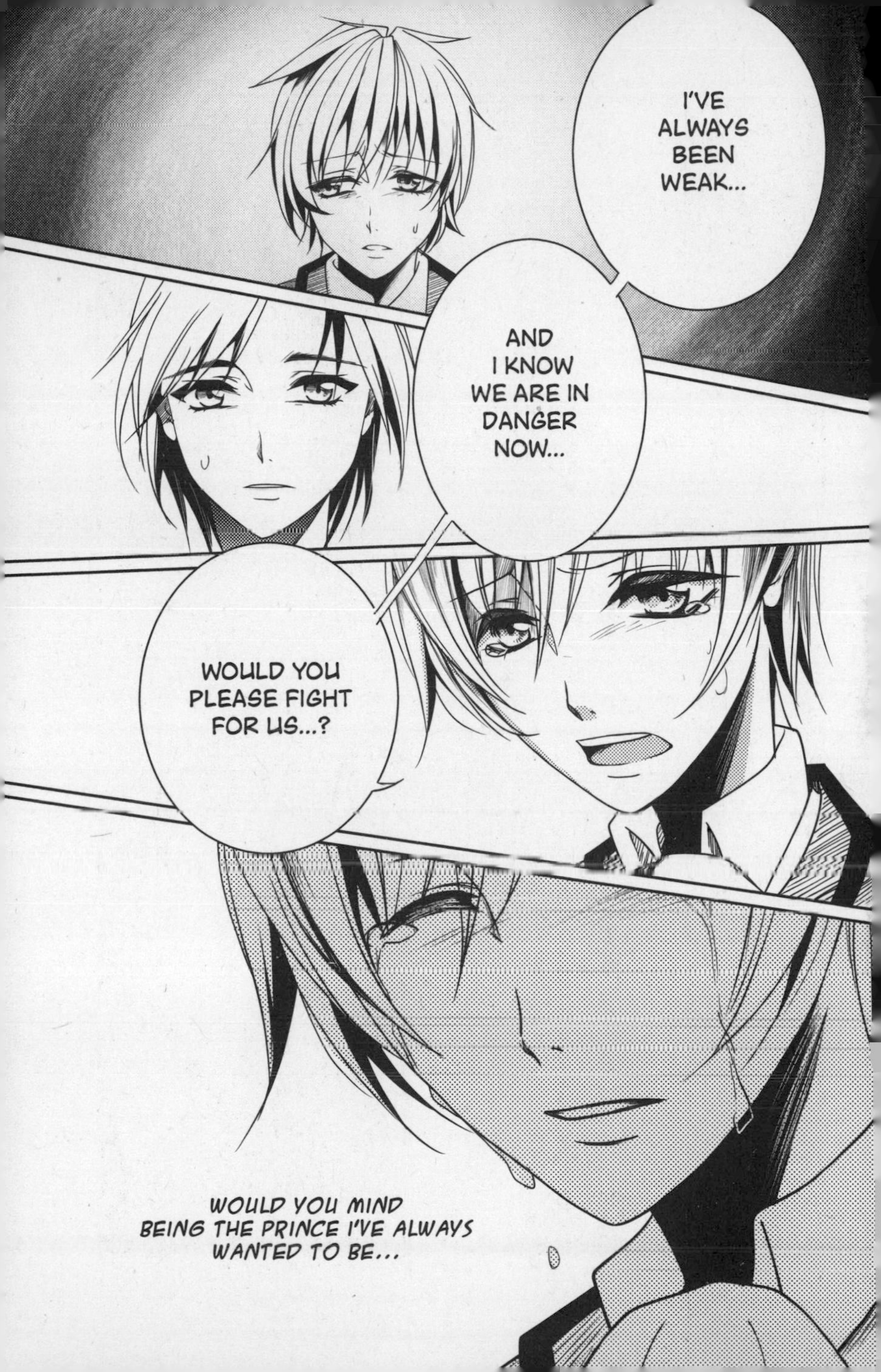
I'VE ALWAYS BEEN WEAK...
AND I KNOW WE ARE IN DANGER NOW...
WOULD YOU PLEASE FIGHT FOR US...?
WOULD YOU MIND BEING THE PRINCE I'VE ALWAYS WANTED TO BE...

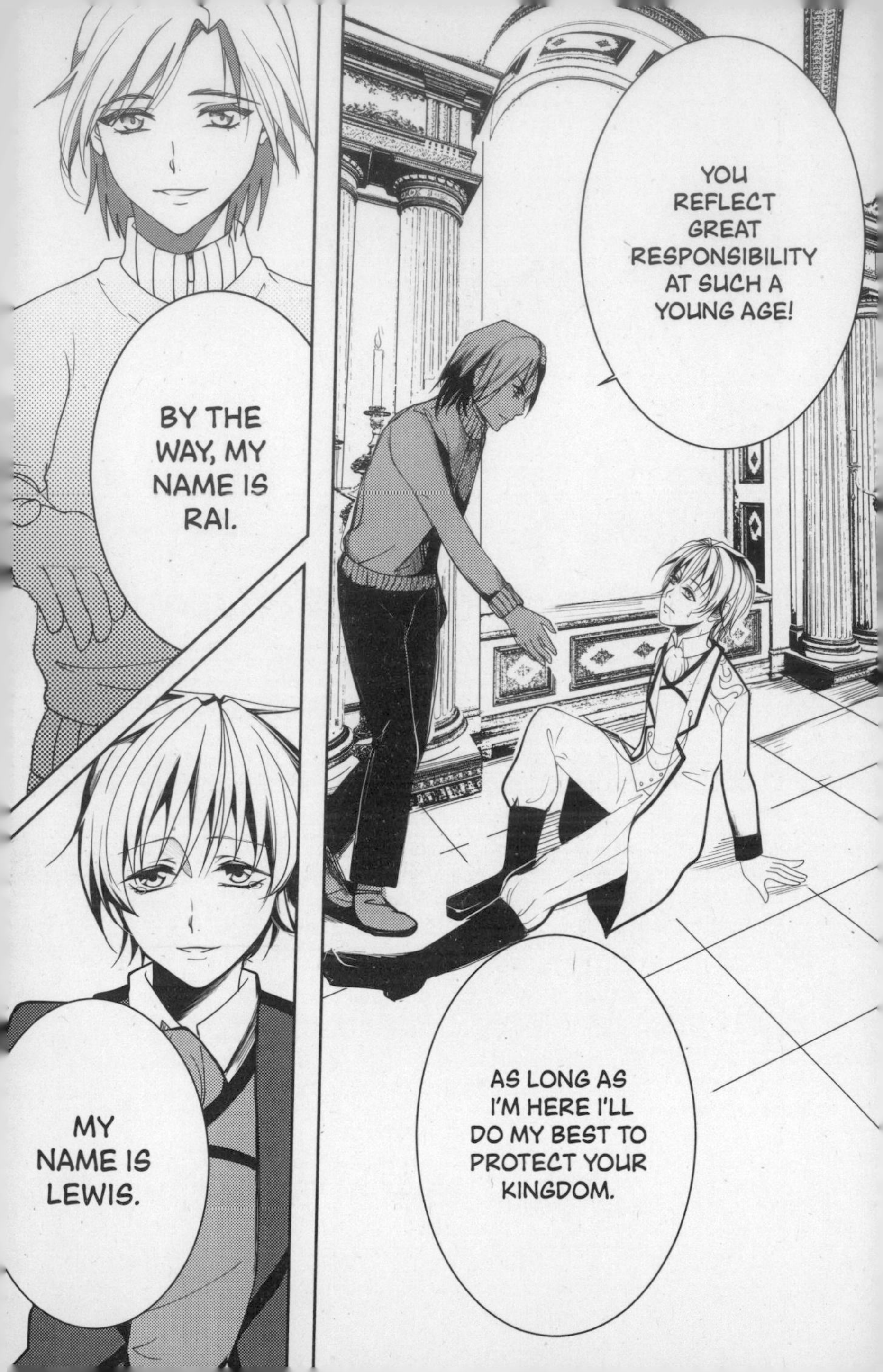
YOU REFLECT GREAT RESPONSIBILITY AT SUCH A YOUNG AGE!
AS LONG AS I'M HERE I'LL DO MY BEST TO PROTECT YOUR KINGDOM.
BY THE WAY, MY NAME IS RAI.
MY NAME IS LEWIS.

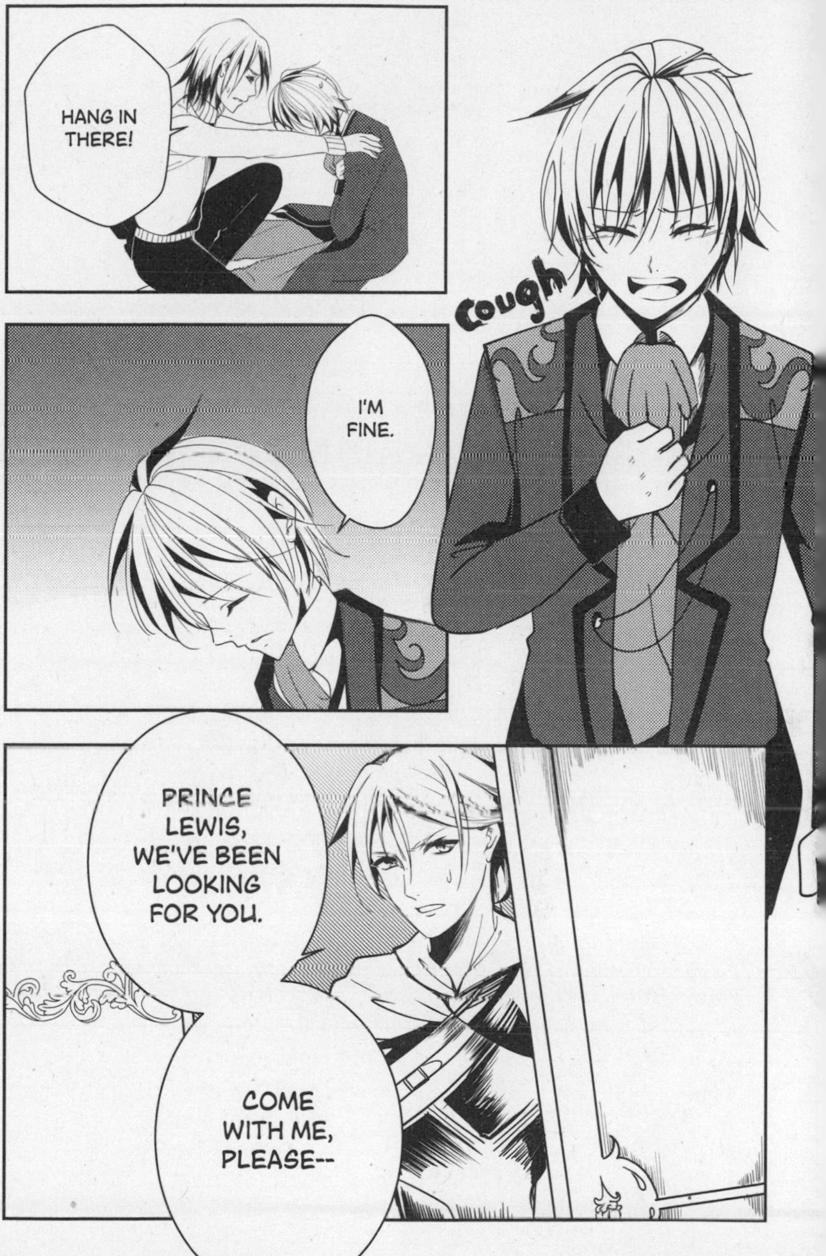
Cough
HANG IN THERE!
I'M FINE.
PRINCE LEWIS, WE'VE BEEN LOOKING FOR YOU.
COME WITH ME, PLEASE--

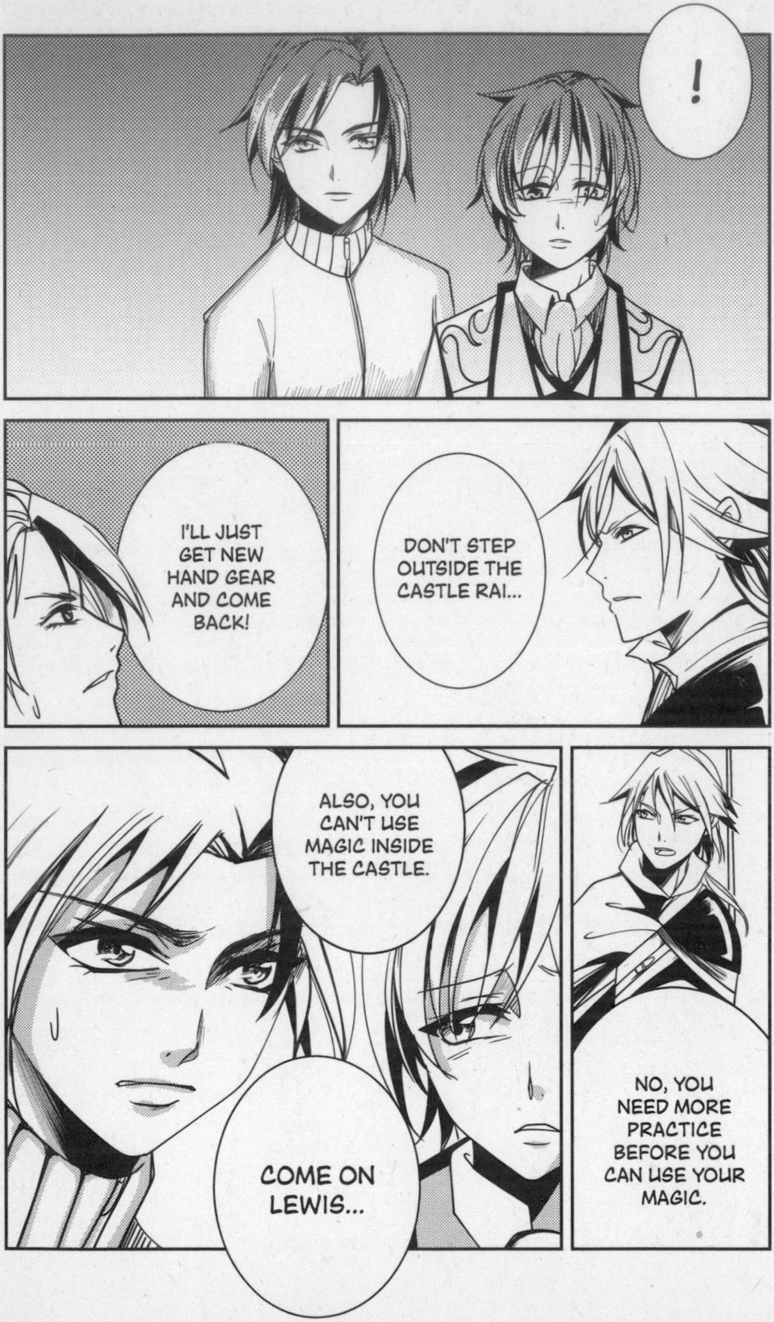
!
DON'T STEP OUTSIDE THE CASTLE RAI...
I'LL JUST GET NEW HAND GEAR AND COME BACK!
NO, YOU NEED MORE PRACTICE BEFORE YOU CAN USE YOUR MAGIC.
ALSO, YOU CAN'T USE MAGIC INSIDE THE CASTLE.
COME ON LEWIS...

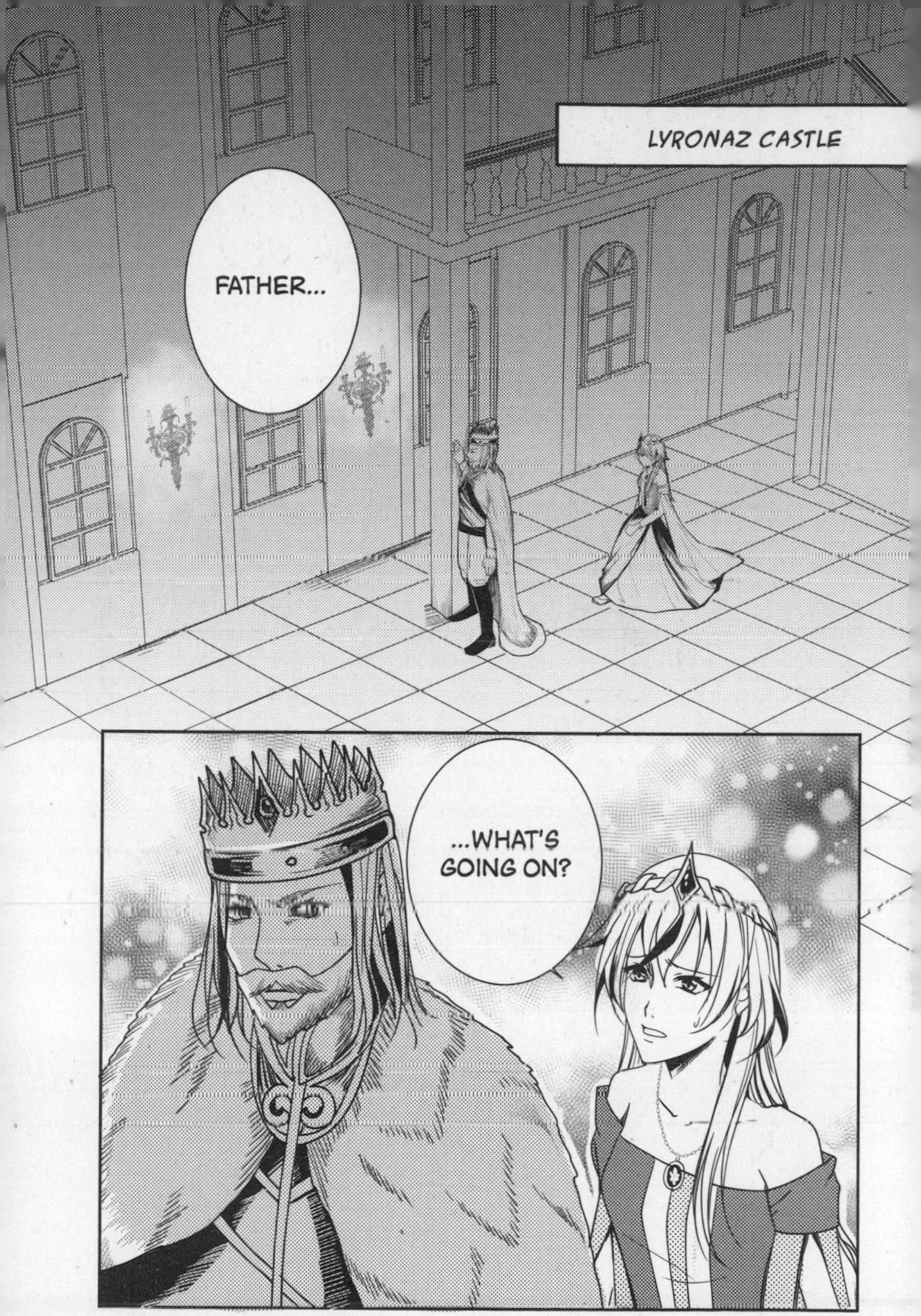
LYRONAZ CASTLE
FATHER...
...WHAT'S GOING ON?

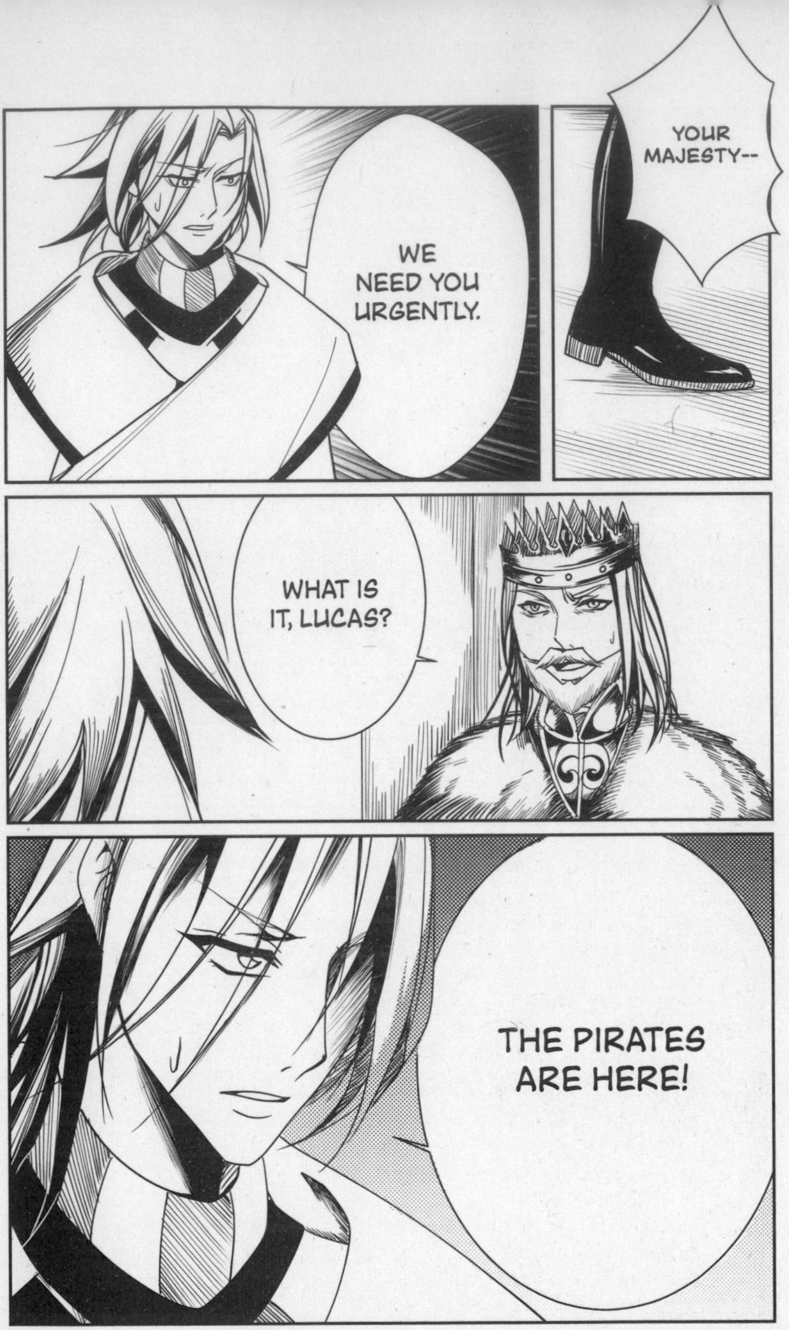
YOUR MAJESTY--
WE NEED YOU URGENTLY.
WHAT IS IT, LUCAS?
THE PIRATES ARE HERE!

01/09/2020

Item(s) Checked Out

TITLE	Ocean of secrets.
BARCODE	33029105476253
DUE DATE	**01-30-20**
TITLE	Harley Quinn :
BARCODE	33029102946522
DUE DATE	**01-30-20**

Total Items This Session: 2

Thank you for visiting the library!
Sacramento Public Library
www.saclibrary.org

Love your library?
Join the Friends!
saclibfriends.org/membership
Visit our Book Den, too.

Terminal #   85

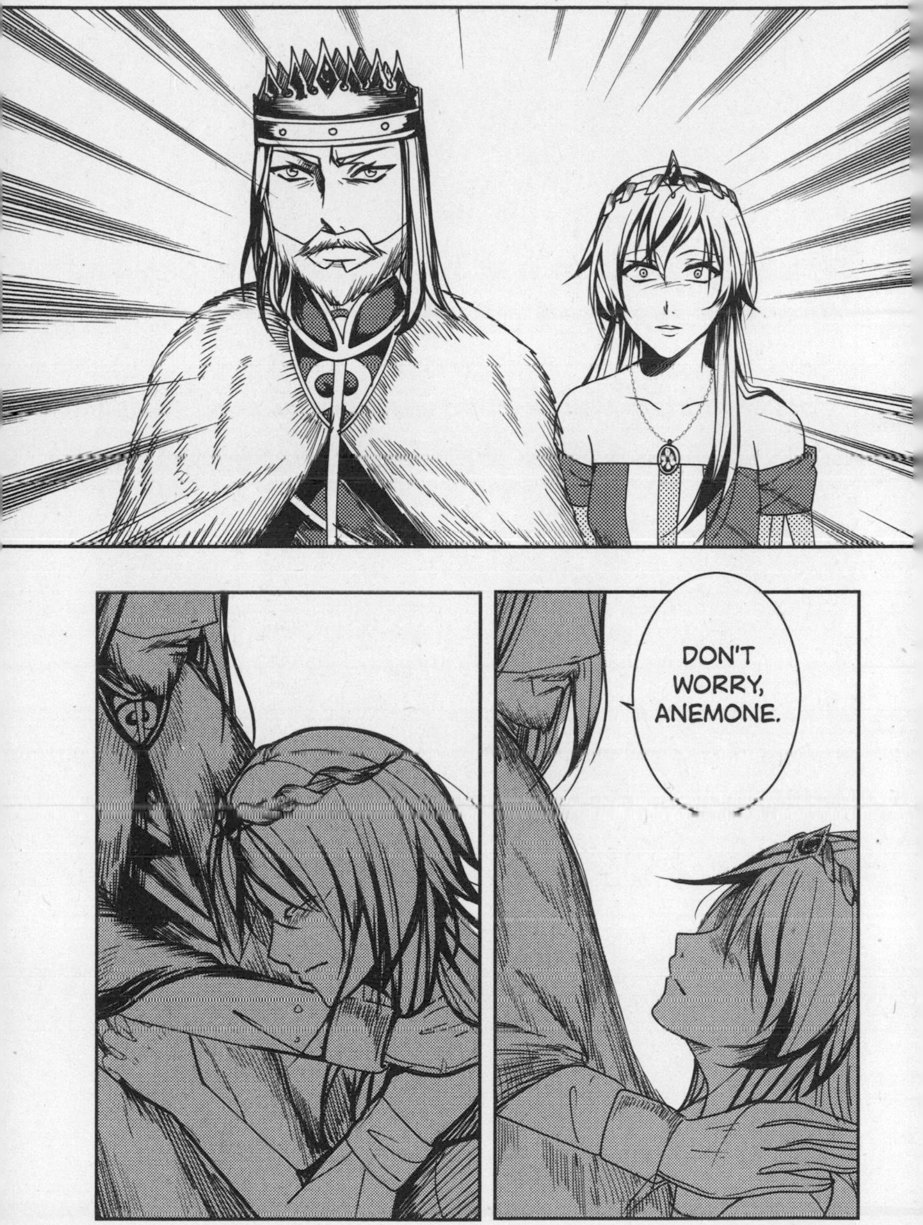
DON'T WORRY, ANEMONE.

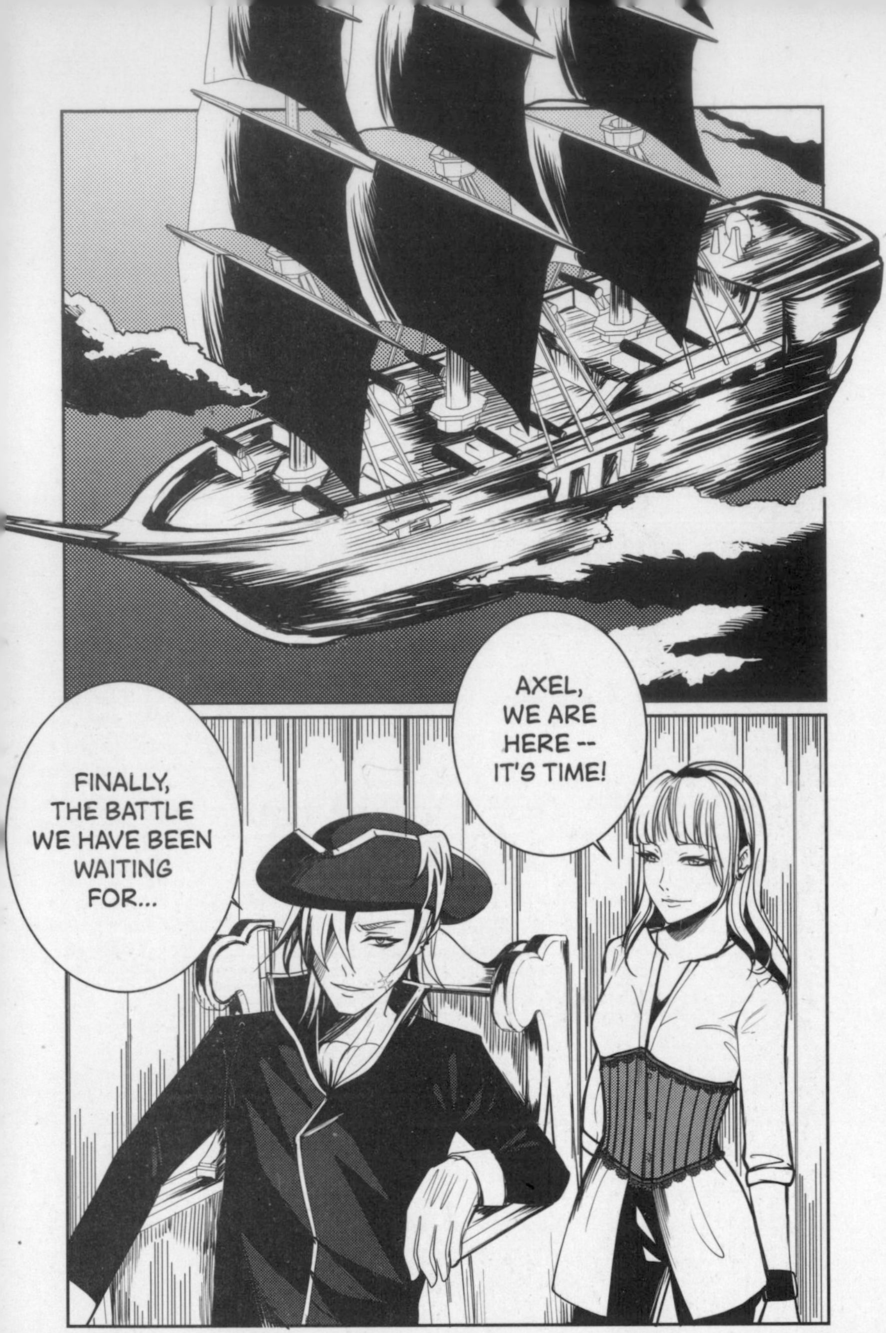
AXEL, WE ARE HERE -- IT'S TIME!
FINALLY, THE BATTLE WE HAVE BEEN WAITING FOR...

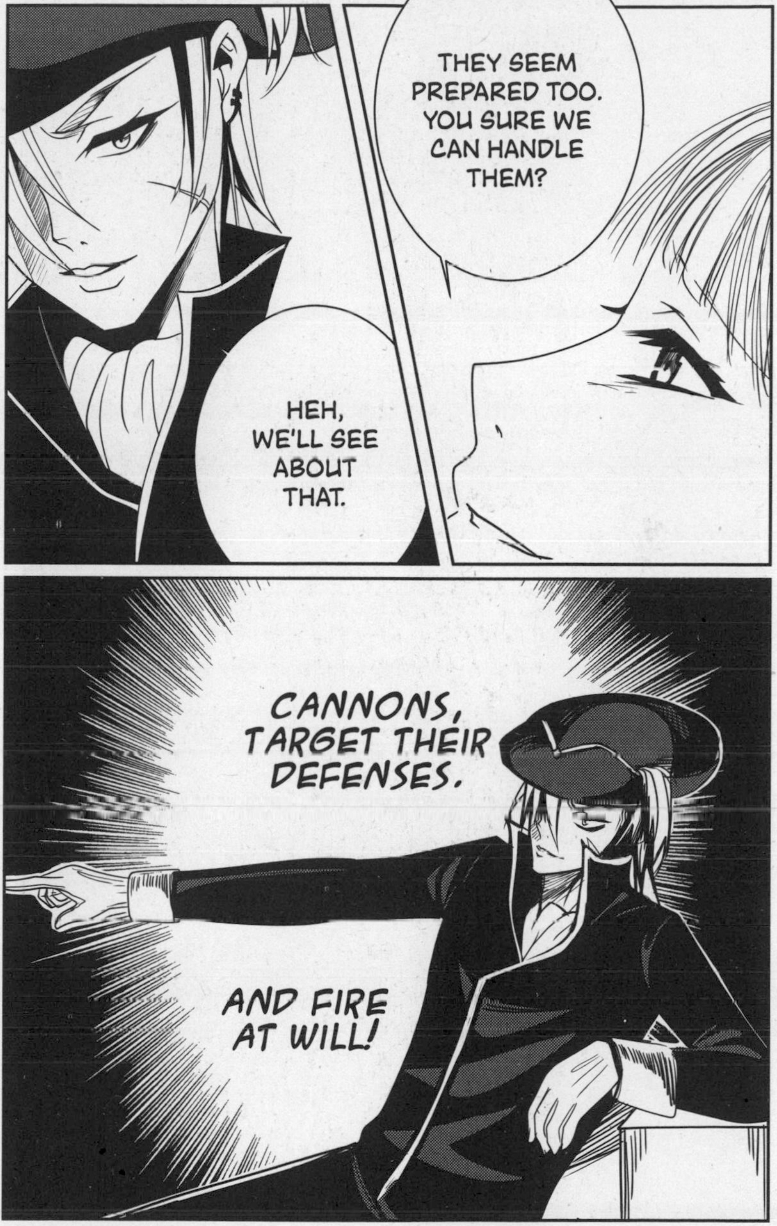
THEY SEEM PREPARED TOO. YOU SURE WE CAN HANDLE THEM?
HEH, WE'LL SEE ABOUT THAT.
CANNONS, TARGET THEIR DEFENSES.
AND FIRE AT WILL!

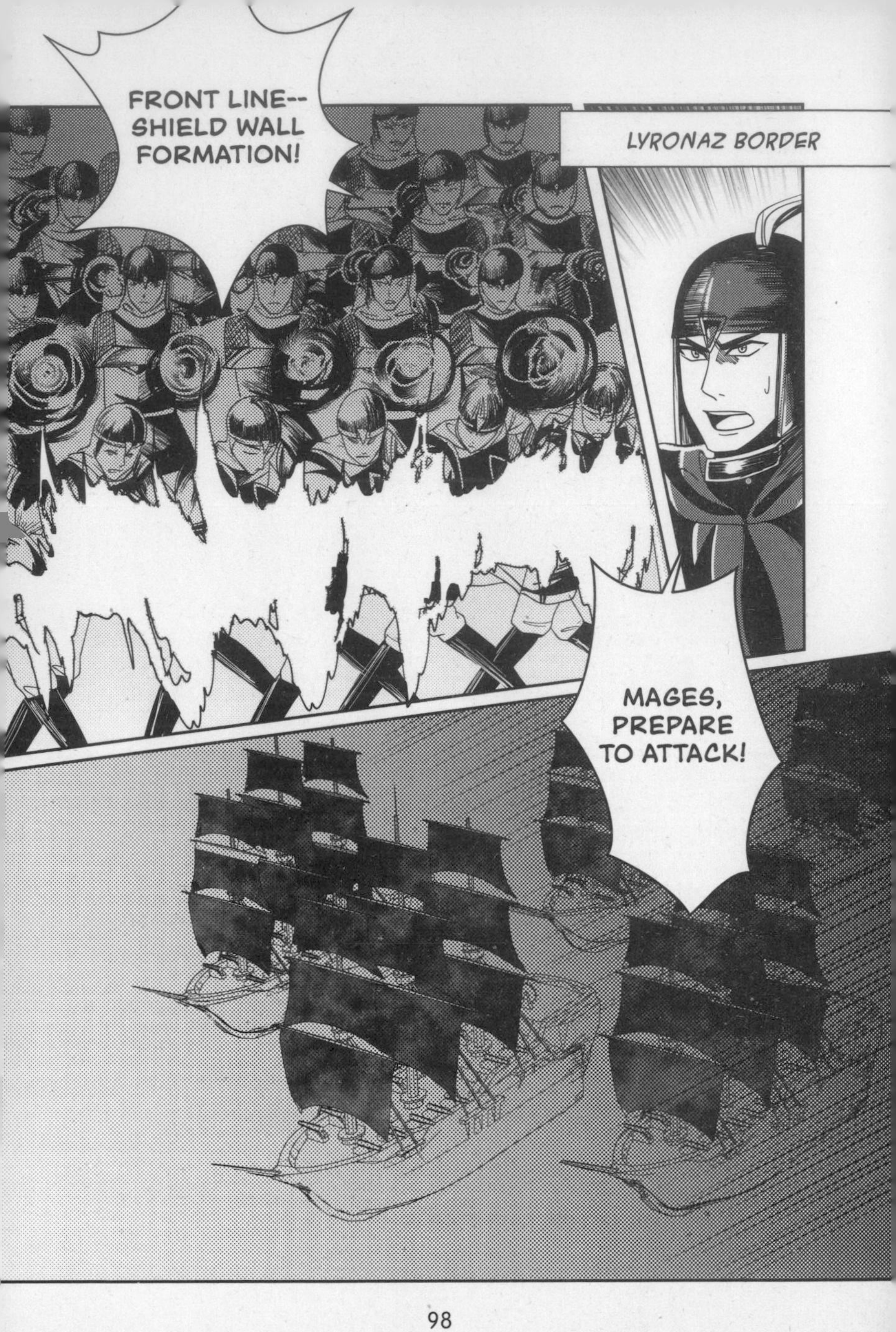
LYRONAZ BORDER
FRONT LINE--SHIELD WALL FORMATION!
MAGES, PREPARE TO ATTACK!

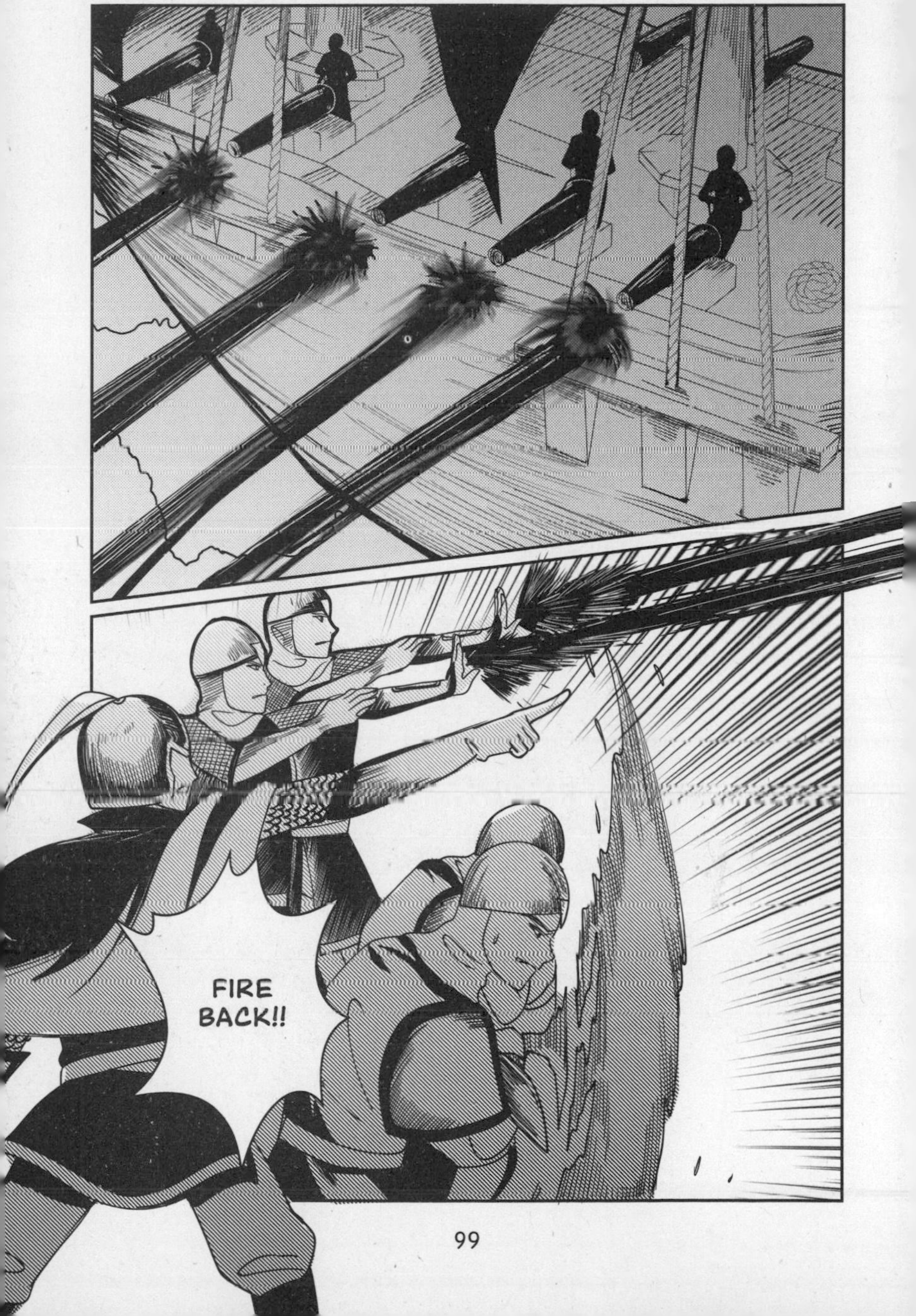
FIRE
BACK!!

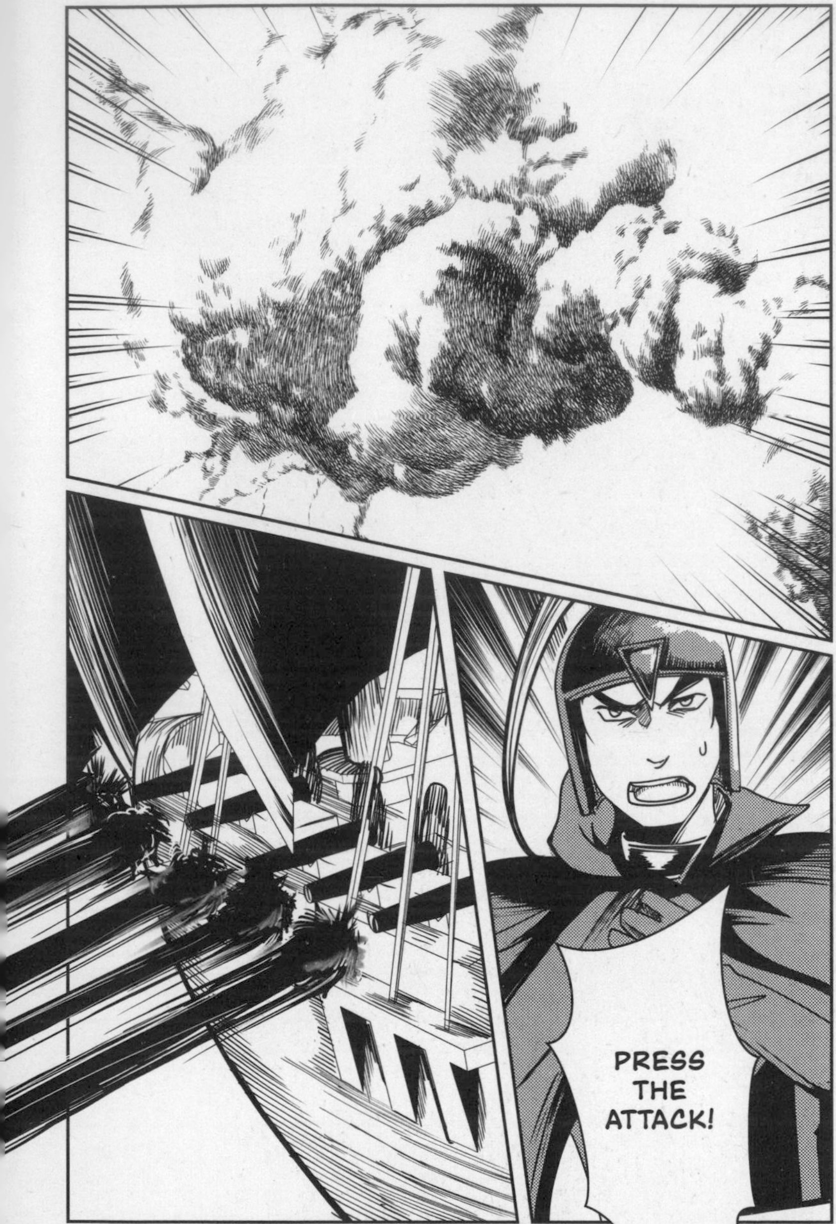
PRESS THE ATTACK!

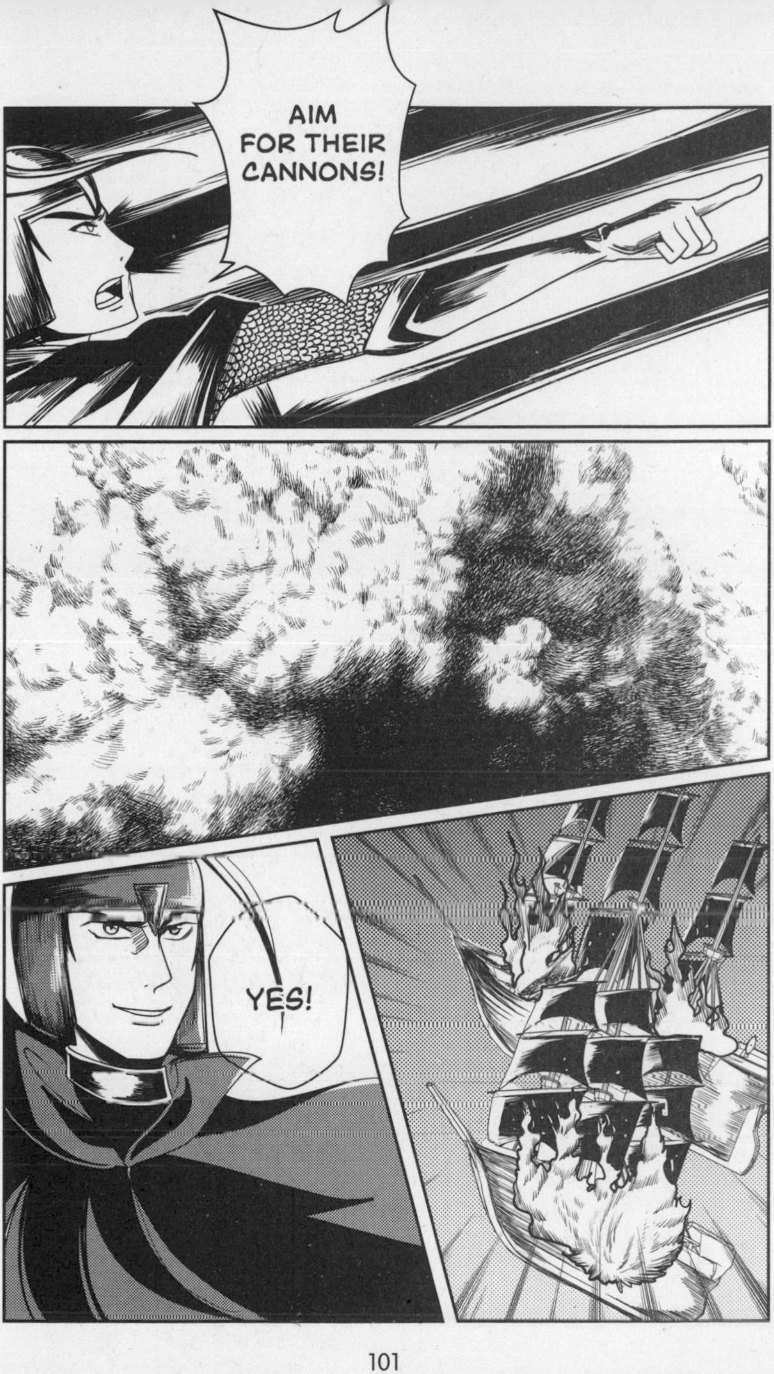
AIM FOR THEIR CANNONS!
YES!

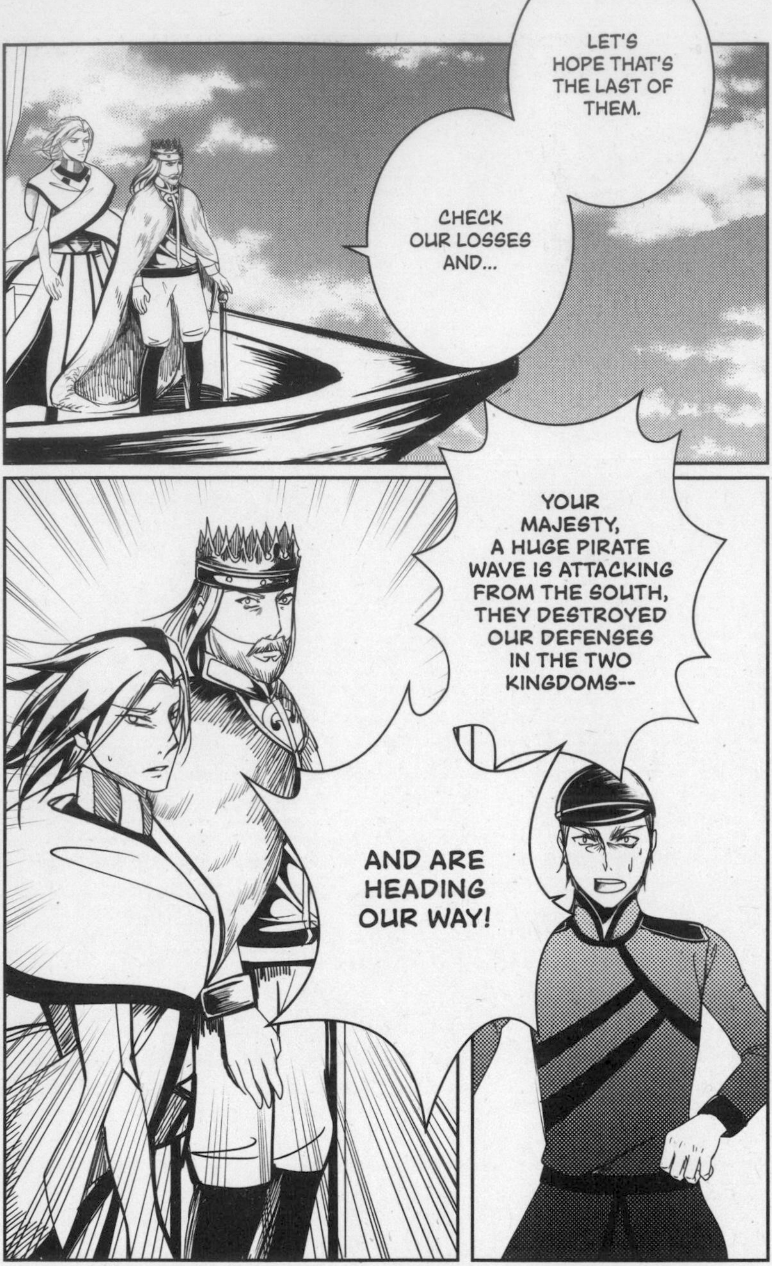
LET'S HOPE THAT'S THE LAST OF THEM.
CHECK OUR LOSSES AND...
YOUR MAJESTY, A HUGE PIRATE WAVE IS ATTACKING FROM THE SOUTH, THEY DESTROYED OUR DEFENSES IN THE TWO KINGDOMS--
AND ARE HEADING OUR WAY!

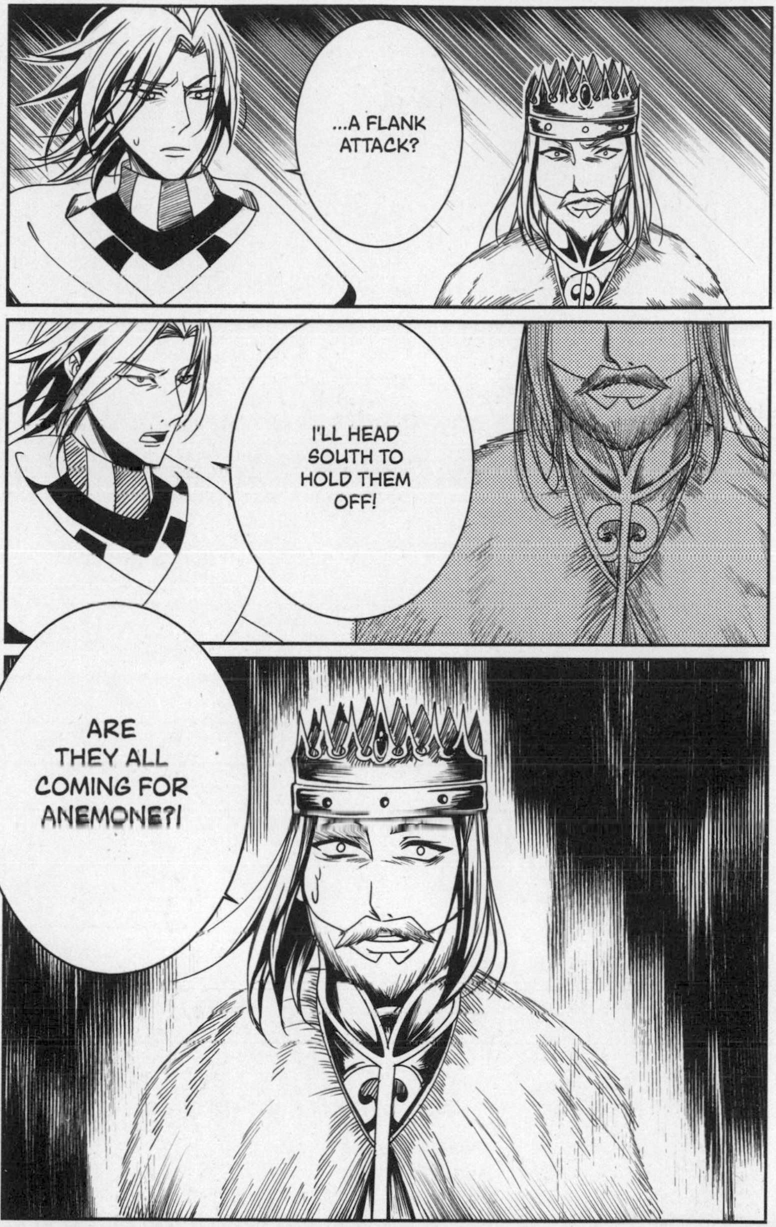
...A FLANK ATTACK?
I'LL HEAD SOUTH TO HOLD THEM OFF!
ARE THEY ALL COMING FOR ANEMONE?!

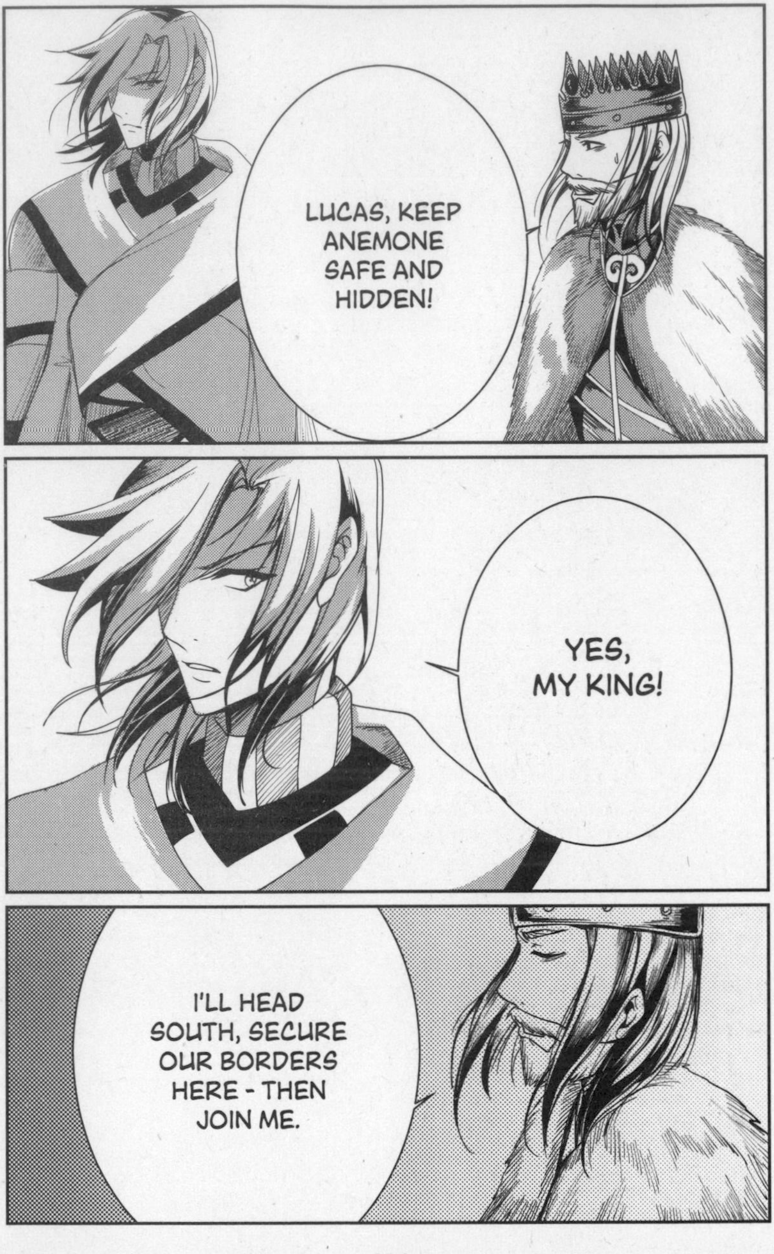
LUCAS, KEEP ANEMONE SAFE AND HIDDEN!
YES, MY KING!
I'LL HEAD SOUTH, SECURE OUR BORDERS HERE - THEN JOIN ME.

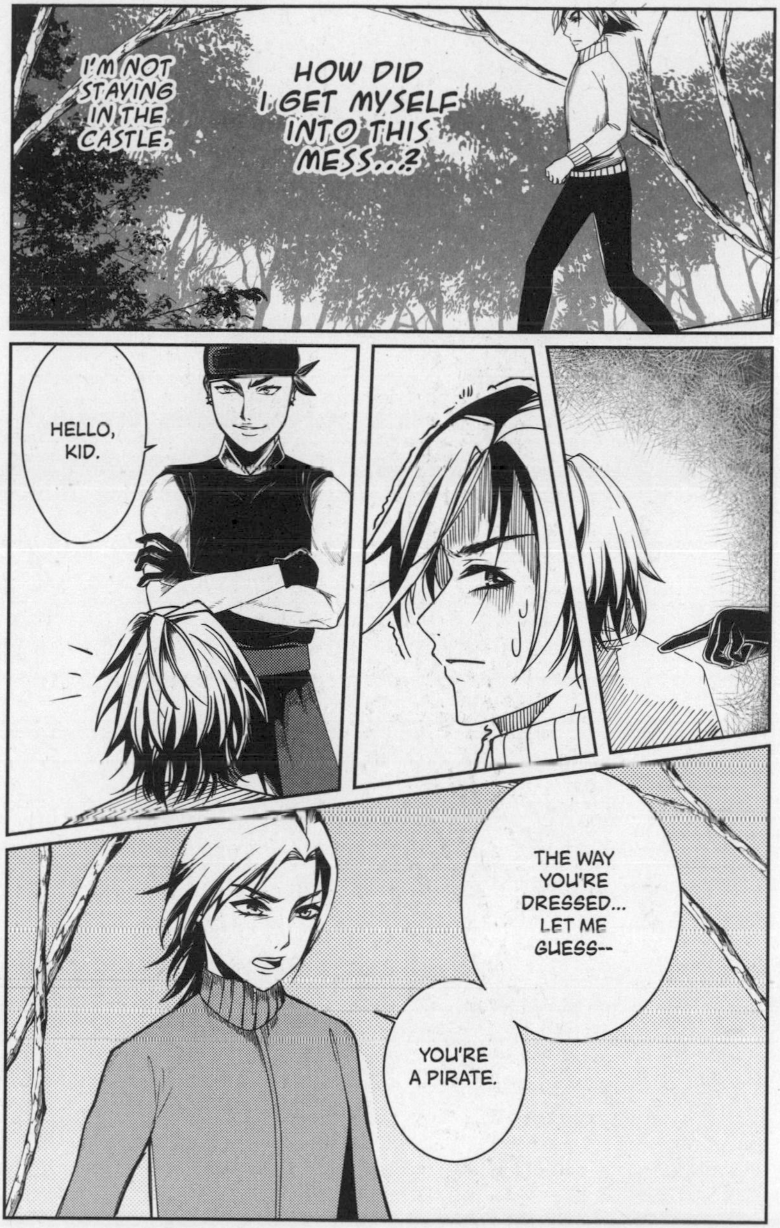
HOW DID I GET MYSELF INTO THIS MESS...?
I'M NOT STAYING IN THE CASTLE.
HELLO, KID.
THE WAY YOU'RE DRESSED... LET ME GUESS--
YOU'RE A PIRATE.

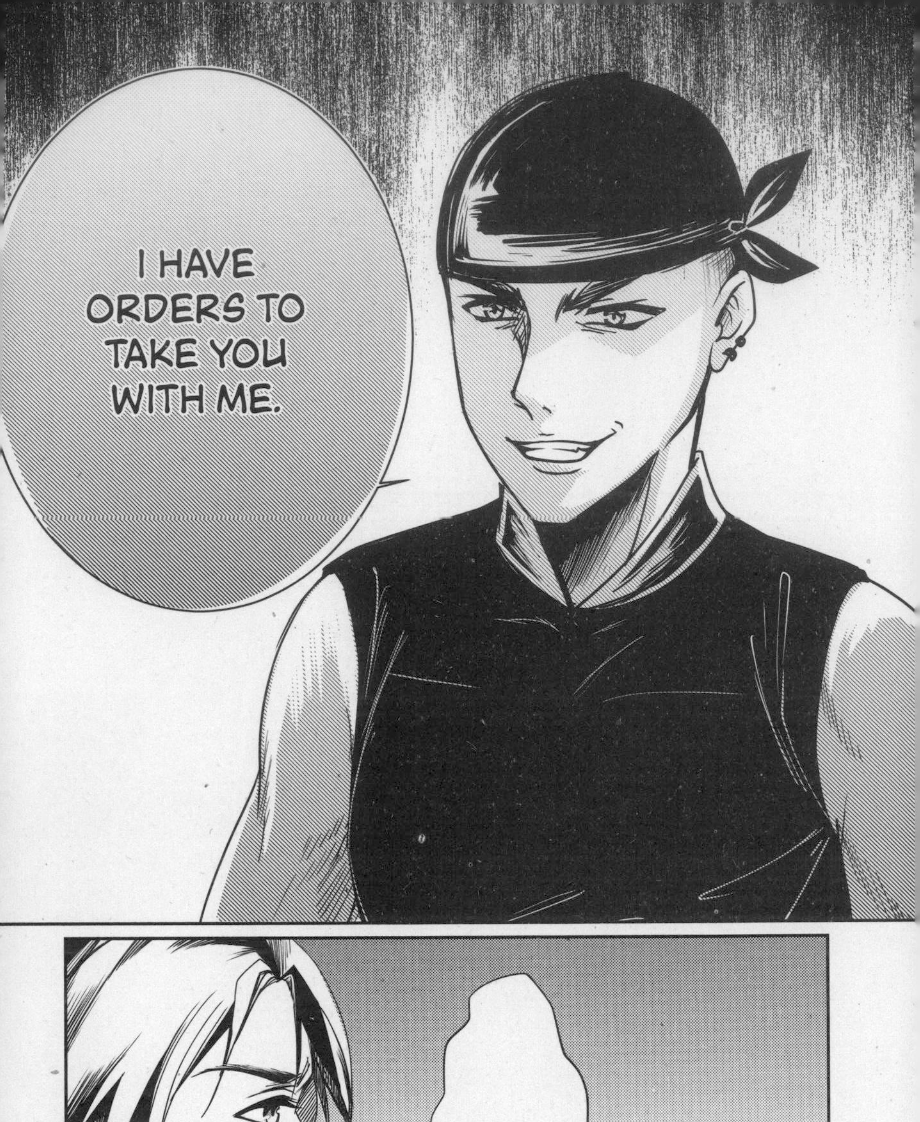
I HAVE ORDERS TO TAKE YOU WITH ME.
WHAT...?

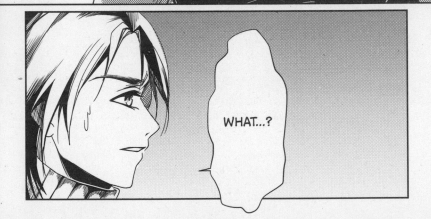

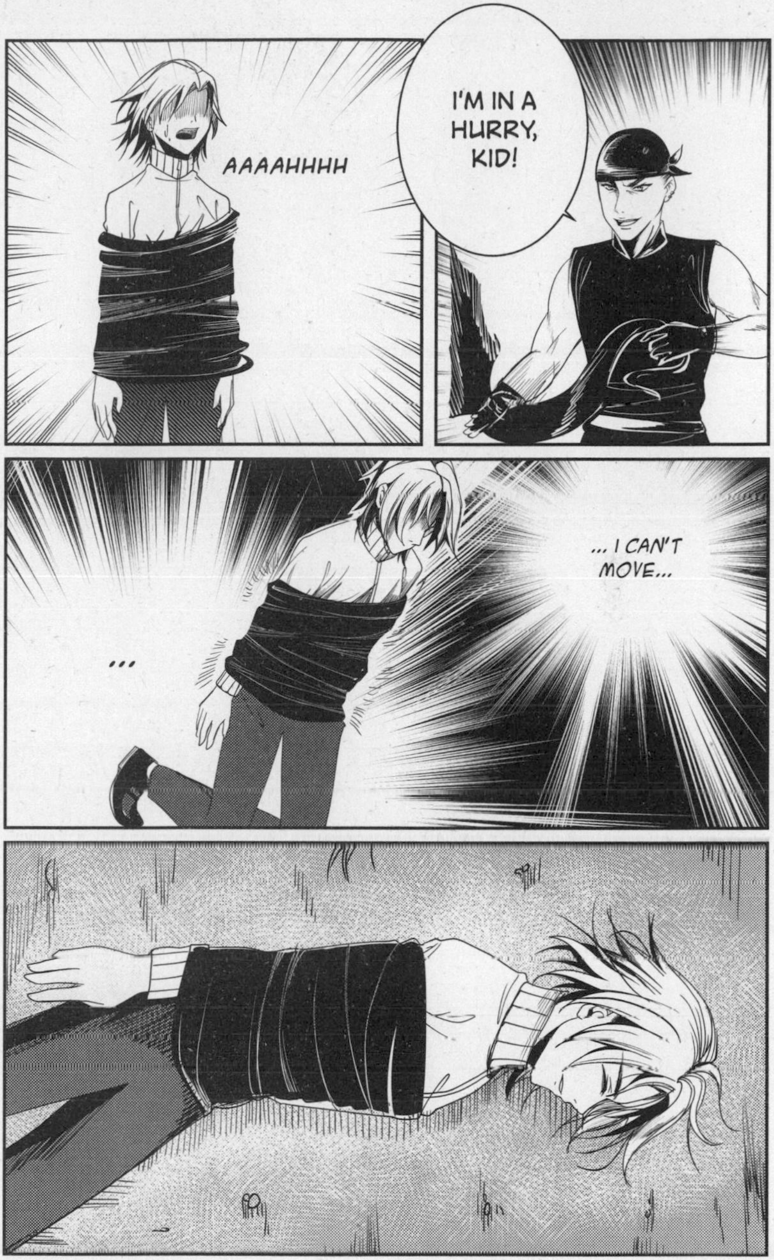
I'M IN A HURRY, KID!
AAAAHHHH
... I CAN'T MOVE...
...

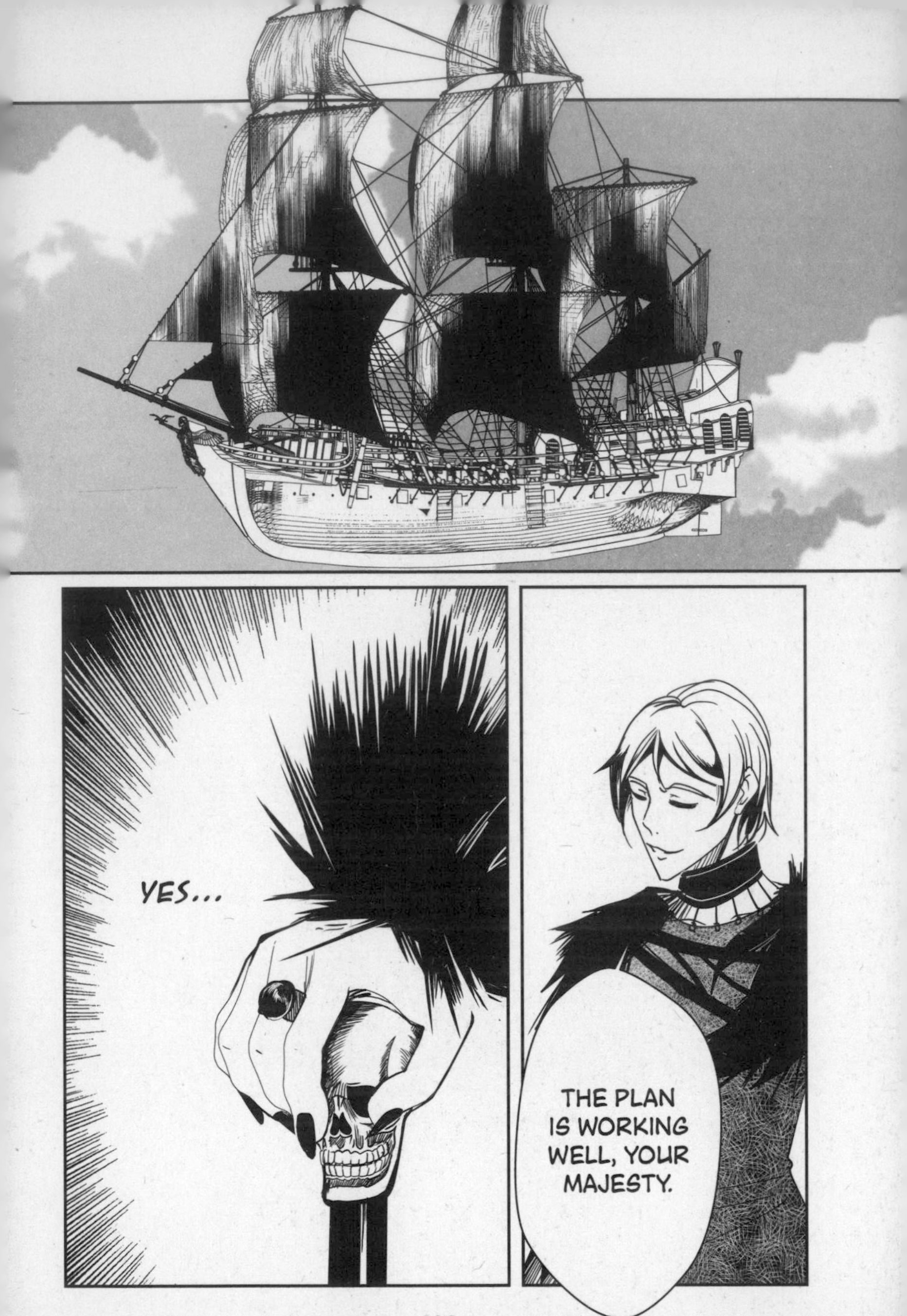
THE PLAN IS WORKING WELL, YOUR MAJESTY.
YES...

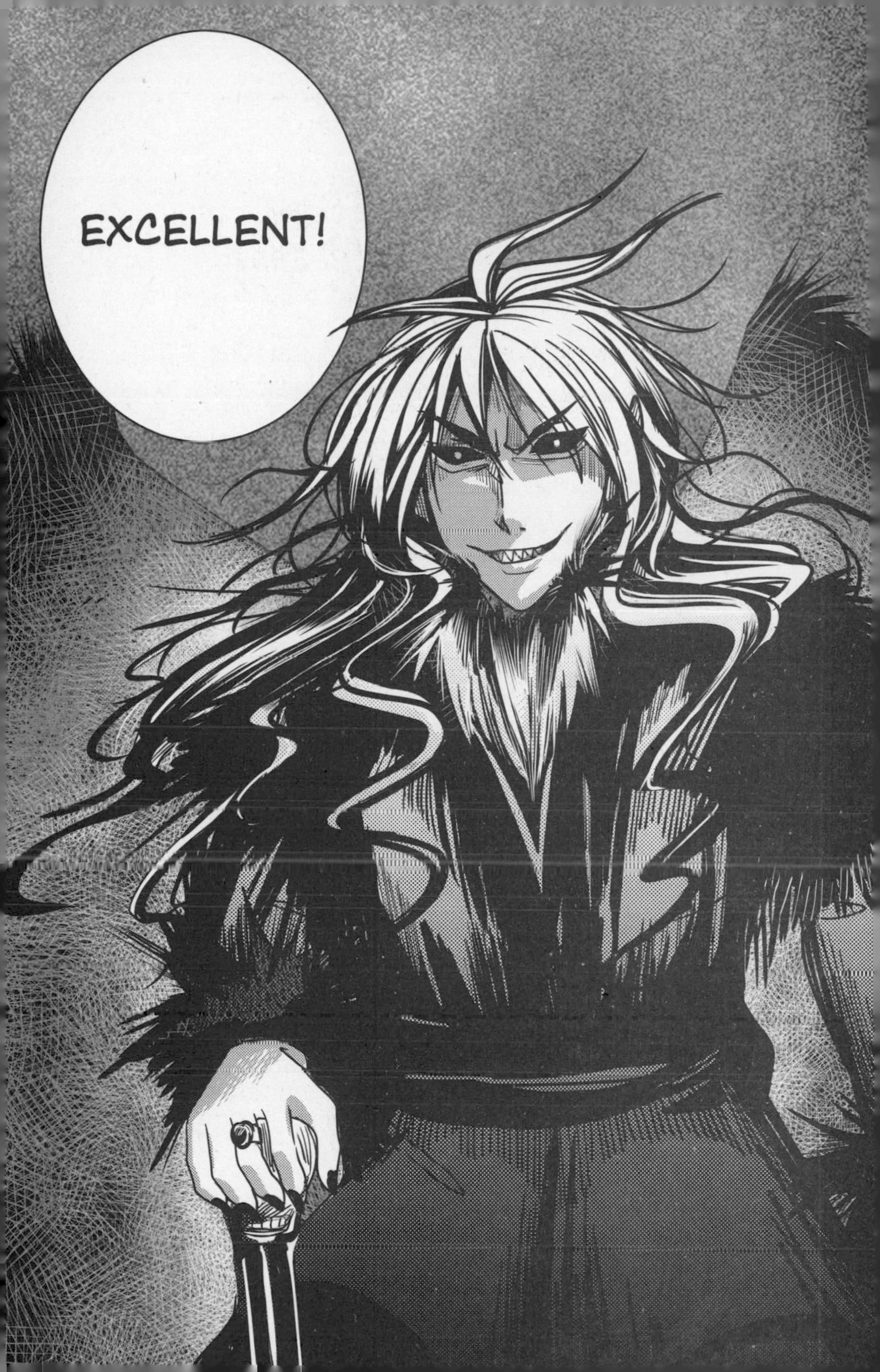
EXCELLENT!

Ocean of Secrets

CHAPTER 9

TRUST IN YOUR KING

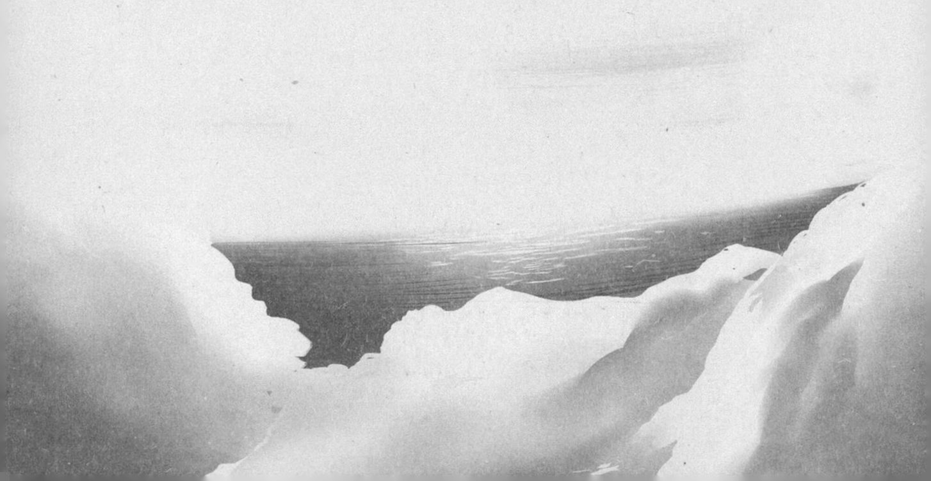

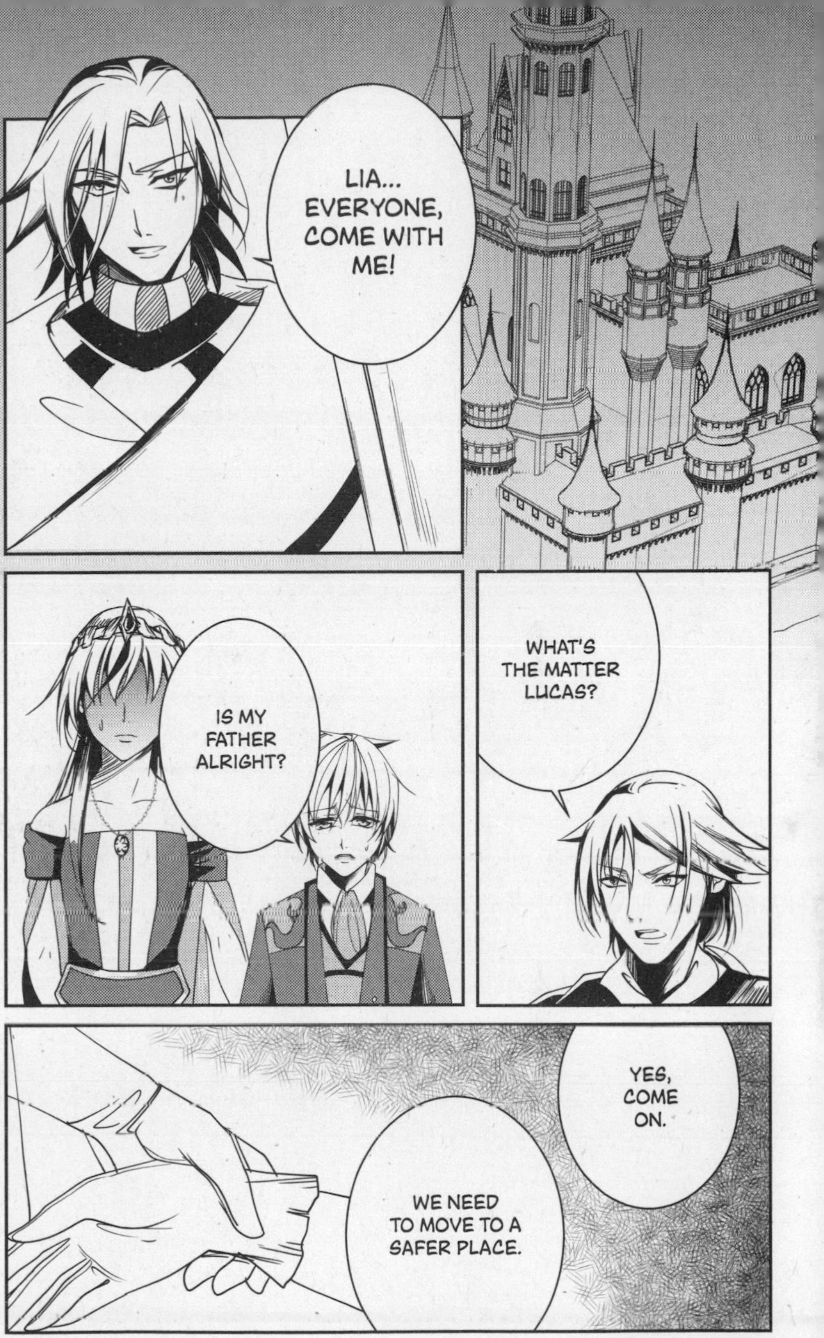
LIA... EVERYONE, COME WITH ME!
WHAT'S THE MATTER LUCAS?
IS MY FATHER ALRIGHT?
YES, COME ON.
WE NEED TO MOVE TO A SAFER PLACE.

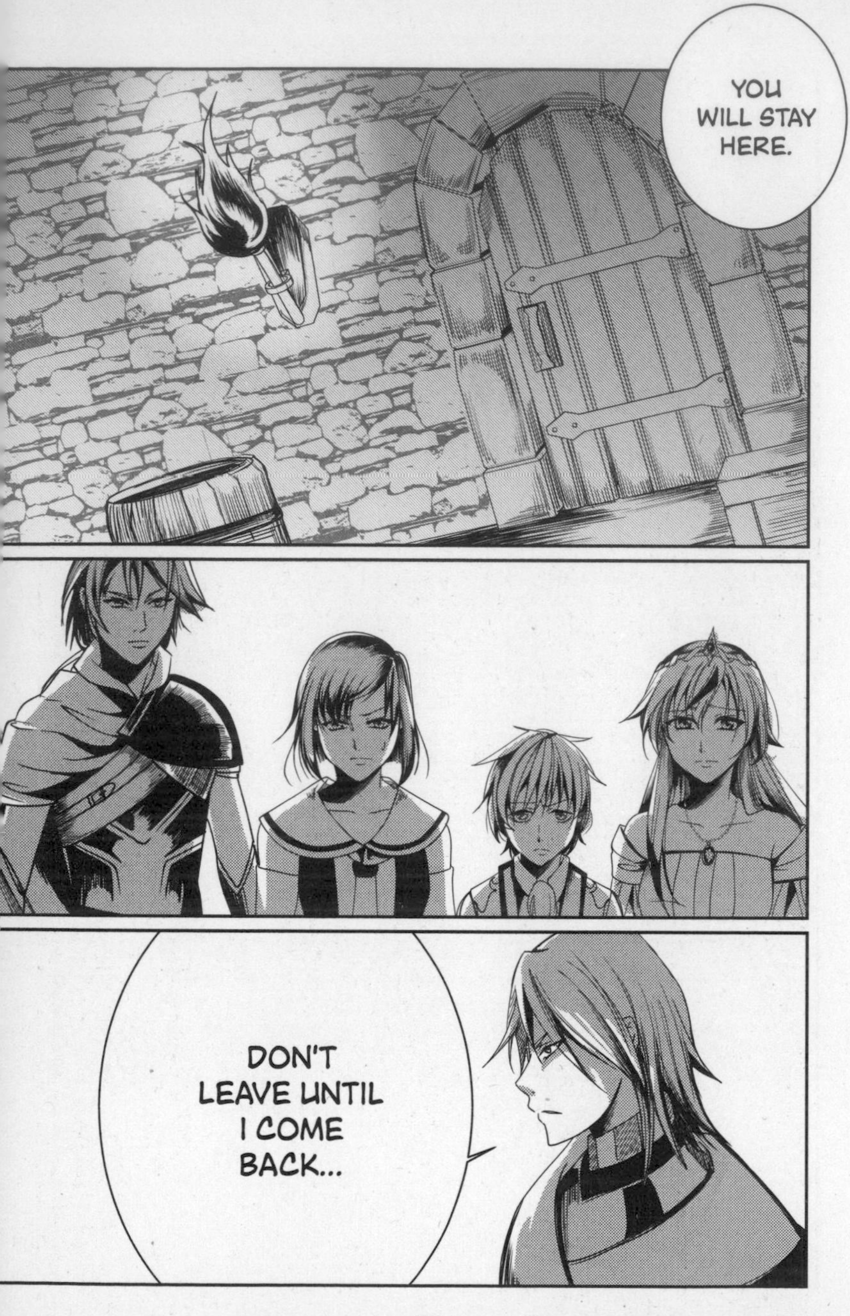
YOU WILL STAY HERE.
DON'T LEAVE UNTIL I COME BACK...

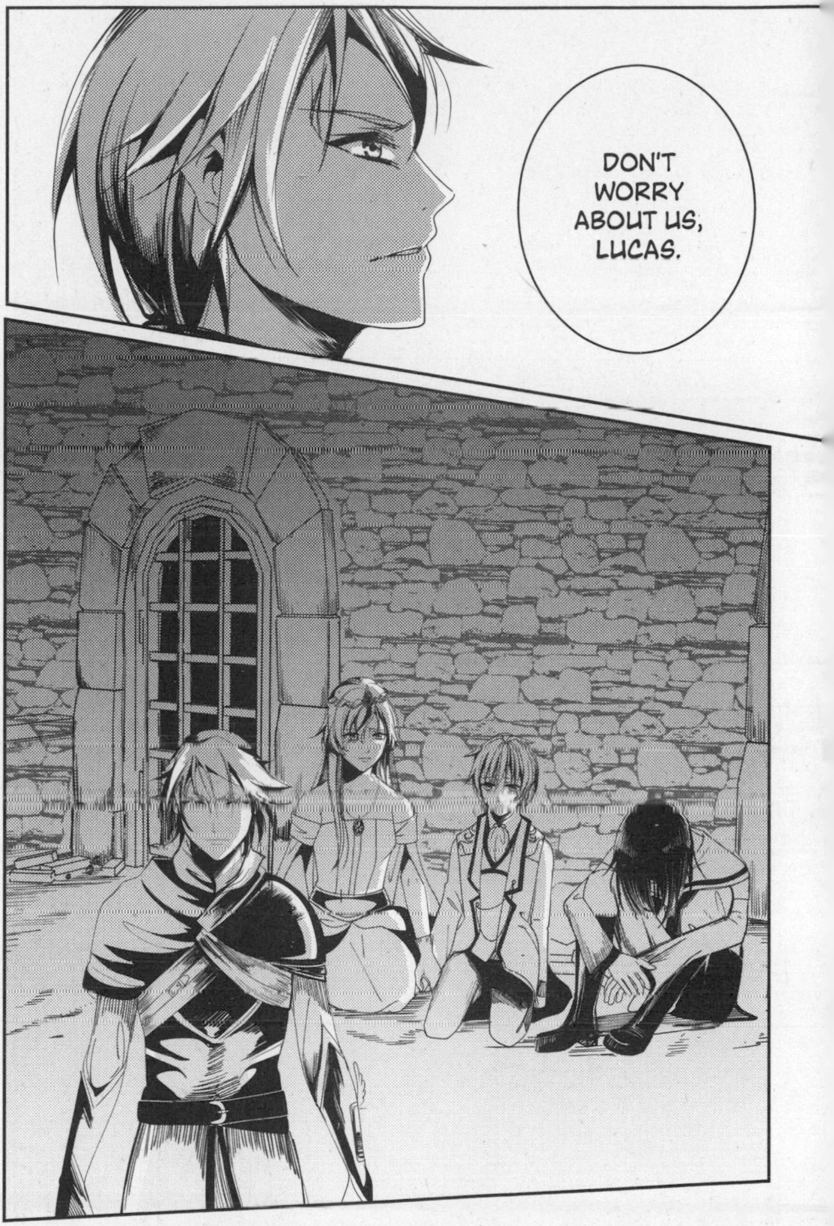
DON'T WORRY ABOUT US, LUCAS.

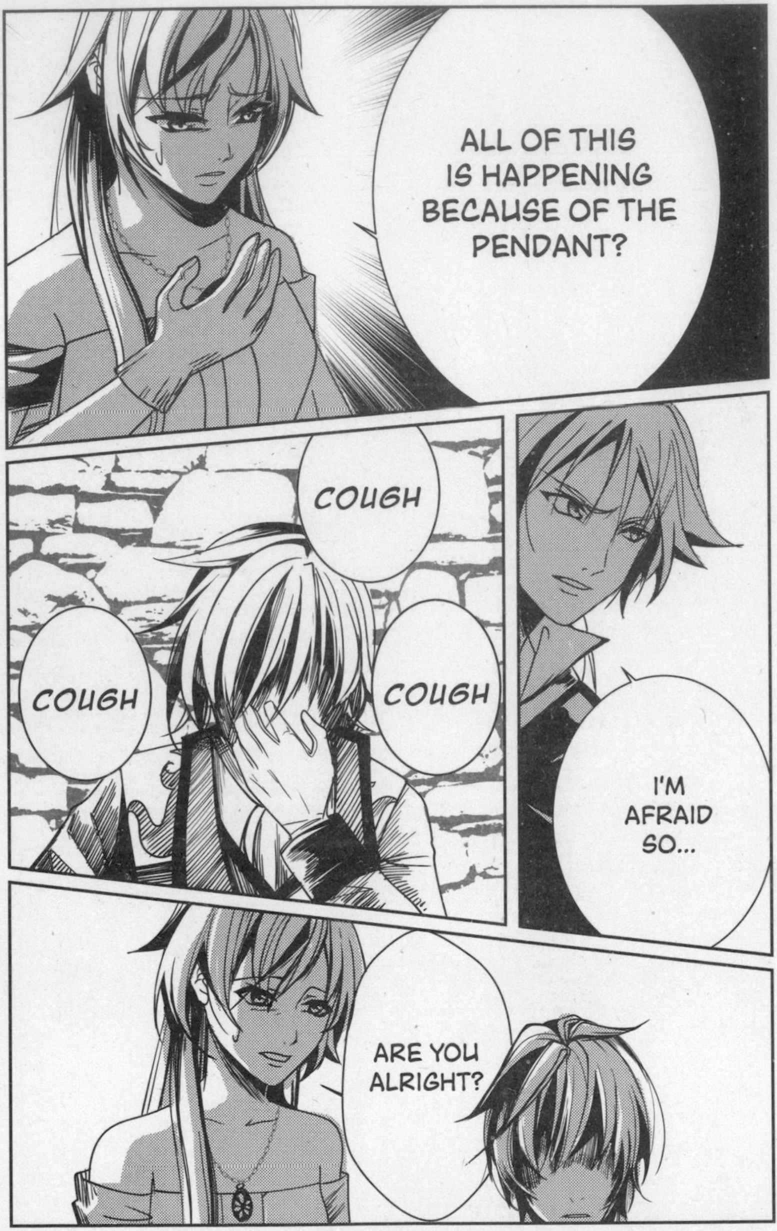
ALL OF THIS IS HAPPENING BECAUSE OF THE PENDANT?
I'M AFRAID SO...
COUGH
COUGH
COUGH
ARE YOU ALRIGHT?

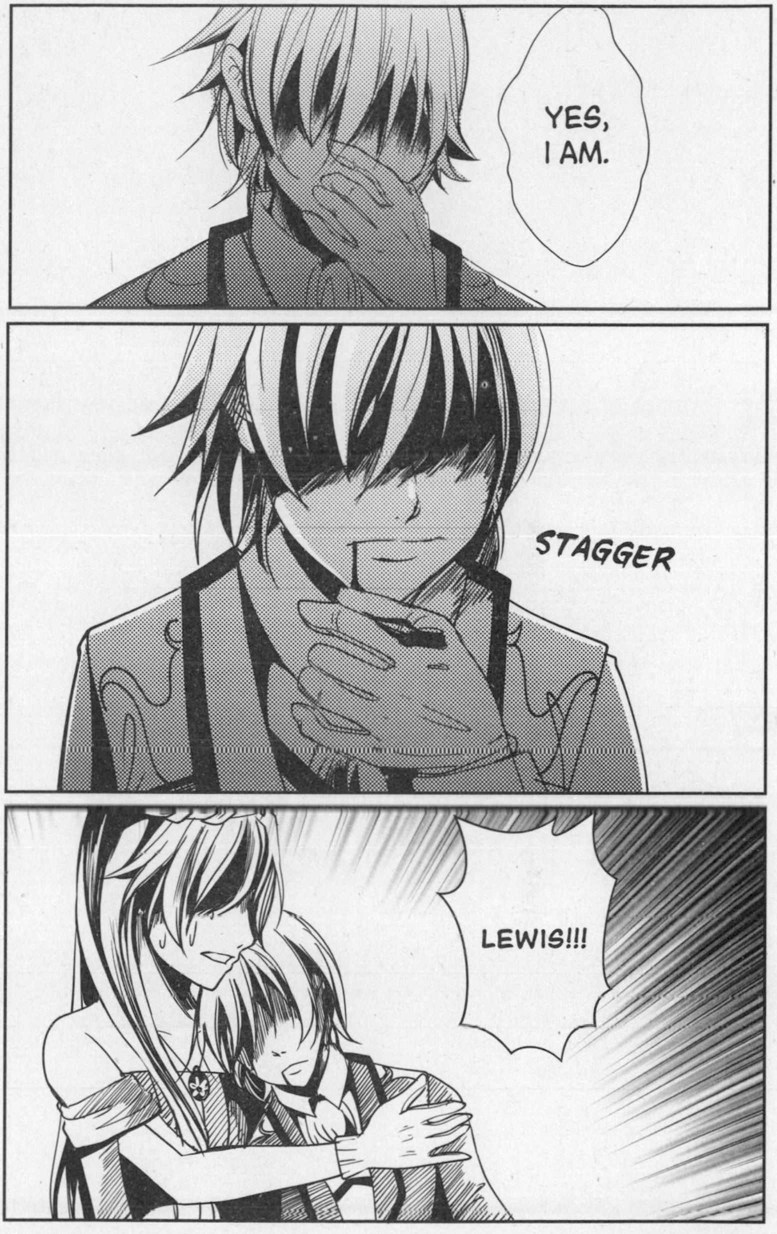
YES, I AM.
STAGGER
LEWIS!!!

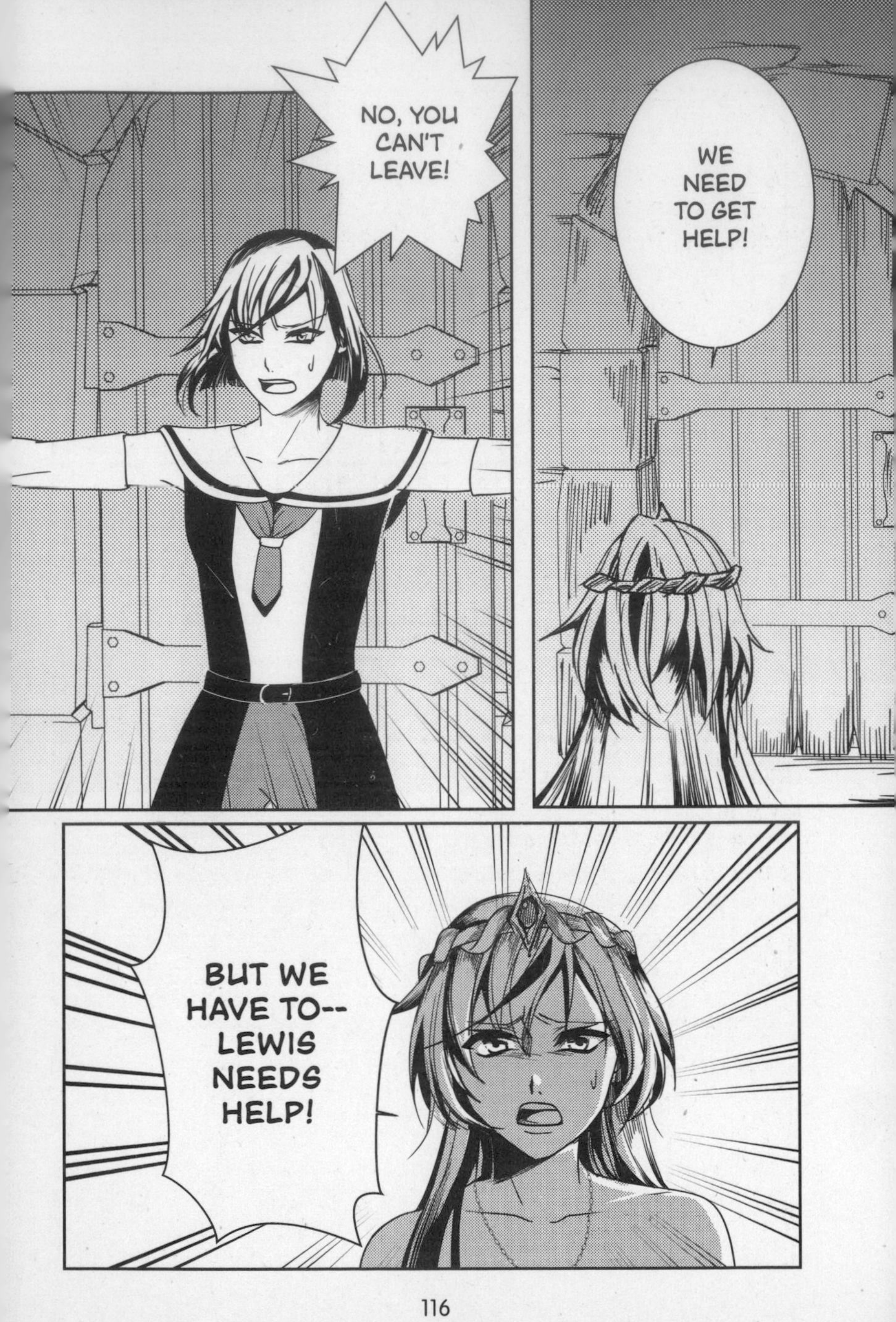
WE NEED TO GET HELP!
NO, YOU CAN'T LEAVE!
BUT WE HAVE TO-- LEWIS NEEDS HELP!

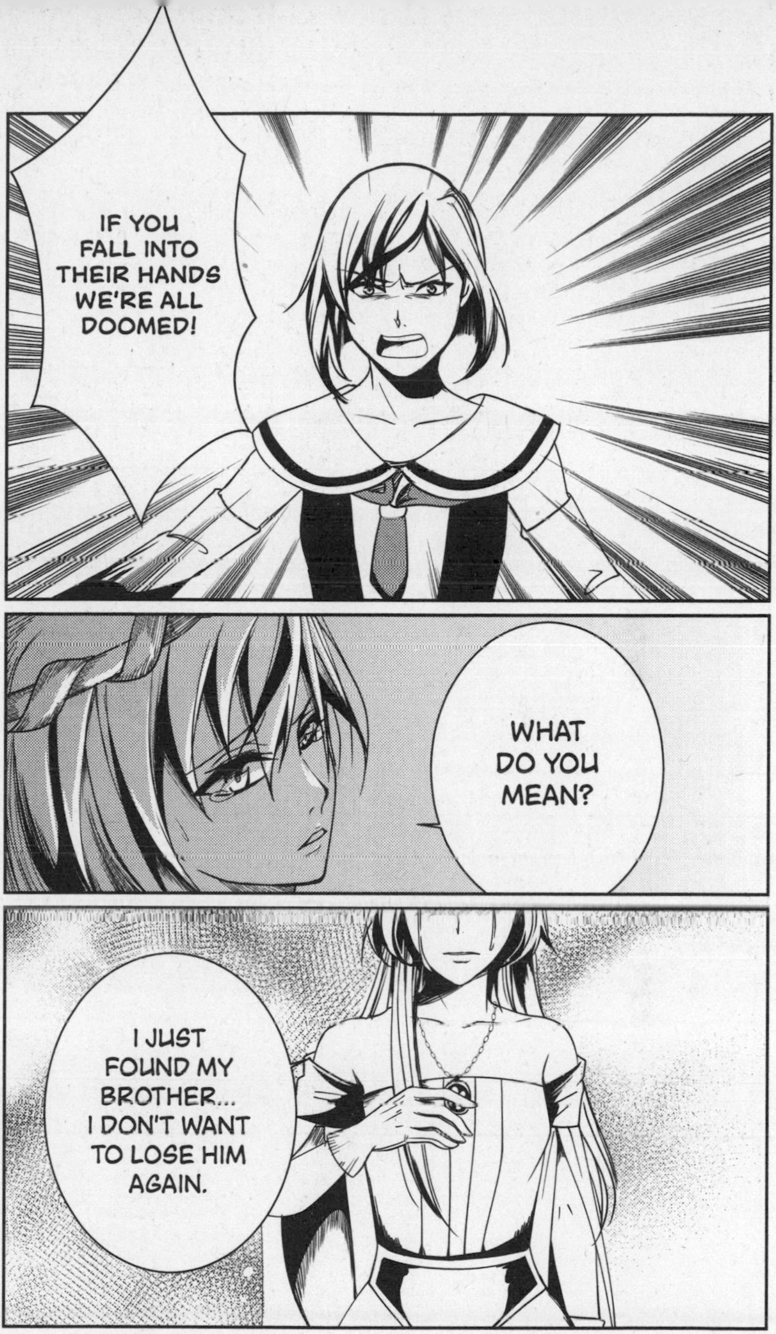
IF YOU FALL INTO THEIR HANDS WE'RE ALL DOOMED!
WHAT DO YOU MEAN?
I JUST FOUND MY BROTHER... I DON'T WANT TO LOSE HIM AGAIN.

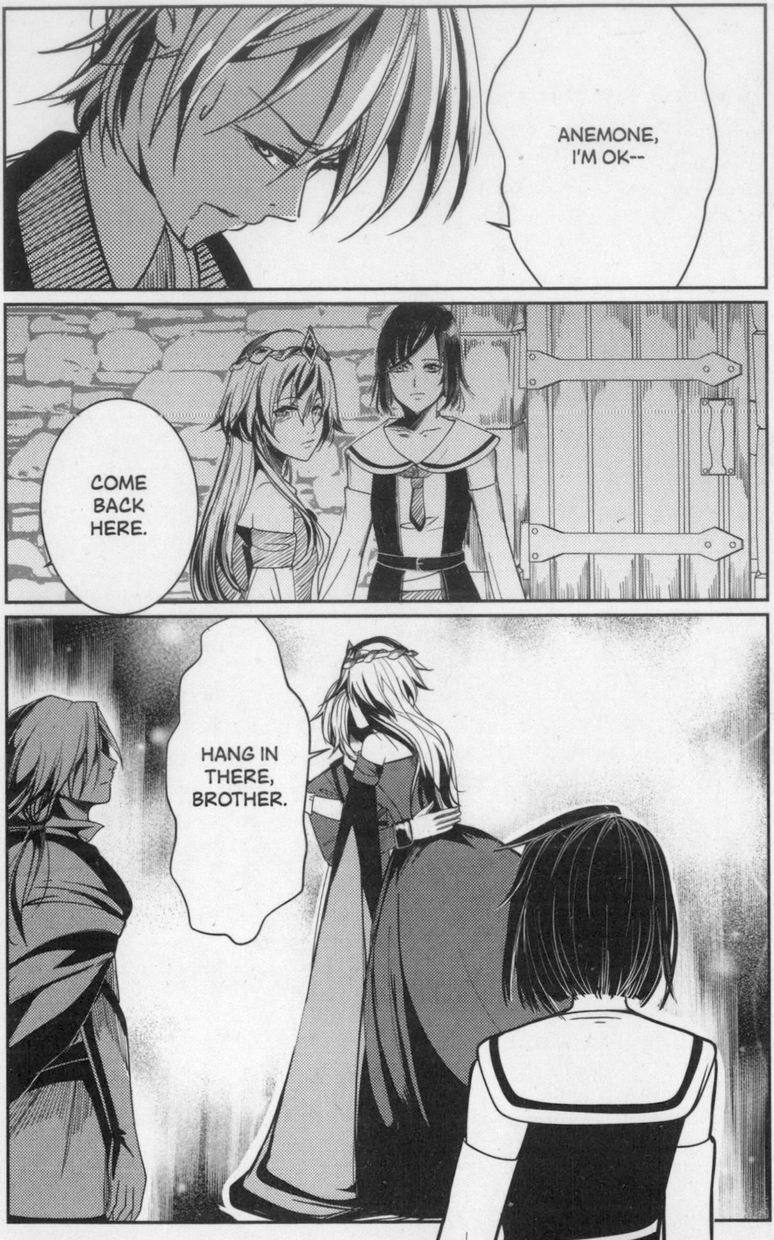
ANEMONE, I'M OK--
COME BACK HERE.
HANG IN THERE, BROTHER.

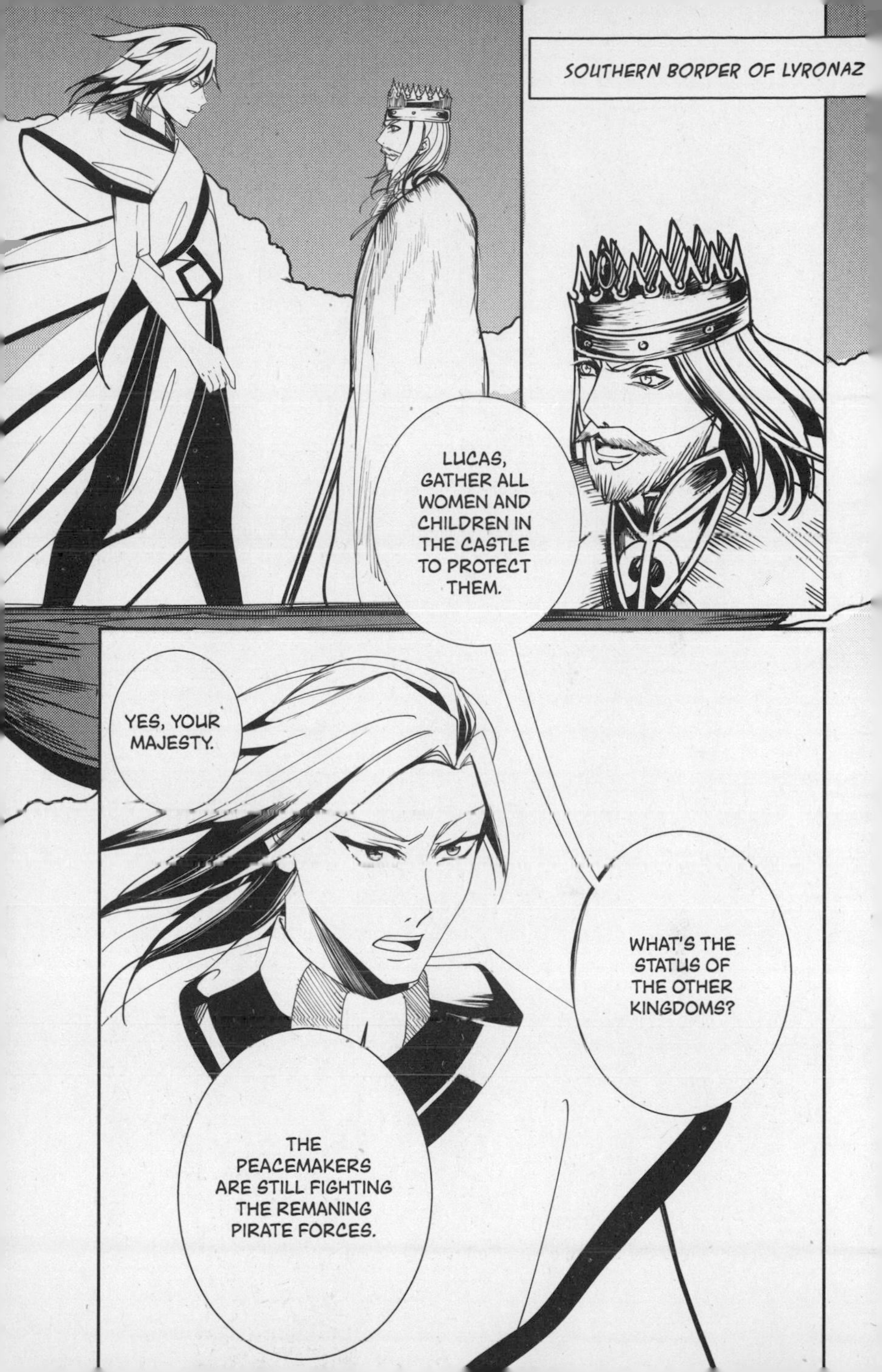
SOUTHERN BORDER OF LYRONAZ
LUCAS, GATHER ALL WOMEN AND CHILDREN IN THE CASTLE TO PROTECT THEM.
YES, YOUR MAJESTY.
WHAT'S THE STATUS OF THE OTHER KINGDOMS?
THE PEACEMAKERS ARE STILL FIGHTING THE REMANING PIRATE FORCES.

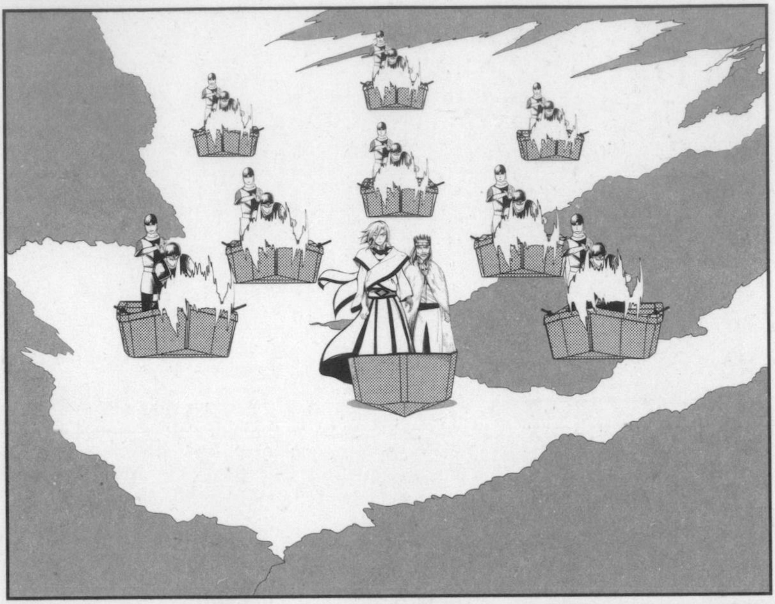
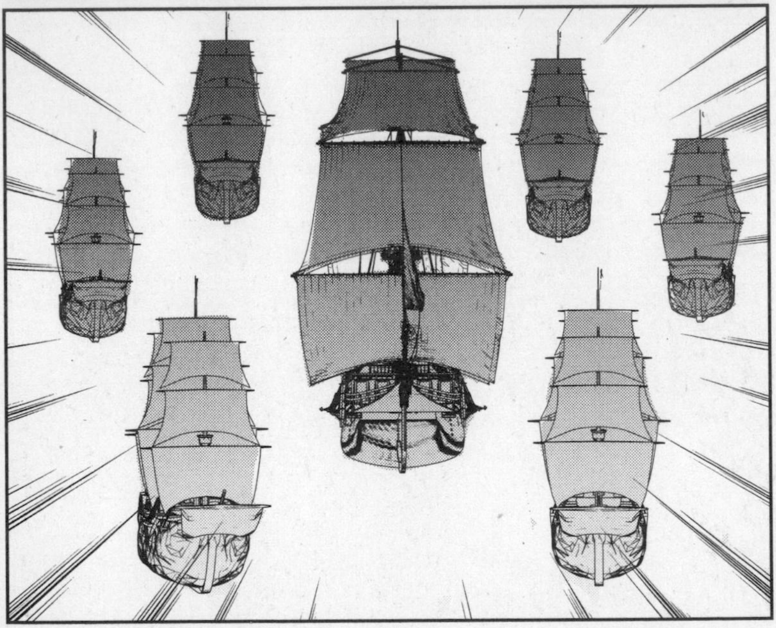

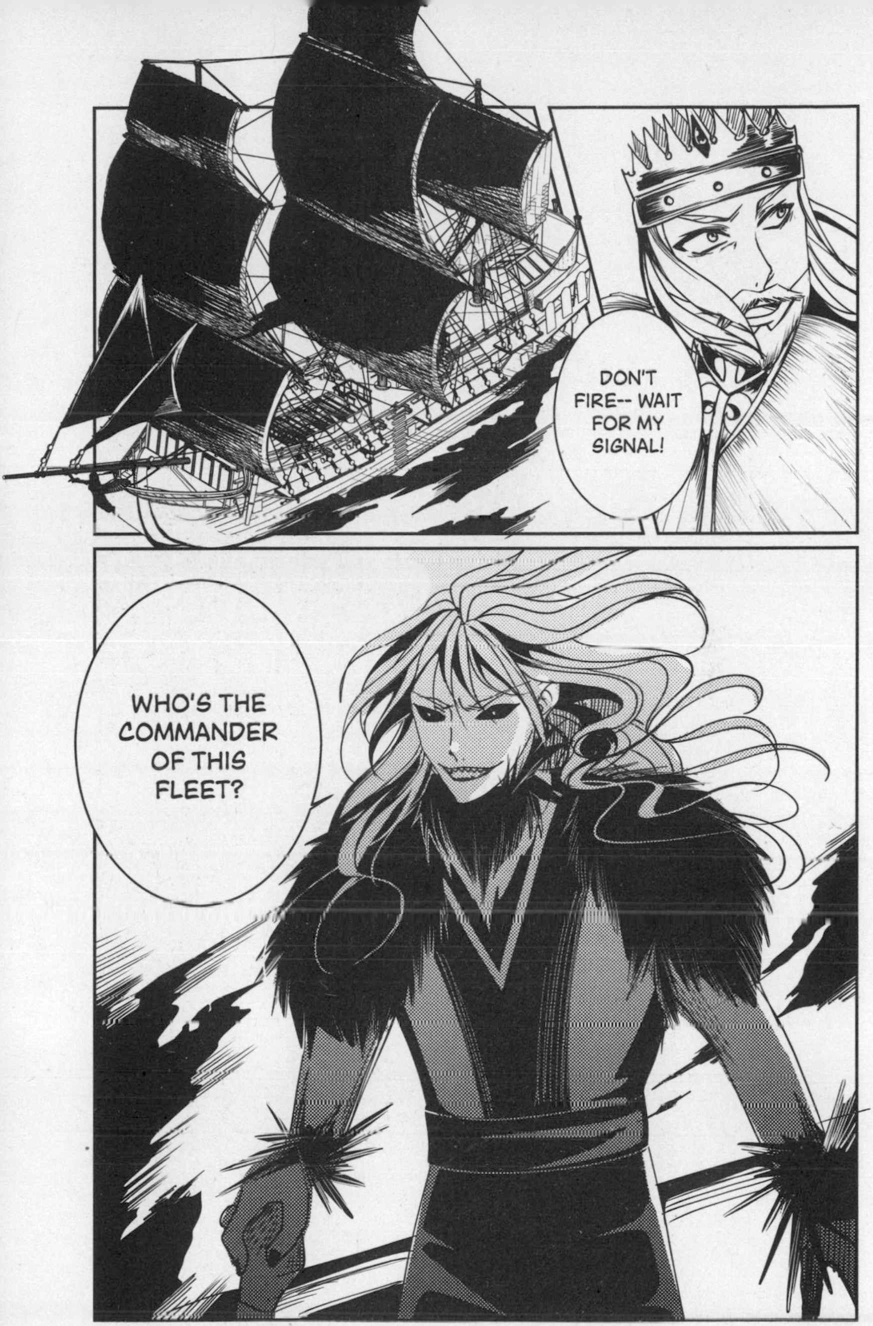
DON'T FIRE-- WAIT FOR MY SIGNAL!
WHO'S THE COMMANDER OF THIS FLEET?

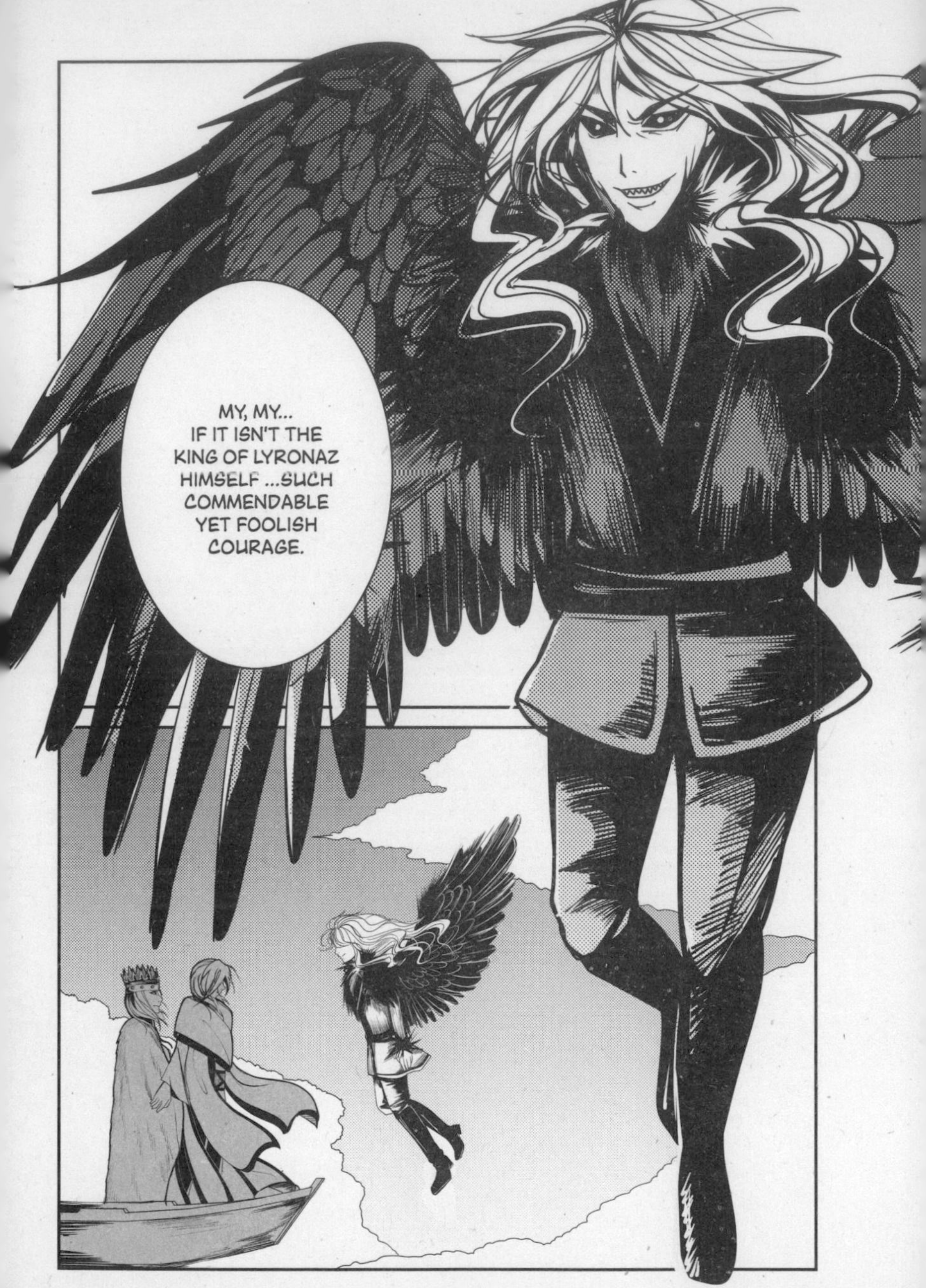
MY, MY...
IF IT ISN'T THE KING OF LYRONAZ HIMSELF ...SUCH COMMENDABLE YET FOOLISH COURAGE.

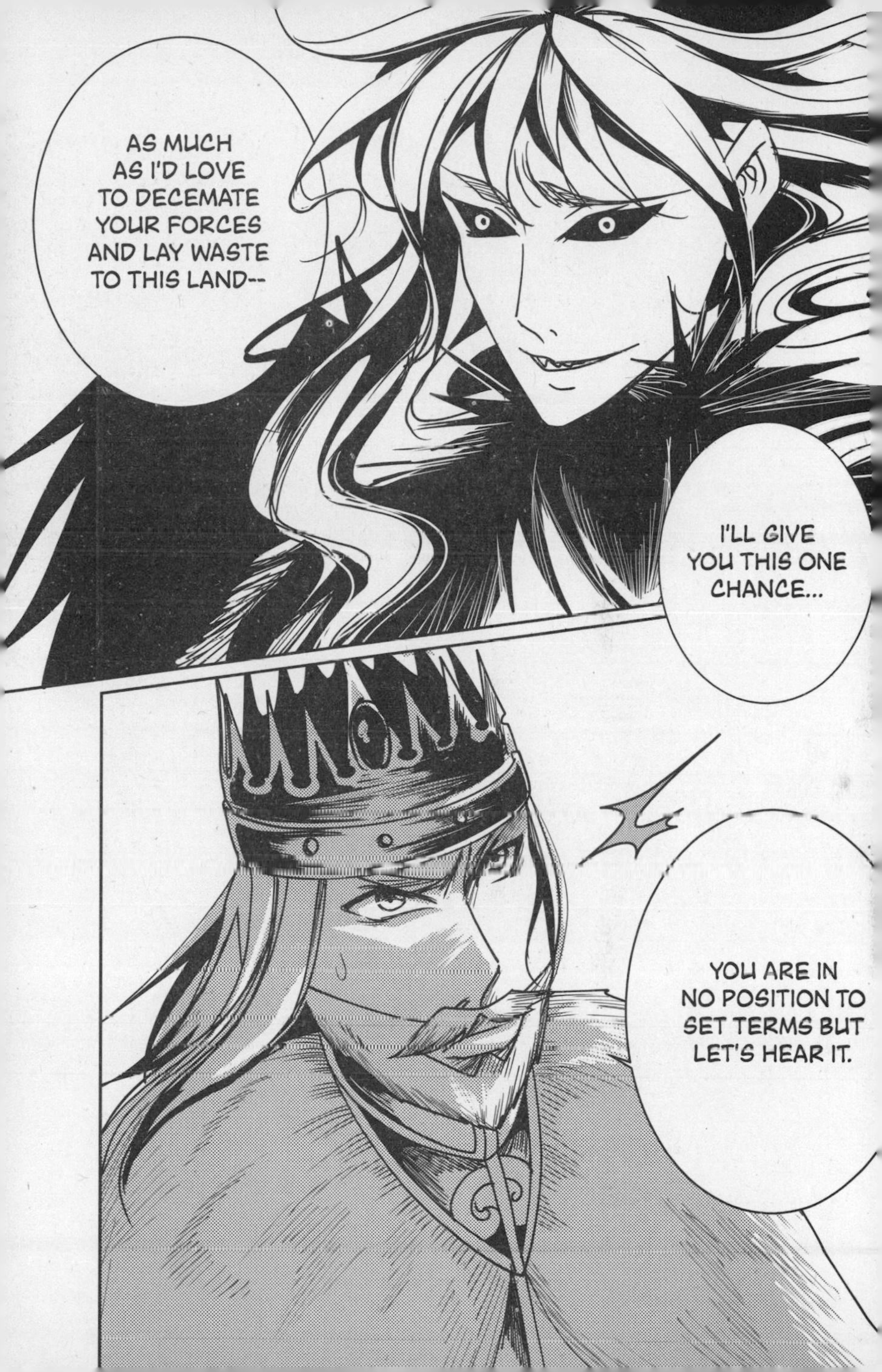
AS MUCH AS I'D LOVE TO DECEMATE YOUR FORCES AND LAY WASTE TO THIS LAND--
I'LL GIVE YOU THIS ONE CHANCE...
YOU ARE IN NO POSITION TO SET TERMS BUT LET'S HEAR IT.

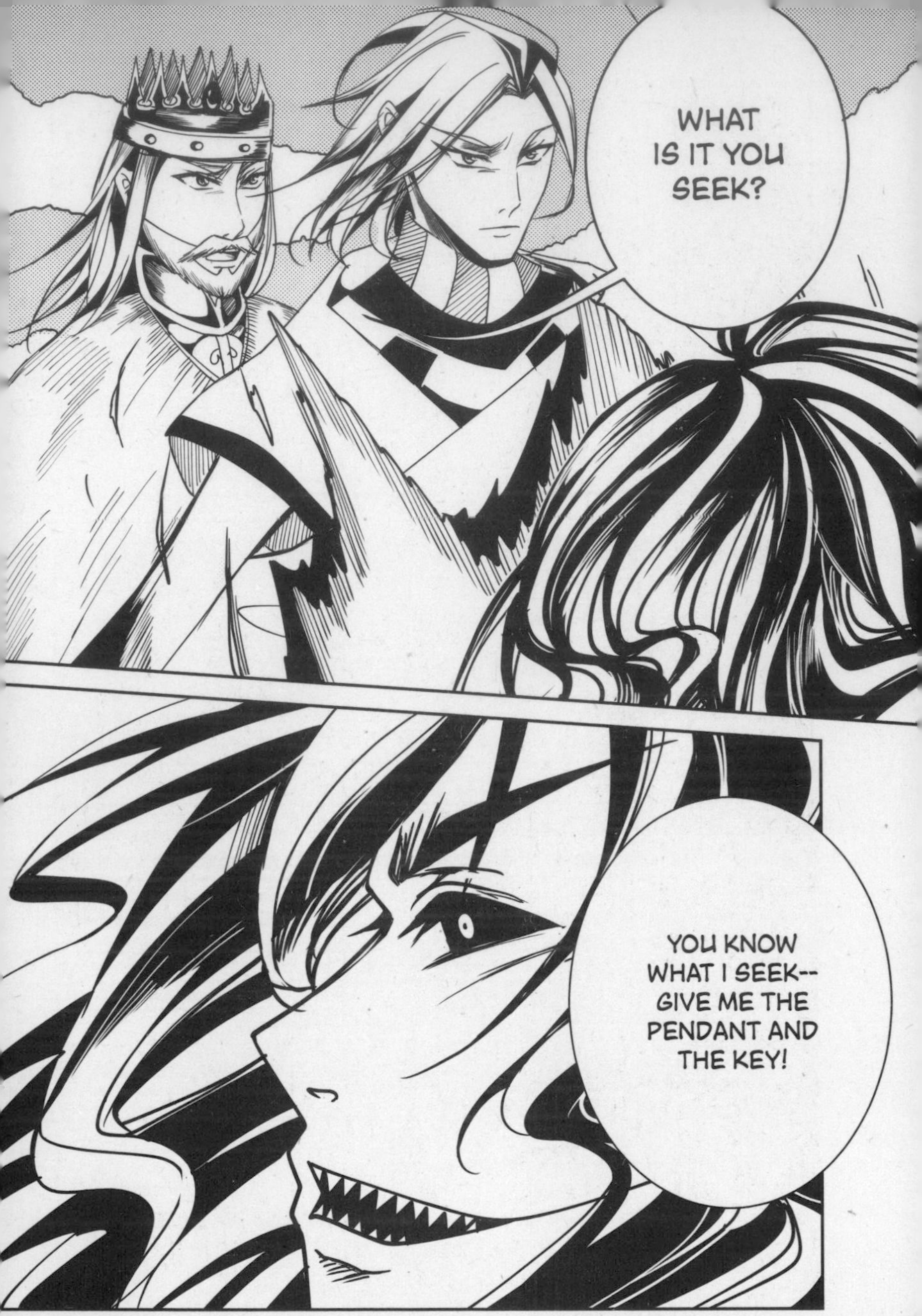
WHAT IS IT YOU SEEK?
YOU KNOW WHAT I SEEK-- GIVE ME THE PENDANT AND THE KEY!

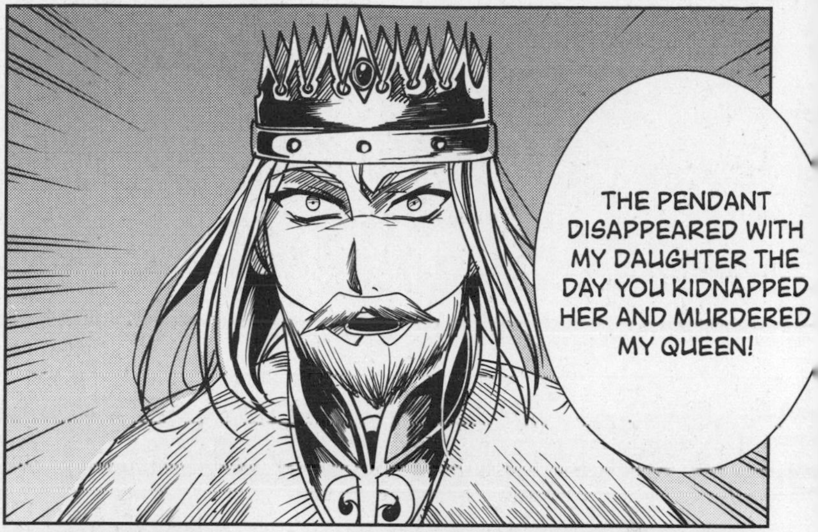
THE PENDANT DISAPPEARED WITH MY DAUGHTER THE DAY YOU KIDNAPPED HER AND MURDERED MY QUEEN!

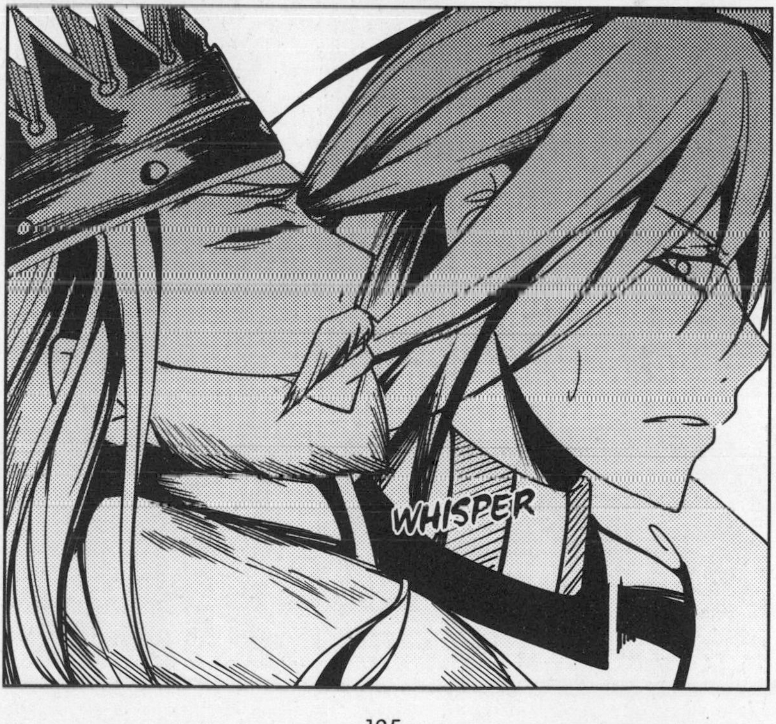
WHISPER

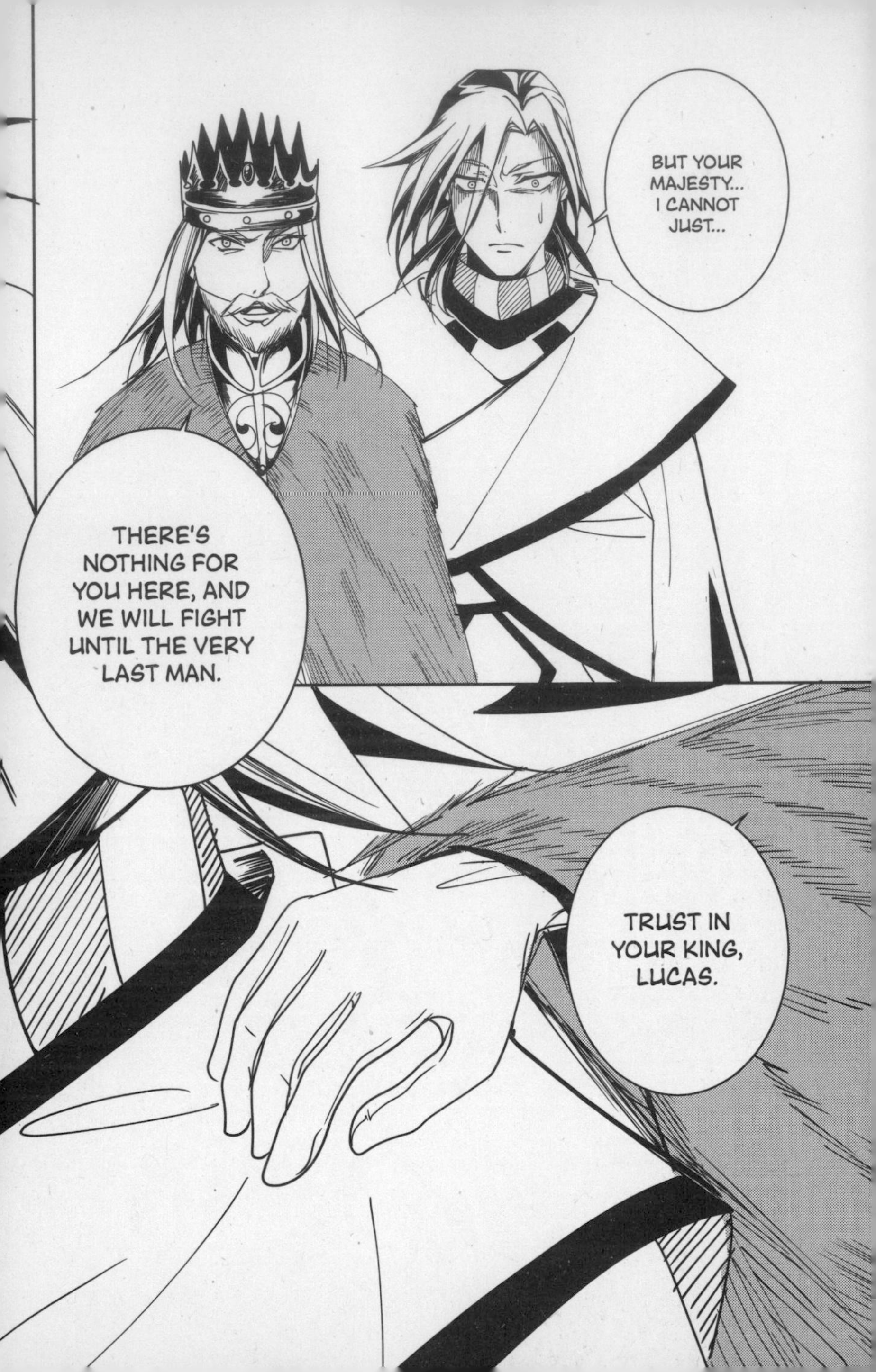
BUT YOUR MAJESTY... I CANNOT JUST...
THERE'S NOTHING FOR YOU HERE, AND WE WILL FIGHT UNTIL THE VERY LAST MAN.
TRUST IN YOUR KING, LUCAS.

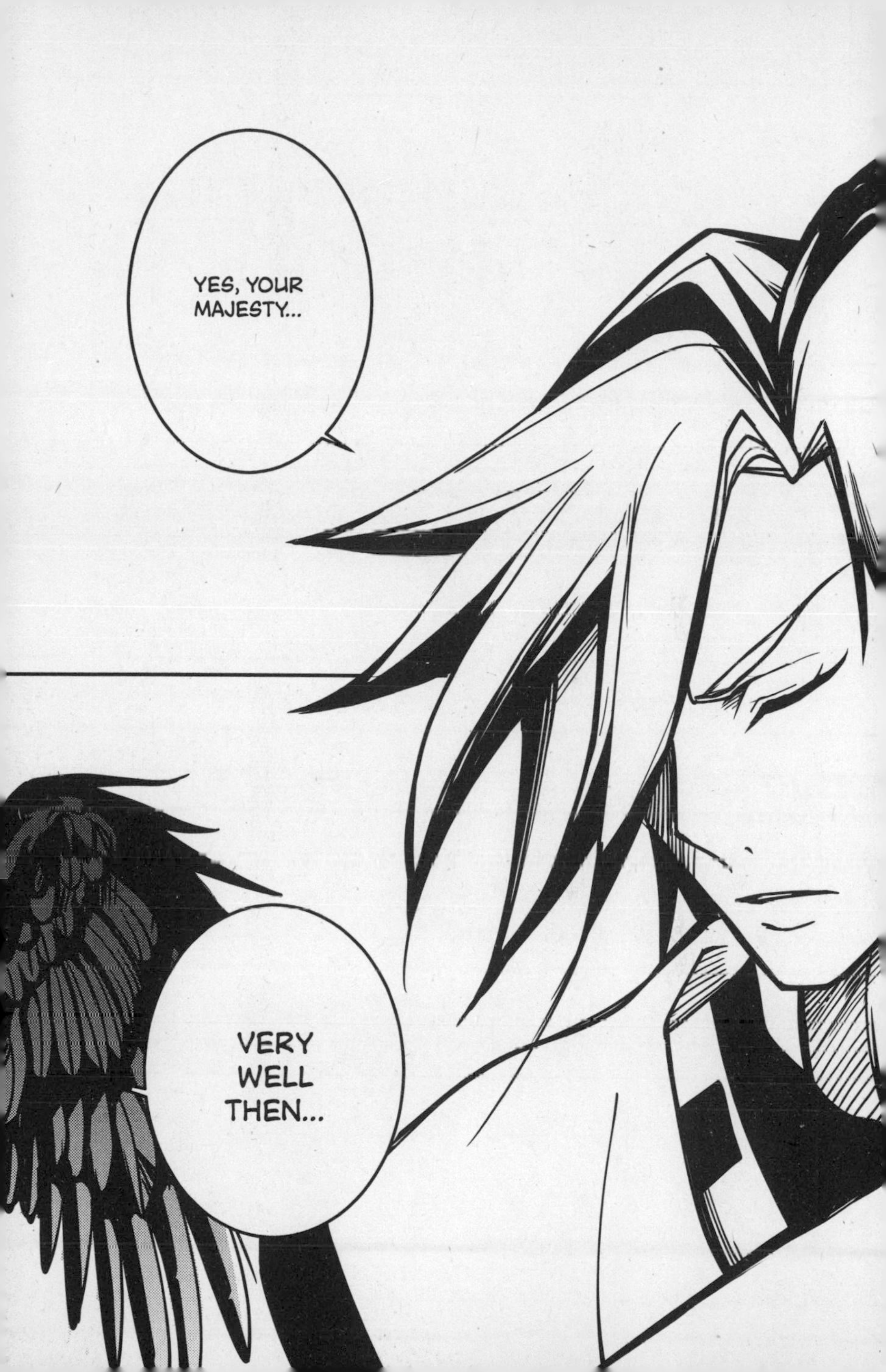
YES, YOUR MAJESTY...
VERY WELL THEN...

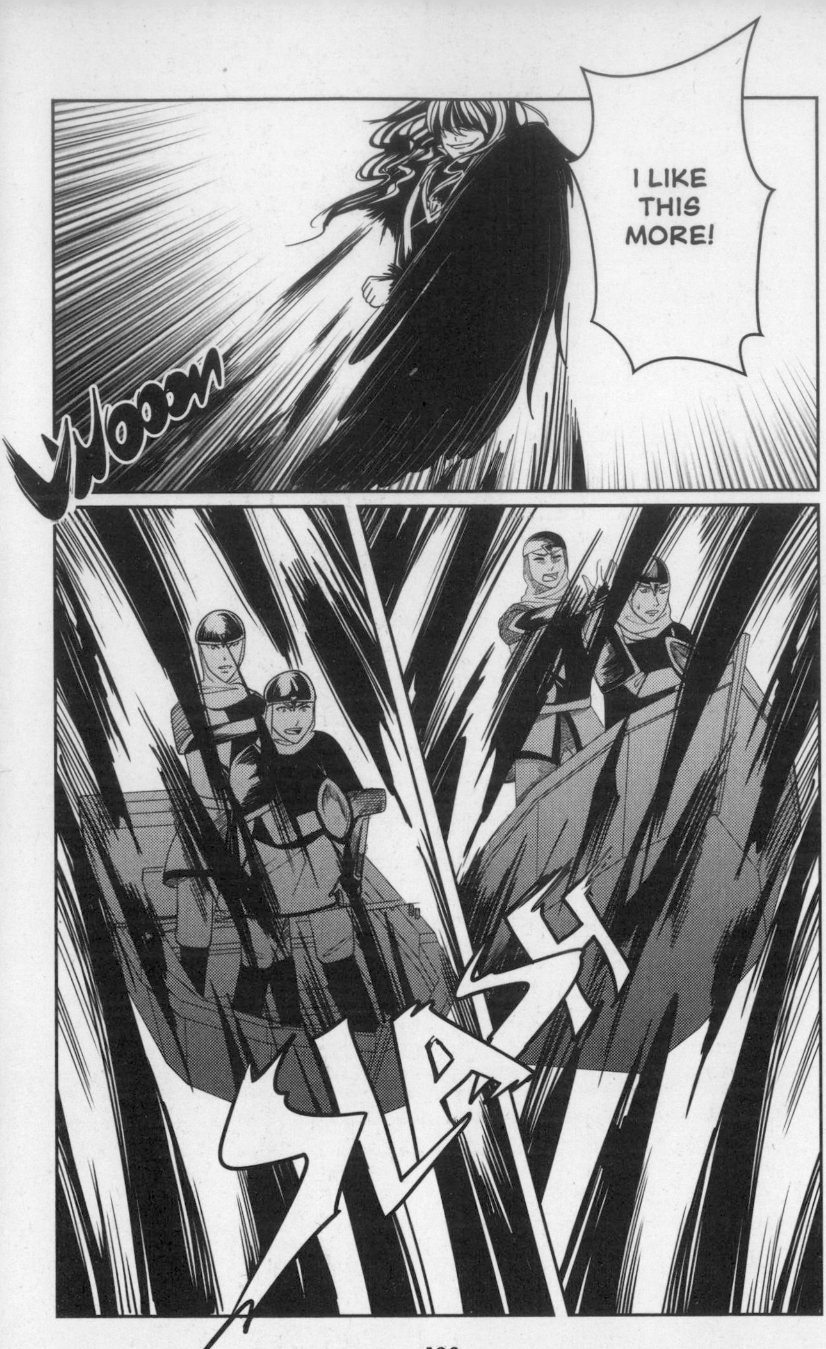
I LIKE THIS MORE!
VWOOOM
SLASH

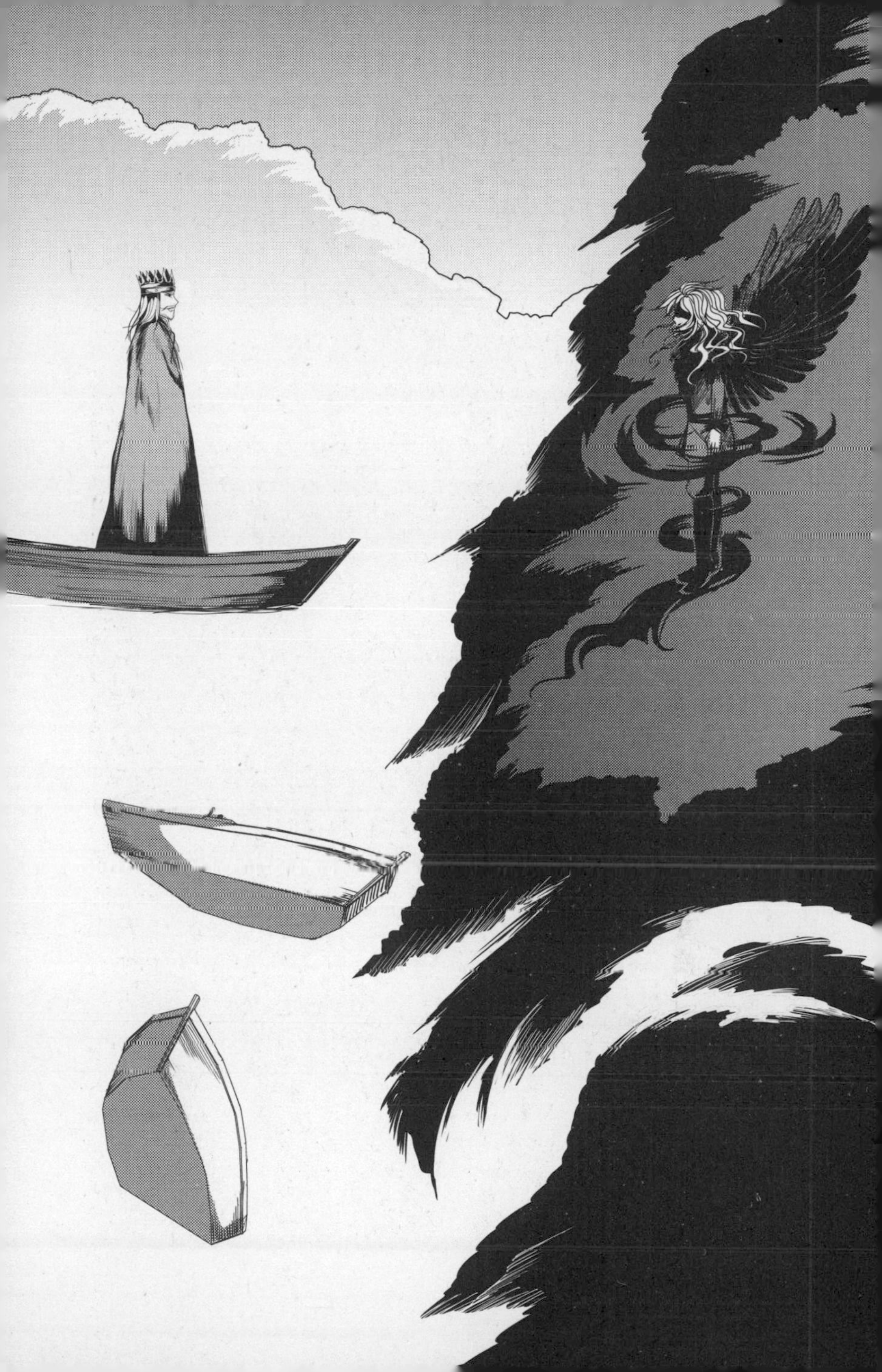

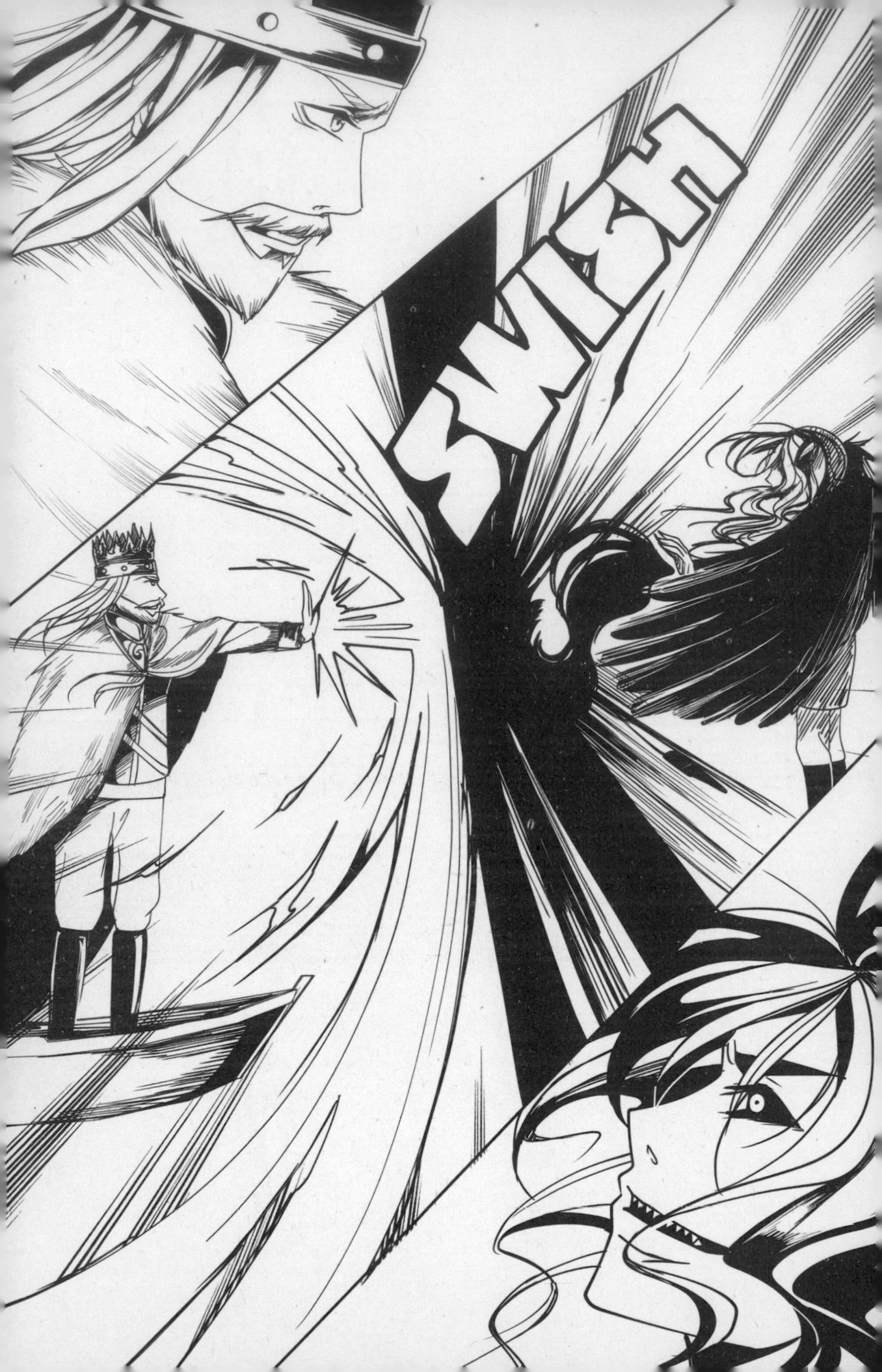
SWISH

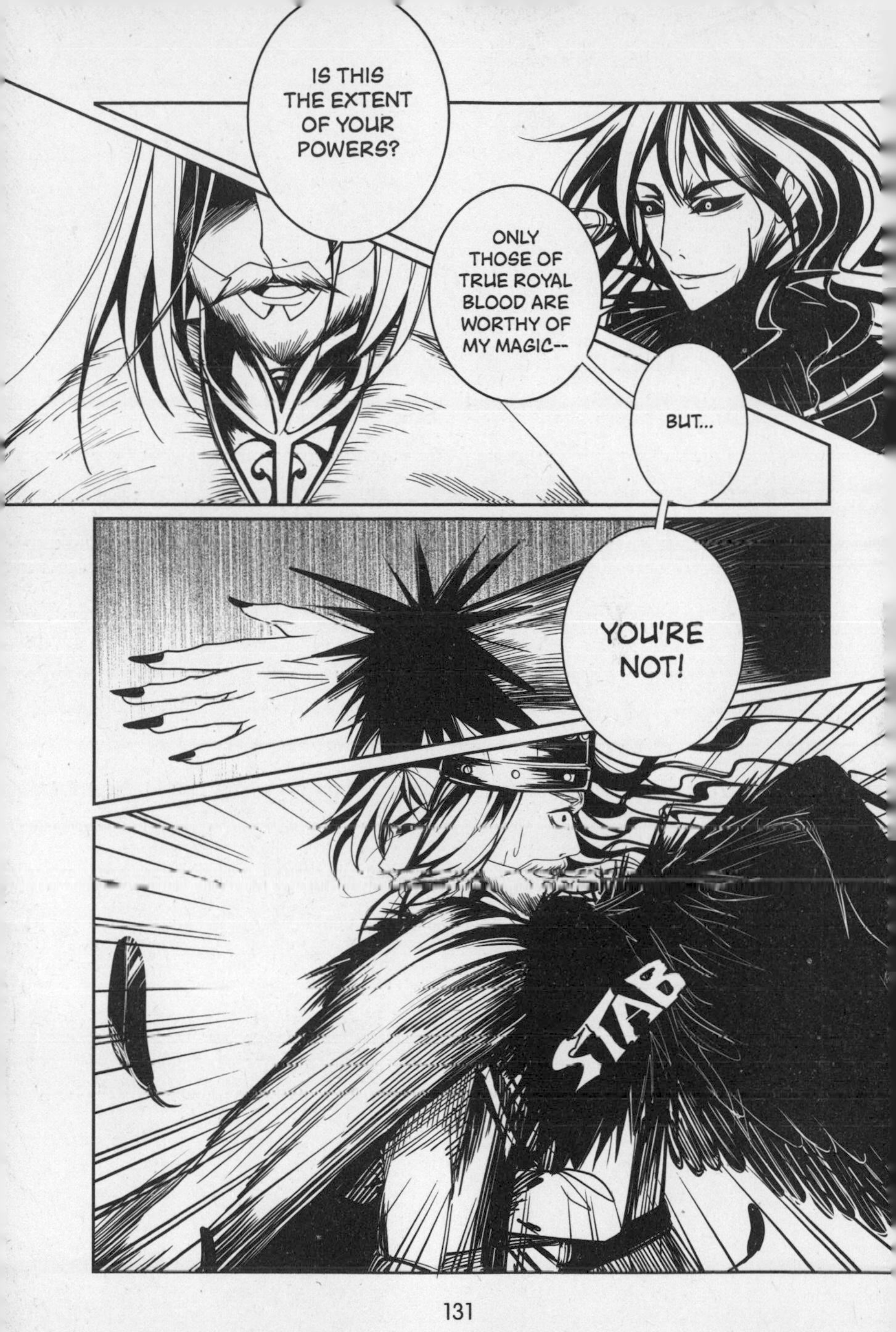
IS THIS THE EXTENT OF YOUR POWERS?
ONLY THOSE OF TRUE ROYAL BLOOD ARE WORTHY OF MY MAGIC--
BUT...
YOU'RE NOT!
STAB

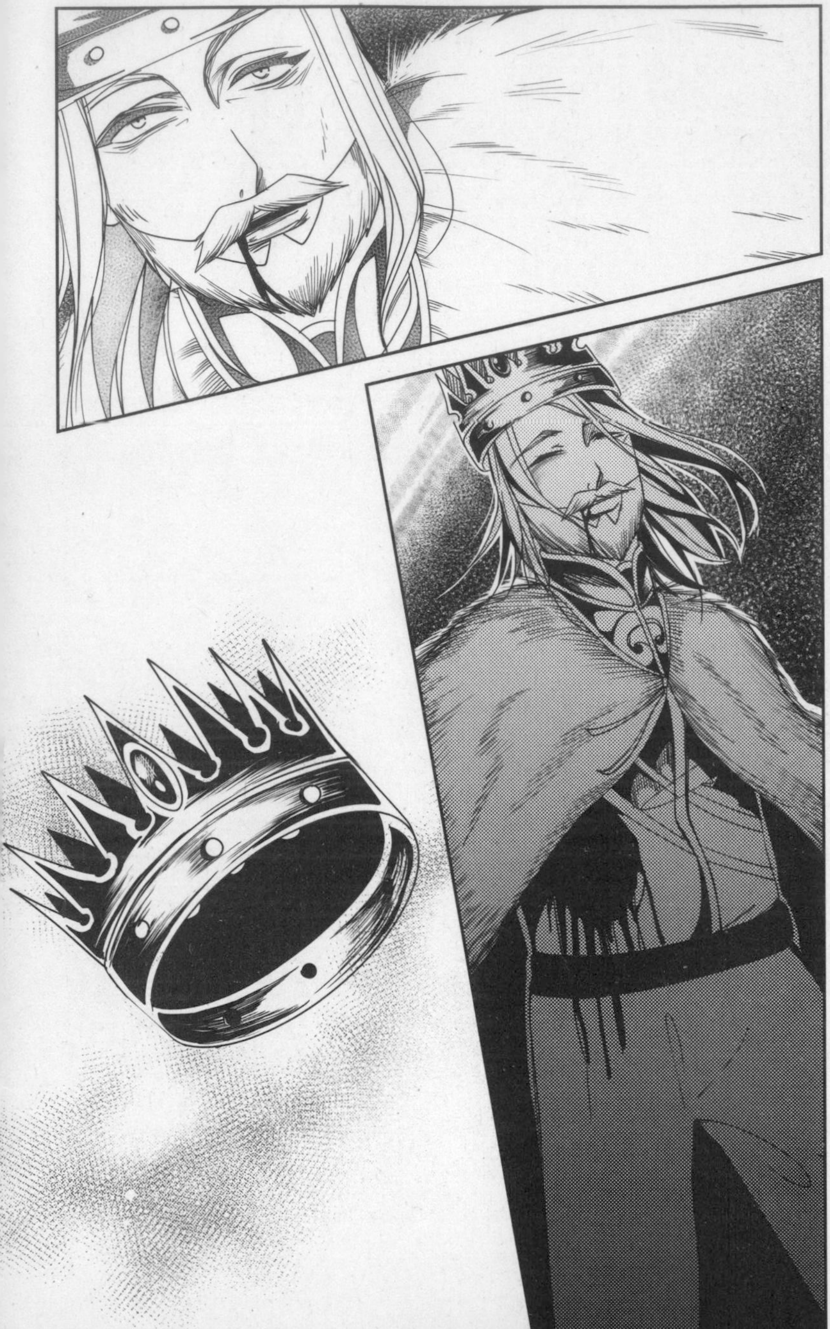

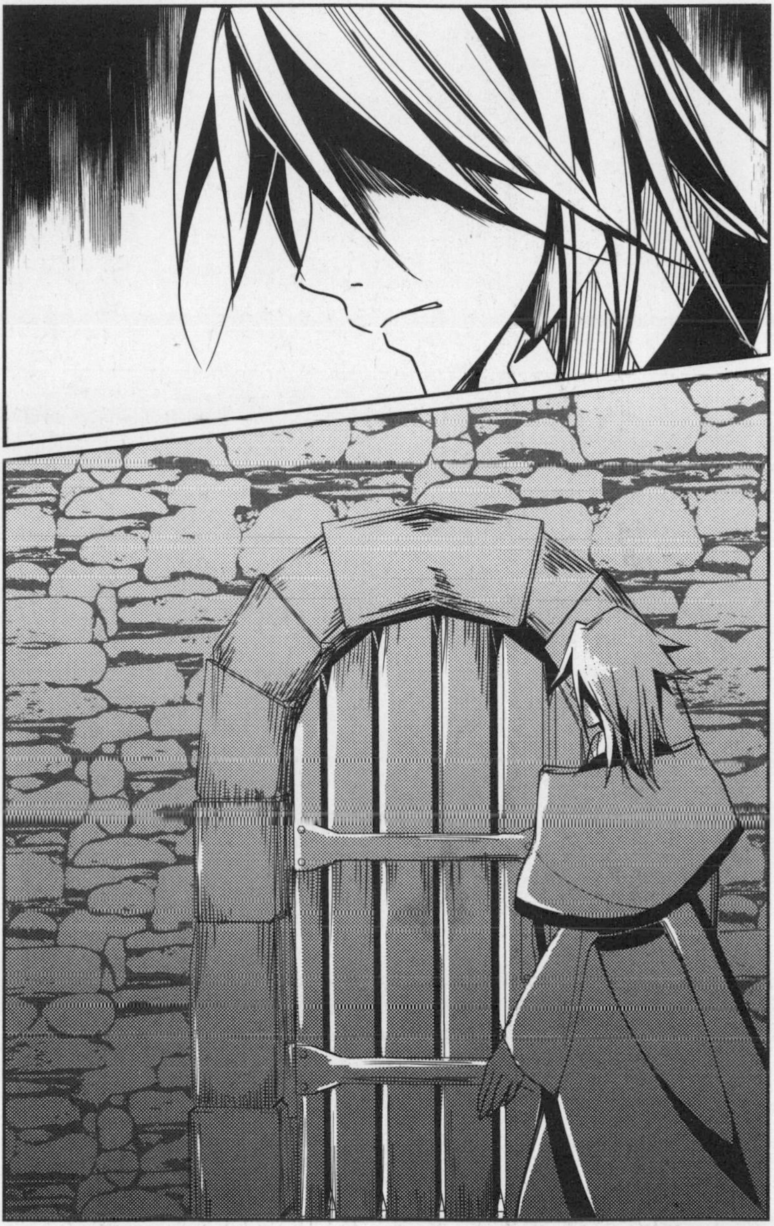

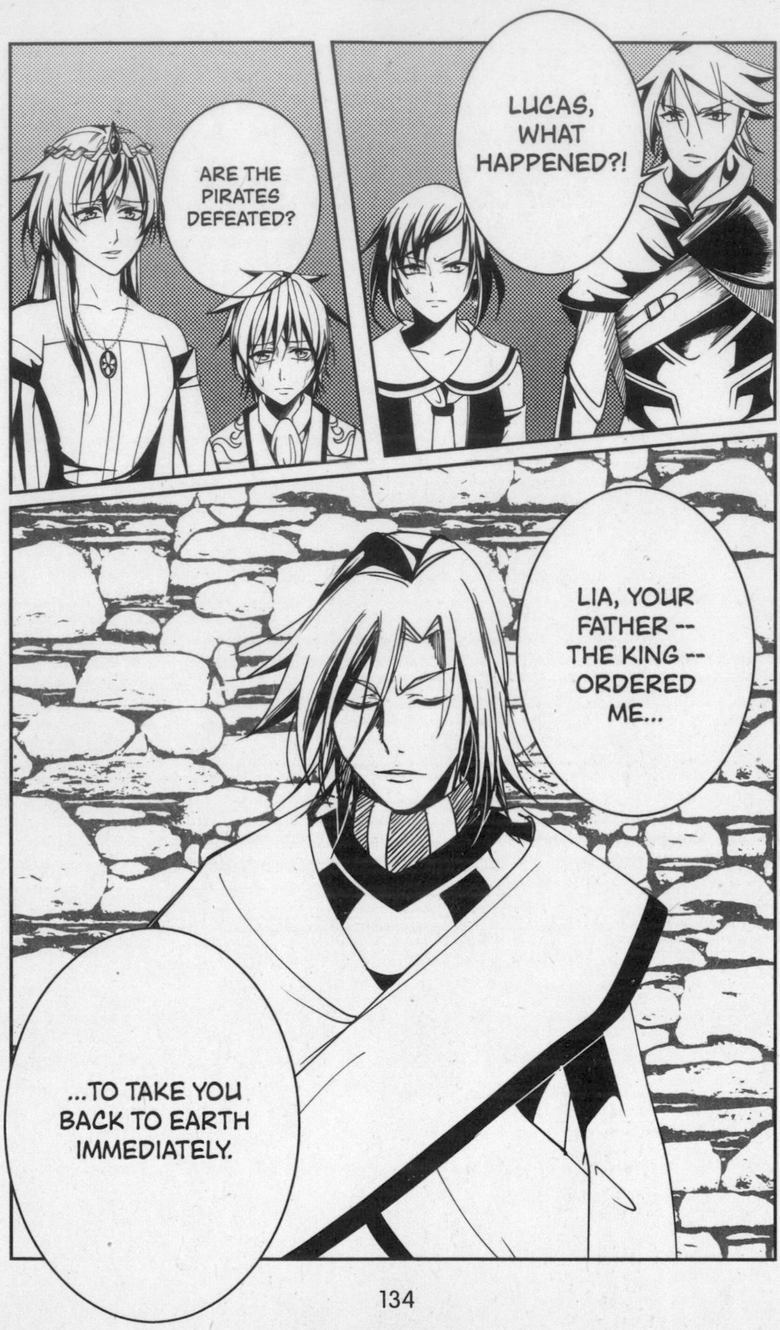
LUCAS, WHAT HAPPENED?!
ARE THE PIRATES DEFEATED?
LIA, YOUR FATHER -- THE KING -- ORDERED ME...
...TO TAKE YOU BACK TO EARTH IMMEDIATELY.

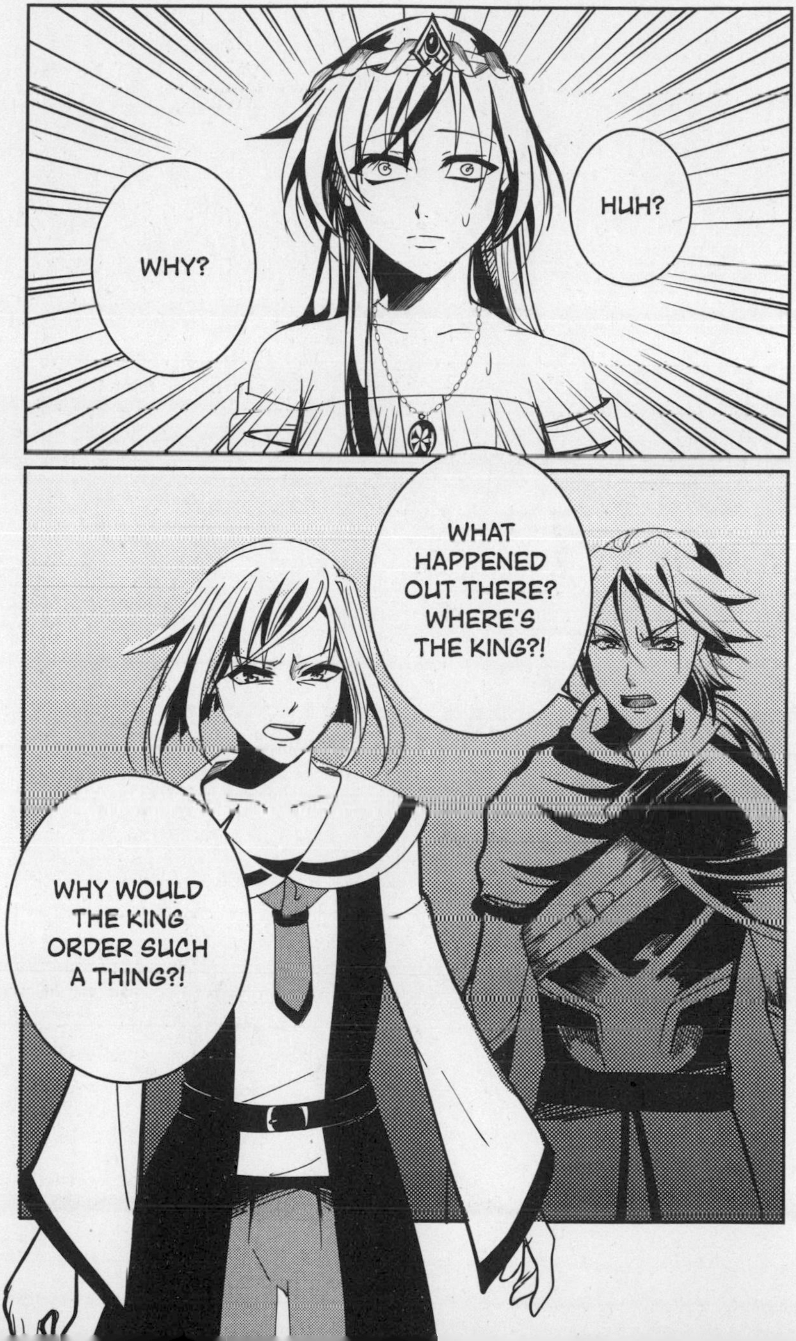
HUH?
WHY?
WHAT HAPPENED OUT THERE? WHERE'S THE KING?!
WHY WOULD THE KING ORDER SUCH A THING?!

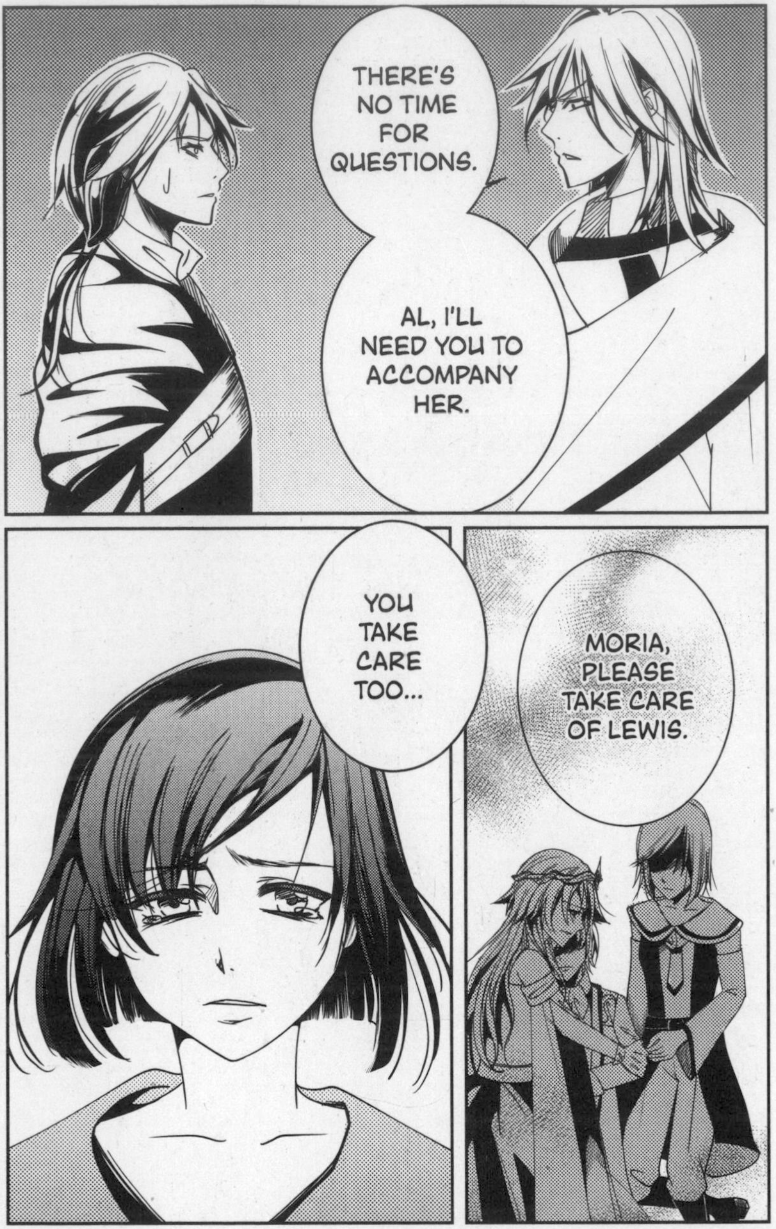
THERE'S NO TIME FOR QUESTIONS.
AL, I'LL NEED YOU TO ACCOMPANY HER.
MORIA, PLEASE TAKE CARE OF LEWIS.
YOU TAKE CARE TOO...

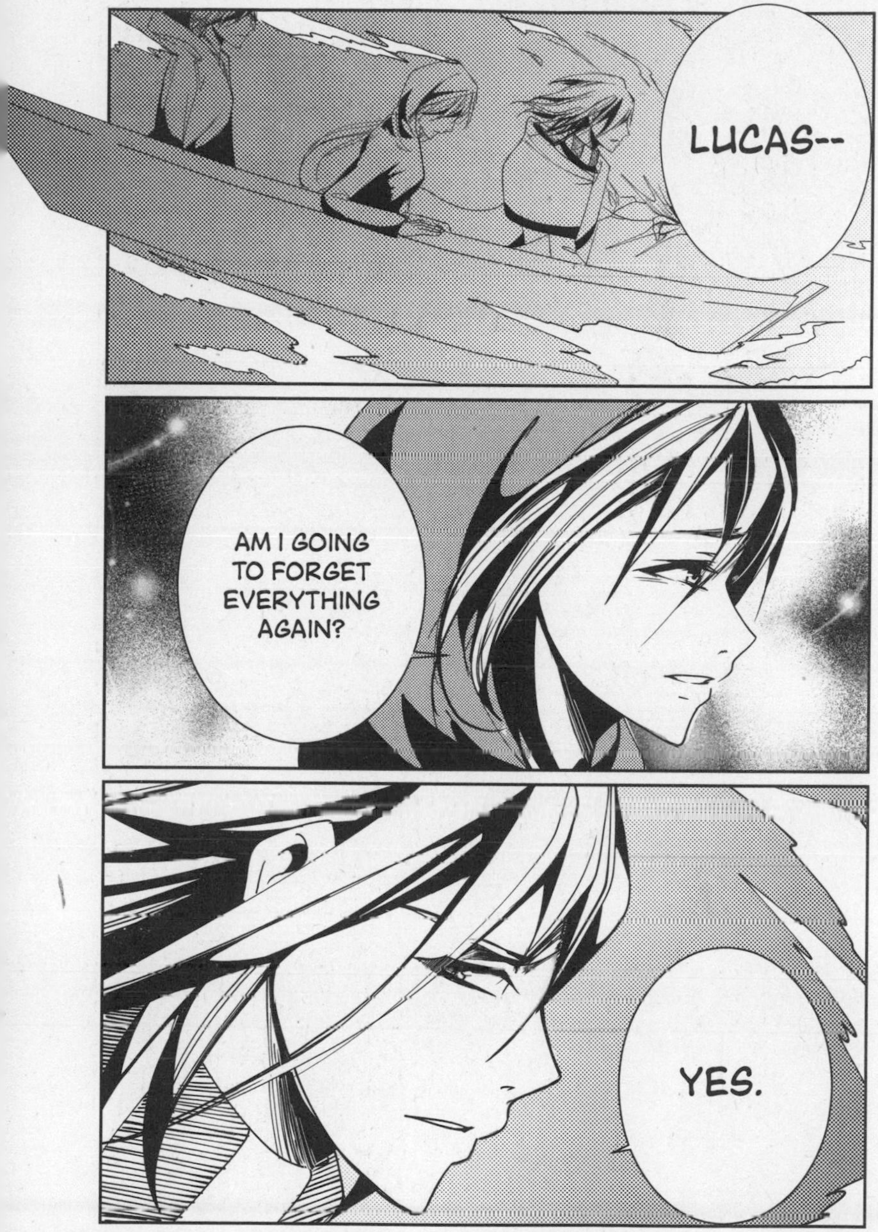
LUCAS--
AM I GOING TO FORGET EVERYTHING AGAIN?
YES.

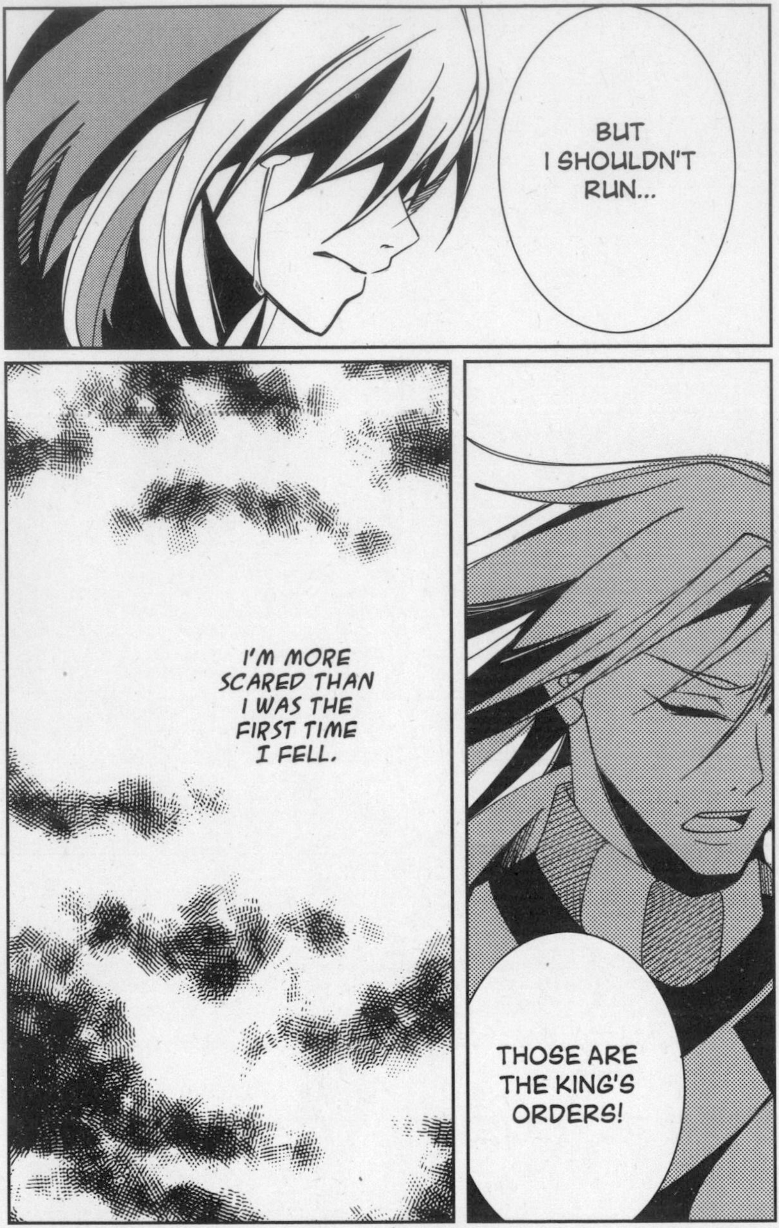
BUT I SHOULDN'T RUN...
THOSE ARE THE KING'S ORDERS!
I'M MORE SCARED THAN I WAS THE FIRST TIME I FELL.

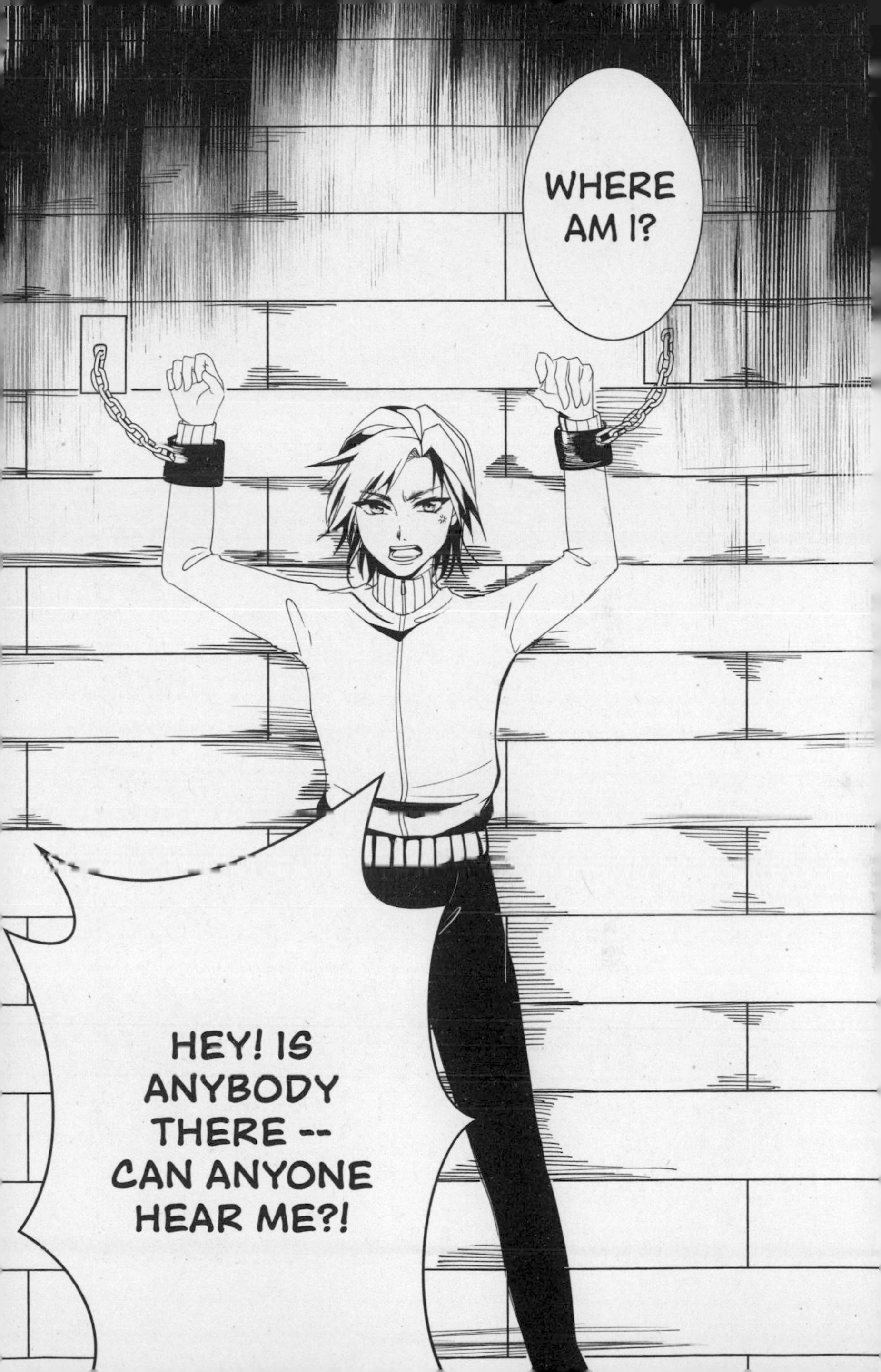
WHERE AM I?
HEY! IS ANYBODY THERE -- CAN ANYONE HEAR ME?!

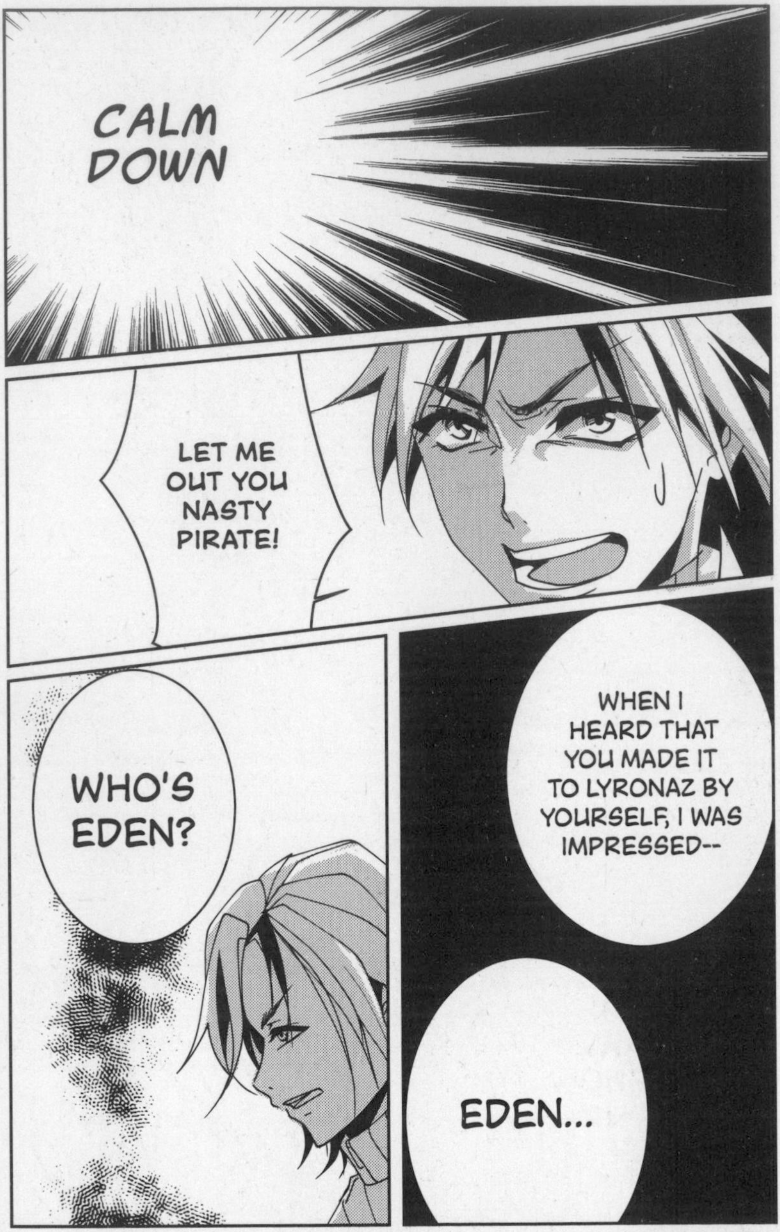
CALM DOWN
LET ME OUT YOU NASTY PIRATE!
WHEN I HEARD THAT YOU MADE IT TO LYRONAZ BY YOURSELF, I WAS IMPRESSED--
EDEN...
WHO'S EDEN?

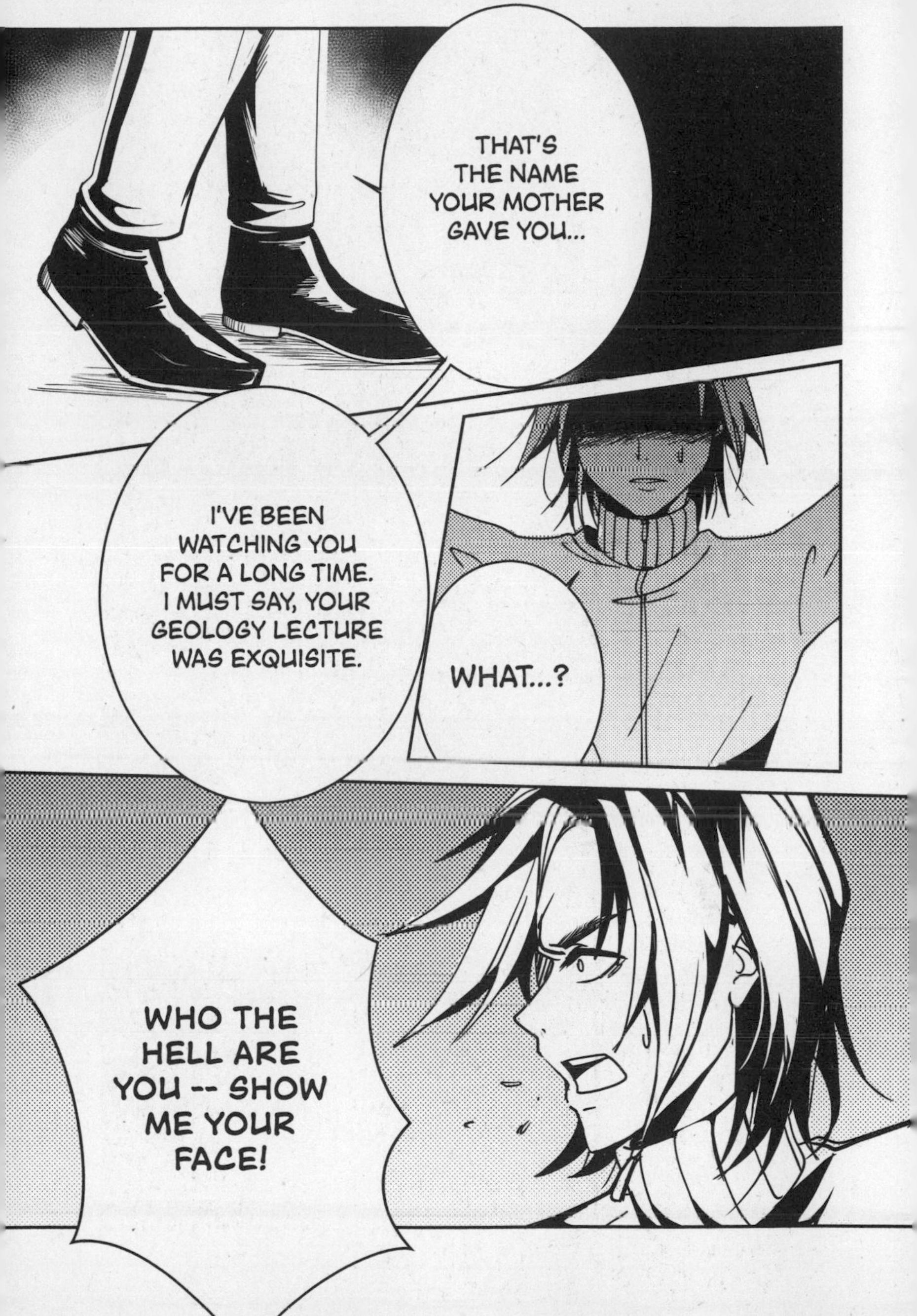
THAT'S THE NAME YOUR MOTHER GAVE YOU...
I'VE BEEN WATCHING YOU FOR A LONG TIME. I MUST SAY, YOUR GEOLOGY LECTURE WAS EXQUISITE.
WHAT...?
WHO THE HELL ARE YOU -- SHOW ME YOUR FACE!

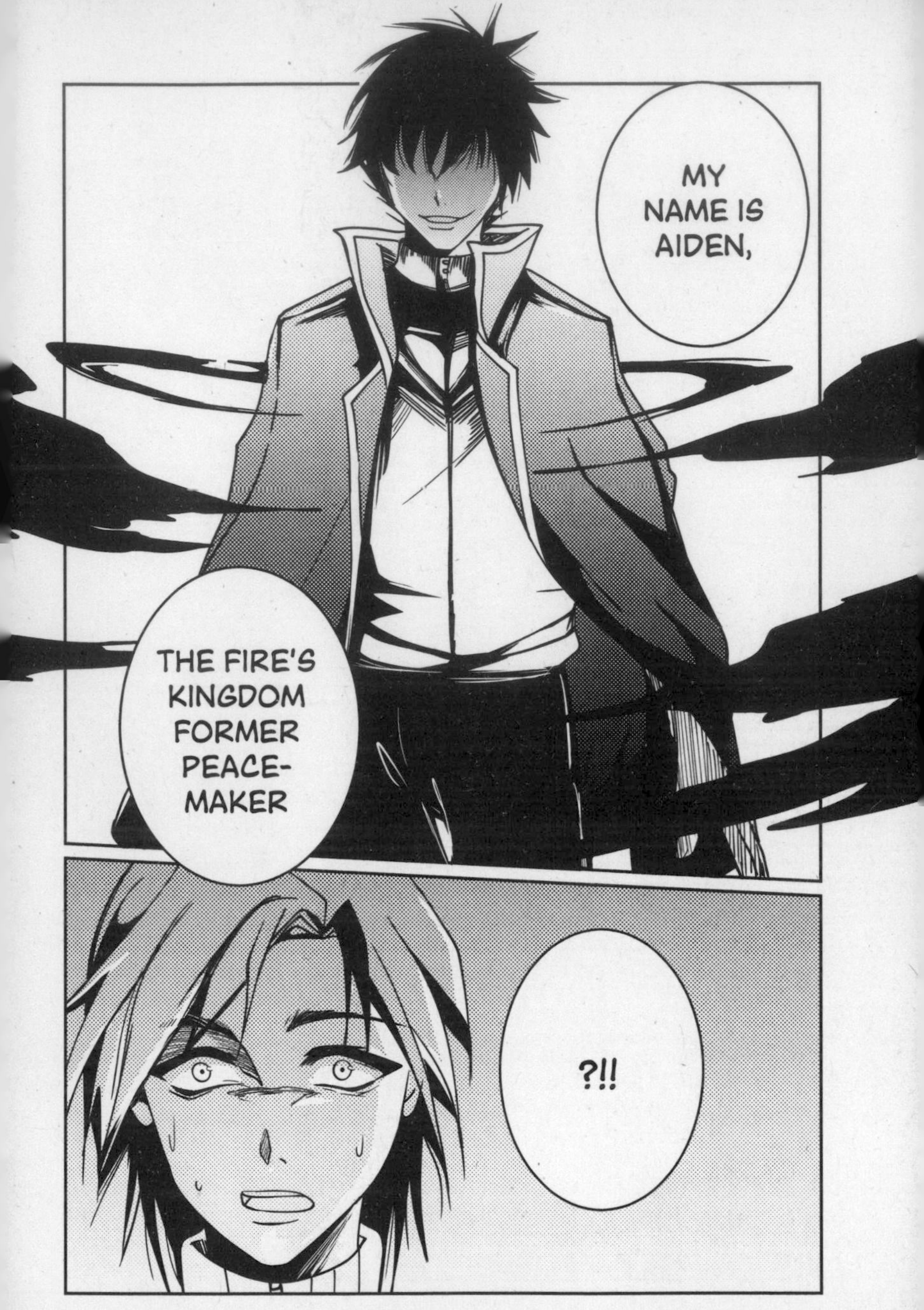
MY NAME IS AIDEN,
THE FIRE'S KINGDOM FORMER PEACE-MAKER
?!!

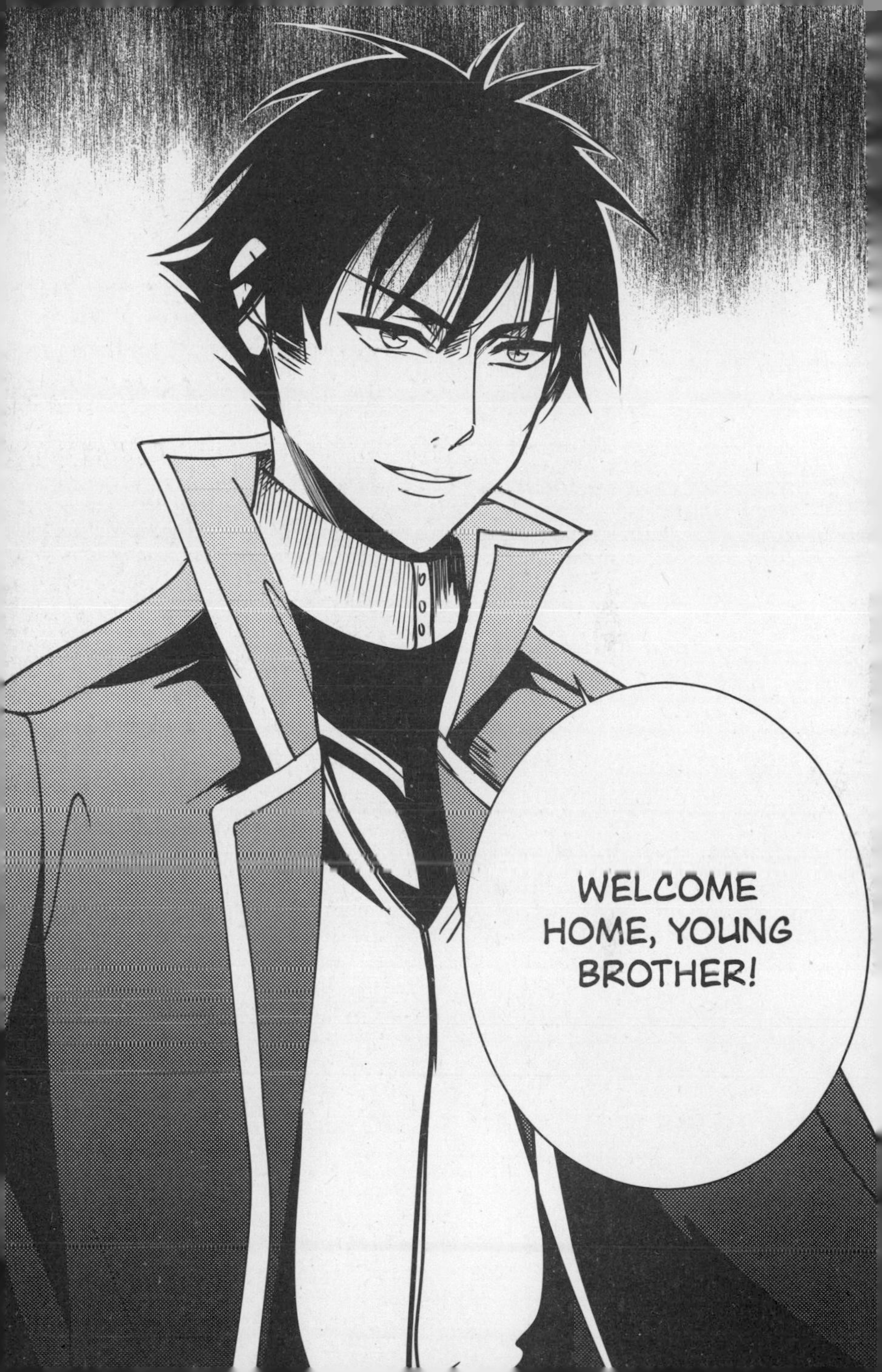
WELCOME HOME, YOUNG BROTHER!

IN THE NEXT VOLUME OF

Ocean
of
Secrets

Lia has returned to Earth with Lucas and Al as part of the King's plan to save Lyronaz. Unable to remember her magical journey, she's eager to return to her home and continue on with her life as if nothing ever happened.

Meanwhile, Rai is shocked to find out his real identity and is faced with a challenging decision; should he fight the Pirates, or join them? What will be the Pirates' next move? And what was the motive behind Aiden's treason?

Find out in volume 3 of *Ocean of Secrets!*

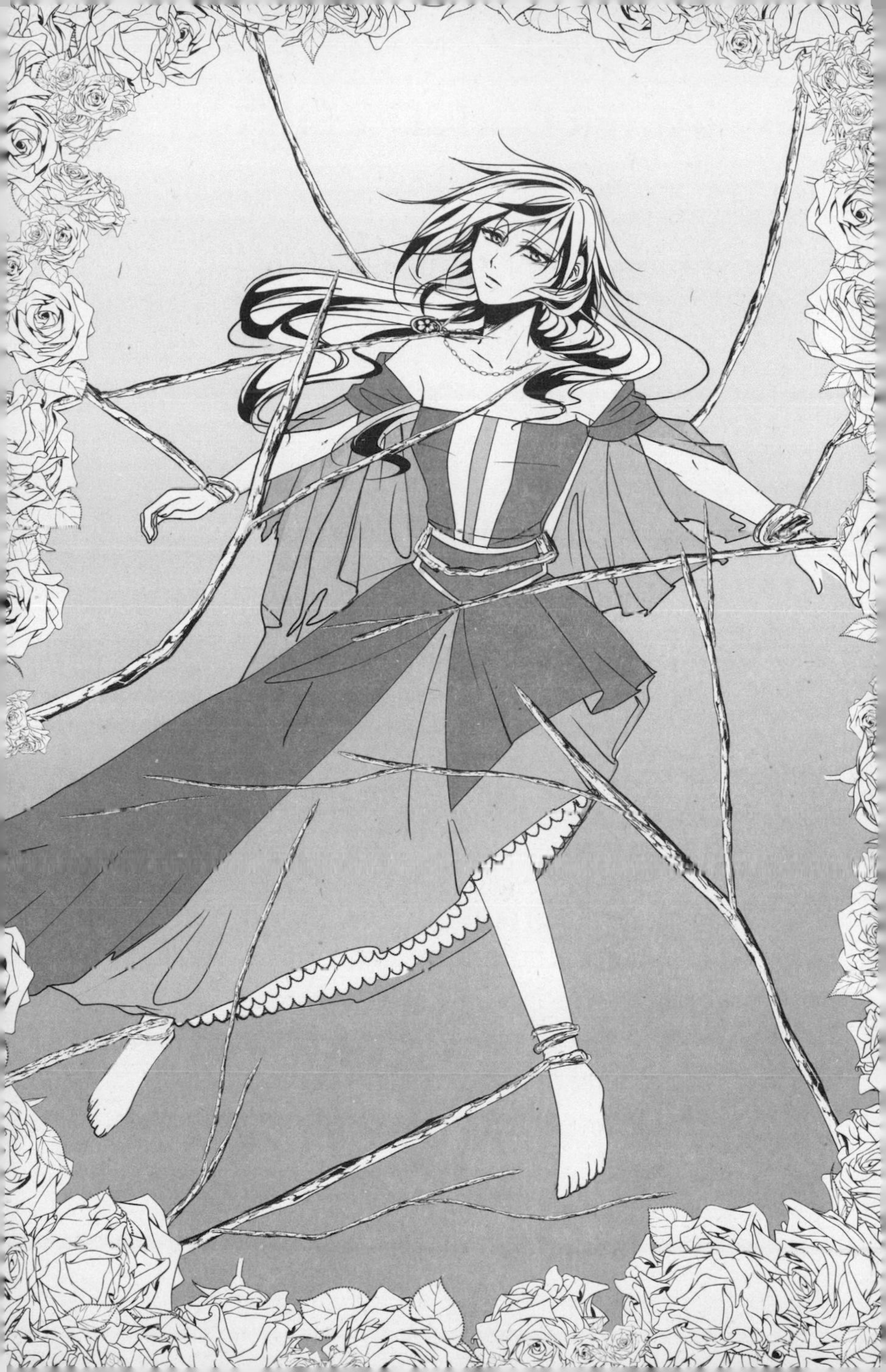

CHARACTER CONCEPT SKETCHES

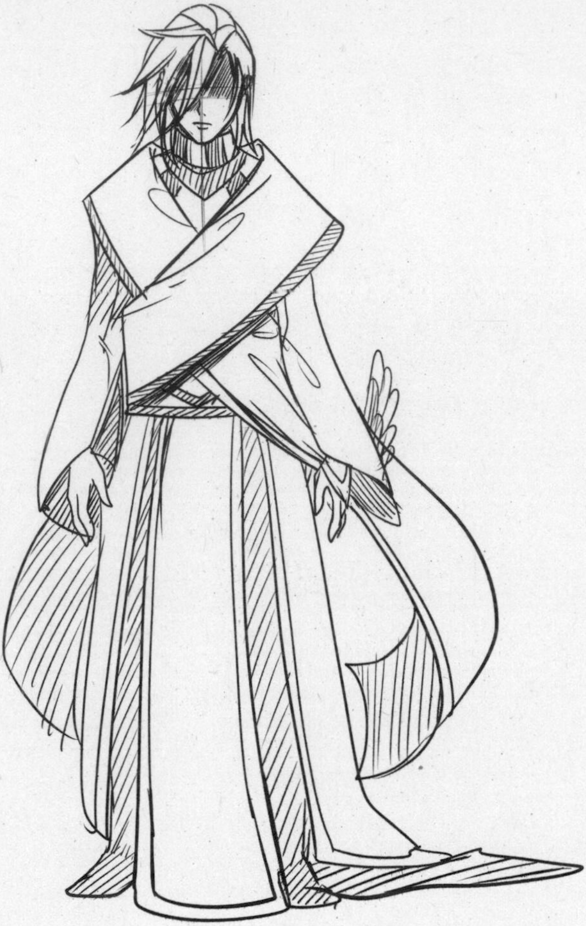

LUCAS OF LYRONAZ
THE PEACEMAKER OF THE WIND KINGDOM

CHARACTER CONCEPT SKETCHES

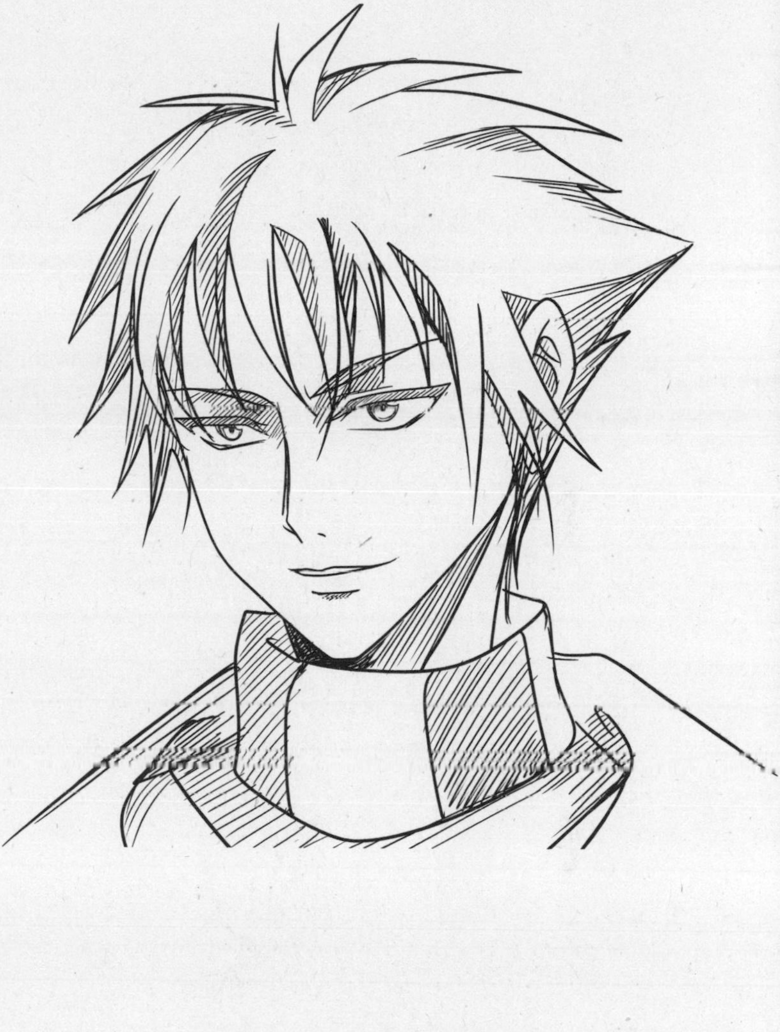

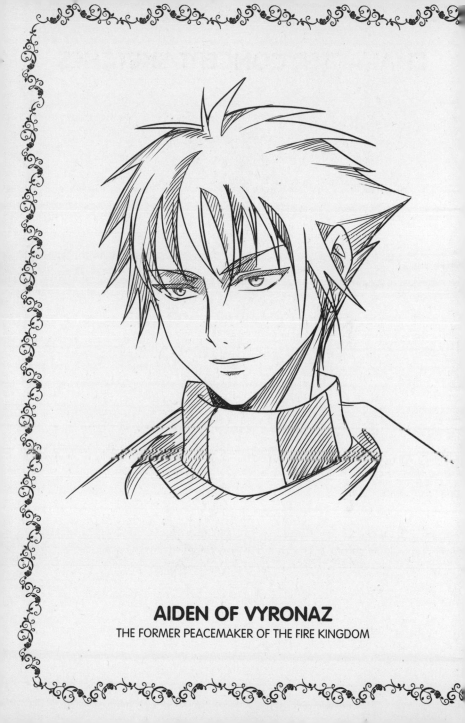

AIDEN OF VYRONAZ

THE FORMER PEACEMAKER OF THE FIRE KINGDOM

CHARACTER CONCEPT SKETCHES

CIAN OF SYRONAZ
THE PEACEMAKER OF THE EARTH KINGDOM

Hey there!

Thank you for buying the second volume of *Ocean of Secrets*. I hope you enjoyed the story so far and you didn't expect an ending like this! I'm sorry for not being as active as I used to be in my social media websites the past year. I'm still holding on to my promises to you and striving to improve my art and story-telling skills. I'm grateful for having you by my side, thank you for your support!

Love,
Sophie

Visit my ▶ YouTube Channel to learn How to Draw Manga!

Step-by-Step
Tutorials

Speed-paint
Drawings

vlogs and
Contests

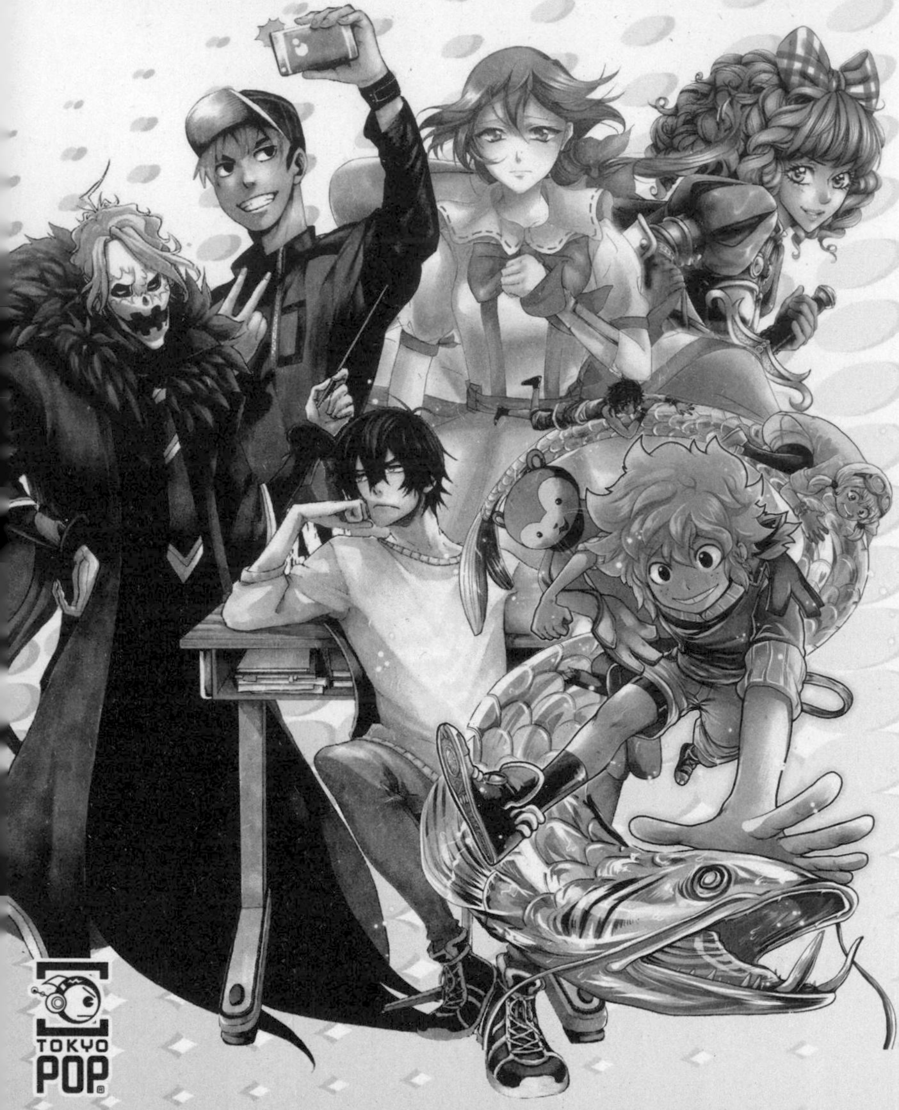

TOKYOPOP
• PRESENTS •

INTERNATIONAL WOMEN of MANGA

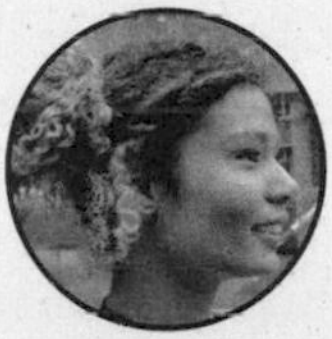

Nana Yaa

GOLDFISCH

An award-winning German manga artist with a large following for her free webcomic, ***CRUSHED!!***

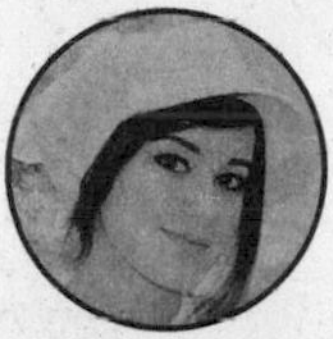

Sophie-Chan

Ocean of Secrets

A self-taught manga artist from the Middle East, with a huge YouTube following!

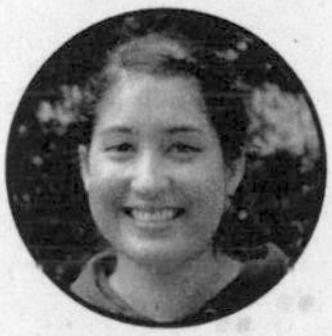

Ban Zarbo

KAMO
PACT WITH THE SPIRIT WORLD

A lifelong manga fan from Germany, she and her twin sister take inspiration from their Dominican roots!

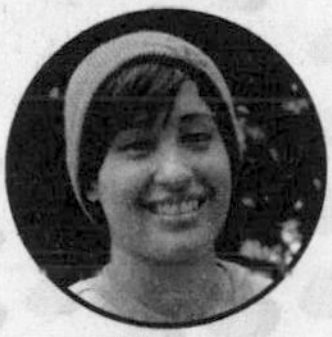

Gin Zarbo

UNDEAD MESSIAH

An aspiring manga artist since she was a child, along with her twin sister she's releasing her debut title!

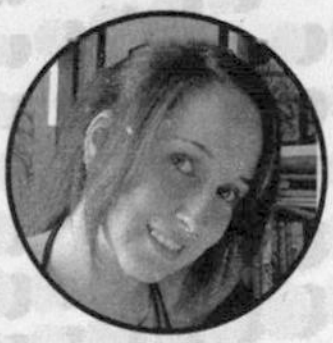

Natalia Batista

Sword Princess Amaltea
Natalia Batista

A Swedish creator whose popular manga has already been published in Sweden, Italy and the Czech Republic!

TO LEARN MORE PLEASE VISIT OUR WEBSITE

www.TOKYOPOP.com

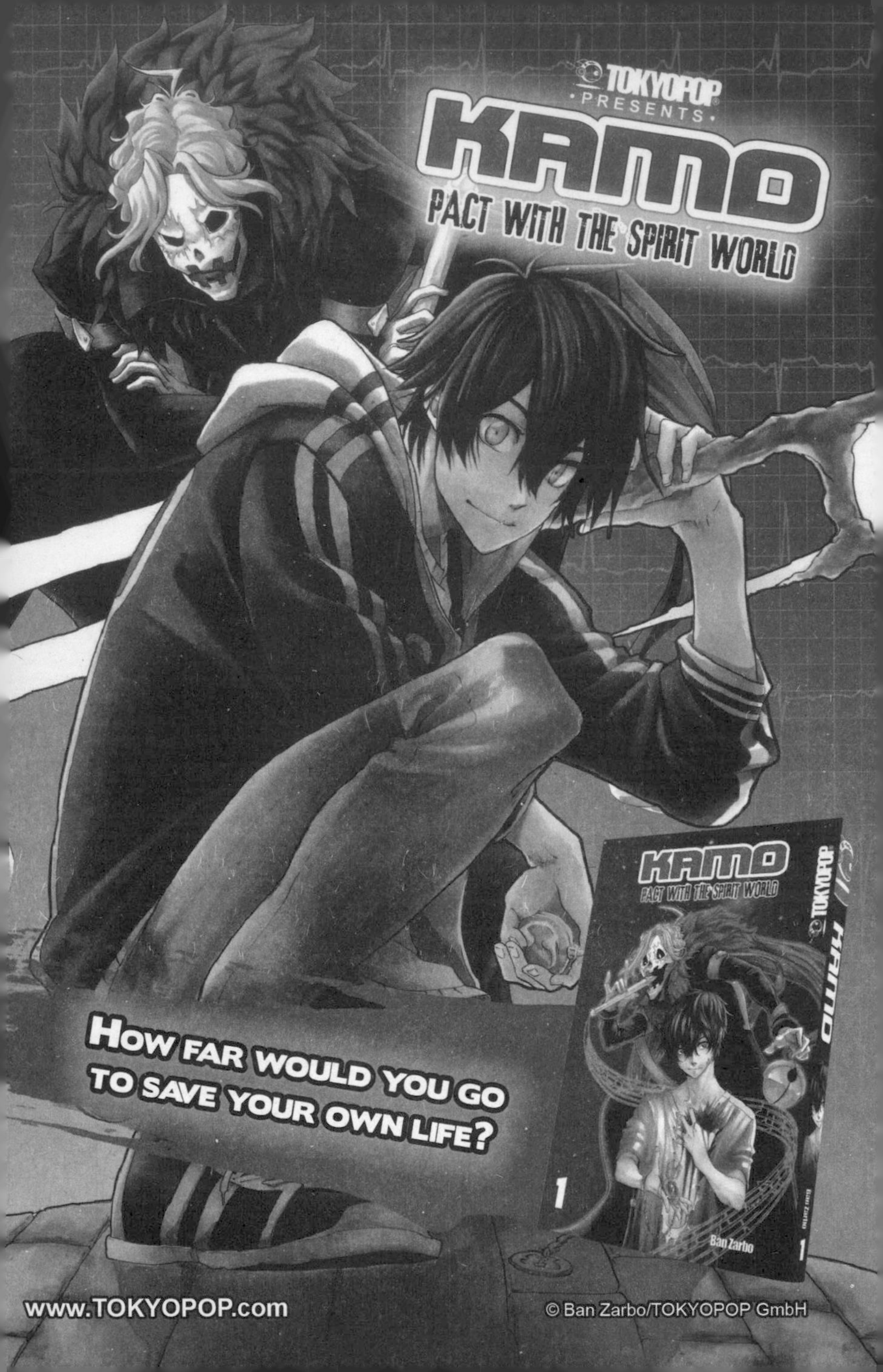

TOKYOPOP
PRESENTS
KAMO
PACT WITH THE SPIRIT WORLD
HOW FAR WOULD YOU GO TO SAVE YOUR OWN LIFE?
KAMO
PACT WITH THE SPIRIT WORLD
1
Ban Zarbo
TOKYOPOP
www.TOKYOPOP.com
© Ban Zarbo/TOKYOPOP GmbH

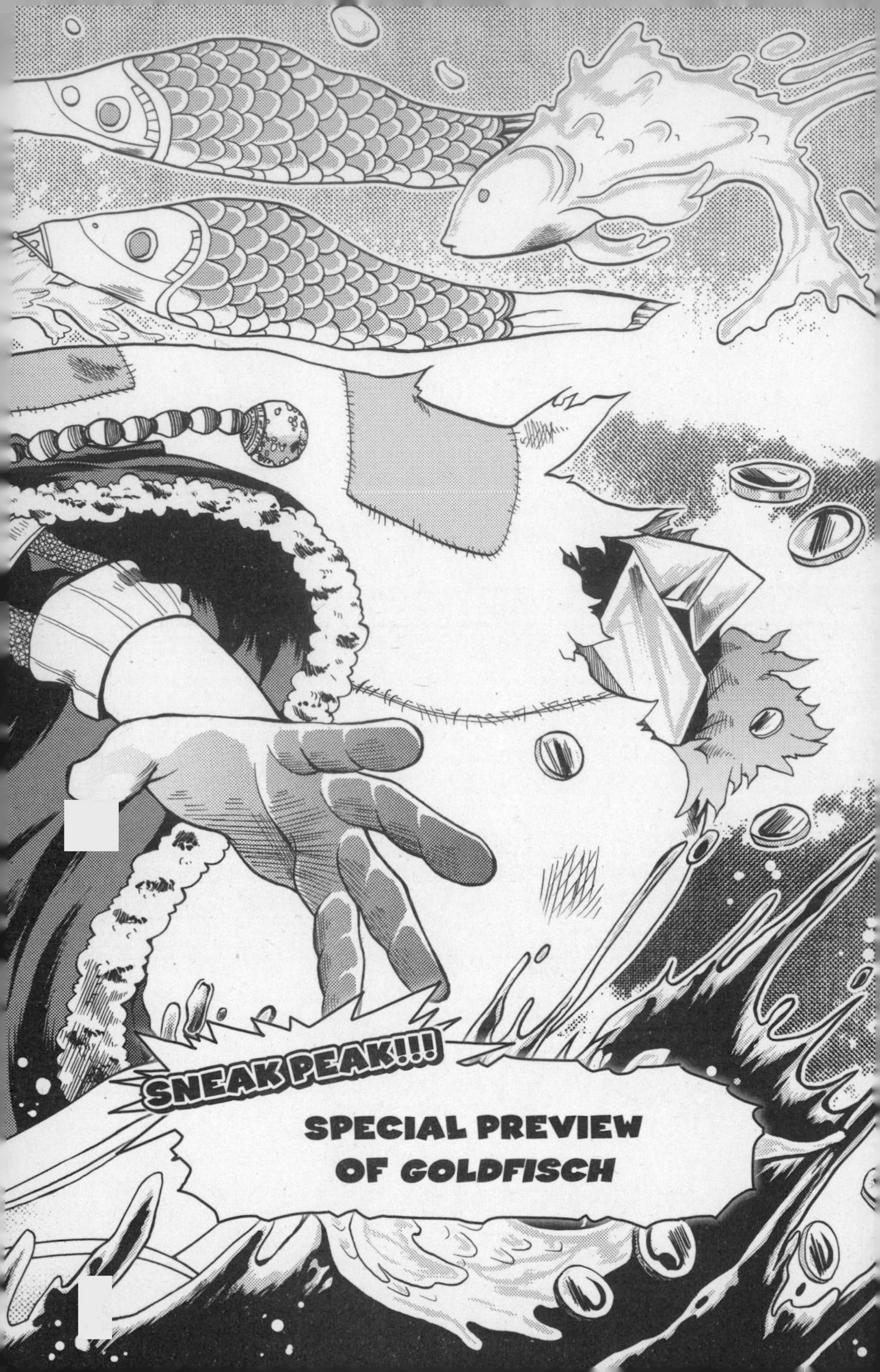
SNEAK PEAK!!!
SPECIAL PREVIEW
OF GOLDFISCH

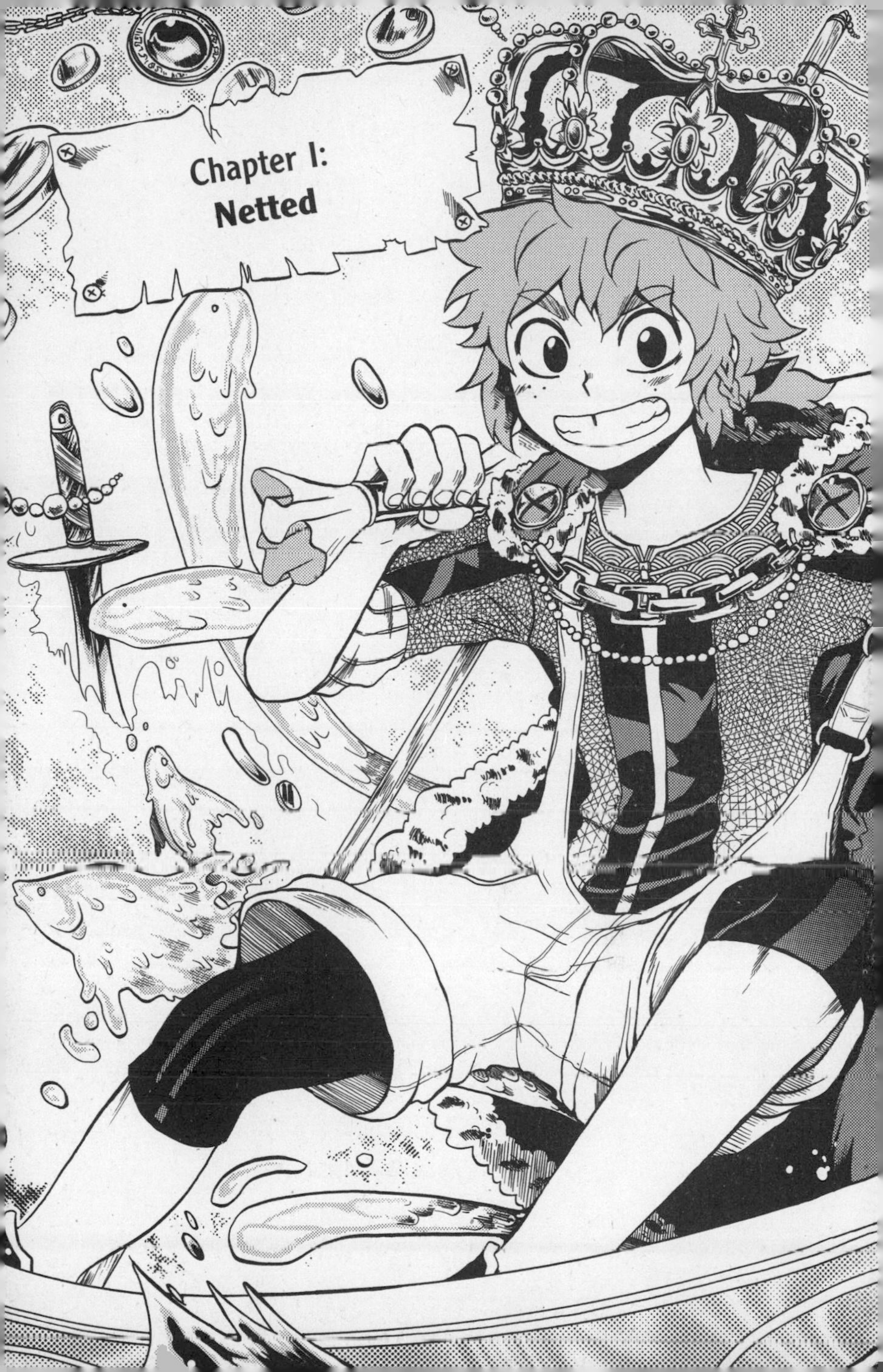
Chapter I:
Netted

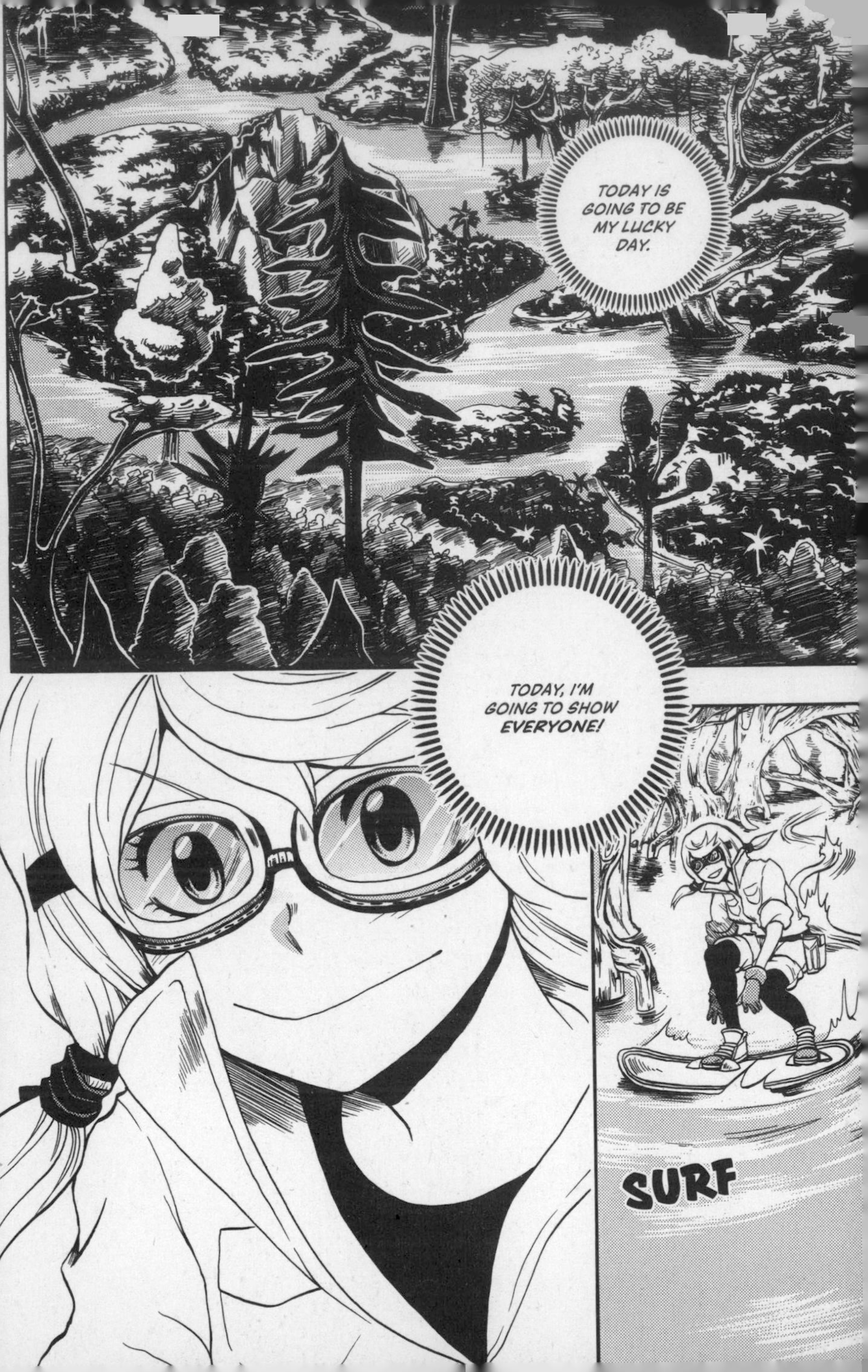

TODAY IS GOING TO BE MY LUCKY DAY.
TODAY, I'M GOING TO SHOW EVERYONE!
SURF

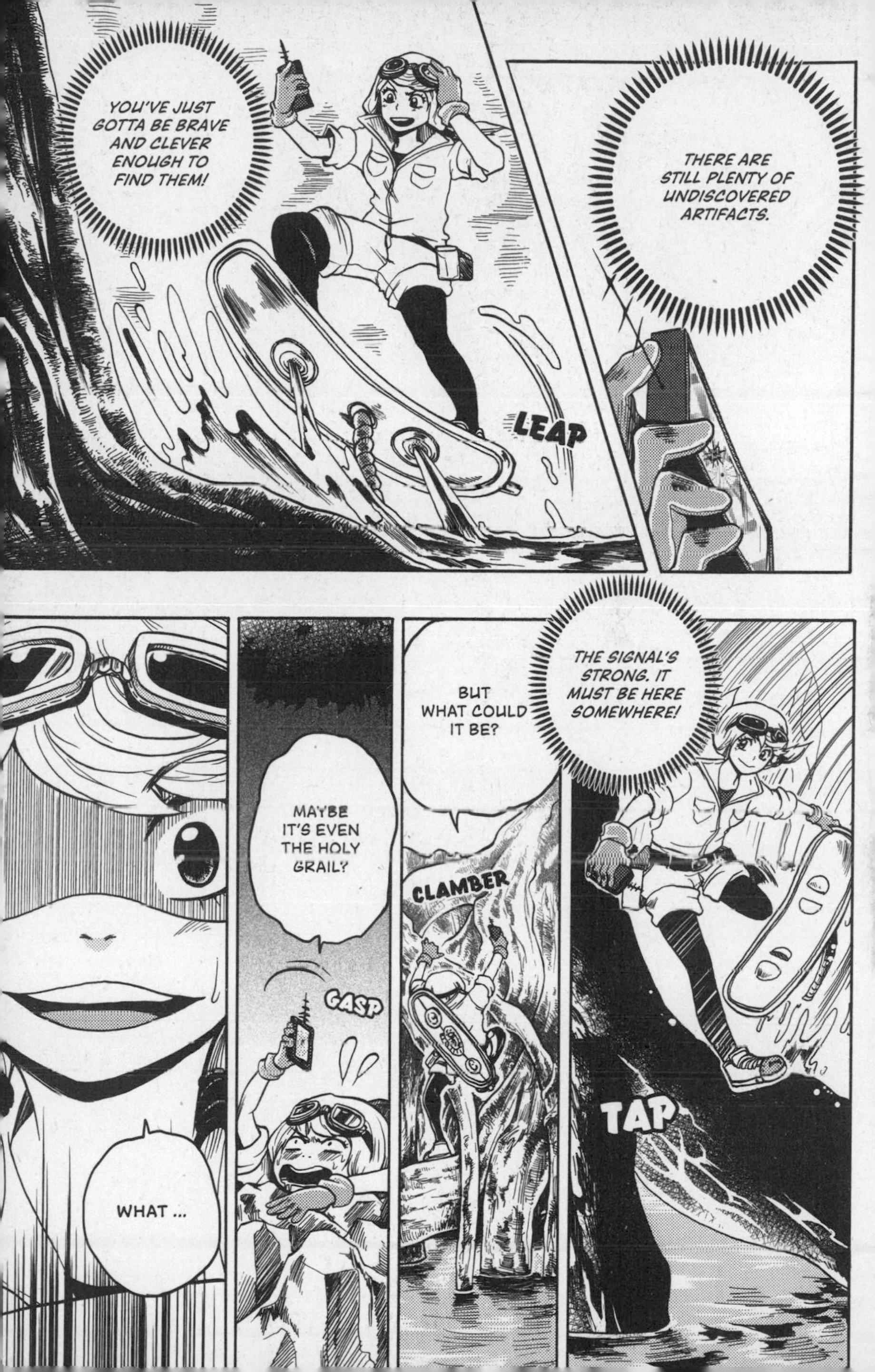
THERE ARE STILL PLENTY OF UNDISCOVERED ARTIFACTS.
YOU'VE JUST GOTTA BE BRAVE AND CLEVER ENOUGH TO FIND THEM!
LEAP
THE SIGNAL'S STRONG. IT MUST BE HERE SOMEWHERE!
TAP
BUT WHAT COULD IT BE?
CLAMBER
MAYBE IT'S EVEN THE HOLY GRAIL?
GASP
WHAT ...

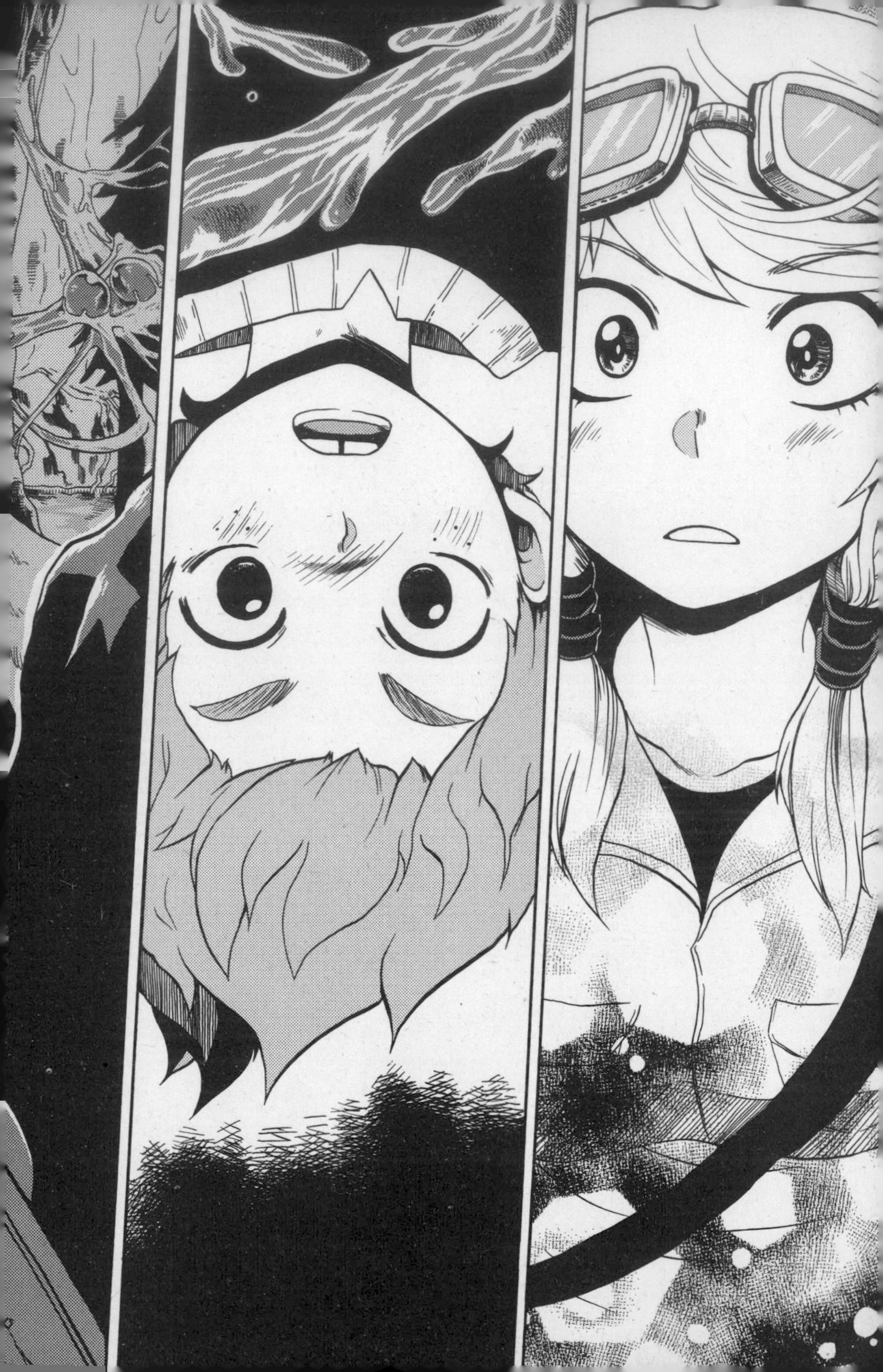

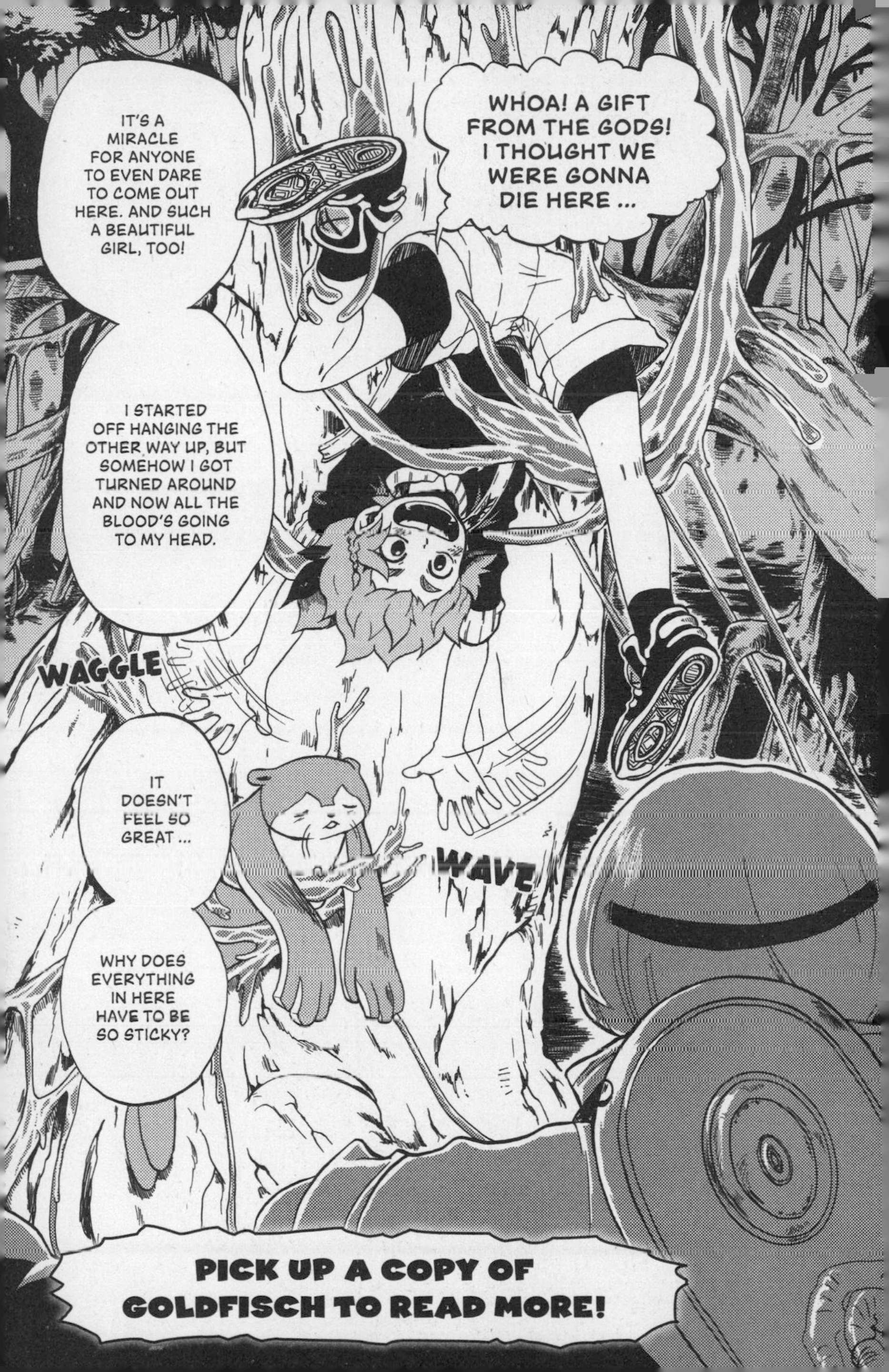
WHOA! A GIFT FROM THE GODS! I THOUGHT WE WERE GONNA DIE HERE ...
IT'S A MIRACLE FOR ANYONE TO EVEN DARE TO COME OUT HERE. AND SUCH A BEAUTIFUL GIRL, TOO!
I STARTED OFF HANGING THE OTHER WAY UP, BUT SOMEHOW I GOT TURNED AROUND AND NOW ALL THE BLOOD'S GOING TO MY HEAD.
WAGGLE
WAVE
IT DOESN'T FEEL SO GREAT ...
WHY DOES EVERYTHING IN HERE HAVE TO BE SO STICKY?
PICK UP A COPY OF GOLDFISCH TO READ MORE!

SNEAK PEAK!!!

SPECIAL PREVIEW OF THE *GRIMMS MANGA TALES!*

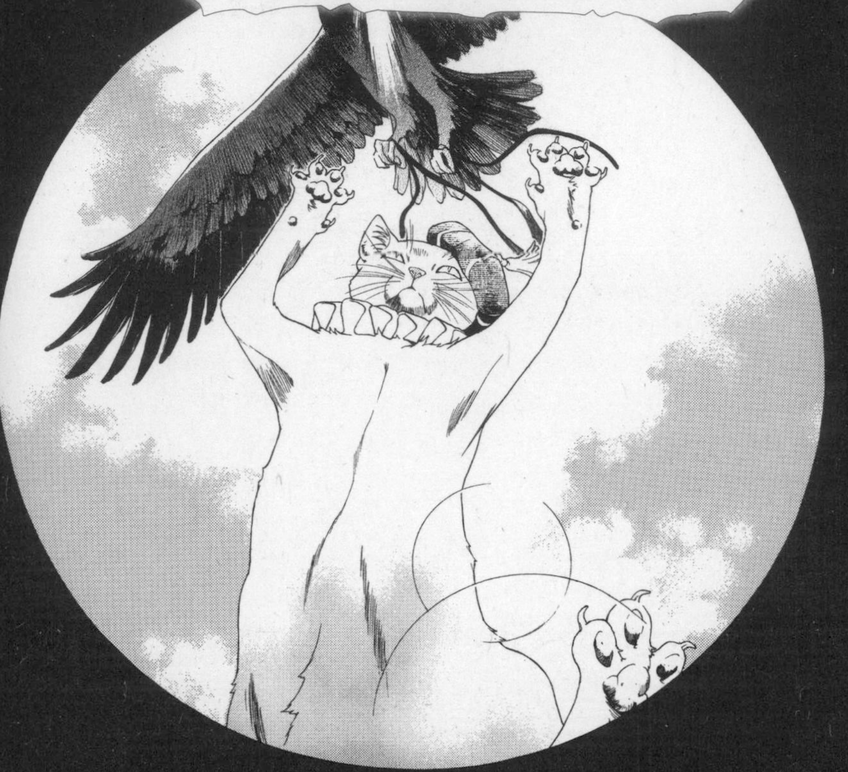

The Twelve Huntsmen

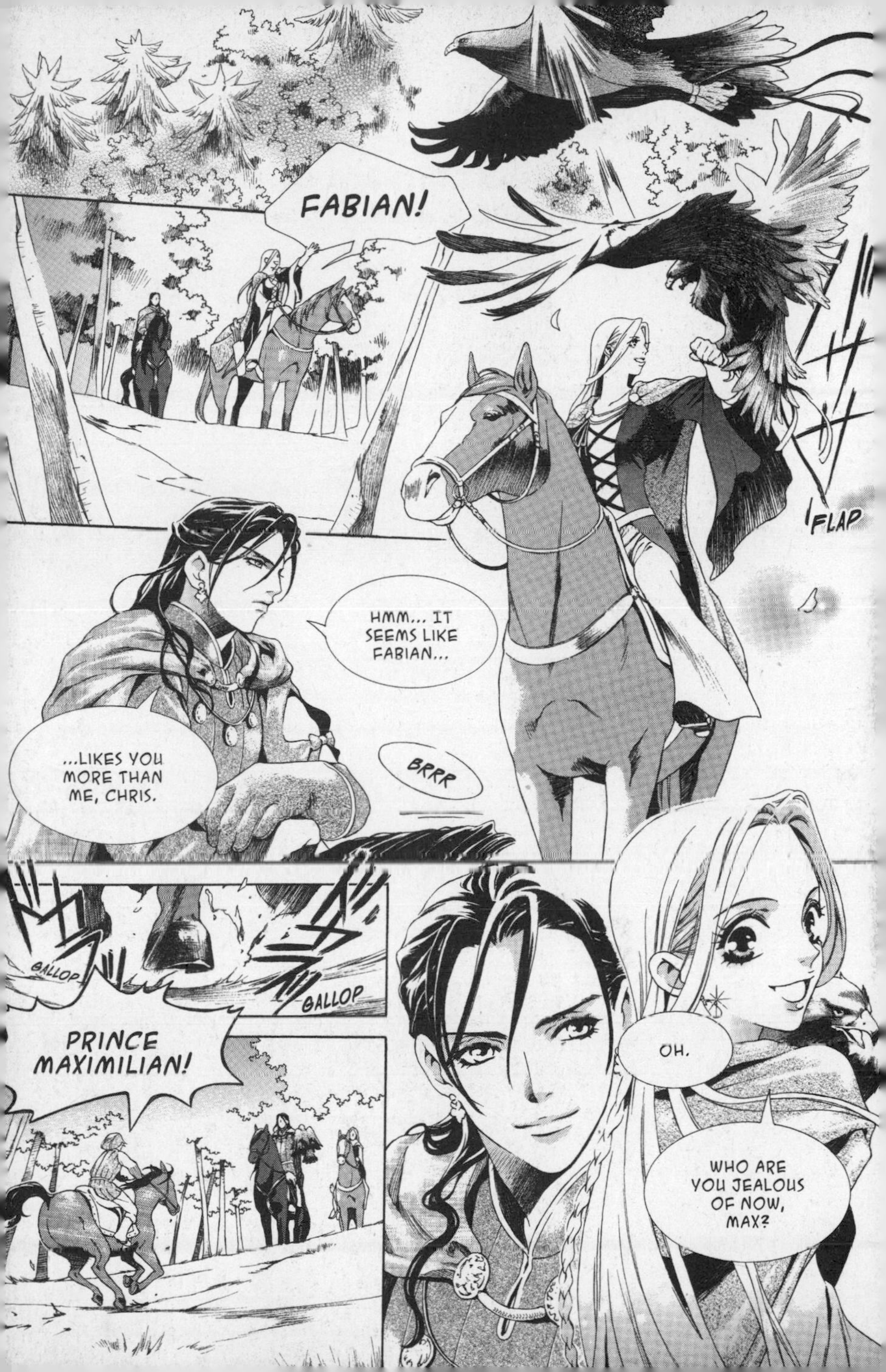
FABIAN!
FLAP
HMM... IT SEEMS LIKE FABIAN...
...LIKES YOU MORE THAN ME, CHRIS.
BRRR
OH.
WHO ARE YOU JEALOUS OF NOW, MAX?
GALLOP
GALLOP
PRINCE MAXIMILIAN!

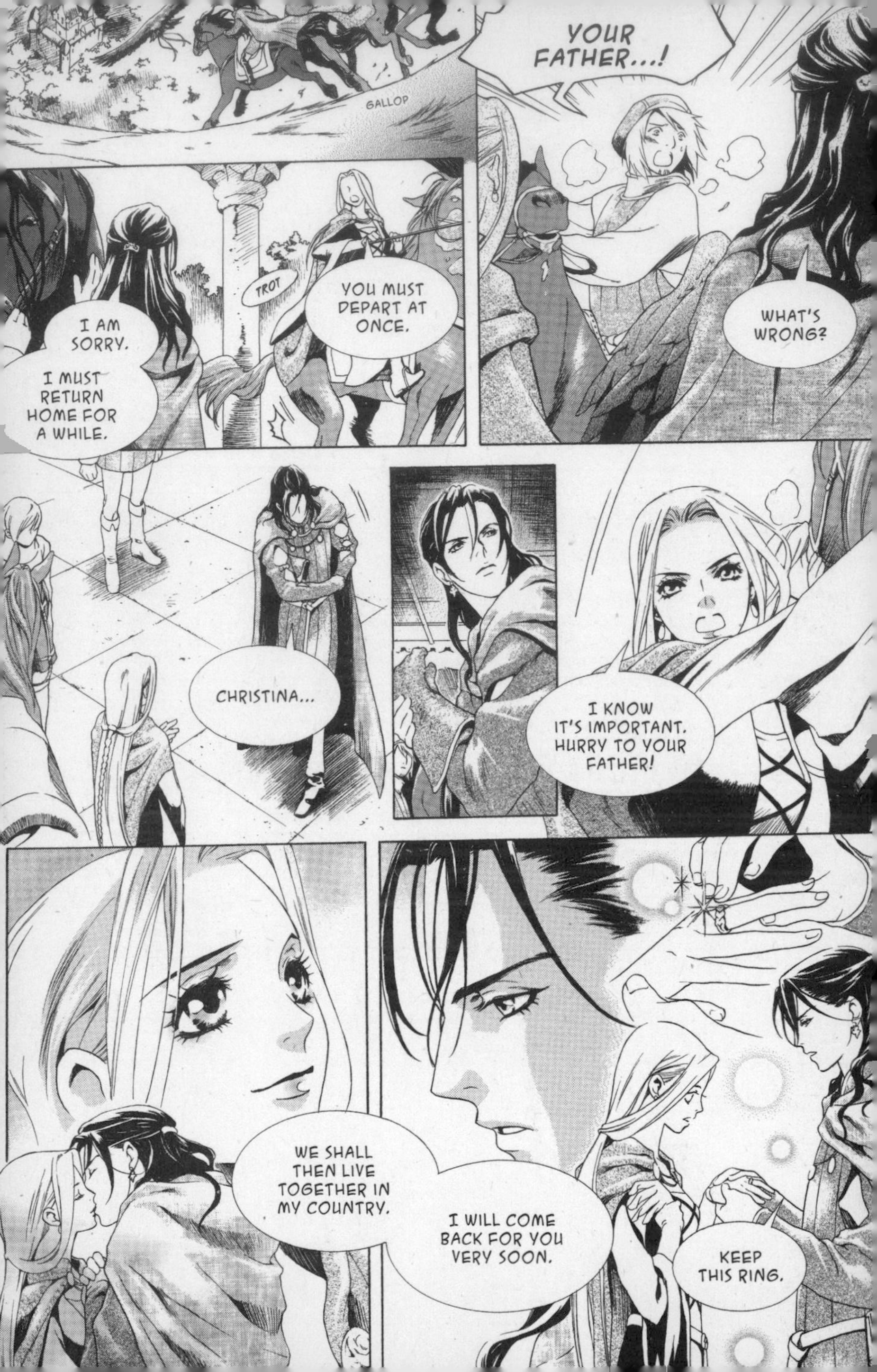
YOUR FATHER...!
WHAT'S WRONG?
GALLOP
YOU MUST DEPART AT ONCE.
TROT
I AM SORRY.
I MUST RETURN HOME FOR A WHILE.
I KNOW IT'S IMPORTANT. HURRY TO YOUR FATHER!
CHRISTINA...
KEEP THIS RING.
I WILL COME BACK FOR YOU VERY SOON.
WE SHALL THEN LIVE TOGETHER IN MY COUNTRY.

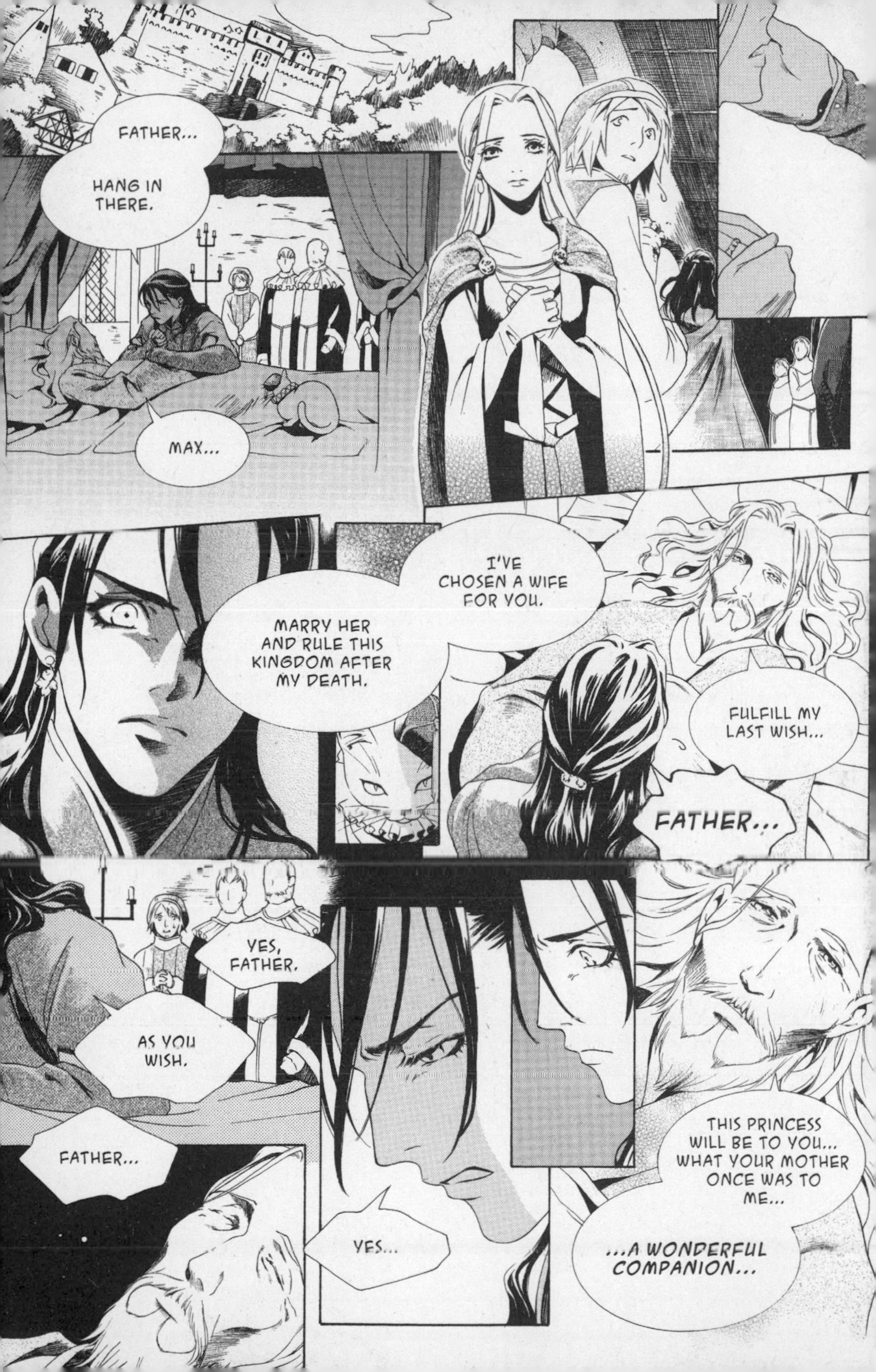
FATHER...
HANG IN THERE.
MAX...
I'VE CHOSEN A WIFE FOR YOU.
MARRY HER AND RULE THIS KINGDOM AFTER MY DEATH.
FULFILL MY LAST WISH...
FATHER...
THIS PRINCESS WILL BE TO YOU... WHAT YOUR MOTHER ONCE WAS TO ME...
...A WONDERFUL COMPANION...
YES...
YES, FATHER.
AS YOU WISH.
FATHER...

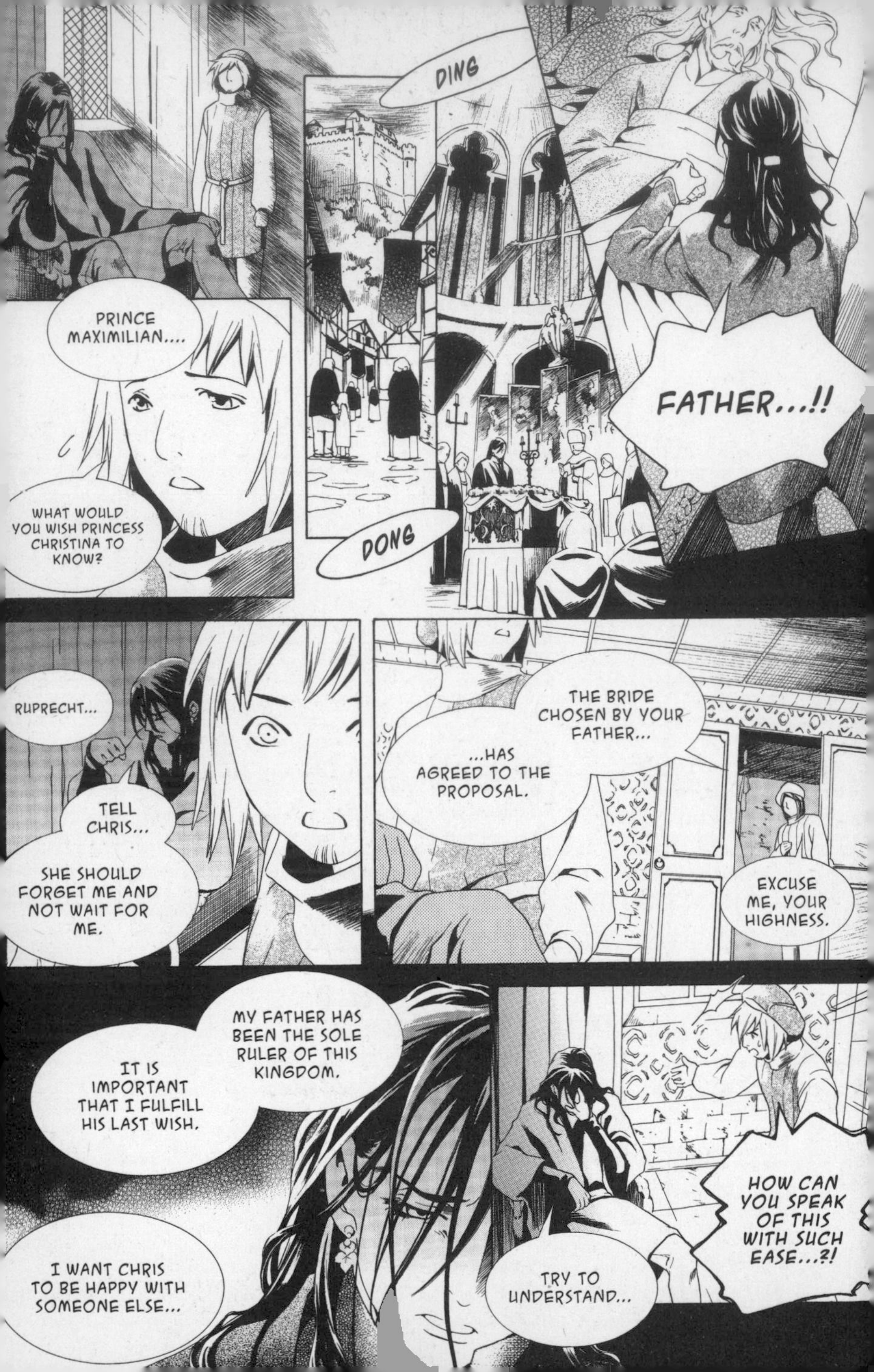
FATHER...!!
DING
DONG
PRINCE MAXIMILIAN....
WHAT WOULD YOU WISH PRINCESS CHRISTINA TO KNOW?
THE BRIDE CHOSEN BY YOUR FATHER...
...HAS AGREED TO THE PROPOSAL.
EXCUSE ME, YOUR HIGHNESS.
RUPRECHT...
TELL CHRIS...
SHE SHOULD FORGET ME AND NOT WAIT FOR ME.
HOW CAN YOU SPEAK OF THIS WITH SUCH EASE...?!
TRY TO UNDERSTAND...
MY FATHER HAS BEEN THE SOLE RULER OF THIS KINGDOM.
IT IS IMPORTANT THAT I FULFILL HIS LAST WISH.
I WANT CHRIS TO BE HAPPY WITH SOMEONE ELSE...

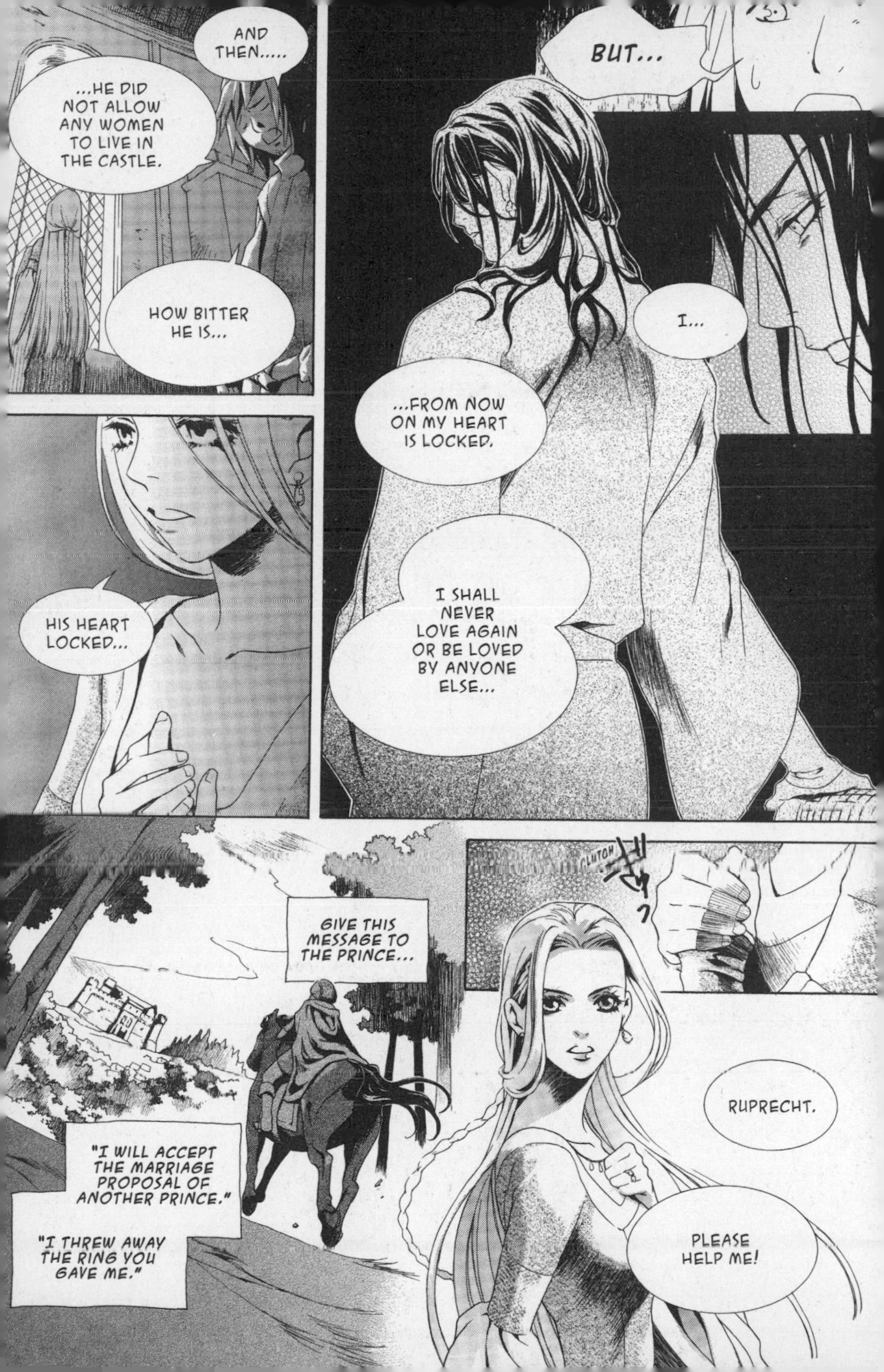
BUT...
I...
...FROM NOW ON MY HEART IS LOCKED.
I SHALL NEVER LOVE AGAIN OR BE LOVED BY ANYONE ELSE...
AND THEN.....
...HE DID NOT ALLOW ANY WOMEN TO LIVE IN THE CASTLE.
HOW BITTER HE IS...
HIS HEART LOCKED...
CLUTCH
RUPRECHT.
PLEASE HELP ME!
GIVE THIS MESSAGE TO THE PRINCE...
"I WILL ACCEPT THE MARRIAGE PROPOSAL OF ANOTHER PRINCE."
"I THREW AWAY THE RING YOU GAVE ME."

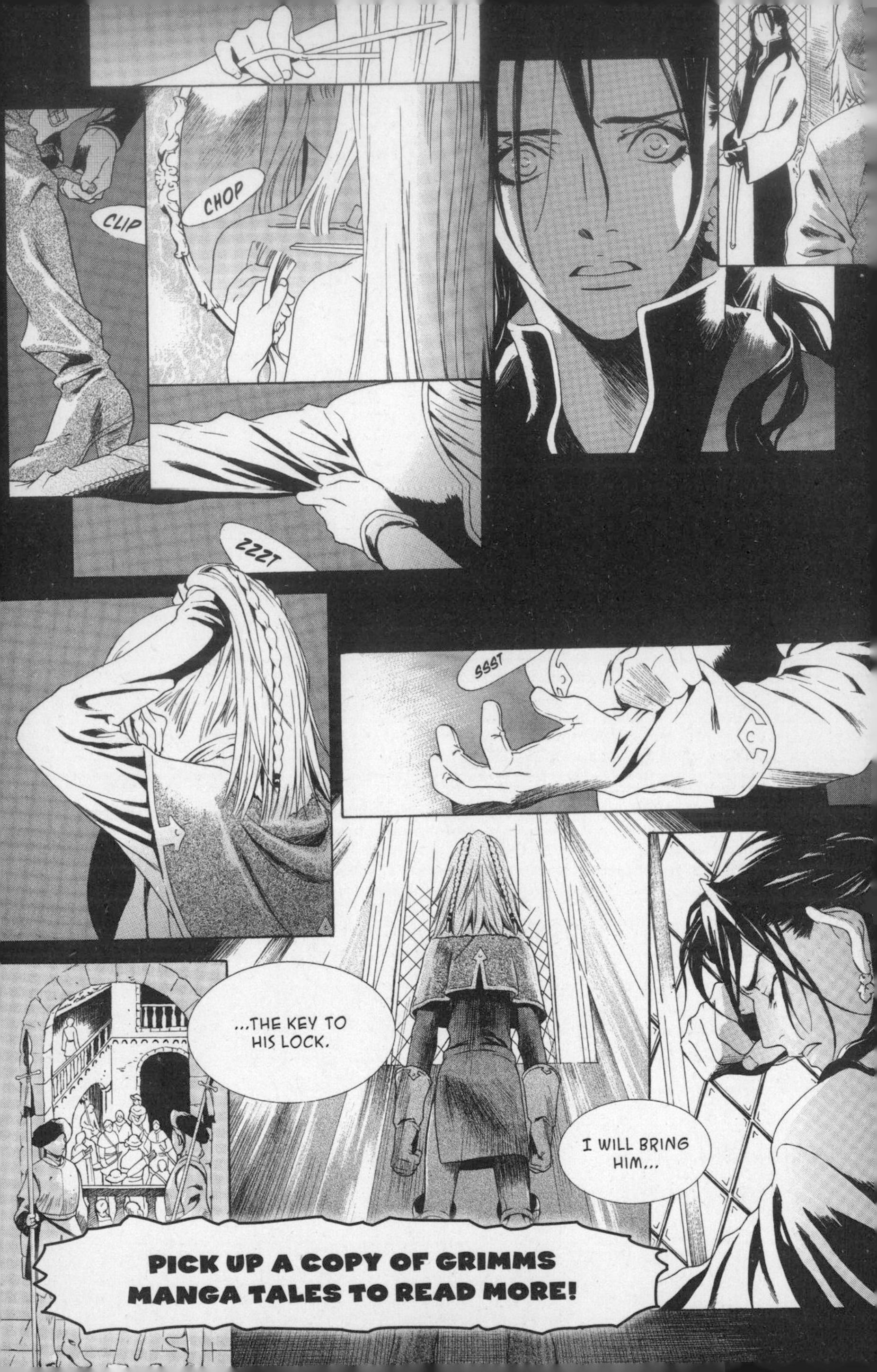
CHOP
CLIP
ZZZT
SSST
I WILL BRING HIM...
...THE KEY TO HIS LOCK.
PICK UP A COPY OF GRIMMS MANGA TALES TO READ MORE!

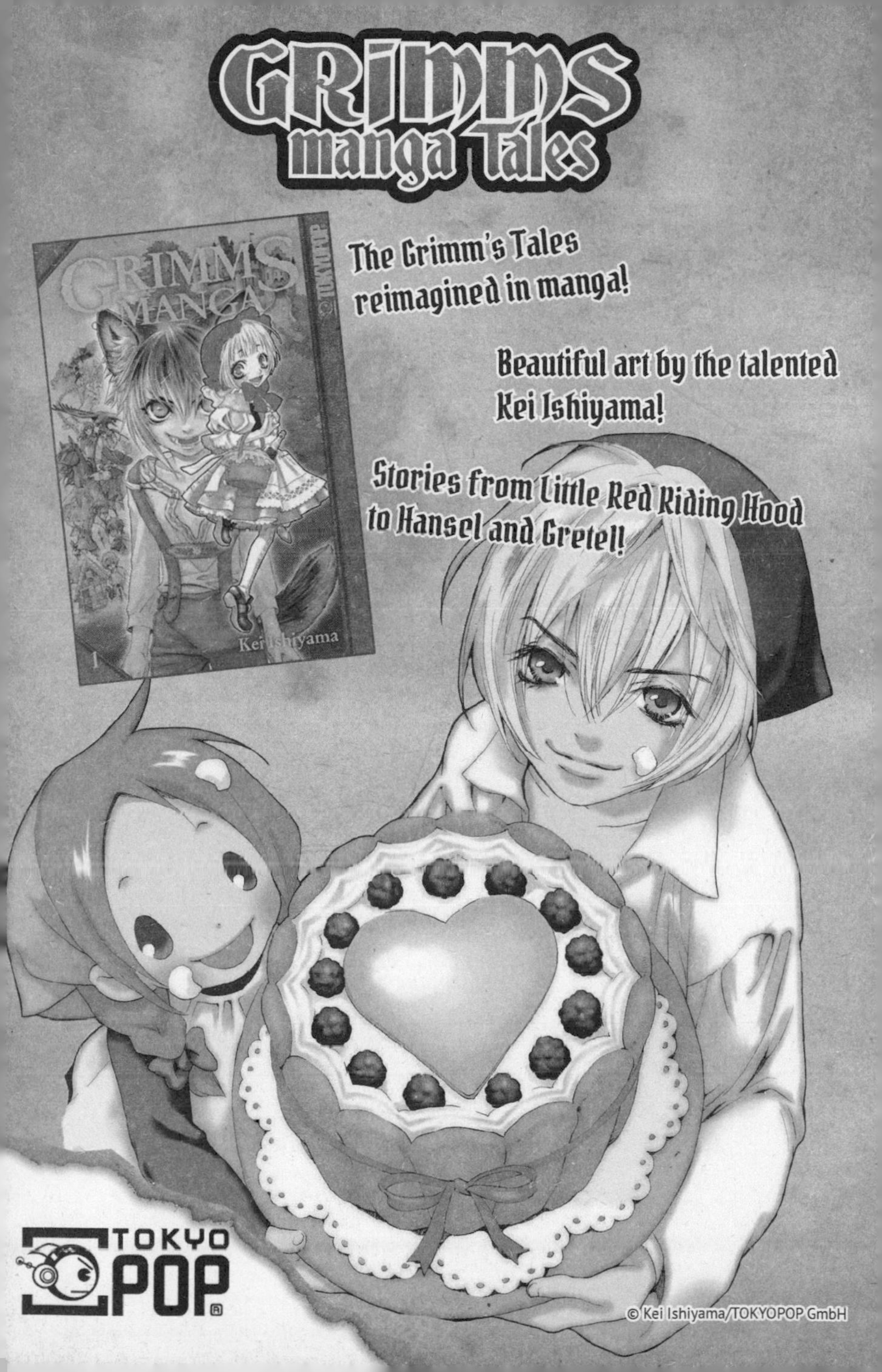
Grimms manga Tales
GRIMMS MANGA
Kei Ishiyama
1
TOKYOPOP
The Grimm's Tales reimagined in manga!
Beautiful art by the talented Kei Ishiyama!
Stories from Little Red Riding Hood to Hansel and Gretel!
TOKYO POP
© Kei Ishiyama/TOKYOPOP GmbH

ABOUT THE AUTHOR:

Sophie-chan (Safa Al-Ani), a self-taught manga artist, born December 1990 in Iraq, gained a following by posting drawing videos on her YouTube channel titled "sophiechan90" with over 30 Million views.

She began drawing and writing stories when she was 7 years old, determined to reach her goal of having her own manga series/anime adaption.

Although Sophie's educational background is in engineering, she continued inspiring artists to follow their dreams no matter where their studies lead them to. Sophie first self-published her graphic novel "The Ocean of Secrets", a full volume manga, in April 2015. Later in November 2015, Sophie created "manga Workshop characters", a how-to-draw book published by IMPACT.

Sophie appeared in several comic conventions such as Middle East Film and Comic Con, New York Comic Con and Anime North. Sophie held several school workshops and a fund-raiser contest for the Syrian Refugees in 2016.